NOMENCLATOR: INITIUM

By Bill O'Malley

For a richer reading experience, visit nomenclatorbooks.com to learn more about the world and times of Nomenclator: Initium

PROLOGUE

To my dear friend Nicarcus, from Lucius Annaeus Seneca:

I was delighted to learn that your son Lucius Mestrius Plutarchus, who impressed me greatly with his intelligence and talent when you both visited Italia (Italy) last year, has the ambition to write history. I too, as a young man, had a great desire to write history. As the years passed, I was drawn more toward literature and philosophy, but I always harbored the intention to write a history of that greatest of Romans, Gaius Julius Caesar. However, as the mound of years behind me grew into a mountain and those before me dwindled and as my duties advising the current Caesar took precedence, I came to accept that this ambition would not be realized. Somehow though, I could never bring myself to discard the notes I had amassed during a series of interviews with a most curious man. I am willing to share them with you with a caveat. Guide your son as to how he uses the material and advise him to publish his work judiciously. While I have no doubt as to the accuracy of the information contained in my notes, you must understand that it is not often wise, nor is it always safe, to present the unvarnished truth. Use discretion when you allow him to write of the lives of the great and powerful and choose carefully the time he publishes what he has written. With my man, Calistus, I have spent many days transforming my collection of notes from a boxful of velum sheets and fading scrolls into a cogent account of my time spent with the freedman of the god Augustus, whom most called by his common name, Polybius, but whose proper name was Gaius Julius Caesaris Polybius Tychaeus. The story I present to you in the following codices:

LIBER I

I met Polyibus in the summer of my eighteenth year during the consulship of Drusus Julius Caesar and Marcus Junius Silanus (15 A.D). One morning, as we prepared to receive his clients, I expressed to my father my adolescent desire to write an account of the life of Julius Caesar. His immediate response was to tell me it was a foolish pursuit as there was already a surfeit of biographies of that famous man.

"Those biographies were all written long after he had ceased to be a man and had become a god. I want to write of the *man*. I want to write a true history!" I tried to sound defiant as I stared into my father's eyes, but I'm sure I seemed quite ridiculous with my overly dramatic adolescent zeal. He must have immediately realized I had rehearsed my side of the conversation.

My father sighed and shook his head. "I doubt there is any such thing as a *true* history, Lucius. Focus on the study of law and rhetoric. That's how a young man makes a name for himself."

I didn't mention it again, but I began to research the life of Caesar. At this time I was required to accompany my father as he went about his daily routine. I was at his side as he met clients and I was on the benches when he was called to testify in court or defend a client against a charge for which there was no valid excuse. I found it all so tedious. I continued to write, but everything I wrote seemed too remote. It seemed more like a catalogue of well documented events than a study of the man's character.

Whenever I would learn of a debate that was expected to be particularly long, I would slip away from the crowd of young men gathered at the doors of the senate house. In those days listening to dreary debates at that open door was considered an essential part of a young man's training. Most of my peers took it very seriously and listened as closely to the proceedings as they did to the odds makers at the circus. Some even scratched notes into their wax tablets. These days, however, many of the future senators left waiting by the doors spend their time playing at dice or engaged in idle gossip. My generation may have been the last to believe the fiction that we were living in a republic. I, on the other hand, would often use the opportunity to spend time at the nearby library on the second floor of the basilica at the north end of the old forum. I spent hours studying the accounts of the lives of Caesar and his contemporaries, trying to glean the man's essence from his letters and speeches. I deceived myself into thinking my father would never know I was not the dutiful son he thought I was.

How he learned of my trips to the library I never found out, but I suspect he was informed by one of the elderly custodians of the library. Like most senators he had clients in every trade and walk of life. At any rate, one day in early Augustus (August), a debate was cut short due to the heat in the senate chamber. I didn't take into account that the chamber filled with hundreds of sweating men in togas would not be as comfortable as the relatively cool corner of the library I had made my place of refuge. I was completely absorbed in the official dispatches of one of Caesar's legates from his year as propraetor of Hispania Superior, when I became aware of someone sitting beside me. I looked over to see my father sitting there, the folds of his toga impeccably in place in spite his having just forced his way through the sweltering crowd in the forum. I started to mutter some excuse about feeling faint

4

due to my recent illness and needing to find someplace cool when he cut me short.

"To write a true and accurate account, you must learn of his life from someone who knew him well. As you yourself pointed out, the official biographers have not been at liberty to present Caesar as the man he truly was since that day your grandfather and his fellow senators made him a god. I've arranged for you to meet one of the last few survivors of that time, an old freedman of Augustus'. The man spent his younger years as Caesar's nomenclator, so he will have known him as well as anyone and certainly better than anyone still living. He's requested you join him at midday on the ides at the Temple of the God Julius. The man is quite old, so do not make him wait. Now come, it's time to eat." With that, my father rose signaling for me to follow him.

As we stepped out of the basilica into the glare of the afternoon sun, he turned to me. The sun behind him hid his face in shadow so I didn't see his expression when he said something I found quite odd. "Anything you write share with no one but me until we have had an opportunity to discuss it." With that he turned and forced his way into the crowd. I obeyed his request but we didn't talk about why he made it either that day at the taverna or, for that matter, ever again. I didn't come to realize why he was insistent on this matter until quite some time later.

In spite of the fact that it was very nearly fever season in the city, I had been staying at the family domus near the Quirinal Hill that summer. My father, mother, and my brother Mela were already spending most days at the country villa, and I would soon join them. But for that month I had the house in the city to myself. I have always seemed to be one

5

health crisis from the grave, but that summer I was feeling better than I had in years, and I was enjoying my relative freedom in the city. Whenever my father would come into the city for business I would meet him to make our rounds, but many days, when it was not lucky enough to transact any public business or a festival shut down the courts or prevented the senate from meeting, I could play the part of a young man out for a good time. However, I made sure I was in bed early the night before the ides of Augustus.

I went early to my scheduled appointment with Polybius, crossing the old forum from the northwest to the east side of the vast rectangle. I enjoyed watching the throngs of people who by midday filled the forum. I used to make careful mental notes of all I saw and would later write it all down in my journal. That day, in addition to the usual assortment of merchants and shoppers, money changers and tourists, vagrants and fine ladies barely visible behind the silk curtains of their litters, I saw an embassy of Aethiopians pushing its way through the crowd. One very tall man with skin the color of oiled ebony and glossy black hair arranged in tight curls was carrying a brightly colored bird on his shoulder. Astonishingly, the bird could talk! I swear by the gods that the bird spoke clear Latin with the same accent as the man who carried it, but in a harsh, raspy voice. The bird was saying "good day citizen," to every man wearing a toga who came within a few feet of the ambassadors. Needless to say, this delighted everyone within earshot and slowed my progress considerably.

Having spent more time than I expected observing this unusual sight, I needed to quicken my pace as I weaved my way through the crowd toward the temple at the far end of the forum. The Temple of Julius the God could be seen from

6

across the forum over the heads of the crowd. I approached the temple on the left side, thinking the old man would be waiting on the shadier side of the building, but there were only a couple of beggars on the steps. Rather than push my way through the crowd in front of the temple, I continued around its less crowded side in the back and came up on the other side between the Temple of Julius and the Regia, that most ancient house of the original kings of Rome. As I rounded the corner, I spotted Polybius for the first time. To my eyes he was impossibly old. He had only a few strands of curly, white hair pressed across his head. Even at a distance I could see his face was lined with countless wrinkles and dotted with the spots that make the skin of the ancient seem to have been spattered with garum and wine. In spite of the heat, he was dressed in an elegant red toga over a saffron colored tunic. Polybius seemed to have coordinated his clothing with his transport or vice versa. He was accompanied by four young men, obviously slaves. Two of the men were sitting next to a litter painted brightly in yellow and red, while the other two were with Polybius on the steps of the temple. One held a red silk parasol over the old man, shielding his fragile skin from the sun, while the other read to him from a codex.

In those days, the steps to the temple rose on either side and joined the Rostra that jutted out in front. The emperor has since remodeled the temple, moving the steps. While they are still on the sides, the steps now face the temple front. The sides of the temple were covered in white marble and the reflected sunlight caused me to squint. I moved in close enough to the old man to cast my shortened shadow over him. That morning I had long debated with my dressing slave as to how I should address the old man. It didn't seem proper to be too formal with a man who had spent more than half his life as a slave, but he had been an intimate associate, (dare I say friend), to both deified Caesars, and that earned a great deal of respect from me. I also didn't feel right about addressing him by his legal name, Gaius Julius Caesaris Polybius Tychaeus, as he shared much of that name with two of the greatest of Romans, the gods Julius and Augustus. Rather than call him by the more familiar Polybius, I hoped by casting a shadow over him he would notice me first and introduce himself. He did, saving me any embarrassment.

"Master Lucius Annaeus Seneca, I presume." His voice was surprisingly strong for one so old.

"Yes, I hope I haven't kept you waiting," I answered, still avoiding his name.

"Waiting is about all I have left to do. You should call me Polybius and I will call you Lucius. I no longer have the patience for formality." My problem was solved. "Now, young man, be a dear and help me to my feet."

I hesitated and cast a glance at the slave nearest him. In that instant Polybius seemed to have heard my thoughts. "Lucius, tell me you are not too good to help an old man to his feet. These poor fellows have to carry me all around the city. Now do me the honor of lending me your arm to lean on."

I reached out my arm and he grasped it near the elbow while I clasped his forearm. His arm, though very thin, was surprisingly strong as he hoisted himself up with my assistance. He signaled to one of the slaves near the litter and the young man scurried over with a silver-tipped staff of gnarled hardwood polished almost black with oil. "I usually don't use the stick, leaning instead on two of these boys, but we are going into the temple, and they're not allowed."

"Are *we* allowed?" I was somewhat surprised. "I thought only the priests and temple slaves could enter the temple at this time."

He laughed a thin raspy chuckle. "To put a fine point on it, *you* are not allowed, but they will not prevent you if you're with me. For me, it's a privilege granted by Augustus when he gave me my freedom. While he couldn't officially acknowledge my relationship with Gaius Julius Caesar, he could do me this one small favor. I can enter this temple whenever I wish and linger as long as I care to. Our current Caesar has yet to revoke this singular honor. I suspect he thinks I am already dead." With that he clutched my left arm with his right hand, disturbing the folds of my toga and with Polybius leaning on the staff in his free hand we began to climb the temple steps.

At the top of the steps, rather than turn toward the temple door, Polybius turned left and shuffled out to the balustrade on the Rostra. From this vantage we had a magnificent view of the forum. Before us swarmed the teeming midday crowd. Mostly men, the crowd seemed a sea of white togas and tunics with the occasional splash of color supplied by a woman out for a day's shopping or a dandy such as Polybius. To our left was the great temple of Castor and Pollux with its gleaming white marble columns and statues of the twin demigods flanking the steps. Beyond that, running nearly the length of the forum, were the columns of the Basilica Julia on the left and the Basilica Aemilia on the right. At the far end was the Rostra, the speaker's platform with its gilded ship's prows glistening in the intense sun while further still, past the Rostra, were the temples of Saturn and Concordia, both towering above the other buildings. Seeing the forum from this elevated platform was like seeing it for the first time. Polybius turned to me. "I very much enjoy this sight. Remarkably, I can still see fairly well, at least when viewing distant objects. The things near me, however, are a blur so, sadly, I can no longer read. Now I must depend on my boys to read to me." He sighed. "It was quite expensive procuring slaves fluent in several languages." He took my arm again and turned me toward the temple doors. "In a way, my eyesight is much like my memory. What happened yesterday tends to fade and blur, while the events of three quarters of a century or more past are crystal clear. When I was a young man I was something of a prodigy. I had the ability to recall everything to the smallest detail. My memory is still better than that of most men half my age."

From the platform we had to ascend another short flight of marble steps to the great gilded bronze temple doors, twice the height of a man. Unlike the doors of most temples, the doors of the Temple of Julius the God are always left open. I suppose it is appropriate as Caesar was much loved by the people and at least presented the image of a patrician who loved the people in return. Whether or not this image reflected his true nature was a question I intended to ask Polybius. From across the forum and through the open doors, the people below could look up into the dim recesses of the temple and see the larger than life statue of Caesar staring out at them. Today the god was dressed in blue. Unlike many of the other statues this one was not painted but was instead gilded. The sculptor had dressed Caesar in the robes of the *Pontifex Maximus*, one of the many offices he held in his mortal lifetime. Special, larger than life, robes had been made to drape over the sculpted ones so the god's clothing could be changed to suit various festivals and occasions. I assumed he was dressed in deep blue because this month all Rome would celebrate the first anniversary of the deification of Augustus, Caesar's adopted son and heir.

10

As we walked through the open doors, a man stepped from the side as if to challenge us before he recognized Polybius. "Good day Master Polybius. I'm glad to see you're in good health. I was worried when we hadn't seen you these past few days."

Polybius turned to me. "At my age people worry when I spend too much time in the latrine. My boys are constantly waking me from naps to confirm I hadn't died. I suppose they want their freedom so it wouldn't be entirely unwelcome for them if I did die in my sleep." He chuckled as he said this. Then, tuning to the slave, "I'm fine Marcus. I was handling some business at my villa across the Tiber. I should have stayed on the far side of the river as I fear the fevers will be bad in the city this year."

The slave smiled and gently and with genuine affection rested a hand on Polybius' shoulder. "I'm so glad you're well, master Polybius." When he returned to polishing the brass lamps on the stand beside the doorway, I noticed that the slave was armed. From one side of his belt hung a short black club of knotted tree root and from the other a long dagger.

Polybius led me by the arm until we were directly in front of the statue. I gazed up at it for a short time and then I looked over to see Polybius, his eyes shut, muttering a prayer I couldn't quite hear. I stood enjoying the coolness of the temple and waited until he finished praying.

"Is that a good likeness?" I asked, as I again stared into the statue's face.

"What, that? No, not good at all. The jaw line has been strengthened and the man has been made to look too

11

serious. More often than not, Caesar would have a smile on his face, but you would never know it from the way the sculptors portray him. This one captures some of his intensity, but none of his considerable charm. The artist's intent was, I suspect, not to create a portrait but rather to help inspire a legend."

"Why did you wish to meet here, Polybius?"

"It's one of the few places in this city where I can find quiet. My hearing is not as good as it once was and I sometimes have difficulty hearing over the din." He paused and then added, "Now tell me, Lucius, why do you wish to write a biography of Caesar?"

I thought carefully before answering. This was a question I had, surprisingly, never asked myself. "I suppose it's because I'm curious about the man. But, it's more than that. I've only lived under the rule of a Caesar, but I have read so many accounts of the Republic before the Caesars rose to power."

"You are a reader." He said quietly.

"I've been sickly most of my life, so I always had difficulty keeping up with the boys my age. But, my mind was sharper than most, so I found my activity in literature. I read voraciously. My father still indulges me in that. He buys me copies of the latest works."

"Yes of course. That is how your father and I met. He is a regular patron of one of my shops. He bought you a copy of Strabo's *History* for your birthday, I believe."

"That's right. You own a copy shop then?" My curiosity was piqued.

"I own three copy shops and several other businesses besides. Let us sit and you can finish what you were saying. It was rude of me to interrupt."

Polybius led me to one of the benches along the side wall. I remember the bench was hard, designed that way, I suppose, to discourage lingering.

"Not rude at all. Well, I have always been curious about Caesar, and it seems odd to me that he is on the one hand held in such high esteem and yet on the other he is sometimes reviled, often by the same author. It's almost as if they are treating him as two separate men." I paused, waiting for the old man's reaction.

"Please continue," was all he said.

"I also need to know what motive Caesar had for bringing down the republic." I said this with more feeling than I had intended.

"The republic was nothing, merely a name without body or shape." Polybius almost whispered the words, sounding wistful.

"You quote him," I said.

"No, young man, I paraphrase. Caesar spoke in the present tense. Caesar *lived* in the present tense." With that he stood up to leave. "To learn what you ask to know you must learn of the times we lived in. I will be happy to instruct you in that."

Halfway down the temple steps Polybius stopped and looked up into my face. "I asked to meet you here because I had business nearby in the forum today and I did not wish to waste even a fraction of an hour on you if you were not serious. I believe now that you are. I also wanted you to appreciate what Caesar has become since that day in Martius (March) nearly sixty years ago, before you begin to try to understand the man he was."

The slaves had moved the litter a few feet from the steps. Somehow they knew he would be leaving at that time. I supposed it was part of a routine that varied little except for his having a companion on his temple visit that day. I helped Polybius lower himself into his litter. When he was settled in he looked up at me, shielding his eyes from the glare of the midday sun. "After the festival you will be spending the rest of the summer at your family villa across the river." He didn't pose this as a question. "Mid-morning four days before the calends of Septembris (August 26) join me at my villa. It's a little more than a mile from your country home. Your father knows it well and can instruct your man as to how to find the place. We will begin then. Until that day, I wish you good health and good fortune." With that the four slaves, moving as one, smoothly hoisted the litter onto their shoulders. They turned in unison and trotted off toward the Julian Basilica with the red and yellow litter seeming to glide over the sea of bodies in the forum like a boat on a calm lake. As I turned to walk the other direction, I heard one of the slaves call to me, "Lucius Seneca!"

I turned back and saw the litter gliding in my direction. When I thought I would need to step to the side to avoid a collision, the four men turned as one, stopping with the side of the litter directly before me. The silk curtain parted and Polybius leaned out toward me. I stepped forward so I could hear what he had to say. "I also meant to ask you why you think *you* can write his biography."

I smiled at him. "I believe my genius has bestowed a gift on me. I seem to have a way with words. I always have."

His response was quick. "Quite so. I myself have the same gift; Caesar had it too. Very good then, I will see you in thirteen days." Polybius signaled his bearers by rapping his heavy rings on the roof of the litter, causing it to swing around and glide back the way it had come. I stood for a couple of moments, being jostled by the passing crowd as I tried to adjust the folds of my toga, watching the brightly colored litter disappear into the distance. I was already eagerly anticipating our next meeting.

LIBER II

I awoke early on the morning of our appointment before the sun rose and even before the household slaves awoke. I had been staying at the family villa on the far side of the Tiber for only three days and I was already bored. Of course, it was deemed necessary to avoid the city at that time of year. With my long history of poor health, every Greek physician, Roman augur, Thracian witch, and half crazed street corner soothsayer I have ever met advised me to leave Rome during the fever season. But, I made the mistake of leaving my collection of scrolls and codices back at the house on the Quirinal. Before, simply out of boredom, going to bed just after sunset the night before, I wrote out instructions, to our slave Cleon, listing which scrolls I needed him to retrieve on his next trip to the city. As a result of going to sleep so early, I found myself wide-awake before anyone else in the house.

I took the opportunity to gather my writing supplies and sharpen my pens. I brought not only pens, ink, and papyrus, but also wax tablets and a stylus for note taking. I later found that Polybius spoke without many pauses, so I had no need for the papyrus and ink. From our next meeting on, I simply transcribed my notes after I returned home. When I had finished preparing my writing instruments, I extinguished the lamp and by the dim predawn light felt my way along the peristyle out to the garden. I heard snoring coming from the kitchen and considered waking the cook so he could prepare my breakfast but then realized my mother would be disappointed. She liked the family to have breakfast together whenever possible. I decided to instead sit in the garden and simply enjoy the morning solitude. I chose the bench on the

16

hill beside the old cypress tree since from that place I could watch the sun rise over the hill beyond the garden wall while enjoying the delightfully cool morning. The summer heat would return as the sun climbed into the sky, but for now I could sit in a cool breeze in the misty light of that time between night and day. It felt to me more like a spring morning than the start of a late Augustus (August) day. I noticed that what I first took as darkness and silence was anything but. Sitting quietly, I could hear hundreds of sounds. There was a chorus of birds in the trees around me and crickets in the grass. In the distance I could hear the bark of a dog answered by another at an even greater distance. I could even hear the shouts of men and the clatter of their cart wheels as the last of the farmers crossed the Tiber Bridge after making the nightly delivery to the city's shops. As my eyes grew more accustomed to the dim light, I could make out the silhouettes of the birds in the tree and over the wall between two pine trees I could see the first morning rays striking the roof tiles of a villa farther down the slope between our home and the river. This was a particularly famous villa; this had been the Julian Villa. Watching the sun come up from this vantage point, I wondered if Caesar had watched the same scene from his garden lower on the hill on that last morning in Martius before setting out for the Senate meeting on the other side of the river.

"Are you not feeling well, Lucius?" My father's voice interrupted my reverie.

"You're awake early." I turned and answered. "No, I'm feeling very well. I just couldn't sleep. I guess I went to bed too early."

17

"Have you thought to bring Polybius a gift?" My father asked this as he sat beside me on the bench.

"Before I left the city I visited the antique dealer near the lion fountain and bought a small, ancient vase from Mytilene. I understand his family is from that city," I replied. My father started to speak, and then paused. "What is it?" I asked.

"I hope a relic from Mytilene doesn't remind him of his family's fall from Fortuna's favor. It was the sack of her home city that led to his mother becoming a slave and to the end of his family's liberty."

"I thought about that, and I'm willing to take the chance. He seems to have recovered nicely from his family's bad luck, and people tell me he tends to take the bumps in the road in stride. Anyway, it's too late to find something else now."

"Yes, you are right. Give it with a generous heart and the gift will be received warmly," After that, we both fell silent and for some time we watched the sunrise and listened to the birds sing. My thoughts turned again to that final spring morning for Gaius Julius Caesar.

Polybius was correct. His villa was just over a mile distant from my own family's villa. I had passed his country home dozens of times as a boy and never once was curious about the sort of people who lived there. I had heard it was a very old man with no young children, so the place didn't hold any interest for my brothers or me. Cleon, our family's most competent slave, guided me there. As we walked along the winding dirt path, I noticed how verdant and full the rolling hills around me were. We even stopped once to sit on a

18

boulder near the side of the rode taking some time to appreciate the scent of the wild roses growing up the slope of the hill. As we neared Polybius' home, I caught sight out of the corner of my eye of a figure running along the crest of the hill to our left. It was a young boy, maybe twelve years old. For an instant, I imagined it might be the shade of my former self, playing in these hills.

A short time later we rounded a bend in the road and, on a slight rise to the northwest, Polybius' villa came into view. I knew at once it was his, for the wall around the front courtyard was painted the same bright yellow as the litter he had used on the day we first met.

We were greeted at the gate by one of the slaves I had seen when I joined Polybius in the Forum. Obviously, he was expecting us. I guessed the boy I had seen running along the hill had been sent out to watch for us and ran ahead to alert Polybius. My suspicions were confirmed when we passed through the gate and I saw the same boy drinking with cupped hands from a fountain in the courtyard. I turned toward the slave who had met us at the gate. "Does your master give you money? Do you like to play dice?"

The slave smiled. "Yes sir, he gives me a little, now and then." He produced three dice from a fold in the cloth belt of his tunic and rolled them in his hand. "Would you care to play a round?"

I laughed. "No, not me, but my man Cleon here loves to test Fortuna's favor. Please don't take all his money, or he'll make very poor company on the walk home." I tossed Cleon a small purse of coins. I expected the slave to lead me into the house, and come back to gamble with Cleon, but instead he led my man away, as the boy ran toward me.

"Lucius Seneca, I'll bring you in to see Caesaris Polybius." He turned sharply and expected me to follow, so I did.

As we approached the front of the villa, I could see that the door was open. The boy led me in through the vestibule, and there in the atrium sat Polybius on a wooden stool with his walking stick across his lap, looking comfortable in a simple linen tunic. "Welcome to my country home, Lucius."

"I am honored to be invited, Polybius," was my response. "Your slave boy is very self-assured." I added.

"I am no slave!" the boy hissed.

"I apologize for greeting you while seated. I should introduce you to this young man. This is my grandson's youngest. Tychaeus is his name. He was named after me. In spite of the fact that he comes from a line of slaves, he is deeply offended if you mistake him for one. He was born free, and all his progeny will live free. At least as free as any Roman can anymore."

As Polybius used his staff to pull himself to his feet, I turned to the boy and gave him a most sincere apology, and that seemed to mollify him. As Tychaeus made his way out the door into the courtyard, Polybius turned to me and said, "Let me show you around before we get started." As we passed the impluvium, I thought the little pond had a fish motif for its mosaic, but then I noticed one of the fish move. Polybius saw my surprise. "My grandson's wife enjoys fish. I myself do not, but for her sake I keep this pool stocked with a few that we catch in the river so she can have fresh fish each day. I'm surprised one of the cats isn't perched on the edge of the impluvium. Perhaps your arrival unnerved them." Polybius led me to the back of the large atrium. To the right was a wing with an open front. This reminded me of our own villa. I was surprised to see the walls lined with portraits. "This is, no doubt, the sort of space where your family keeps the funeral masks of your ancestors. I don't have any ancestors. Instead, I keep portraits of my progeny." I saw in the lower right corner a portrait of Tychaeus. I looked around for the boy, but he had vanished.

"You said the boy was named for you, but Tychaeus isn't your name."

"No, it's not, and it has not been my name for many years, but Tychaeus is, as you will learn, the name my mother gave me."

"Polybius is the name your first master gave you when he bought you?" I asked.

"My first master did not buy me, at least not directly. Come with me and I will tell you about my childhood."

"I think I'd rather hear about Caesar." I was a little irritated as I didn't wish to sit through Polybius' life story. I came to hear Caesar's story.

"In due time, young man. I need to tell you my story so you will see how I came to know Caesar. Without the background information, you may find it hard to believe what I have to say of the great men and women I came to know."

21

He led me to the tablinum. In most domi and villas, the large open room served as a meeting room. In our family villa my father used his tablinum for meetings with clients, and he kept the room open both front and back. My father always said it is important that others can see when he is meeting a client. People need reassurance that a senator is willing to listen to the concerns of others. Polybius used his tablinum as a sort of office and library, so in his villa the room was closed off in front with a huge woven tapestry of Aegyptian design. I stopped to admire the heavy cloth. The tapestry was magnificent. In Its center stood Isis, the Aegyptian goddess of the earth and protector of the dead. Around the border was a design of lotus flowers and river birds. "It's beautiful," I said.

"Yes, in spite of its age the colors are still strong. If you look closely you can see that some of the threads were actually spun from gold."

"Where did you get it?"

"It once belonged to Cleopatra, the last legitimate Pharaoh of Aegyptus (Egypt)." He smiled. "She left it behind in her haste to leave Rome after Caesar's assassination. Octavianus gave it to me a few years later. I suppose it was meant to be some sort of compensation for denying me my freedom. I would have much preferred freedom, but the cloth is nice."

I hoped he was not planning on spending the day in the enclosed tablinum. I could imagine how warm the room would become once the sun was overhead. Polybius held aside the tapestry so I could pass through and followed me into the room. "I keep the room closed so my pages stay in one place.

22

If the cloth is pulled back on a windy day, it becomes like a vortex in here. As you can see, my documents are already in enough disarray without the four winds contributing to the chaos." He gestured to the piles of parchments and papyrus scrolls stacked on a large round table in the center of the room. On a shelf near the back I could see a stack of codices. "I have been having my slaves read to me. I've been brushing up on the past, so I can keep the events I tell you in proper chronological order."

"I'm grateful to you for taking the time to share your memories, Polybius," I said.

"No gratitude necessary. I'm glad to have the opportunity to relive the past. The past is all I have; my future grows very short."

"Well, at any rate, to show my thanks I brought you a gift." I took the vase out of the bag I was carrying and presented it to him.

Polybius held the vase at arm's length, straining to see it clearly. "Hold that tapestry back, will you please? I need more light." I did as he asked. "Is that a Mytilenian fish motif on this vase?" He smiled.

"Yes, I bought it from an antique dealer on the Quirinal."

"It is lovely. I saw some like this when I visited Mytilene many years ago. You commemorate my origin. This is quite appropriate, as I planned to start my story with the story of how my mother became a slave, and that begins with the Roman sack of Mytilene."

Polybius picked a broad brimmed hat from the top of a pile of papyrus sheets and began shuffling out the back entrance of the tablinum. I was grateful we would not be staying in the dim room. As he led me through the peristyle, we passed another, larger pool in the center of the open room. This too was stocked with fish. The pool was at least two feet deep and sitting on its edge, dangling his hooves in the water, was a statue of a satyr with a fishing pole. We moved back to a passage that led out to a veranda running the entire length of the back of the house. From the veranda I could see a vast walled garden, and in the center of the garden was a small lake. In the middle of the lake rose a tiny island connected to the rest of the garden by a stone bridge. "We will talk out there on the island," Polybius said, as he put his hat on and adjusted it to shield his eyes from the sun. "Help me cross the lawn, please. The terrain is quite uneven."

Polybius slipped his arm into mine, and leaning on the staff in his other hand, we slowly made our way to the bridge. I wondered why he insisted we move to the island, when there was a table and two chairs on the veranda. The island was furnished with three large stone couches surrounding a low table, also made of stone. Upholstered cushions were piled on the couches. This island was apparently intended to be used for dinner parties. Polybius lowered himself onto one of the couches and gestured for me to sit on the one that would put me nearest to his head. "I prefer to lay down when I reminisce about the past. The prone position seems to stimulate my memory."

"Why are we meeting out here," I asked.

"Why not? Is it not lovely?" He could see I wanted more of an explanation. "We are meeting here because it is

24

wise our current Caesar does not get wind of my dredging up the past."

"Surely your slaves are loyal. They wouldn't eavesdrop, would they?" I was surprised.

"Trust me, Lucius, all slaves eavesdrop. And, all slaves are disloyal to some degree. This is something I am quite certain of."

"You're right. It is a lovely spot." I smiled conspiratorially, but I didn't understand why Polybius believed Tiberius Caesar would have the slightest interest in what we were doing.

"Please, pour the wine." Polybius gestured toward a heavy earthenware pitcher and two goblets on the table. The wine was refreshingly chilled, diluted with just enough water for a mid-morning drink.

"This wine is excellent. Is it from your own vineyard?" I asked.

"Yes it is, but you didn't come here to talk wine. We can have that discussion another time. Now take out your stylus and tablet. You may wish to take notes. I shall begin at the beginning. My beginning, for that is where the story starts for me." We had been speaking in Greek, but Polybius, when he came to the word "beginning," paused and rejected the Greek word for the Latin word, "*initium*."

LIBER III

"I do not know who my father was, but I have a strong suspicion, and he most certainly was an officer serving under Marcus Minucius Thermus. My mother was taken into slavery the year Sulla and Metellus were consuls (80 BC). She was captured after the fall of Mytilene. As you may already know, Mytilene is a delightful city on a tiny island that is connected by bridge to the much bigger island of Lesbos near the Asian coast. I had an opportunity to visit the place once. The city is an ancient Greek colony and the city fathers followed a long history of independent action when they sided with Mithridates, the upstart king of Pontus, when he rebelled against Roman rule. They were so independent minded they actually refused to surrender long after the king himself capitulated. After seven long years, a Roman army at last took the city."

"The city was under siege for seven years?" I was incredulous.

"No, of course not. Not continuously. There was much posturing and negotiating with the occasional armed conflict. Nearer to the end, the city's leaders knew disaster was coming and chose to make a stand. They stocked the city, armed the citizens, and barred the gates, awaiting their fate. If anyone had thought to study the Roman military mind they would have known that the Romans would never give up. A well-supplied Roman army will fight for years. I would guess generations of soldiers would fight for a city if it ever came to it. To back down would be an insult to Roman *dignitas*."

26

"At any rate, the city was taken. Shops and temples were looted, homes were burned, men were slaughtered, and women and children were taken captive. Many of the women and some of the children were, of course, raped before being enslaved. Boatloads of slaves were shipped to Italia. Some of the more useful captives were kept behind to work for the proconsul and his staff. My mother was a beautiful young woman. Artemisia was her name. She had dark hair and green eyes. She was an intelligent, clever girl who made the best of any situation. My mother was sixteen years old when the city fell, and she was to be married that year, but her future husband had been killed in battle a couple of months before Mytilene was sacked. Her family was well connected in the city and she suggested to her captors she might have information regarding the pockets of men holding out on Lesbos. The Romans were anxious to depart the island, but did not like to leave unfinished business."

"Duty demands she help the proconsul. Did she?" I asked.

"Her duty at that time was to her city and to herself. It was too late for Mytilene, but she could help herself. She knew nothing useful, but the ruse was enough to keep her from being loaded onto a cramped leaking ship full of sick and broken women and children. It turned out the only useful thing she had to offer to the Roman officers was her beauty and charm and that was enough to keep her from being tortured or killed. She used them both during the month or so the Romans were left putting things back in order."

"She prostituted herself then?" I regretted asking the question as soon as it left my mouth.

"Young Lucius, I would be neither so harsh nor so quick to judge. Did she have sex with the men? Yes. In fact, she granted more than one that honor. That is why I do not know for certain the identity of my father. But, she had no choice as she was acting to save her life. Have you never compelled a slave to have sex with you?"

"She was willing, I assure you." I answered.

"If you say it is so, I will believe you." Clearly he didn't believe me, and I was for the first time unsure myself. For an instant, I disliked him for that. "Anyway, it was rumored that Caesar at about this time sold his own favors for much less than his life."

Polybius could see I was about to speak and anticipated me. "That is something we will touch on later, Lucius. For now let's keep to the topic. When she realized she was pregnant, Artemisia did not dare to reveal it for fear she would have been killed. She had hopes one of the young patricians would take her home to be a household slave in a fine villa. She knew a young man would not want her if she were discovered to be pregnant. If a rich man owns a slave there is at least a chance she will have a decent life. If she were to be sold at a discount price in the slave market, there was almost no chance. She also knew she would be worth much less should her pregnancy be revealed. The slave traders are required by law to disclose such things. So she kept me a secret, and one of the young men took her home to Rome."

I'd heard pregnant slaves often sold for less, but was never sure why, so I asked him.

"As I'm sure you are well aware," he answered, "many women die during the birth of the child they bear. For

28

most, the chance of gaining two slaves for the price of one is not offset by the chance of losing the one that was initially desired."

"What did he do when he found out she was pregnant? She couldn't have hidden it for long." I pointed out.

"It never came to that. When he returned with her, the man's wife was furious. The woman was the jealous sort and not half as pretty as Artemisia. My mother told me the couple fought over her for several days before the wife insisted they let the *paterfamilias* settle the matter, so the three of them went to visit the man's father. In order to keep the family peace, he told the young man to sell his slave and use the proceeds to buy his wife a fine jewel. That is how my mother ended up naked and in chains at the slave auction.

As it was, it all worked out. A man named Titus Virinus purchased her. He was a copyist and purveyor of literature by trade, and he made a substantial living from his copying business. He had brought an old slave tunic with him to the auction and made her put it on before he led her to his home in the Argiletum Street at the edge of the Subura. Once there he had her washed and dressed properly and brought into his tablinum. When she was brought into the room he instructed her to stand to one side of the room. At that point, she made an effort to turn her charm on him. He was about fifty years of age, turning fat in the middle, and he was losing his hair, but I was important for him to like her before he discovered she was pregnant.

He instructed her to remain quiet, as he finished making some calculations with an abacus and notating the figures on a sheaf of papyrus. Just as he was putting his abacus back in its box, a young male slave entered the room.

'You wish to speak to me Master Titus?' the slave asked.

'Yes, Marcus, I would like you to couple with this girl I just purchased." As my mother told the tale, she was shocked and let it be known that she was not inclined to put on a lewd show for the man.

His answer was swift. 'I do not care one whit what you are or are not inclined to do.' The young slave's face brightened in an eager smile. Titus ignored him. 'You are mine now and you will do as I wish. But no, girl, I do not want you to engage in sex with this young man right here, right now. I want you to do it as frequently as is necessary for you to become pregnant. I met an Aegyptian who says he is able to, by starting them young enough, train children to excel in almost any pursuit. I wish to try this myself. I would like to breed copyists for my business. The slave trader said you could read three languages fluently. I hope that is so, as it indicates that talent courses through your blood stream.'

Now my mother smiled with relief. 'Coupling with this man won't be necessary. I am already pregnant, nearly two months along. The baby's father is one of Minucius Thermus' legates. The man can also read three languages. I've seen him do it.' The male slave was apparently crestfallen."

At this point I interrupted. "I thought she didn't know who your father was."

"You're quite right, Lucius, but she was not about to tell that to Master Titus. Now, let me continue. Titus rubbed

30

his chin. 'Hmmm, I wish I would have known this before I bought you. I could have negotiated a better price. Perhaps I still can. Marcus, take this girl to see Lydia. She will be in charge of this pregnancy. I want all to go well. If you are lying about this, girl, you will be sorry.' My mother and the other slave turned to leave. 'Wait,' Titus stopped them. 'What's your name, girl?'

'Artemisia,' my mother answered.

Titus thought for a moment and then replied, 'That's fine. You can keep the name.' The two slaves again turned to leave. 'One last thing, girl. You are to address me as either Master Titus or simply Master. Now, go.'

The slave boy led her out a side door and up a staircase on the outside of the building, holding her tightly by the wrist as they went. He didn't want her to run, as new slaves were sometimes inclined to do, for that would almost certainly earn him a beating. Before climbing the stairs Artemisia stopped him. 'You don't need to hold so tightly Marcus.' As she told me the story, she smiled broadly with that smile of hers that was like a sunrise. 'I am not so stupid as to try to run away. She used her free hand to, with the gentlest touch on his cheek, turn his head to face hers. 'You, Marcus, are a very handsome man. Perhaps I will couple with you anyway.' This of course brought the smile back to his face. He continued to hold her by the wrist, but more as a potential lover would rather than a captor.

She was brought to the apartment on the second floor of the domus. None of the apartments on this side of the domus were connected to Titus' living space; each had an outside entrance. This apartment was where the midwife Lydia

31

lived. The midwife inspected my mother carefully. I suspect she was looking for physical defects that could interfere with a successful birth, or perhaps she was looking for signs of one of those diseases that Venus bestows on those she wishes to curse. At any rate, my mother passed the inspection and was sent back to the domus in the company of Marcus.

As Artemisia told it, the next several months were a time of relative ease. She was set to work for five hours each day at either weaving or preparing stacks of papyrus for Titus' copying business. She would then spend an hour with Lydia, describing in detail how she felt that day. In the later part of the day she would spend hours reading and writing. Titus believed that if she spent time at these tasks while I gestated in her womb I would develop a talent for them. I think he may have been right, as I showed great promise at a very early age.

In due course I was born in the small apartment Lydia shared with her husband, Alexander the physician. Titus entered the cubicle to inspect me. That is when my mother told him she had named me Tychaeus. He casually replied, 'No, I am naming him after my favorite author. He is to be called Polybius.' Of course, when we were in private, Artemisia always referred to me as Tychaeus.

I was told I spent the first three years of my life as my mother's constant companion. She was required to read to me, and as soon as I was old enough to hold a sliver of chalk I was set to scribbling on the paving stones of the kitchen floor of the domus. All the household slaves were required to speak to me as often as possible, and the Greek slaves were to speak in their native language so I would be bilingual from the outset. In my fourth and fifth years I began to spend one hour each morning and one each afternoon with a grammaticus

32

hired by Titus. He would stop by in the morning before going to his school to teach and again in the afternoon on his way home. Under his harsh tutelage I was writing in both Latin and Greek before my sixth birthday. Correct spelling was paramount, and I could spell many more words than I knew the meaning of. He was a very cruel man, as many in his line of work are, and I do not have a single fond memory him. Fortunately, I had a natural aptitude for what he was trying to teach. There was another pupil who was not so fortunate.

Quintus was near my age. He was born six months after me to one of the household slaves, and Titus considered him to be a lucky accident. He tried to train Quintus to be a copyist alongside me, but the poor boy had no talent for it. He struggled to put the letters in the correct order, and would even sometimes write letters in reverse. The beatings from our teacher only made him more nervous and led to more mistakes. I later learned that Titus gave up on him and was on the verge of selling my companion when his mother somehow convinced the gardener to insist he needed a young assistant, and from that time on Quintus divided his time between working in the garden and doing many of the menial tasks in the kitchen. He was also required to keep the lavatory spotlessly clean as a sort of punishment for not having my talents, but he didn't seem to mind at all. I continued my studies alone.

During this time, my mother became pregnant twice by the slave named Marcus. Each baby was a boy and each time he died shortly after birth. One of my brothers lived for eight days, the other just a few hours. Of course, my mother was blamed for the unsuccessful births. She lived almost as a wife to Marcus, sharing a cubicle on the second floor of the domus with him and two other slaves in addition to myself, but she never became pregnant again. This was without a doubt bad luck for her. Her ability to produce talented sons was her greatest value to Master Titus. I didn't realize it at the time, but the possibility of my mother producing a brother to me was the only reason she continued to live at the domus on the Argiletum.

By the time I was eight years old, I was spending every morning working in the copy room on the second floor at the front of the domus. Most of the rooms lining the front and the sides of the building were rented out to shopkeepers and didn't have doorways to the domus, but the corner literature shop out front led by a short passage directly into Titus' atrium. Above the shop was the copy room. This room had rows of tables and benches. Each table was supplied with an inkpot and a lamp. Unlike all the other rooms in the building, this room was equipped with large windows of many small glass panes. The glass must have cost Titus a fortune, but this room, above all others, needed adequate lighting. At that time, window glass was extremely rare and costly to make. The glass was so precious that all day and all night one of two burly former slaves, each armed with a dagger and a club, was stationed on the street corner to convince anyone passing by that it was ill advised to try and break the window with a stone. The glass was so dear to Titus that he had spent almost as much on the two former gladiators that guarded the windows as he had on the glass itself. On a table along the back of the room the supplies were kept. There were stacks of parchment, stacks of velum, and stacks of papyrus on one side of the table. There were various inks lining a shelf above the table, kept in bottles with their names carefully incised on a thin brass label hanging around the neck, while under the table were boxes of scrolls of an assortment of sizes. Along the front of the room was a low platform, and on this platform sat

34

a stool and a large podium. Here sat the reader. This man had a clear melodies voice. He would sit for hours, reading the text of various documents, while the rows of slaves would sit scribbling away, each making an identical copy. I was one of those slaves.

When I was not working at making copies, I was either spending time with a spelling tutor or working with individual clients. Very often, men would come into the shop to have a private letter, business document, or will composed. Most often these clients were the less wealthy equites who didn't trust their own educations and couldn't afford a literate Greek slave of their own. Others who used Titus' services were men of substance and prestige who did not want their own slaves to know the contents of what was being composed for fear they would let the information leak out. Very often a man would not want the slaves to learn how he planned to disposes of them after he died, so I helped write many last wills. I would work six hours each day, four between breakfast and the mid-day meal and two after mid-day. While working with these clients it became apparent I had an almost preternatural memory for details. More than a month after copying or composing a text for a client I could quote it almost verbatim from memory. In this way I got to know details of the lives of many of the most influential citizens of Rome. Once these prominent Romans learned I was capable, they trusted me to work on many of their most sensitive documents. Because no one ever suspects a child will retain or understand much, I was in great demand.

At this time I also discovered another talent I had. At first it happened by accident, but later I learned I could quite easily copy a document in the writing style of the original author. I found I could imitate anyone's handwriting. This

35

talent made me much sought after by busy clients, as an important man will often want others to think he had cared enough to personally write a letter with his own hand rather than having dictated it to a slave. Sometimes the slaves of the more prolific letter writers would drop off stacks of letters that had been dictated to them along with a sample of the master's handwriting, and I would be required to render convincing forgeries.

After working on my copying, I would either find time to play with Quintus or I would join my mother, helping her with her household tasks. During this time with my mother she would often tell me stories of our family history back home in Mytilene. On some days she would be particularly sad, and while I never knew why at the time, looking back I understood the sadness would come upon her when she thought about her lost freedom and the life she might have led. On those days, I would often sit near her while she worked and read to her from the scrolls of stories and poetry I would borrow from Titus' vast and eclectic library. Sometimes, on days when Artemisia was too busy to spend time with me, Quintus and I would go around the outside and visit Lydia the midwife or her husband Alexander, the local medicus who had been trained at a famous school on the island of Cos. Alexander had a thriving practice, and he was much sought after for his ability to cure disease, but his real specialty was patching up injuries. He was always being called on to set broken bones or stitch up some bloody wound. He told us he learned the art of patching wounds when he acted as a field medicus for the tenth legion. It was his belief that those years were far more valuable than his training in Cos. I once saw him remove part of a man's broken skull and replace it with a thin piece of silver, stitching the skin back over the patch. The victim was never again quite as he had been and spent his days

36

wandering the streets, going wherever his disordered wits directed him, but he lived for at least ten years after his accident. As young boys, Quintus and I were fascinated by the physician's work.

It was during my ninth or tenth year, (70 or 69 BC), I first met Caesar. On that particular day I was working in the shop downstairs. While it was unusual for me to be sweeping up the shop, I would sometimes do so when we were ahead in our copy work. I enjoyed working the shop as a change of routine, and this particular day was quite pleasant. Like most of the shops, ours had a front that opened to the street, and there was a delightful early autumn breeze coming in. A sacrifice had occurred in the forum, and the smell of roasting meat was enticing. I had, of course, heard of Caesar. Some ten years before, Caesar was the daring young man who had defied the Dictator Sulla's order to divorce his wife, setting them off on the run and putting their very lives in jeopardy. A few years later he had been captured by pirates and held for ransom. After gathering the treasure needed to secure his release, he famously raised a small force and returned to retrieve the money. Upon defeating the pirates, he made good on a promise he made while they held him by crucifying them all. Now he was a pontiff and military tribune and had just returned from fighting in the war against the renegade slave, Spartacus. Yes, Caesar was making a name for himself. Since he often spoke in favor of legislation meant to improve the lot of the plebs, he was well regarded in the Subura. My mother once whispered to me she hoped Spartacus would defeat the Romans, and then in her next breath she added that she did not want him to kill the famous Julius Caesar. She would sometimes say that if she was a free woman she would find some way to marry him. This was of course an idle dream, because we both knew that even if she was free she would still

37

be a foreigner, and Caesar, a patrician, could only marry a Roman citizen.

I was, of course, just a young boy, and since my entire world consisted of the block around the Titus domus, I had never laid eyes on the man in spite of the fact that he lived just a half mile down the Argiletum. When he walked into the shop followed by two slaves, one carrying a basket of scrolls and the other a wax writing tablet and stylus, I knew instantly who he was. As a younger man, Caesar had scandalized high society by wearing tunics with long sleeves and fringes, and he continued to do so. There seemed nothing very remarkable about the man. At least nothing you could put a name to right away. He was about thirty years old, of medium height, somewhat thin, and had wavy, dark brown hair. Most days, Marcus, my mother's 'husband' manned the shop. Naturally, he knew Caesar on sight having been often sent to deliver finished copies to the forum or the homes of the better off. Marcus had a good heart, but he was not the most intelligent man. He could run the counter of the shop, but he knew his limitations, and when he saw the large number of scrolls Caesar needed to have copied he realized he wasn't up to the task of negotiating the price, so he politely excused himself and hurried into the domus to get Master Titus, leaving me alone with Caesar and his slaves.

Most of the customers ignored me. I was a slave, and a very young one at that, so I wasn't prepared when Caesar first spoke to me. 'Hello, boy, what's your name?'

I looked up at him, and couldn't find my tongue. I simply stared at him for a moment and then looked past him at the slave standing behind him for help. The slave, an older man with graying hair and big ears, winked and smiled at me. 'You can speak, can't you?' Caesar asked, smiling.

'Yes, sir,' I managed to say. 'My name is Polybius.'

'Ah, your most literate master named you for the great historian. Perhaps one day you too will be a historian.'

'No, sir, I am only a slave,' I replied. Caesar had the most interesting conversational style. It was not what he said but rather the way he said it that was at once both disarming and utterly charming. Here I was, a slave boy, and Caesar was looking at me with his intense, dark eyes and talking to me as if I was the only person that mattered. When I spoke to him, he actually seemed to listen to and consider my words.

'But you don't always need to remain a slave. Many slaves are freed and go on to have great success. You need only look at Titus, your master. His father was born a slave of the Cato household and he not only earned his freedom, but he also became a rather wealthy businessman. Of course, he only was freed after having been sold to the Titus family. The gods know the Catos work their slaves until they drop. The only reason the elder Titus was sold by the elder Cato was because he broke his ankle, and the medicus had been bribed by Gnaeus Titus' wife to lie and say the slave would never walk again. She had wanted to own the man for years. She had a rather intense infatuation with him, or at least with certain parts of him.' I didn't know what was more shocking, that my master was the son of a slave or that Caesar was taking the time to share gossip with me. At that time, I wasn't even aware that it was possible for a slave to be made free.

'I enjoy reading histories. Herodotus is my favorite.' I boldly answered, making conversation as best I could.

39

'You prefer him to your namesake?' Caesar asked.

'Polybius is a fine writer, of course, but my family is Greek, and I enjoy reading the history of my people.' I was so enthralled by the conversation with Caesar I didn't hear Master Titus come up behind me.

'Polybius, don't bother the customer.' I started at the words.

Caesar spoke to my master but didn't take his eyes from mine. 'You have an exceptional boy here, Titus. He seems to have a remarkable mind for one so young.' Caesar looked over to Titus for the first time. 'If you would ever consider selling him, let me know.'

Turning back to me, Caesar asked, 'Did you read Herodotus in Latin or the original Greek?'

'Greek, sir, I prefer to read authors in the language in which they wrote.'

'Splendid. The boy reads both Latin and Greek.' Caesar patted me on my shoulder.

'That will be all, Polybius. Leave us now.' Titus glared at me as I glanced over my shoulder while pushing the curtain aside and stepping through the doorway.

I lingered behind the curtain long enough to learn that Caesar had been elected quaestor and was going to serve in the province of Hispania Ulterior (Further Spain) on the Iberian Peninsula. The scrolls contained important information on the province, and he needed them copied so he could study them on his way to the west. I felt a little sad that I would not see him again."

At this point Polybius stopped his narrative and struggled to push himself up into a sitting position. "I'm afraid Lucius, we will have to end our meeting for today. I need to urinate. This is perhaps the longest I've gone without pissing in months. Lately, it seems I need to go each hour." I was disappointed. He had finally started to talk about Caesar and now he wanted to cut our meeting short so he could take a piss.

Polybius read the puzzled look on my face. "Cheer up Lucius. We can meet again the same time, day after tomorrow. I'm not stopping just to pee. I have an appointment. I've borrowed a man from old Rusticus down the road. He is coming over to give me a massage. My young physician tells me it will help with my sluggish circulation. He seems to think the right treatment can cure old age." Polybius sighed and shook his head. "If only that were so."

I helped Polybius back across the lawn. He moved more swiftly this time. I surmised it was the urgency of a full bladder propelling him. Before we got to the house he led me off to the side. He had a small shed that held nothing but a wide pot to piss in. I waited outside while he relieved himself and he then saw me to the door where I found Cleon sitting, dozing on the floor of the colonnaded portico, the empty money purse beside him.

I spent the next day organizing my notes into a readable form and then reading everything I could find in our villa that related to the time of Caesar.

41

LIBER IV

The morning of our next appointment I awoke to the sound of thunder. I left my cubicle while running my hands over my face to wipe the sleep away. Down the colonnade I could see Cleon was already awake, sitting on the floor, shaking a dice cup. He whispered rather loudly to me, "Someone has made Jupiter angry today."

"So it would seem. Are you practicing at dice?" I asked.

"Yes. I'm bringing my own this time. I think that man cheated. Something wasn't right about those dice he had."

"What makes you think I'll be giving you any money today? You seem like a bad investment." I laughed.

He looked a little anxious about that as he scrambled to his feet, "I'll win for sure today. I've been practicing."

"You can't practice at dice. Once a die is cast, the outcome is up to Fortuna. Go and get us a couple of oiled cloaks. We'll probably get caught in a downpour. If you win today, I'll want my original stake back from both days." I turned him around with both hands and gave him a playful push to get him moving. "I slept late today, so we'll be leaving right after breakfast."

After relieving myself and splashing water on my face, I returned to the peristyle for breakfast. When it was warm enough, my mother preferred we all eat together under the portico. My father and mother were already at the table where a slave was laying out the plates of food. Before I could sit, my mother said. "Go fetch Mela. I think he's out in the garden. We're having boiled eggs with our bread today. One of the hens is a prodigy. I've never seen such egg laying."

A short time later I returned with my brother. He was fifteen and always in a bad mood. "I'm not hungry," he snapped at no one in particular as he pulled over a stool and sat at the table. He then proceeded to eat three eggs, two breakfast loaves, and a handful of olives.

After breakfast I took a bit of bread out to the atrium. In the open wing to the left of the tablinum was our family altar. I made an offering to our Penates and our family Lares and then another to the Divine Julius. Two days after my father let me know he was aware of my research on Caesar, I set a small statue of the god Julius on the altar. I half expected my father to ask me to remove it (with the appropriate prayers of course), but he said nothing and the statue remained. Of course, it did not hold the same place of prominence as those of our family gods.

After the small offering, I returned to the peristyle to let my parents know I was leaving. As I entered the room, the sky opened up and rain poured down through the open part of the roof. The roar of the rain on the roof as it rushed in toward the   center   and   crashed into the open garden in the middle masked all the other sounds of the house. I found my parents still sitting at the table. My father was munching on olives and spitting the pits onto the floor. "Well," I said, "I'll be getting pretty wet."

"Surely, Lucius, you're not still going?" my mother asked.

43

"He has made an appointment, Helvia. It would be disrespectful for him to not keep it," my father answered for me.

"Don't be silly, Marcus. It is just an appointment with a slave."

I found myself angry with her for the remark. "He has not been a slave for half a century or more, and he has agreed to help me. I owe it to him to keep the appointment." I was harsher than I intended.

"Don't get angry, Lucius. You know what I mean. And besides, you'll get soaked." She answered with a conciliatory smile.

"He will not dissolve. After all, he's not made of salt." My father said this with a tone of finality.

"At least bring an oiled cloak and a pair of boots then." My mother said.

"Cleon already has the cloaks, and the boots are an excellent idea. I hadn't thought of that." I said this as I gave my mother a quick peck on the cheek and headed to the back door where Cleon was waiting. As I turned into the hallway, I nearly ran into my brother.

"Can I come with you? I'm going to *die* from boredom if I stay here."

"You'll be even more bored sitting for hours listening to an old man go on and on about the past." I answered him.

"How come you don't get bored?" He was being insistent.

44

"I find the past fascinating. I'm much more interested in life than you are."

"The life you find so interesting has been dead for ages!" He said this over his shoulder as he moped away.

I felt sorry for him, so I left him with a bit of hope. "I'll ask Polybius if you can come next time." He continued walking without looking back.

At the back door, Cleon was waiting with the cloaks and the boots. I pulled the moneybag from the belt of my tunic and tossed it too him. He nearly dropped the cloaks as he reached to catch it. I noticed he thought of the boots when I hadn't. I changed shoes and wrapped myself in the cloak, and we set out. I no longer needed him to find the way to Polybius' villa, but it was safer to travel the roads in pairs. In those days, the far side of the river was not as built up as it is today. There was never much danger, but it is better to plan ahead rather than end up beaten and robbed.

We arrived at the gate to Polybius' villa much more quickly on this day, as the driving rain made the prospect of a casual stroll very unappealing. When we arrived, there was no one to meet us. We stood at the front gate for quite some time, pounding the ring that dangled from the mouth of a massive bronze wolf's head knocker onto the plate behind it. Finally a slave rushed out holding a cloak over his head. He shouted his apologizes over the rush of pouring rain. "Sorry sir, I couldn't hear the knocker with all the rain!" We ran to the front door.

Once again, Tychaeus was waiting for us. Smiling broadly, he said, "You look a little wet, Lucius Seneca."

45

"Do I?" I put on a puzzled look. "I hadn't noticed anything out of the ordinary." I said this as I passed my wet cloak to a waiting slave.

"Come with me, Polybius is waiting." I expected to see the old man sitting at his place in the atrium, but the stool was empty. Instead, Tychaeus led me out through a passage in the side of the Atrium. After passing outside through a colonnaded walkway, we came on the most remarkable room. To the side of the villa was a large room with a heated pool in the middle. In the steaming water sat Polybius, quite naked.

"Welcome, Lucius." Polybius smiled and waved me closer. "Come into the water and join me." I stood at the edge of the pool staring at Polybius who was shrouded in steam.

I said rather stupidly, "You have your own private bath."

"Yes. On cold damp days like this I take two hot baths. Sometimes I'm afraid spending too much time in the water will wrinkle my skin," he said holding his hand before his face. "But, it seems too late for that," he laughed. He seemed in a very good mood. For some reason, I was uncomfortable with the thought of climbing into the water with him. His body had the withered misshapen look of the very old, and I found him difficult to look at.

Polybius had a habit of seeming to hear my thoughts. "Don't worry, you will get used to seeing my desiccated old bag of bones. And don't be concerned about me leering at you when you take your tunic off. You're not really my type," he laughed.

46

I shrugged, and dropped my bag and peeled my wet tunic over my head, laying it on the bench near the pool. I slid into the hot water, feeling my skin tingle. 'I've never taken a bath this early in the day," I offered. The hot water felt extraordinary against my cold skin. It was the perfect antidote to the cold, wet day. As I slid into the water, I noticed an orange cat sitting in the corner of the room eying me warily.

"When nature sends a flood, who am I to argue. I just make sure I get as wet as possible" Polybius looked up at Tychaeus. "Please see that we are not disturbed. Come back in about an hour to make sure we have not dissolved completely." The boy picked up my wet tunic before he turned and walked briskly out the one door to the room, pulling it shut behind him.

"Where did we last leave off?" I asked, my voice echoing off the stone walls of the room.

"That is another aspect of this experience I enjoy," Polybius replied, "I can hear everything that is said to me when I'm in here, and no one in the greater world outside can hear a thing we say. I left you with a young Julius Caesar in Master Titus' shop," Polybius quickly answered. "Or, more accurately, with Caesar leaving the shop and heading off to Further Hispania."

"When did you next meet him?" I asked.

"We will get to that in due time. How and when I met Caesar again is a result of the winding path my life began to take at this time. You see, up until this point I was scarcely aware my life was any different than anyone else's. I was not even fully aware of my own enslavement. I just assumed all boys my age worked hard each day. My only child companion

47

was the boy slave named Quintus. As I told you earlier, he didn't work in the copy room with me, as his talents lay elsewhere. He divided his time between helping the cook and assisting the gardener. He knew more about plants than most adults and nearly as much as the old slave who tended the gardens. In our free time, of which we had little, we would play with each other. When we were stuck indoors due to bad weather, we would play hide and seek or other children's games. Some of the older slaves even taught us how to play dice and games such as duodecim. We were all part of the extended family of household slaves, and we had our own world existing side by side with the Titus family's world, but they really didn't care much about us and we didn't care much about them.

As it was, I enjoyed my life. At this time Titus was single again. He had divorced his wife for suspicion of adultery, and for about half of a month it was all the slaves talked of before we settled back into our old routine. And, for the next three years, the doings of the Titus family once again became of little concern. Master Titus was often irritable, so we learned to avoid him when we could, but, all in all, everything seemed fine to me.

However, it was at this time that I realized how little regard Titus had for us. Between the calends and the ides of Aprilis (April 1 - 13) in my thirteenth year, I discovered just how subject we household slaves were to the whims of our master. As was often the case, either I would spend the night in the cubicle Quintus shared with his mother, or he would spend the night in ours. On this occasion, I was spending the night in his family cubicle on the second floor. Just before dawn, we were awakened by the sound of heavy feet coming up the wooden staircase. We both simultaneously sat up in the

48

bed we shared and looked around the room. Oddly, we were alone. Quintus' mother would never leave without waking us, so we knew something was wrong. I can still remember the frightened look on Quintus' face. I reached over and laid my hand on his shoulder. 'Don't worry,' I said. 'I'm sure she's alright.'

At that moment, the wooden door swung open. The heavy feet on the steps belonged to a burly man who was badly in need of a shave. The metal identification plate that hung by a bronze collar around his neck identified him as one of Titus' slaves, but neither of us had ever met the man. Quintus' mother followed him into the room. She was softly crying. Before the stranger could take more than two steps into the room, Quintus' mother slipped past him and knelt in front of her son. She took him in her arms and held him. At this point, they were both weeping, but my friend had no idea why. After a moment, his mother released Quintus from her embrace and instead, took his hands in hers.

'I'm afraid I have some bad news, Quintus.' Tears came to her eyes again. 'Master Titus has decided to send you to his country villa to work in his herb garden. You won't be living here any longer.'

'But I like it here,' was all he said.

His mother took him in her arms again and they both cried. 'You have to leave now,' she said. 'Aulus here will be taking you.' With a nod in his direction, she indicated the man she had come in with.

The stranger spoke for the first time. 'Now don't be a pain in the ass about it, boy. You must do what the master says.'

49

Quintus' mother picked him up and took him out of the bed. He was small for his age, and she could easily lift him. She hugged him tightly and quickly before setting him on the floor. 'Go to the latrine now. I'll put your things in a bag.'

Quintus just stood there with tears in his eyes. He looked to me for reassurance or hope, but I had nothing to offer. I felt physically sick like I had been punched in the belly. Aulus took him by the back of his neck and steered him out the way he had come in. I began to cry. Quintus' mother sat beside me and putting her arm around my shoulder we both cried together. After a short time, she stood up, wiping her tears away with the back of her hand. She began collecting Quintus' few possessions and putting them in a canvas sack. I felt numb, but I helped her as best I could. After she left with the sack I thought of a gift I could give Quintus. In reality, it was nothing, just one of the four mismatched dice I owned, but my dice were my most treasured possessions, as they were the only toys that I could call my own. Every other plaything in the house was communal property, but these dice were all mine and I kept them hidden. I slid over the loose floorboard and took a look into the recess. There they were, and taking one out I looked at it hard, knowing I might never see it again. I then ran quickly down the steps and into the atrium. Near the front door Quintus and his mother were talking quietly. I walked swiftly up to them but stopped a few feet short, respecting their private moment. Quintus looked at me and smiled through his tears. My stoic façade crumbled and I ran to him and hugged him. We had wrestled together, and even sometimes fought. We had raced and tumbled and played rough, but we never had hugged like that, with that level of emotion. In that instant, I realized how much I loved my friend. I pressed the die into his hand and Quintus tried to refuse it, but I would not let him give it back.

50

I leaned into him and whispered in his ear, 'I'll come find you. We'll run away.' He just looked at me and shook his head.

'Be good,' was all he said. Then in the next instant he was walking out the door with Aulus and we were left standing there watching him leave. I tried to run out after him, but his mother held me back. 'We can go visit him,' she said, but I could tell from her tone that even she didn't believe that was true.

"Hmmm." Polybius said. "I hadn't expected that emotion to come rising up with the memory. Now my spirits have been dampened." I was surprised to see, amid the sweat running down his wrinkled cheek, what was unmistakably a tear. "Well, I might as well compound the grief. Perhaps it is the dismal weather that brought it on." Polybius sighed. "That was just the start of my troubles. I shall now relate what was to follow in the days ahead. The events of this short span of time set my life down a very different path than I might have been on, but I didn't know it at the time. Of course, every event and each choice changes everything. Life is a series of dice throws, and luck is the key factor.

For a couple of months, just below the surface, preparations had been taking place for Titus' wedding. Since this was his third marriage it would be a relatively modest affair, but there was still the ceremony and the dinner party to attend to, and Titus wanted to impress his new bride. I was told she was considerably younger than he. Her name was Porcia, which was appropriate, as she was quite full figured. Porcia was a distant relation to Cato, Titus' patron, and they had met at a dinner party at Senator Cato's house. Since the night they met, she had been to the Titus house on several occasions, but I had never seen her. Each day she had visited, I was working in the copy room. One day the copy room was shut down early, because it was a day quite like today. The air had been heavy all morning and about mid-day the sky opened and the rain came pouring down. The dark clouds and driving rain limited the amount of light coming in and the roar of rain on the roof tiles made it impossible to hear the reader, so work for the day was done. Normally, such an event would have filled me with joy, for I would have an afternoon of play, provided no one found any work for me. But, with Quintus gone I dragged myself down the steps. I entered the Atrium from the southwest, planning to cross the house by following the colonnaded portico to avoid the rain. As I turned into the passage, I nearly ran into Porcia and Master Titus. She was clearly vexed. Perhaps the weather had disrupted her plans for the day. I took an immediate dislike to the woman when she glared at me in a menacing manner and turning to Titus said, 'You need to teach your slaves to behave better.' With that she roughly shoved me to the side, pushing me out into the torrent of water pouring off the roof and splashing into the impluvium. I sat in the downpour glaring up at her back as she continued her progress. I limped to our family cubicle, blood from my skinned knees mixing with rainwater. When I got home to our cubicle, it was empty. I pulled off my soaked tunic and crawled under my blanket where I spent the afternoon.

Porcia was a rather large woman and not very pretty. She compensated for what she lacked in natural charms with an expensive taste in clothing and jewelry. I believe her primary appeal for Titus was her money. He was already quite wealthy, but the man was greedy and she had recently been widowed and came to him with a rather substantial amount of

52

property that she owned in her own right. Needless to say, I didn't look forward to her joining our household.

I went about my work for the next several days in a considerable funk. I missed Quintus very much and his departure spread a pall over the mood of our entire extended slave family. I had no idea things could get worse, but they did. Four days before the ides of Aprilis (April 10), I returned, as was usual, downstairs into the domus after being required to work an extra-long shift filling the inkpots and sharpening pens in the copy room, and I went across the atrium to search for my mother. Since she was not anywhere to be found downstairs I walked the stairs up to our cubicle. I pulled the curtain aside and entered the room. The small shutter on the single window was closed, which was unusual since it was a warm and sunny spring day. I walked across the room and opened the shutter, letting a shaft of light shine into the dark room. As I turned to leave and continue my search, I saw Marcus seated on the floor with his back to the wall. I could tell he had been crying. I had never seen a more dejected look on another's face. 'She's gone,' he said, rising to his feet.

'Who's gone,' I asked stupidly.

'Artemisia.'

I didn't understand what he meant. I just stared at him waiting for him to say more. Finally after what seemed an eternity, he said, 'Your mother's been sold. They took her to the slave market an hour ago. You were kept upstairs so there wouldn't be a big fuss.' He lowered his voice, and added with a hiss, 'That fucking bastard Titus has gone and sold her!'

I ran at him, my eyes filled with tears of sadness and rage. I began to pound my fists on his chest. Marcus just

53

wrapped me in his arms and held me tightly until my rage was gone and I leaned against him sobbing. To this day, I cannot believe that damned son of a wolf bitch was so cold, so unfeeling, so evil. To this day, I hope the infernal gods have damned him to an eternity of pain. I have never before, nor since, hated anyone so much. He has been dead some seventy odd years now, and I still hate him.

Polybius went quiet. I let him sit in the hot bath water with his ancient pain. There was nothing I would dare say to interrupt his sad reverie. He was no longer fighting it, and tears flowed down both cheeks mixing with his sweat, dripping into the gently steaming water. I was surprised to find that my own eyes were filled with tears. After a few moments, Polybius coughed once to clear his throat. "I think we have had enough of the bath for now. Let's continue this inside."

"Should I go out and find one of your men?" I asked.

"That won't be necessary. If you move to the other end of the pool and pull that chain, it will ring a bell on the other side of the wall. He will come."

I did as he asked and in an instant the heavy door opened and one of the young slaves I had met in the forum came in carrying a tray stacked with towels and fresh tunics. Another of the houseboys followed him with a tray with bottles of oil and a large brass bowl. For the first time I truly noticed the two men. They were both quite handsome, maybe five or six years older than me. They were well-built and both tall, but one was just a bit taller than the other. The two looked more like athletes than laborers. Both had the same cleft chin and dark curly hair, so I surmised they were brothers. They set their trays on a table along the wall and the one who carried

54

the oil turned and asked, "Will you need the oil, Polybius?" I was surprised he didn't call him 'master.'

"Not for me, thank you," Polybius answered.

"Would Master Seneca like a rub down?"

"No, I'm fine, thank you." I studied the two slaves. Their manner was just a little different than all the other slaves I had ever known.

"Would you like help getting out of the bath?" one slave asked Polybius.

"No, thank you, I'm sure Lucius can manage us both."

"Then we will leave you," the other slave said as the two men moved toward the door. When they had nearly reached the door, I stopped them. "Pardon me."

"Yes, sir?" the taller slave asked.

"What are your names?" I was surprised I cared to ask.

The shorter man answered for them both. "My name is Milo and my brother is Telemon, but everyone calls us Castor and Pollux because we are twins."

I again surprised myself by saying, "Please, call me Lucius." I wondered what my mother would say if she learned I allowed slaves to be so familiar.

I was somewhat uncomfortable helping Polybius towel dry his ancient frail body but I had no choice, as he had dismissed the slaves. While helping him, I had an opportunity to see his naked back. Ancient scars from long ago beatings crisscrossed the fragile old skin. When we were both dried and dressed, I helped Polybius out of the room and we made our way down the colonnaded walkway into the living quarters of the villa. I noticed Polybius did not seem to like to talk while he walked, concentrating all his strength on each slow shuffling step. The air was heavy as we shuffled over to the tablinum, and I dreaded the thought of spending the rest of the morning in the closed room. To my surprise, Polybius steered me to an opening at the side of the room. This doorway led to a staircase that brought us to a room above the tablinum. It was difficult for Polybius to make his way up the staircase, but with my help he managed. The room was longer than the room below and to one side was a large open balcony that was protected from the rain by the overhanging roof of the home. The walls were painted with a woodland scene filled with satyrs and nymphs cavorting among the trees. It was skillfully done and the artist had so accurately used perspective that in the dim light it appeared as if we were in a forest at dusk. We made our way out to the balcony. A low table and two small couches had been arranged facing the balustrade so we could look out and up the hill at the estate's vineyard and beyond the wall into the wooded area still further up the slope. The mosaic floor of the balcony continued the theme of the interior walls, and a dancing satyr was under my feet as I sat on one of the couches. The sky still hung low and gray, but the rain had diminished to a drizzle and the air smelled fresh and clean.

Seeing Polybius naked and helping him make the slow painful progress through the villa and up the stairs piqued my curiosity as to the true age of my host. "If you don't mind my asking, how old are you, Polybius?"

56

"I am as old as those hills beyond the vineyard wall."
He laughed a little.

I guessed he wouldn't tell me, but when he had settled into the pile of cushions on his couch, and I had poured two cups of wine from the pitcher that had been set out on the table, he looked over at me and said, "The young are always so curious about the old. I don't know if it is a dread of the slow decline that awaits them, or just wonder that someone could live so long. The gods have blessed me with many more years than most men are given."

"I apologize for asking," I said.

"No apologies needed," he answered. "I understand your desire to know. My age makes me a bit of a prodigy. I quite surprise myself when I think about it. I was born on the day before the nones of Septembris (September 4) in the year when Servilius Vatia Isauicus and Claudius Pulcher were consuls (79 BC), making me ninety-four years old. I hope to make it to the century mark. That would be something to marvel at, but I am more than content with the years I have been allowed." Polybius settled back to continue his story. "Now, where was I?"

"Your mother," I answered him.

"Yes, we left off with some painful memories. You know, I've often been told my prodigious memory is a blessing from the gods, and I suppose it is. However, like many blessing, it is also a curse. I remember both the happy times and the sad." Then with a sigh Polybius continued his narrative. "Artemisia was gone. The loss of my friend and my mother in that short span of time made me, for the first time, truly aware of how subordinate my place in the world was.

Until then I had neither witnessed nor given much thought to how we were absolutely under the power of our owner. Without giving me the opportunity to say goodbye to my mother, Titus tore our family apart and used his power to create a new family more to his liking. Later in the day, after the shock had subsided some, I asked Marcus why Titus had sold Artemisia. "She couldn't have any more babies. The gods blessed her with you and they would allow no more. Master Titus wanted her to produce more clever boys like you to work in the copy room, but that was not to be."

That evening, just before sunset, Marcus helped Quintus' mother, Clodia, move her few things into our cubicle. The space where she had lived was being vacated to make room for some of Porcia's slaves who would soon be moving into the domus. Clodia seemed embarrassed to be moving in, as if it was somehow her fault that Artemisia was gone. As she slid her small trunk under the bed I asked her, 'Will you and Marcus be having sex together now, you know, so you can have a baby?'

She turned and looked at me. Marcus started to blush. 'Why do you ask that?' She answered my question with her own.

'Marcus told me my mother was sold because she couldn't have more babies.'

Clodia came over and sat next to me on the bed and took my hands in hers. 'Master Titus will probably expect us to do that, but that isn't the sole reason your mother was sold. That was just the excuse he used to justify selling her.' I could see even Marcus was surprised to hear this. 'I overheard Porcia tell Titus that Artemisia is too pretty. She is jealous of

58

your mother's good looks. It's not a good idea to be prettier than the master's wife, but that isn't something your mother could change, so she was sold.'

LIBER V

That night, as I lay awake in bed, I made a promise to myself and to the gods. I would do whatever was required to be free. In my childish mind, it was only a matter of running away and finding Quintus and Artemisia and creating the life I wanted. I thought about moving to someplace far away. Names like Narbonensis, Asia, and Bithynia filled my thoughts. I had only heard of these places through the letters and documents I copied for clients, but I knew they were far from Rome and far from Titus and Porcia. Over the next few days I plotted. I began to save extra crusts of bread and dried fish and meat in a canvas sack I kept in the secret spot under the floorboard. I stole a knife from the kitchen and hid that with my food. I removed a wool cloak from the basket of laundry being sent out for cleaning and hid that in my trunk. My plan was to wait for the night of Titus' wedding when the entire household would be distracted. My worst fear was getting caught by one of the gladiators who guarded the windows of the copy room.

As long as I could remember, I had feared the two men who acted as the domus guards. The older man, Felix, was a tall, ugly fellow with silver gray hair cut short. He had a long jagged scar that ran down the left side of his face, only allowing him half a smile. The scar on his face was one of about two-dozen scars visible on this man. He was marked by the many battles he fought in the arena with scars on both arms, both legs, and across his barrel chest. It was said he had only three scars on his back because he never turned it to a living opponent but one time and that was when a net and trident man feigned being dead only to rise up and stab him in the back with his fork. The wound left three marks, one for each of the trident's prongs. Felix used to laugh loudly at a joke, but flare to anger at the slightest provocation.

The other gladiator was named Achilles. He was a few years younger and half a head shorter than Felix and not as scarred as the older man, but he was just as fearsome. I can only recall having seen him smile once. Achilles was frightening to look at. His cold blue eyes seemed to radiate danger. This was a man who seldom spoke, and when hid did it was usually to threaten someone with serious harm. Everyone in the household avoided both men.

These two men sat, day and night, on a stool under the balcony that projected from the corner copy room. They would only leave their post to pace along the front of the domus or to cross the street to the public urinal, all the while keeping a watchful eye on anyone who looked like he might like to throw a stone at one of the precious windows. They would divide their watches, each working half the day and half the night. They lived like slaves, their lives bound to Titus and his home and business, but, in reality, both men had purchased their own freedom several years earlier. After purchasing these two men, Titus paid them a small stipend each month and both had managed to save enough to buy his own freedom. It was said that Felix bought the freedom of both himself and a slave named Niobe on one day, married her on the next, and then continued his life exactly as it had been two days prior. He continued to live in the same small cubicle he had lived in for years, only now he had to pay rent. Quintus and I used to compete with each other to discover who was the braver by each trying to get closer than the other to the guard on duty. We would take turns inching our way along the wall toward the hulking figure before turning to run in terror as soon as the gladiator would look in our direction. When I was a young child, my mother would frighten me into good behavior by threatening to feed me to Felix or Achilles. I did *not* want to be caught escaping by one of these men.

My plan was as simple as it was misguided. After the wedding, there was to be a dinner party. Porcia was a very demanding woman, and since Titus and his betrothed had not yet melded their staffs of slaves together, Porcia decided her cook and household slaves would handle things while we stayed out of the way. Every slave of the Titus household was quite happy to oblige her wish. Marcus, Clodia, and I were directed to spend the evening in our upstairs cubicle. Earlier in the day, when everyone was busy cleaning the domus, I removed my sack of food and my stolen cloak and knife from the hiding place. I also had a few silver coins I had found over the years and my two remaining dice in a small purse made from a young boar's scrotum. This I tied to my tunic belt with the drawstring and tucked it under so it wouldn't be visible."

At this point, I thought I had caught Polybius in an inconsistency. Part of me wanted to find a reason to not believe him, as I thought it was the duty of a conscientious historian to doubt his source. "I thought you had four dice, and gave one to Quintus. That would leave three remaining."

"Quite so," Polybius answered without hesitation. "I too thought I had three dice in my hiding place, but when I went to retrieve them, I could find only two. I had no time to search for the other, so I contented myself with what I had. After that, I hid my supplies on a shelf behind some tools in the gardener's small shed to the side of the peristyle. When night fell I was going to wait until the others were asleep and sneak downstairs and slip out through the service door near the kitchen. Once outside I would make my way across the city, find the river and follow it to Ostia. Of course, I had no idea how far it was to Ostia, nor did I know which direction to travel. From documents I had copied I knew Ostia was a port city near the sea and that it was sixteen miles from Rome, but never having traveled more than a couple of blocks from the Titus domus, I didn't even have a clear conception of how far a mile was. None of this deterred me from my plan. I was sure that once I reached Ostia I could stow away aboard a ship and take it all the way to Syria or Aegyptus.

I lay awake listening to the sounds of the dinner party coming from the triclinium downstairs mingle with the snores coming from Marcus. I had no way of judging the time and I was afraid I would be seen by one of Porcia's slaves as he or she moved between the kitchen and the dining room. I nearly changed my mind, as one often does when the moment for action arrives, but I reminded myself of how cruel Titus had been when he sold my mother and my only friend to satisfy the she wolf he was marrying. So, I chose to go through with my plan. Quietly, I slid out from under my blanket and crept across the floor where I slept. As I pushed aside the curtain hanging over the doorway, a sliver of light entered the room. At that instant I heard Clodia stir. 'Quintus, where are you going?'

I became as rigid as a statue. 'It's Polybius. I need to pee, and the chamber pot is full. I'm going down to the latrine.' Clodia, realizing her mistake, remembered her son was gone and sighed.

'Of course. I'm sorry, Polybius. Be careful on the stairs. It's so dark.' With that she rolled over.

I no longer had to be especially stealthy. I had a reason for being up and I had a ready excuse for anyone who might question why I was on the first floor. Once downstairs, there was enough light to see where I was going. The atrium was dark, but light filtered in from the triclinium and the kitchen. I realized I did need to use the latrine, so I moved across the atrium and through the passageway near the kitchen and out to the latrine off the side of the peristyle. When I had urinated and adjusted my tunic, I left the small room. Rather than turn right back to the front of the house I turned left and moved into the colonnaded passage around the peristyle and to the shed where I hid my supplies. I collected my things and felt my way along the dark passageway to the service door. To my dismay, the door was not just bolted shut but was locked with a padlock. This was clearly another change brought about by Porcia. She didn't trust her own slaves, and she clearly didn't trust Titus' slaves either. Of course, my actions that night more than justified the lock.

I was in a panic. It was difficult enough to hide my things in the daylight, so I was not at all sure I would be able to abandon my plan and conceal them again in the dark. If I brought them to our cubicle, it would bring trouble to all the household slaves. My only choice was to go out through the small service door on the side of the front shop. There were two problems with this option. The first was that I would need to creep past three or four slaves sleeping along the walls of the atrium. The second problem, and the one I feared most was that I would need to exit dangerously close to the gladiator guarding the front of the domus. Unfortunately, I could see no other choice. I felt my way along the wall and through the passageway leading to the atrium. Moving as quietly as I could, I crept to the front of the atrium and found the door to the shop up front. For an instant I feared Porcia had that door locked too, but to my surprise it was only held shut with the slide bolt. I was able to slide the bolt back without making too much noise, and once inside the shop I slid a box of scrolls in front of the door to keep it from swinging open. After entering the shop, I could barely see. I took a moment to allow my eyes to adjust to the darkness, but it didn't help much. While feeling my way along the wall I nearly tripped on a broom that was left leaning against the wall. I stopped in my tracks when I sent it clattering to the floor and I stood there as motionless as a statue. I could feel the sweat trickling down my back and sides, but I dared not move. I could feel my heart thumping in my chest and hear the blood rushing in my ears. I tried to not breathe, as I listened for any sign of the guard. After what seemed a century, I took a deep breath and continued my journey along the wall, being careful to feel for any more obstacles. After a short time that seemed like half the night, I found the narrow service door. This door was at the side of the shop and just around the corner from where the guard sat, resting on his stool. As quietly as I could, I slid the bolt back on this door and opened it just a crack. I felt a rush of cool night air as I peered out into the darkness. The cool air reminded me how much I was perspiring and also that I had forgotten to take the stolen cloak I'd hidden on the top shelf of the tool shed. My tunic was wet with sweat and clung to my chest and back. I could see the glow of the guard's lantern around the corner at the front of the building. I decided to turn right and make my way to the back of the building and around the insulae to the north and out to the street further down the block.

As I made my way along the side of the building, feeling the rough bricks with my hand, I was overcome with a sudden rush of panic. Just as I was about to break into a run, I felt a huge hand wrap around my face, covering it. I could smell the garlic on Achilles' breath as he whispered in my right ear, 'Don't make a peep, not a sound.' If I had wanted to scream, I couldn't. Achilles' hand covered my entire face. I couldn't even breathe. All I could do was nod my head. As he relaxed his grip a bit, I could see out of the corner of my eye and what I saw terrified me even more. In Achilles right hand I caught a glimpse of his dagger just before I felt the cold steel brush the back of my neck. I imagined my severed head being kicked down the street in the morning. Rather than cut off my head though, I felt Achilles knife twisting on my metal slave collar and I heard the bent pin that held the collar securely around my neck bounce with a small ping on the pavement at my feet. In one swift move, the gladiator caught the collar in his left hand before it too could hit the ground. In doing this he had to let go of me and I was tempted to run, screaming, but I was rigid with terror.

'You won't get too far with that hangin' 'round your neck.' Achilles said in a hoarse whisper, spinning me around to face him. 'What does it say? I don't read so good.' Polybius imitated the gladiator's crude speech as he said this.

I stood staring into the face of the monster that haunted my dreams, and what was happening felt more like a dream than reality. It took me three attempts to find my voice before I rapidly squeaked out, 'I have fled my master. If found return to Titus on the Argiletum. Reward assured.' It was too dark to read, but I had memorized the words on the round bronze plate that had hung around my neck for as long as I could remember.

'For such a skinny little rat, you got some big balls. I never had the nerve to try and run. By Dis, I didn't even have the nerve to leave after I got freed. I'm still sittin' here,

66

workin' for Titus, and now the wolf bitch he's gone an' married. You're most likely gonna die out there, ya know,' Achilles sighed as he said this.

'I have a plan.' I said, relaxing just the least bit.

'Oh, a plan! I see. Well, it better be a good one, 'cause these streets are full of thieves and thugs and they'd just as soon slit your throat as look at ya.' He was starting to make me doubt my plan, but it was too late to turn back now. 'You better get pretty far away from here tonight. Come daylight, everybody in the house will be out lookin' fer ya.'

'Do you know how far it is to the river?' I asked him.

'Not too far, that way.' He indicated the direction by pointing his dagger. 'But I'd avoid crossin' the forum if I was you. All that open space will make ya easy prey for someone out lookin' to take advantage of a street kid, if ya know what I mean.' I had no idea what he meant, but I simply nodded.

'Now ya better get goin',' he said with a smile. 'Hang 'round here and you'll make trouble for us both. I'll tell Master Titus I saw ya run off into the dark jus' before daybreak. That'll give ya a couple hours lead on 'em.' Achilles turned me around and gave me a friendly shove. Just as I was about to break into a run, he called to me in a hoarse whisper, 'Hey kid!' I turned back to him. By the light of the lantern I saw my collar arcing through the air and I reached out to catch it, just as it was about to hit the street. 'Get rid of that, quick as ya can,' I was about to turn away again, when I saw something else flying through the space between us. I instinctively reached out for it and caught a small purse full of coins. 'That might help ya. Hide it someplace and don't go showin' nobody ya got money.' Achilles smiled at me.

67

'Fortuna's favor to ya, kid.' With that, he picked up his lantern and turned to walk along the front of the domus in the other direction, but he stopped and once again whispered, 'Hey kid.' I turned and looked back into the glow of light around him. 'Your mother wasn't sold in the market ya know. Titus likes to settle debts by tradin' slaves he has no use for no more. I heard she went to some rich, important patrician to work on his farm in Picenum. Jus' in case you was thinkin' of lookin' for her. Now get outta here.'

I nodded and smiled, as much from relief that he didn't kill me as from the clue as to where my mother was. I turned and ran as fast as I could down the dark street. In almost no time though, I had to slow my run to a trot as I was enveloped in darkness. When I was forced to slow to a hesitant walk, I realized I should have planned my escape for a night when there was a full moon, but it was too late to do anything about it now. At this hour there was almost no light by which to see my way. If I had left a couple of hours earlier there may have been light sneaking through the cracks of the shutters over the upper floor windows of the apartments that lined the street, but this late in the night it seemed all the lamps had been extinguished. I was reduced to slowly moving to the side of the street and feeling my way along the building fronts. My eyesight had adjusted enough to the darkness for me to distinguish between the walls and the boards of storefronts, and the doorways of the insulae, but it was still a slow journey. After traveling what I assumed must have been miles, I heard the splash of a fountain near an intersection ahead. I left the security of the shop fronts I was following as a guide and ventured out into the middle of the street and made my way closer to the sound of splashing water.

The fountain was constructed as a large square basin with a limestone water nymph standing waist deep in the pool. Above her head she held a tilted amphora from which there came a constant flow of water. I was happy to see the fountain, as I had worked up a great thirst with the tension of my escape and my run down the street, but I was disappointed to realize it was the very fountain I had seen hundreds of times from the balcony of the copy room. I had traveled barely two blocks. I gulped down handfuls of water and splashed water over my head to clear my mind before sitting on the edge of the basin to collect my thoughts. The area around the fountain was not quite as dark as the street down which I'd just felt my way. Along the Argiletum the street was wider than most of the streets of the Subura, but to make use of the precious little space it was lined with four and five story insulae, each with a dozen or more apartments. Even the few domi such as the Titus home that remained on the street had over time had second and sometimes third stories added to them. Many of these buildings had balconies that ran the length of their fronts and blocked out what little light there was from the stars and crescent moon. Here at the fountain my eyes began to adjust to the dim light and I could make out the shapes of buildings. Just down the street I could see shapes that didn't seem to represent homes. These buildings were large and imposing and without balconies. I correctly surmised that I was nearly at the edge of the forum and seeing the grand temples and basilicas and the curia, that ancient meeting place of the senate. I knew the Forum Boarium was somewhere beyond the Forum Romanum, and the Tiber River docks and warehouses fronted that great cattle market. Now I was faced with a dilemma. I asked myself if it would be better to cross the open space and risk encountering the mysterious predators Achilles had warned me to avoid or to take the long way around the forum and risk losing my way in the dark narrow streets. In spite of my fear, I decided to risk crossing the open space of the forum.

I made my way toward the side of the great Basilica Aemilia and then followed the wall until it ended and I was forced to turn into the forum proper. At the front of the basilica, I darted across the open space to my right and found myself up against the Rostra. In spite of having never set foot in nor eyes on the forum, I immediately recognized, from descriptions I had read, the great speaker's platform. I sat under one of the gilded ships prows that jutted from the front of the Rostra and hoped I was deep enough in its shadow to escape detection. My heart was pounding and I was already out of breath, but I didn't see another living creature save a couple of rats darting across the forum. I slowly made my way along the front of the Rostra until I reached its end. I knew I would need to make another dash across open space. Maybe forty feet away was the huge dark silhouette of the Temple of Concordia. I thought if I could make it to the temple steps I could rest a short time and make another dash across to the temple of Saturn on the other side of the forum. To the right of the temple of Saturn I could make out an open space that looked to be the start of a street."

At this point I once again felt compelled to interrupt Polybius. "How is it you didn't encounter any farmers trucking their supplies into the city to stock the tavernas and shops. I've seen *and heard* the parade of carts that make their way into the city all night long."

Polybius looked a little irritated that I seemed to doubt his story. "I'm sure you have, as have I," he answered. "Remember, young Lucius, wheeled traffic in the city was not banned during daylight hours until Caesar's dictatorship, and that was still many years in the future. In the time of my youth, produce was brought into the city the evening before and fresh fish was brought in all throughout the day." At that I felt rather foolish and nodded for him to continue. I was coming to realize it was not wise to question his veracity.

"At any rate," Polybius continued, "I was able to make it to the steps of the Temple of Concordia without incident, and there I sat for a moment as I said a silent prayer of thanks to the goddess. I was still very nervous, but not nearly to the degree I had been when I started my progress across the open space of the forum. From the temple steps, I could indeed make out a narrow street. I decided to avoid the Temple of Saturn to the left of this street and just take my chances dashing right into the darkened lane. As I left the relative light of the forum, I found myself once again enveloped in darkness. I could barely make out the landscape in front of me but I ran ahead anyway. After running blindly about fifty feet or so, I raced headlong into a flight of low, wide steps. I later came to learn that I had run into the narrow street that leads up the side of the Capitoline Hill. Crashing into the steps, I badly scraped my knees and my forearms and sent my small canvas sack of supplies flying. I cursed rather more loudly than I had intended and followed that with a stifled cry of pain as I tried to push myself up and crawl ahead looking for my lost sack of supplies. Just as I found my canvas bag, a light appeared at the top of the hill. I could make out the silhouette of a man holding a lantern above his head with his left hand; his right hand held a sword. Between us was a winding lane of sloping road that turned to steps wherever the incline became too steep. Behind and to the right of the man, I could make out the form of the Temple of Capitoline Jupiter.

My pain was quickly forgotten as I turned to run back the way I came. From the top of the steps came a shrill whistle. This was answered by another whistle coming from the Temple of Saturn. Trapped between them I had no choice but to leave the path and take my chances running along the back of the Temple of Saturn. As I rounded the back of the temple I tripped and fell, once again losing my sack of supplies, but I had no time to search for it in the dark. Scrambling to my feet and running at full speed, I nearly ran into the side of the basilica that bordered the left of the temple. This was the Basilica Sempronia, a smaller version of the basilica built by Caesar that stands on the spot today. I ran around the far side of the temple and I could hear what seemed like at least two other men whistling to the others. I thought these men must be the mysterious predators I was warned to avoid. I made my way to the front of the row of shops and tavernas, and was faced with a choice; should I attempt to run back across the open forum or make my way into unknown territory and run along the portico that fronted the row of shops spanning the length of the basilica. My decision was made when I heard the heavy steps of booted feet running in my direction. I turned and ran down the length of the portico. Looking over my shoulder, I could see the light from the man's lantern growing brighter and could hear at least four men shouting to one another. I remember feeling sad that my brief taste of freedom was so short lived as I slowed to a trot, accepting the inevitable. The men would find me and in all likelihood I would either be killed or returned to Titus, where I might also be killed. I was hurt and exhausted and feeling utterly beaten. I eventually came to a stop and looked back, waiting for the men to see me.

Then, for the second time that night, I felt a hand reach out and cover my mouth, stifling a shout of protest. This

72

hand was not nearly as large nor as strong as Achilles' hand, and the voice that whispered in my ear belonged to a much younger man, or, to be more accurate, I should say a boy, not much older than me. 'Don't make a sound or you'll get us both caught.' I didn't put up a struggle, letting the young man drag me back into a recess in the portico. He pulled me back around a large ceramic pot and as he sat hard on the stone floor behind it, wedging himself between the pot and a wall, he pulled me onto his lap, still holding his right hand over my mouth. With his left hand he dragged a filthy blanket over us both. When he realized I was not putting up any sort of resistance he first eased his grip on my mouth and then released my face altogether so he could use both his arms to pull me closer to him and wedge the two of us into the narrow space between the wall and the pot. He then dragged my feet up under the blanket and adjusted it so it would cover us both completely. I tried to catch my breath while sucking in air as quietly as possible. Sitting motionless in total darkness, I began to notice my surroundings, and as I tried to make sense of where I was, I could smell the stench of stale urine mingled with the sweat of both my captor and myself. I could hear or feel, I'm not sure which, both our hearts beating rapidly. I could feel his warm breath on the side of my face and I could feel the grip of his arms around me, holding me tightly, but not too tightly. It was then I realized my captor was, in reality, my protector.

'If they have dogs, we run in different directions. If a dog catches you, go for its eyes. It won't do any good, but try anyway,' he whispered in my ear.

'How will we know if they have dogs?' I whispered back.

73

'You'll know,' was his reply. 'For now, we don't make another sound and we don't move.' I decided to trust his judgment. He no longer needed to keep his arms around me, but he continued to do so.

We sat like this for a very long time. In spite of my state of anxiety, or perhaps because of it, I drifted into a sort of half waking, half sleeping state. I seemed to be aware of my surroundings and yet, I had a most curious dream. In my dream, I was right in the very spot I occupied in reality, under a blanket and on the lap of a strange boy. I could see a light powerful enough to show through the weave of the blanket, so I pulled the cloth down a bit to see where it originated. Standing in front of the pot was a beautiful woman. At first I was frightened that we had been discovered, but she was smiling and holding her right hand out to me. 'It's alright. You can come out. Don't worry, no one will see you.' She spoke in a voice that sounded like music. I crawled out from behind the pot. 'You are willing to risk so much for your freedom. I am moved by your daring and it pleases me. It shows you have faith in me. Many would call you a fool, but I know you are very brave.' She took my hand and we began to walk along the portico past the row of closed shops. In the distance it was still night but all around us it was bright as midday. I looked back toward the boy who had rescued me, and the woman seemed to know my thoughts. 'Don't worry about him, he will be fine.'

'Who are you?' I asked.

She laughed as she answered, 'Don't you recognize me? I am Fortuna.'

'The goddess?' I foolishly asked.

74

'Yes, Tychaeus, the goddess.'

'How do you know my name? Nobody calls me that, anymore.'

'I have known you since before you were born. I know more about you than you yourself will ever know for certain,' she answered.

'Will my gamble pay off? Am I truly free or will those men catch us and send me back,' I asked her.

She stopped walking and in an instant was no longer at my side but was instead standing in front of me staring into my eyes. She was still incredibly beautiful, but now there was an aspect of danger about her. 'Yes,' she said.

'Yes, I'm free, or yes, they will catch me?'

'Yes, your gamble will pay off,' she answered. 'I have a plan, and you will play a part in it. Now go back and join your new friend and remember what I have said when you return to Master Titus.' Those last words struck me like a blow to the belly, taking my breath away. The shock caused me to awaken with a start.

LIBER VI

I then heard new sounds. I could see sun light and hear the sounds of the boards being pulled from one of the nearby shops. I could also smell bread baking and hear the birds chirping. There was that smell of urine again and I could hear the sound of water flowing nearby. I pulled the blanket from my head and noticed a fat man with his tunic hoisted up, pissing in the large pot we were wedged against. It was then I realized we had spent the night in a public urinal. When he had finished and shook off the last drops he looked down at me and scowled. 'You're a new one. You little shits multiply like rats.' I stared dumbly up at him. 'You're lucky I didn't piss all over you. Now get away from here. I have a business to run and I don't like beggars chasing my customers away.' When I twisted around and crawled from the space where we had wedged ourselves, the man noticed the older boy. 'I shoulda know you'd be around here.' He kicked the boy, as he too crawled from our hiding place. The boy grabbed his blanket and started running down the portico. I took off after him, not knowing what else to do. A short way down the portico we ran past the bakery that had just opened for business. The smell of baking bread reminded me that I was hungry, but I had no time to lament my lost food, as I was surrounded by the threatening glares of the shopkeepers removing the boards from the fronts of their stalls. I just continued running behind the boy who had protected me the night before.

I followed as the boy ran to the end of the basilica and turned right onto Via Tuscus. We took this road a short

76

distance until we came to the end of the temple of Castor and Pollux, where he ducked into the bushes behind the temple. I crouched down and followed him in through a well-hidden path to a small clearing where we sat down in the dirt. For the first time we got a good look at each other. I studied this stranger carefully. He had dark curly hair and in spite of the dirt I could see he had strong regular features with a straight nose and full lips. His eyes were blue and his cheeks were coated with a first beard of fine light hairs with a few dark curls mixed in. His moustache and chin hairs were just a bit further along. I guessed him to be about fifteen or sixteen years old. As we were running along the portico I noticed he was taller than me, but as we sat there in the small clearing I could see he was thinner than I and not very well-fed. His collarbones jutted out from the top of his oversized tunic and his legs and arms were quite thin.

My companion seemed very relaxed hiding in the bushes, as if this was home to him. I didn't know what else to do, so I thanked him. 'You saved me last night. Thanks.'

'I was only watching out for myself. If you got caught they would've found me too.' He tried to sound tough, but then he smiled and his whole demeanor softened.

'Well, thank you anyway. My name's Polybius. I lost a sack with some food in it last night behind the big temple at the other end of the forum. We should go back and look for it.'

'I'm Gaius Antistius,' he answered. 'You're new out here, I can tell. Your food is long gone. If some stray dog didn't get it, somebody like us is eating it for breakfast by now if a stray dog or the rats didn't get it.' I was crushed, as my adventures the night before had given me a huge appetite,

77

'We'll get something to eat as soon as the baker puts his bread out.'

'I have no money,' I lied. I didn't want to spend my money too soon.

Gaius smiled and gave me a pitying look. 'We don't need money. We wait 'til no one is looking and we grab a couple of loaves and run like our asses are on fire.' He seemed to know what he was doing.

'Where do you live,' I asked. I immediately regretted the question, realizing it would lead to Gaius asking me questions I was reluctant to answer.

'Right here, when nobody else gets to the spot first. I'm a citizen though.' He seemed to want to make that point clear. 'I live here 'cause after mom died and then dad lost the farm and he couldn't find a job in the city so he joined the legions. I'm gonna sign up next year when I'm old enough.' He talked about these problems casually like they were common and I'd understand. At that time I was still quite ignorant and never knew there were hordes of people without homes living on the streets of Rome. 'Last night I came here to sleep but there was a man here with a prostitute. I watched for a while, but it was getting dark and I didn't want to get caught out in the open so I went to sleep by the piss pot after the fullers had collected the urine.'

'I'm a citizen too,' I lied. 'Doesn't it stink sleeping there?'

It's not so bad; you get used to it, and nobody else wants to sleep there so it's safe. Where do you live,' he asked.

78

'No place. I ran away.' I was truthful about this at least. From this point I began to invent freely. 'My mom died too. My dad married a wicked woman who treated me very badly, so I left. We lived in a nice place over on the Argiletum. I'm going to find a job and get my own place.'

'How old are you?' Gaius let out a little laugh when he said this.

'Fourteen,' I lied again.

'You won't find a job. Grown men can't find jobs. Every day families get kicked off their farms and come to Rome looking for work. You should go back home and tell your father how sorry you are. Maybe he won't kill you.'

'I'm not going back.' I was firm.

'Well, you can hang around with me if you want, but don't get in my way. I'm gonna go take a piss.' With that Gaius moved crouching through the bushes to the back of the temple. I realized I too needed to piss, and followed him. Along the back of the temple there was room to stand up, and we both stood side by side pissing on that sacred wall. Gaius finished first and as he turned to walk away he said, 'Now let's go get some breakfast.'

I hesitated as we stepped out of the brush and onto the street. Gaius turned with an exasperated look. 'What? Are you scared to take a loaf of bread? Just do what I do. Feel it first to make sure it's not too hot to carry.'

'It's not that. Who were those men that chased me last night? Won't they be waiting for us?' I could tell by the look on his face, Gaius thought I was a little stupid.

'Gods! Haven't you ever noticed the temple guards hanging around the forum? At night when there's nothing to do they'll chase down vagrants and give 'em a good beating or maybe catch a runaway slave they can get a reward for. Don't be stupid, Polybius. Now let's get going.'

The mention of runaway slaves made me blanch. Gaius didn't seem to notice or if he did notice he chose to ignore it. I never knew there were temple guards, although it made sense. I'd made copies of hundreds of documents listing valuable gifts donated to various temples and priesthoods. I'd seen that wealthy citizens could deposit money in temples for safekeeping, and often had their last wills kept securely in temple vaults. In my naiveté I assumed no one would ever violate a sacred place and risk the wrath of a god. I covered my ignorance with a lie. 'I thought they stayed in the temples at night.'

As we came to the end of the street and entered the forum proper, I was struck by a new fear. That early in the morning it appeared about half the people in the forum were slaves and the others were mostly poor plebeians. I'd heard the forum was always crowded, and I expected to see hundreds of equestrians and patricians in togas, but this was not the case. Almost everyone there at that hour was wearing the plain tunic of the working class pleb or the slave. My plan was to be halfway to Ostia by dawn and now I realized I could run into a slave belonging to Titus or, even worse, Porcia. I gave thought to turn and run, but hunger or perhaps a sense of obligation to Gaius made me take the risk. It was surprisingly easy to steal the bread. The baker and his wife were very busy helping a line of customers, and the slave working in the shop didn't seem to want to notice us standing off to the side waiting for the right moment. Gaius had pulled his blanket over his head

80

like a hood. I noticed he had it fastened at his shoulder with a pin of some kind and was wearing it like a cloak. I thought this only made him appear more suspicious, lurking in the shadows with a dirty blanket over his head, but I was new to this and didn't want to question his judgment. There was a double line of people waiting to get their morning bread. At the precise moment both the baker and his wife turned back to their oven, Gaius darted in front of the person waiting at the head of the queue and snatched a loaf from the row lined up on the counter. I followed and did the same. The baker chased us, brandishing a club and screaming curses, but those waiting in the line held him up, and by skillfully weaving around people we were soon lost in the crowd. I noticed that a couple of the plebs in the crowd briefly joined in the chase but soon lost interest. Not a single slave appeared to notice anything amiss.

We ate our bread behind the Temple of Saturn. I found the canvas sack I had lost the night before but, as Gaius had predicted, it was empty. While eating our breakfast I asked Gaius a question that made him give me that suspicious look I'd noticed earlier that morning. 'Why were some of those people not paying for the bread? They just seemed to be trading small sacks of something for it.'

'Are you from Parthia?' He seemed annoyed at my ignorance. 'Those are the people on the free grain dole. They bring the grain to the bakers to mill and bake it for them. In exchange the baker gets to keep a little of the flour to make the bread he sells. They drop the grain off one day and pick the bread up the next. I thought you said you were from around here!'

'It's just that our domus has a kitchen.' I covered quickly.

'Well, most of the plebs don't. And, the landlords don't want them cooking anyway. That's how fires get started.'

I decided to keep my mouth shut and eyes open and figure things out for myself until I could find a way to get to Ostia. I certainly didn't want to arouse his suspicion. We spent most of the day wandering the streets. I was again in a panic when about mid-morning Gaius led me across the forum and onto the Argiletum, but we turned off onto a side street well before we got to the Titus domus. The streets that led off the Argiletum were narrow and dirty. The insulae were so close together they blocked out most of the light. Balconies that projected from apartments on opposite sides of the street sometimes nearly touched each other. Because they were so narrow the streets were always jammed with people. Almost all the insulae were lined with shops on the ground floor and, unlike in the forum, there didn't seem to be the orderly and patient wait for service at the counters of these shops. Instead there was a good deal of jostling and arguing with the occasional scuffle. Gaius led me through the streets pointing out the sites and describing the people like I was a visitor to the city. In a sense, I was new to Rome. I had never ventured farther from the Titus domus than the nymph fountain, and I never had occasion to visit this section of the Subura. Gaius instructed me in the ways of living on the street as well. He explained that it was better to steal from the shops in the forum, because the better class of citizens it attracted would be less likely to join in the pursuit and the slaves of the rich never bothered a fleeing thief. He also explained that it was often easier to find charity in the poorer neighborhoods. In spite of

82

the fact that they had little, the plebeians were more generous when approached by someone less fortunate. The rich, he said, held their money tightly in their clenched fists. A beggar was also more likely to earn a beating and be robbed of that day's gains if he ventured onto the Palatine Hill. Robbery and assault seems to be the punishment the patrician class likes to mete out for what they seem to see as the 'crime' of poverty unless it happens to be one of their own who falls on hard times. In that case the transgressor is just allowed to accumulate enormous debt until he can be posted to some province where he can regain his fortune.

After the midday meal, when the tavernas had quieted down, Gaius, with me in tow, made the rounds of nearby eating establishments. He said the managers would sometimes let him eat the table scraps in exchange for sweeping the floors, but we had to time our arrival carefully. If the taverna was too busy, the workers would chase us away for fear we would disturb the customers, too late and some other boy would have gotten the job before us. He instructed me carefully to never under any circumstances steal from these shops, as we would never be allowed back. After being turned down twice, the third manager we approached not only let us eat whatever scraps we could find, but gave us each a big bowl of soup. This meal was at least as good as what I had been eating all my life in the Titus household.

The Subura was a strange place unlike any I have yet experienced in my long life. As I said the streets were narrow. They were so narrow, in fact, that it was impossible for two carts to move down the same street in different directions. Because of this there was a tacit understanding that the carts only traveled alternating ways from street to street. On each side of the narrow streets were ramshackle insulae, most of

83

which were in various stages of collapse. Indeed, it seems the only thing that did keep them from collapsing was the fire that often consumed them before the natural pull of the earth could bring them down. Dirty people lingered in dirty doorways or in front of shops that sold second or third hand goods or fruits and vegetables left over from what wasn't sold on previous days in the shops in the forum or on the hills. The crime of theft would have been a serious problem if anyone who lived in the valley between the hills had anything worth stealing. If there was ever a reason for a man of substance to enter into the Subura he had the good sense to dress in a plain tunic and leave any money or valuables at home, else he would leave without them or never leave at all. As it was, gangs of thugs ran various blocks, demanding protection money from shop owners and doing violence to those who didn't pay, when, in fact, the greatest threat the merchants needed protection from was the gangs themselves. In those narrow streets it was common to encounter men and women in the grip of some madness, talking senselessly to people they alone could see or hear or raging at the real people who passed close enough to capture their attention. It was common by midday to see the same men and women who had become slaves to wine passed out in doorways or on the streets, sometimes soiled with their own urine, filth, or vomit.

At the same time, there were often great acts of kindness with people uniting to help each other out. Those who were in the same trade would band together and if one of their 'brothers' had a problem, the group would provide what assistance it could. There were two or three physicians who would visit the Subura a few times a month and provide their services for little or even no pay to those who needed it. There was a widow who reportedly had a farm in the country that gave her a small but regular income. She took in young

84

orphans too small or weak to fend for themselves, teaching the girls to embroider cloth and the boys to work the counter of the second hand shop she kept for no other reason than to give these poor children a safe place to do something useful. The only patricians I ever saw move freely and unmolested through those streets were Gaius Julius Caesar and his family. Of course, they always had slaves or freedmen attending them, but not for protection. Because the Caesar branch of the Julian family had maintained a home in the Subura since ancient times, many of the residents became their clients and had a fierce loyalty to the family. These common people of the Subura provided all the protection needed when Caesar or his mother ventured into the streets. Whenever I saw Caesar and his tall, gray haired slave moving through the streets, I was reminded of our first encounter in Titus' shop and it gave me a thrill that I couldn't explain.

I had noticed there were many homeless boys wandering the streets of the Subura, but I didn't see any girls except those with some deformity or infirmity. I asked Gaius why this was so.

'The girls are married young or sold. The ones who do get orphaned usually become prostitutes. I can show you some if you like, but you can't get that for sweeping the floor.'

I blushed when I realized he thought I wanted a girl. The Titus household had no girls my age, so I had no experience with sex, at least none involving another person. 'I was just wondering,' I said, betraying my embarrassment. Of course I had witnessed people engaged in sex. The slave quarters of the Titus household were small and our three rooms were shared by many. Some of the slaves didn't even have rooms, and were forced to sleep on the floor in front of

85

the bedchamber of Master Titus or on the floor of the kitchen in front of the hearth. The front door slave slept in the vestibule of the domus. I don't believe he ever ventured farther from that post than the latrine off the peristyle in the back. Day and night he could be found at his post by the door. At any rate, it was not uncommon to enter a room and encounter a couple stealing an amorous moment. A few times I even found my mother and Marcus engaged in intercourse. Of course, I found this quite disconcerting. Most often, she would warn me ahead of time to avoid the room. There was also a universally understood signal; if the toe of an empty sandal was visible protruding beneath a doorway curtain, it would be impolite to enter that room. Observing sex and having the actual experience, however, are quite different matters.

Since around my thirteenth birthday, I had found myself becoming more and more preoccupied with sex. Marcus told me it was natural; he said that the obsession started when a boy sprouted his first pubic hair, and ended when he turned gray and wrinkled. He told me I would spend my life trying to steal a glance at a girl or dreaming about the soft touch of a rich man's daughter or wife. I can tell you from experience that the obsession diminishes with age, but never entirely leaves a man, even when he is gray and wrinkled. Perhaps it will at the magic age of one hundred. The female form fascinated me, but I was as much if not more attracted to the male body. In spite of the fact that I have fathered children, I have always preferred masculine companionship, both as friends, and as romantic partners."

I was a bit startled by this, and looked up from my note taking. "You actually prefer men to women?" I, of course, knew there were men who were attracted to other men,

86

but I had never heard anyone address the subject so easily and admit he was more attracted to men than women.

"Quite so," he answered casually. "In fact, somewhere about my thirtieth year, I no longer bothered to seek out female company. Caesar's soldiers sang a bawdy song as they marched in his triumph saying that he was 'every woman's husband, and every man's wife,' or something to that effect. That used to make me smile, because it was not at all true of Caesar, but could have been said about the two of us if we were considered together, and by that time we were rarely publicly seen apart. I certainly was not *every* man's wife, but I had played the part for more than one."

"You took the feminine role then?" I asked uneasily.

"You are asking if I have been fucked by men. Yes," he casually answered, "and I have also fucked men. I have physically enjoyed men and they have enjoyed me in myriad ways."

All I could say was, "It is unmanly to be a passive partner to another man."

"So you say," he replied. "That is your father talking, and his father, and his father's father." Polybius sighed. "One of the few freedoms reserved for one of my standing in society is that I have no standing in society. You, young Lucius, are shackled by the constraints applied by your ancestors. All those death masks your father proudly displays in the wing off his Atrium compel you to behave a certain way. I, on the other hand, have no ancestors glaring at me from beyond the grave. There are no expectations of how a slave or a freedman must behave, save obedience and fidelity. I have the one freedom you will never have. I can love whom I choose. More often

87

than not, my choice has been another man." With that Polybius struggled to move into an upright position on his couch. "I'll leave you to ponder that thought while I visit the chamber pot." I helped him to his feet and watched him shuffle off to move behind a curtain at the far end of the room.

While Polybius was gone I thought about what he had said. I knew in my heart that it was wrong for a Roman citizen to assume the feminine role in a sexual relationship with another man, but I couldn't apply logic or reason to make that argument. I also knew that men frequently forced themselves on male slaves. It never occurred to me that a man could not just tolerate the passive role, but even enjoy it. What he said made sense. In many ways my life was laid out for me. Decisions that directed how I led my life were not only made by my father, but also by my long dead ancestors. Ultimately though, I was glad I was strongly attracted to women, and only women. I was so deep in my thoughts that Polybius had emerged from the shadows of the room before I noticed him shuffling slowly forward supported by his staff.

"Ahhh, I have made you uncomfortable with what I have said." He smiled as he said it. "I'm sorry. I didn't mean to disturb your mind. I'm afraid, as my story progresses you may be even more disturbed as you hear me tell of a few 'great' Roman citizens I have met who, from time to time, enjoyed playing the part of the wife." Now, I was curious. As Polybius settled himself back onto the cushions of his couch, I excused myself and found the chamber pot.

When I returned, I ran into Castor as he was leaving with the empty wine pitcher. I looked at him curiously, wondering if he had ever been the recipient of Polybius' amorous advances. When I returned to the balcony I saw a

88

fresh pitcher of wine. "How did Castor know it was time for more wine," I asked.

"I throw coins to my boys. They wait on the terrace below. It is how, one day, they will buy their freedom. That is, if I don't die first, bequeathing it to them in my will."

"How is it that a former slave can, with a clear conscience, own slaves of his own?" I was bolder than usual because of the wine I had consumed.

"I treat them well. I give them far better lives than the poor plebs they see every day," he replied.

"It's not the same," I said.

Polybius sighed and looked long into my eyes before he spoke. "I know that. I, of all people, know that it's not the same. But, I need these boys. I'm very old. My conscience isn't clear, but if I lost them, I could not go on."

"Surely, if you gave them their freedom, they would stay on as your freedmen." I said it as much as a question as a statement.

"If I gave them their freedom, they would, more likely than not, leave this very day. You do not understand the allure of freedom. Instead, I hold it out as a reward for serving me until I die, all the while hoping they don't kill me."

I was surprised by what he said. "As far as I have observed, Castor and Pollux love you."

"Love and murder are not exclusive of each other, as you will undoubtedly learn in your life. Now, let's go on." With that, he settled back on his couch and I refilled our cups.

89

He continued his story. "I still intended to find my way to Ostia and stow away on a ship bound for some far away port, but my days with Gaius turned into months. There was an easy rhythm to living on the streets that coexisted with the constant threat of danger. The community of homeless people and those so poor that they were living on the edge of homelessness often helped each other out while at the same time they competed for survival. There was a man who would trade haircuts for food. He was a barber by trade, but a fondness for wine led to shaky hands and shaky hands led to bad haircuts and at least one ear that was clipped nearly in half. As a result, he was forced to lower his prices and could not afford both his rent and food.

There was a widow named Camilla, who was lonelier than she was poor. This woman was past her fortieth year, but she was very attracted to teen boys. I was shocked when Gaius explained to me that she would trade a clean tunic and a meal for sex. I was extremely nervous the first time we visited her. I almost turned and ran as we made our way up the dark dusty steps of an insulae to a fourth floor apartment. The apartment was small, but clean. It was only one room, but it was large enough for a bed and a small table and stools. When we arrived together, she seemed quite excited to see the two of us, but I was so nervous and I found her fat sweaty body and bad teeth so unappealing that I couldn't actually participate in the sex act. I was also surprised to find I felt jealous. I guess I would have to say I was in love with Gaius, but it wasn't a mature love, rather it was the kind of infatuation only a boy on the cusp of manhood could feel. I didn't like the idea of sharing my friend with this woman. But, I could do nothing to alter the situation, so there I sat naked on a stool. I was clutching my money purse since our tunics were soaking in a tub nearby, watching Gaius make clumsy love to Camilla. I was grateful to see he never kissed her, as that would have been far too intimate. Seeing him naked and engaged in sex, I found myself aroused, so I masturbated as they had intercourse. This seemed to excite Camilla almost as much as if I was actually involved in the act, and she watched me with the intensity of a bird of prey as she pulled him tightly to her.

When they finished, we took turns washing off our bodies in one small wooden tub, while Camilla, still naked, washed our tunics and underwear and Gaius' blanket and hung them on a line strung in one corner of the room. She then gave us bowls of cold soup from an earthenware pot and some hard bread. She sat contentedly watching two naked boys eat their meal. After we ate, I began to worry we would be trapped there for hours, while our tunics dried. To my surprise, when our bowls were empty, she stood up and went to a chest in the corner of the room. All I could see was her large bottom as she bent over rummaging through the trunk. She stood up and called me over. I felt rather embarrassed to walk over to her still naked, so I covered my genitals with my hands while at the same time clutching my coin purse. She turned and held a tunic up to me, checking it for size. 'Too big,' she said as she turned and traded it for another from the trunk. 'This one will do.' She then found a tunic for Gaius, and underwear, and we got dressed. At first I thought she must have a son around my age, but then it occurred to me that she traded clean tunics for sex with many of the homeless boys, and rather than waiting for them to dry after the washing, she just passed along those of the previous owner. I assumed we would be leaving, but I soon found there was more to the ritual. Gaius and I had to dump the tubs that had been used to wash our tunics and the sex from our bodies over the wooden rail of Camilla's balcony. Gaius shouted a warning as we hoisted the first tub, but some people on the street still got splashed. When we hoisted the second tub up they cleared a sufficient area to avoid getting any wetter. After that, we had to each carry two large pails down to the fountain on the corner and fill them. It was hard work carrying the water up the stairs and it took three trips to bring enough water to refill both tubs.

This whole process lasted until late in the day. The shops had all been closed for hours, and the streets began to fill up with people returning from the baths, so we made the rounds of our usual sleeping spots. The rest of the day, Gaius was strangely quiet. The blanket was still damp, so we needed to find a place near a branch where we could hang it to dry. The spot behind the Temple of Castor had no large trees, so we found a level spot, surrounded by trees, on the slope of the Palatine Hill. For a time we sat watching the sunset, but Gaius still wouldn't respond to my attempts at conversation. 'Is something bothering you?' I asked.

'It's nothing,' he answered before going quiet again. After a few moments he looked at me angrily. 'I thought we were friends,'

This hurt me. 'We are friends! Right now you're my only friend.'

'Then why have you kept secrets from me?' He looked at the belt around my tunic, where I kept my purse as I pretended to not notice.

'I haven't kept secrets,' I lied.

'What do you have in the purse?' He sounded hurt and angry

92

Then it was my turn to be silent. We both sat watching the sky darken for a long time. He got up to test the blanket for dryness. He seemed satisfied, so he spread it on the ground and laid down on his side with his back to me. I saw he left enough room, so I lay down beside him, staring up into the darkening sky. We said nothing for some time, me deep in thought and Gaius deep in hurt. I knew if I told him the truth I might lose his friendship but if I continued to lie to him I would lose it for certain.

'You're right, I have lied to you. I'm sorry.' I finally said. I was worried I would need to find a new place to sleep that night, but I went on anyway. 'I have dice I keep for good luck.' I paused and took a breath. 'And, some money.'

He didn't answer, but once I started telling the truth, I didn't want to stop. 'I lied to you because I thought I would lose you as a friend. I'm not a citizen. I'm a slave.' I waited for a reaction. I knew he wasn't asleep, but Gaius said nothing so I continued with my story. I told him everything. I told him about my job and my life in the Titus house and finally about Quintus and Artemisia. 'I was saving the money so I could take a ship from Ostia to Picenum to find my mother.'

Gaius rolled over on his back. I braced myself for his inevitable anger. I was sure he would hate me. 'You don't need to take a ship to Picenum,' he said. 'It's on the other side of Italia. You could walk there in half a month or less.'

I was relieved he didn't respond with anger. 'I'm sorry I lied to you,' I said softly.

'I know, you told me,' he answered, 'Promise you won't lie to me again.' Then he rolled toward me, threw his

93

arm across my chest and said, 'Let's get some sleep, I'm tired.'

'I promise,' I said, smiling in the dark.

The following morning, Gaius asked how much money I had. I was reluctant to show him, afraid he would want to spend it, but I promised not to lie to him. 'I don't know,' I answered truthfully. 'I don't know how to count money.'

'Let me see. I can tell you,' he said. I took my purse out and untied it from my belt, emptying it into his hand. He first examined the dice and smiled as he gave them back to me. He then carefully explained the coins. He pointed to a silver coin. 'This is a denarius. It's worth the most.'

'I thought the larger coins were worth more.'

He then pointed to one of the larger bronze coins. 'No, this is a sestertius. It's only worth a quarter of the silver ones.' Finally, pointing to one of the copper coins he said, 'This is an as. It takes ten of these to make a denarius. We're not supposed to use these anymore, but a lot of shops still take them.' He poured them back into my hand and I, in turn, poured the coins back into my purse. 'It all adds up to about ten denarii. We'll need to get more if we're going to Picenum.' With that, I had a traveling companion.

We couldn't steal food too often or the vendors would retaliate. There seemed to be an understanding that if we only took a little it wasn't worth the trouble to stop us, so we spent the rest of the day making our usual rounds, scrounging for food and begging for coins. Gaius folded his cloth tunic belt so that when he tied it a space was made for him to put coins he managed to beg from people on the street. At the end of the day, we returned to the spot on the slope of the Palatine and counted out our money. I always earned more. I was smaller and had a way to make myself look pitiful. Gaius let me do the counting and I only made one mistake before getting it right. I was surprised when he gave it all to me. 'Put this in your purse.'

As we watched the sun set that day, we made plans as only two boys, ignorant of the world, can. We imagined ourselves taking to the road and finding my mother working on a farm in Picenum. In one plan, we would rescue her, while in another, we would find jobs and earn enough money to buy her and set her free. We invented scenarios about how we would spend the rest of our lives, eventually earning enough to buy a farm together and settle down and raise families. In each of our plans, we would have long and happy lives. Of course, we both knew in our hearts these dreams were not realistic, but it provided a welcome alternative to the belief that we would spend the rest of our days living like stray dogs on the streets of Rome.

At one point in our discussion, I even suggested Gaius' father could marry my mother once we freed her. When I said this, the smile left Gaius' face and he went silent, scratching in the dirt beside him with a stick. I thought he was offended by the fact that I suggested his father marry a former slave, and this, in turn, offended me. I tried to not say anything, but I couldn't stop myself. 'You don't like the idea of your father marrying my mother.' He looked at me with a pained expression on his face but didn't say anything, so I did. 'That's a real asshole attitude. Just because she's a slave doesn't make my mother less worth marrying. She was born into nobility in her city.'

95

Gaius reached out to touch my arm, but I pulled back in anger. 'Polybius please,' he pleaded with me as I got to my feet, intending to walk away and find someplace else to stay for the night. I waited for him to say something, and when he didn't, I turned and began to walk down the hill. 'Polybius, wait! It's not what you think.'

I turned back in anger and shouted up to him. 'Then what the fuck is it?'

'It's that I think my father wouldn't be good enough for your mother. You're not the only one who lied about his past.' That brought me back up the hill. Once I was in front of him, I could see tears welling up in Gaius' eyes as he tried to avoid mine. 'I lied about my father. He's not a soldier. I'm not even sure he's still alive and I pray to the gods he isn't. My mother and father had five children. I had three brothers and a sister. I had two older brothers and one who was a year younger than me, but he died when he was a baby. My sister was two years younger than me. My father worked on the docks, unloading ships. We lived in Ostia. Everybody said he was a good worker, and maybe he was when he was younger, but when I was about seven or eight he started to drink a lot of wine. He always liked his wine, but something happened at that time and he started to get drunk ten or twelve times a month. I didn't realize it at the time, but now I think he didn't like his kids. We took too much attention from our mother and for that he resented us. When he got drunk he turned mean, really mean. This went on for a couple of years before he started to get drunk every night. He started to beat our mother and then us. We always would pretend we were asleep when he came home so he might not beat us, but he always woke my mother for sex or so she could fix him some food. When he started getting drunk during the day, he lost his job and we

96

were all forced to beg for food and money, which he would take from us and spend at the local taverna on wine or prostitutes. My mother and eldest brother always took the brunt of the beatings, but one day Marcus never came home. For a long time I hated him for leaving us, but then we learned he had been beaten to death by a group of boys who wanted to rob him. This broke my mother's heart, and her health began to fail. She died later that same year. She'd had fevers before, but this one was very bad and she just grew weaker and weaker. My brother Gnaeus and I were at her bedside when she died. She made us both promise to care for our sister, Antistia. About three months later, my father came home, drunk as usual, and tried to force Antistia to suck him. Gnaeus and I both laid into him. During that fight, my father struck my brother hard enough to knock him to the floor, unconscious. With my brother out of the fight, I was no match for my father, and he managed, after leaving me bruised and bloody, to throw me out of our apartment and bar the door behind him. I could hear through the door what he did to my sister. After he fell asleep, my sister unbarred the door and let me back into the apartment. Together we were able to move Gnaeus onto the bed we shared, but he never woke up. The next morning he was dead. For about three months after that, every few days my father would rape my sister. She was only twelve years old. I was too underfed and weak to match him in a fight and I feared he would kill me too, but I continued to fight him. One morning I awoke to find my sister dead. In the middle of the night, she had ripped the seams on an old tunic to twist it into a rope. She tied one end of the twisted cloth around the metal bracket that held the board that barred our door at night, and the other end around her neck. She knelt down and leaned forward, putting enough strain on the cloth to choke the life from her.'

97

After hearing this, all I could do was hug Gaius as he softly cried into my shoulder.

That night, as I lay beside Gaius in that place halfway between sleep and wakefulness, I remembered my dream of Fortuna. I could hear her say, '…remember what I have said, when you are returned to master Titus.' At that, I started awake. This in turn woke Gaius who, as usual, had protectively placed his arm across my chest.

'Are you okay, Polybius?'

'It was just a dream,' I answered, as much to myself as to him. 'Go back to sleep.'

The following morning I awoke to find Gaius already up, sitting with his knees drawn up to his chest, appearing deep in thought. 'What are you thinking?' I asked.

'I'm thinking we'll never get enough money begging on the street,'

I knew he was right. 'What can we do?'

'We need to find some way to rob someone.' I was surprised by his answer. I never really thought taking a loaf of bread or a radish as stealing, but robbing someone of his money was quite different.

'That would be wrong.'

Gaius flared at me in anger and frustration. 'Isn't it wrong that some people have so much and I need to screw an ugly old woman to get a clean tunic. Isn't it wrong that they can throw half their meals away and we get to eat their scraps we find on the floor?'

'Please don't be angry with me Gaius.'

'It's not you! It's everything! What we talked about last night was great, about moving away and finding your mother and making a new life, but it's not going to happen unless we make it happen. We can't leave it up to chance. I'm afraid Fortuna doesn't favor people like us.' Gaius sounded like he was pleading with me. At that point I almost told him about my dream, I almost said that Fortuna did favor us, but I was afraid it would make me sound foolish. Instead I remained silent, and for a long time he fell silent too. Then he got up, as if everything was alright, and said, 'Let's go get some breakfast.'

LIBER VII

Later that same day, late in the afternoon, Gaius and I had a chance to witness one of the many fires that plagued the Subura. I'm not certain you have ever had the pleasure of closely examining one of the poorly constructed insulae that house the poorest people of Rome, but if you have done so you will have noticed that the skeleton of the structure is built of wood timbers, and the facade is often of the lowest quality bricks. Sometimes they are even made of mud brick, especially on the upper floors where there is less weight to bear. This sort of poor construction has caused many of the men who own these properties to prohibit their tenants from doing any cooking in the apartments. Of course, the ban on open fires is often ignored, and it would be impossible to expect anyone living in such dismal quarters to go without the meager light from a lamp or two. Thus, there are fires.

On that bright and sunny day a fire broke out in one of the insulae on the street of the pawnbrokers, just off the Argiletum. My attention was first drawn to the place by the sound of a woman screaming. Looking toward the wailing, I noticed thick black smoke billowing from a window on the second floor, causing me to stop in the street and draw Gaius' attention to it. Soon a large crowd had gathered in the street, attracted like insects to a lamp by the orange and yellow flames climbing up the side of the building from the first window and the two most adjacent to it. In a very short time, the fire had spread across the second floor through the third floor and into the fourth. Just as women, men, and their children came swarming like roaches onto the street from one

100

of the doors, a fight broke out among the people pushing their way out through the narrow opening. Quite soon, unconscious or dead bodies were blocking the doorway making it all but impossible for anyone else to evacuate. The screams were agonizing to hear, but I stood there watching the chaos around me until Gaius dragged me away just before a section of the front wall came crashing down into the street. All the pawn brokers had been trying their best to empty the most valuable items from their shops, but as soon as they would drop an arm load of goods on the street and turn back for more, greedy men and women from the crowd would pounce on the pile like hungry dogs on a fresh carcass and fight over it until there was nothing left behind. This frenetic activity came to a halt when the bricks fell, carrying a large burning timber with them, killing several people and scattering many more in a shower of sparks and ash and a cloud of smoke.

Gaius and I continued to watch from a safe distance, sharing the limb of one of the few trees on that street with three of four other boys and young men who were nimble enough to scale the branches. Eventually, a man came with a troop of slaves to prevent the fire from spreading to neighboring buildings, but only after the owners had negotiated their sales. I was fascinated by the events I'd witnessed, and didn't take my eyes from the scene until Gaius tugged on my sleeve and indicated with a nod of his head that I should look at a man in a toga who had wandered down the street from off the Argiletum. Once he was sure I'd seen him, Gaius scrambled down the tree, and not knowing what he had in mind, I followed. When we were about twenty feet from the man, Gaius leaned in toward me and whispered, 'See that man?' I nodded so he continued. 'He goes to the races nearly every day. On days like this, when he's frowning, he didn't do so well, but if he's whistling and he's got a smile for everyone he passes, he's won big. We should watch for him, and go for his purse.'

It was around that simple observation that we would hatch a plan to steal what was for us a fortune. Later that night we learned of the women, the men, and saddest of all, the children who had perished in the blaze. Most we knew of, and a few we knew personally, but we didn't have time to mourn. We had a robbery to plan.

The plan we devised was as ill-conceived as it was simple. Gaius knew when the races were scheduled in the Circus Maximus and he knew the route used by the man he had pointed out to me when he returned from the track. It was also very simple to tell when he had won, as he carried his winnings, tied up in a canvas purse, gripped tightly in his right hand. Our plan was for me to approach him and distract him by begging for a coin or two, while Gaius came up behind him and snatched the purse full of coins. We were then to run in opposite directions and later meet up behind the Temple of Saturn. We even gave ourselves code names with which to communicate so we wouldn't reveal who we truly were.

Of course, two days later when we put our plan into action, events didn't go as we had hoped, as they seldom do. The man immediately sensed what was happening and was able to turn in time to see Gaius going for the money. Just as Gaius snatched away the purse full of coins, the man swung wildly hitting him on the side of his head, knocking him to the ground. Gaius shouted, 'Run, Ajax!' as he scrambled to his feet. I too scrambled to my feet and ran in the opposite direction. As I ran I looked over my shoulder. The man was shaking off his toga so he could give chase to Gaius who was just now running away. I noticed the man had a dagger in his hand. Against all we had planned and not knowing what I would do, I turned back and ran in their direction.

The man was running after Gaius and shouting for help. Others joined in the pursuit but didn't appear to know whom they were supposed to be chasing, so they were running in all directions. I was relieved that Gaius seemed to have lost himself in the crowded street, so I circled around, moving along the perimeter of the crowd that had gathered to see what the excitement was about. I caught sight of our intended victim when he climbed up on the low wall of a fountain to survey the crowd. He shielded his eyes from the sun with his left hand while holding the dagger up in his right. Turning first one direction then the other, he nearly caught sight of me once, but I managed to hide behind a very tall man. Just as I was about to turn away and go to meet Gaius at our predetermined meeting place behind the temple, the man excitedly jumped from his perch on the fountain wall and started pushing his way through the crowd, I made my way after him.

I could follow his path by watching the movement of the people in the crowded street as they tried to clear out of his way. I followed the wave of movement until I broke through the crowd where the street intersected with a narrow lane. There was almost no one in the lane, but I guessed the man must have chased Gaius that way as there was no longer any jostling in the crowd. I paused only for an instant and ran off down the lane. I caught up with them a short way down the narrow, dead-end street. Gaius and our victim were scuffling in the back of an empty taverna of an insulae that was being constructed. Without giving it any thought, I jumped on the man's back, clawing at his face with one hand while putting the other around his throat. He tried to shake me off but I held

103

on tightly. With one quick lunge backward, our intended victim slammed me into the half-finished brick wall of the small room we were in. Stunned, I was forced to let go and fall to the floor. The man charged at me with his dagger held high. From behind, a brick thrown by Gaius hit him hard on his back. This was enough to stop him from killing me. He turned back toward Gaius and was met with a handful of quicklime thrown into his face. Fortunately for us, the stonemasons had left a box of quicklime behind when they finished for the day. The man covered his face and screamed in pain and rage. We saw our chance and ran together for the door. I noticed Gaius had dropped the purse full of coins, but there was not time to back for it.

Turning to run the way we had come, we both stopped short when we saw two men coming down the lane in our direction. We had no choice but to run the opposite way. The lane came to a dead end with a high wall blocking our escape. At this point we were both out of breath and in pain. We limped to a stop, but just for an instant. Turning back we could see our intended victim had recovered sufficiently to continue the chase and the two others joined him. I thought for certain we would both die that day. When I heard Gaius shout 'In here!' I followed as he darted in front of a man paying the slave who guarded the door. We found ourselves trapped in a public latrine. The room had ten seats with six of them occupied. The slave had followed us in, but stopped at the doorway. Evidently, he had seen that men were chasing us, and rather than try to catch us both he just blocked the door so our pursuers could do the work. We could see through the doorway that he was very soon to be joined by the other three. The six men, sitting on the stone bench, each over an open hole, just stared at us. Some laughed at our predicament. One threw a wet sponge at me. A nervous looking man quickly

104

finished his business, got up and adjusted his underwear as he made his way to the door. He reached the door just as the others arrived, and there was some confusion as they tried to push their way past him. I could see only one option. 'In here,' I said, grabbing Gaius by the tunic and spinning him around. I jumped up on the bench and quickly slid myself through one of the open holes. I dropped down about four feet into a two-foot deep stream of cold water. Gaius quickly followed me.

The men peered through the open holes, but they were all too large to fit through them. If Gaius had been properly fed he too would have had trouble getting through the opening. However, if we would have remained there, it would have been only a matter of time before they found someone to come in after us, so we crawled forward into the darkness. The floor under us was slippery and the water smelled foul. I knew that at any moment a turd could drop from each of the occupied seats above, so I moved to the side away from the openings and crawled in the direction the water was flowing. The water all seemed to rush toward an opening. The opening was just wide enough to fit through, but as I extended my legs through the hole I found there was no longer a floor. The water simply cascaded down into the darkness. I turned and slid my legs through trying to feel for a floor under me. Clinging to the sides I stretched deeper into the opening, but I went too far and lost my grip on the slippery stones and fell through into the darkness. I splashed into still deeper water below gulping in the foul water as I went under. In a panic I scramble to get my head above water. I found I could stand with the water at the level of my chin.

'Polybius! Are you alright?' Gaius forgot to use my code name, but I didn't think it mattered since we were both going to die.

105

'I'm fine.' My words echoed off unseen walls.

'Move out of the way, I'm coming down,' Gaius said as he dropped down sending another rush of water into my face.

Now we were both in the water. I turned and moved my way deeper into the dark away from the opening. It was just a few feet before I encountered a stone wall. Gaius followed me as I moved down the passage feeling the slick wall as we went. As my eyes adjusted to the darkness, I noticed up ahead there was light coming from the roof of the passage. As we drew nearer I saw it came from four small oval holes in the roof. This provided enough light to see that the wall we were up against didn't go all the way to the ceiling. Instead, it formed a ledge that was about two feet above the water line. I was able to pull myself up onto the ledge. I turned and offered Gaius a hand. He winced and cried out as I helped pull him up onto the ledge. The ledge, it turned out, was wide enough for us to walk on with the roof of the chamber arching overhead. We walked for a considerable distance, guided by the dim light coming in from the small holes in the ceiling above. Finally, Gaius turned to me and said, 'I need to rest.' We slid down and sat with our backs to the cool stone wall.

I looked around. There was mold and fungus higher up on the walls, just above an obvious high water mark that ran along the wall about level with my shoulders as I sat on the cold hard stone ledge. The water filling the channel beside our ledge slowly but continually flowed, reeking of the offal that came along with it. Along the ledge I noticed there was every sort of trash, from pieces of broken wood, old cloth, the rotting corpse of what appeared to be a small dog, as well as broken pottery, an old shoe, and a piece of knotted rope. These items were just the few I could discern in the narrow range of my sight afforded by the slivers of light from the covers above our heads. I could hear the screech of rats in the distance, but fortunately, I could not see the creatures.

'Where are we?' I didn't expect Gaius to answer, assuming he was as confused as I.

'The Cloaca Maxima. We're in the great sewer that runs under the center of the city.'

Gaius seemed to be having trouble breathing. I looked down to where he was holding his side and noticed his tunic was stained dark.

'You're bleeding!'

'He stabbed me,' Gaius answered.

On closer inspection I could see there was a good deal of blood. His tunic was soaked in blood in the area around his hand. I pulled his hand away from the wound. At first he resisted, but then he let me see it. I tore the cloth away, ripping it where the knife had made the hole. Blood trickled from the wound. It was not a large cut, but it looked very serious. 'We need to get help,' I said.

'No,' he protested. 'I'll be fine.'

'You won't be fine. You'll die!' I'd made up my mind. I was going to find help. 'Is there a way to get out of here?'

'I don't need help. The bleeding will stop.' Gaius tried to sound confident, but I could tell he was frightened. 'Besides, who can help me?'

107

'I know a medicus. I'll go to him. Now, how can I get out of here?'

'Polybius, please! They'll make you a slave again.'

'If I don't go you'll die down here. I'm not going to let that happen.' I was insistent.

Gaius relented. 'There's an opening on the south end of the forum just beyond the basilica. Workers use it to make repairs to the sewer.' Gaius sounded weak. 'It's closed by an iron gate. Usually it's locked though.'

'I'll find it. I'll come back with help.'

'Don't go. Please, Polybius, they'll make you a slave again.' Gaius was pleading, but my mind was made up.

'Then I'll just have to run away again,' I answered him. Taking his face in both my hands, I moved in close so he could see me and I looked into his eyes. 'Do not die! I'll be back soon.'

With that I stood and moving as close to the wall as possible I nearly ran along the ledge. I tripped once on an uneven stone and almost fell into the water, but that barely slowed me down. I would move even faster each time I approached one of the openings in the street above. I realized these four holes were the ventilation holes of the covers that blocked the larger holes on the street above. I had seen these covered openings many times, but never considered where they led. At last, I found the opening Gaius had indicated. A tunnel branched off to the side and led to a rusty iron gate blocking a narrow arched doorway. Sunlight streamed in and I could smell the clean air of the outside world. To my dismay the gate was locked. A padlock was secured around the hasp that held the gate shut. I reached out and tried to pull the lock open, but it was secure. I rattled the gate in the foolish hope it would open and I then slumped to the ground and began to cry. I was then overcome with a burning rage born of my frustration, directed at nothing and everything all at once. I shouted curses at fate and the gods as I began kicking the gate that prevented me from saving my friend's life. I kicked and screamed and cried until my rage was dissipated. Then I pulled myself up by the rusty iron bars to go back and be with Gaius when he died.

Only then did I notice the gate was loose. All my kicking had no effect on the bars or the lock, but I had managed to loosen the rusted iron fasteners that held the hasp into the stone. I sat down and started to once again kick the gate. But now, instead of a haphazard frenzy, I kicked with controlled force using both legs and all my strength. With each kick the gate moved a little further. It was not long before one last mighty kick sent the gate swinging open. My legs were exhausted and my feet sore, but there was no time to waste. I ran up the short flight of stone steps leading from the opening and stopped for just an instant to determine my location. I found myself in the velebrum, the low area between the Forum Romanum and the Forum Boarium. Just ahead was Tuscus street. I ran north along the street and into the forum. Fortunately, it was late enough in the day for the forum to be relatively empty. I was able to cut straight across to the Argiletum. Without thinking of my own safety, I ran down the street I had avoided for the past months toward the Titus domus. As I approached the domus, I noticed Achilles was at his post on the corner. He saw me and looked surprised, but made no move to stop me. I cut down the side of the building and ran to the narrow stairway that led to the second floor

109

apartments while praying to the gods I had just cursed a short time earlier that Alexander would be home.

I ran up the stairs and through the open door to the apartment Alexander shared with his wife and his apprentice. Lydia saw me first. 'Polybius!' She sounded excited, but in an instant looked sad.

I had no time for small talk. 'Lydia, where's Alexander? I need him!'

'He's in the other room. Are you hurt?'

I didn't stop to talk, but darted into the second room with Lydia following behind. Alexander sat at the long table along the wall, grinding something into a powder with a mortar and pestle. His apprentice, Leonidas sat at the other end of the bench, sharpening surgical tools on a whetstone. They both turned at once. 'Polybius, whatever is wrong?' Alexander sounded calm, as always.

'My friend is dying. He needs your help.' I gasped out the words as I bent over with my hands on my knees and gulped in air.

'Calm down. Tell me what has happened.' The medicus said this in his most reassuring voice.

'My friend has been stabbed. He is bleeding to death. I have some money. Not much, but I can pay you what I have.' I handed him my purse.

'Where is your friend?' the physician asked, putting his arm reassuringly around my wet shoulder.

110

'He's in the great sewer under the forum near the Basilica Aemilia. He's bleeding.' I was becoming more desperate the longer we stood there.

I stood watching as the three others in the room began to move quickly but efficiently. There was a clear sense of urgency, but not panic. Lydia handed me a large pitcher of water and said 'drink.' With no cup in sight, I gulped straight from the pitcher while watching her gather clean dressings for the wound. The apprentice lit a fire under a small grate and placed a bronze pot on it. He took the cover off a pail on the floor and filled the pot with water and then began carefully placing surgical instruments into the water. Very soon we were all moving as one.

'The entrance to the sewer is at the south end of the forum past the basilica. I broke the gate open,' the medicus didn't seem to be listening and I was getting more worried. As I followed the three out into the other room, my heart sank and I was overcome with panic. Achilles was standing in the center of the room and had been listening to the conversation. I feared he would drag me back to Titus, and Gaius would die alone in the sewer. To my surprise all he said to me was, 'Hello Polybius, I see you've got a problem.' Then, turning to the medicus, he said, 'Felix will take my place out front. Follow me.'

We all followed Achilles down the stairs. At the bottom, the group turned to the back of the domus. 'No! We need to go this way!' I shouted as I turned toward the street.

'We've got this, Polybius,' Achilles said as he walked quickly to the back of the domus. I ran after him, thinking the man had lost his senses. As I rounded the back of

111

the house, I saw Achilles crouched over, pulling a heavy stone slab up from the ground. It was then I realized he was opening a sewer cover. I never knew that our private latrine at the back of the peristyle connected to a great underground sewer. Achilles knew exactly what he was doing. He dropped down into the opening followed by Leonidas. Lydia handed down a lantern she had brought with her. I moved to follow, but Alexander held me back.

'They will find him. You've done well. Now, we wait.' I slumped down on a stone bench at the back of the house. I realized how exhausted I was, and I simply buried my head in my hands and wept. Lydia sat beside me and wrapped an arm around me pulling me close. In a short time I found I was too tired to even cry and I just sat staring into the dirt at my feet. I hadn't even noticed Alexander had left us until he returned with a narrow wooden ladder. After he lowered the ladder into the hole, Alexander sat down on the other side of the bench and rested a hand gently on my knee. 'Polybius you must understand, Titus is my patron. I owe him my loyalty.'

I knew it would be painful for him to say what he had to say so I spared Alexander and finished his thought for him. 'I know. You must return me to my master. I understood that when I came here. Please, don't let Gaius die,' I pleaded.

'I'll do what I can. The rest is up to nature,' he answered.

After what seemed a lifetime, I finally heard voices coming from the opening. Leonidas emerged first, carrying the lantern. His hands and arms were stained with blood, as was the front of his tunic. The same calm efficiency returned to the group, and I was once again standing to the side helpless.

112

Before he cleared the opening, Leonidas was sharing what he knew with the medicus. 'The wound is deep but not large. I've managed to slow the bleeding, but it will need to be cleaned before we close it. It is truly filthy down there.'

'I've sent for fresh water and put a sheet on the table. Clean yourself and join me as quickly as you can.' The physician extended a hand, helping his assistant pull himself out of the hole. Right behind him was Achilles with Gaius over his shoulder. Gaius was naked save for a cloth wrapped tightly around the middle of his torso. He looked thin and pale in the bright sunlight. The bones of his spine jutted up along the center of his back, his ribs were clearly evident, and he was motionless.

'Is he dead?' I asked softly.

'No, he's alive thanks to the gods and to *you*,' Lydia answered.

Achilles moved quickly, bringing Gaius around the side of the house and up the stairs. Alexander followed right behind with Lydia ushering me along. They carried Gaius in and laid him on the table, and then Lydia led me out of the room and drew the drape to cover the doorway. I was too weak to protest, so I let her take control. She helped me undress, and then standing me in a washtub, she cleaned the filth of the sewer from my body. I could hear voices through the doorway leading to the steps. It sounded as if most of the slave family had gathered below. Clodia appeared in the doorway with a small loaf of bread and a clean tunic for me. She didn't say a word, but after I had dried myself and dressed, she took me in her arms and held me for a moment. Finally, she whispered, 'Welcome back, Polybius,' her voice

113

filled with sadness. As she left, she looked back at me and gave me a melancholy smile. I sat and ate my bread in silence, dreading what would come next.

After what must have been at least an hour, Alexander came from behind the curtain. 'The knife penetrated the liver but it should heal. He lost a good deal of blood, but I was able to close the wound. If it does not putrefy, he will live.'

'Can I see him,' I asked.

'Just for a moment,' the physician answered. 'He is very weak and he needs to sleep.'

I moved hesitantly through the curtained doorway. Gaius was no longer on the table. They had moved him to the bed against the wall and it occurred to me that Leonidas would need to sleep on the floor that night. Gaius was on his back with his arms out to his side and a white wool sheet pulled up to his armpits. His skin was nearly as white as the sheet and there were beads of sweat on his forehead. I thought he was asleep, so I quietly knelt down beside the bed and took his hand in mine. Lost in thought, I didn't notice he had opened his eyes until I heard Gaius weakly say, 'I told you not to go, Polybius. They'll make you a slave again.'

'Don't worry about that. Just get better. We can run away again after you're well.' We both knew that wouldn't happen. 'I've got to go,' I said as I rose from the bedside. 'Remember me.' I smiled weakly as I backed out of the room. Gaius smiled back. Just before I reached the doorway I impulsively returned to his bed and taking one of my dice from my belt I pressed it into his hand. 'Keep this,' I said. 'It's good luck.'

'I can't take this,' he said weakly.

'They'll only take it from me when I go down to the domus. Keep it. You can give it back to me when we next meet.' Gaius tried returning the die to me but I backed away again and left the room after leaving my purse on the table.

LIBER VIII

What happened next seems like a dream. Achilles came back and put chains around my wrists and my ankles and led me down the stairs. I was taken around the front of the house, even though the side entrance was closer. As I passed the other slaves they each, with furtive glances, whispered something encouraging. Marcus boldly gave me a pat on the shoulder, knowing full well it could earn him a beating. I realized I was being paraded around the front of the house to show the people on the street that a runaway slave had been captured. I wanted to shout to the gathering crowd that I had returned of my own will. I wanted to tell them I did it to save the life of a Roman citizen. But, I played my part and shuffled ahead of Achilles with my head bowed low. Once inside I was brought up to the small second floor room behind the copy shop where I was stripped naked and left sitting on the floor in the dark. The door was bolted behind me from the outside. It occurred to me I had left my purse on the table in Alexander's apartment and I had hoped he would keep my remaining die safe. I cared nothing for the money.

The room I was in had no window. I suppose that's why this cubicle was chosen, that and the fact that it had a heavy wooden door in place of the usual curtain. There was another smaller door that led to the copy room itself. This door was also bolted shut from the outside. A sliver of light slipped in beneath each door leaving all but the area immediately in front of them in darkness. The room was hot. This room had been used to store papyrus and other supplies for the copy business and I could tell it had just been cleared out, as the air

116

still smelled of velum and ink and the dust left behind after shifting the crates that had been so long in the same place. I was miserable, but at the same time I was at peace with what I had done. I was glad to have saved my friend from death. Being as tired as I had ever been, I crawled over to the corner and lay down on the floor, arranging my chains in such that they would chafe the least as I slept. Soon I was fast asleep.

Once again I dreamt of Fortuna. As in my first dream, I thought I had awakened and was aware of a light in the room. I opened my eyes to see a cornucopia on the floor. Spilling from the horn was fruit of every variety. There were pomegranates, and apples, and grapes, and nuts. I reached out my hand and the cornucopia and all its contents quickly slid backward along the floor, eluding my grasp. It came to rest at the feet of the goddess, standing near the door. I looked up at her pleadingly, but she simply shook her head and said, 'Not yet, Tychaeus.' With that, I truly awoke. The room was totally dark now. It was night, but I had no way of knowing how long I had been asleep. I sat in the dark, reliving in my mind my days of freedom.

I was left in that room for days. I counted at least three sunrises under the bottom of the door, but I had no real sense of time. I found that a chamber pot had been left for my use, but no one came to empty it. After the first day I hardly used it. With no food or water I didn't need it often. On the third or perhaps the fourth day, I contemplated drinking the urine but changed my mind when I brought the pot near my face. The smell of feces floating in the liquid reminded me of the sewer under the forum. I was strangely calm. I accepted the fact that my dream of Fortuna had been just that, a dream without any meaning, and I resigned myself to the idea that I would be left to die of thirst and starvation. I didn't pound on the door or yell for help. At night, I sang songs my mother had taught me as a child until my mouth was too dry to continue. Then I relived memories of my childhood, trying to recall every detail of the domus or the copy room or the street out front. In the daytime, I pressed my ear to the copy room door and tried to listen to what was being read. I slept a good deal.

One day I awoke, my head leaning on the copy room door, startled by the sound of the sliding of the bolt on the other door. I was grateful for something to be happening, but I was also filled with dread. The door swung open, and after my eyes recovered sufficiently from the sudden brightness, I saw, standing in the doorway, a strikingly handsome young man whom I had never before seen. He had thick blonde hair, a strong chin, a straight nose, and piercing blue eyes. He appeared to be in his teens, but since his face was shaved clean he must have already come of age. I guessed he was about seventeen or eighteen years old. In one hand he had a slave collar and the other held a wooden rod about three feet long and as thick as a man's thumb. Standing behind him was a slave I had also never met holding a tray with a chamber pot and two bowls on it. I hoped one had food and the other water. He was a big man and I guessed he was there to offer protection for the younger man in the event I became violent.

'I am Gnaeus Titus Livianus. I am your new master. You are to stay here in this room until I determine you have been sufficiently punished for your ingratitude.' I surmised from his name that he was Porcia's son, and Titus had recently adopted him. Without warning, he quickly stepped forward and began to strike me with the rod. The first blows fell on my upraised arms and then I turned over and let the blows rain down on my back and shoulders, protecting my head as best I could with my chained hands. A stream of curses spewed from

118

his lips as he repeatedly hit me. He seemed genuinely furious. Finally, his fury spent, he stopped hitting me and stood there smiling, sweating and out of breath. Turning to the slave behind him he said, 'Put the collar on him.' With that he dropped my new collar on the floor and turned and left the room.

The slave set down the tray and did as he was told without ever saying a word. He had some sort of special tool with him to twist the links so I couldn't remove the collar. He placed the full chamber pot on the tray and he too left the room, pulling the door shut behind him. When I heard the bolt slide back, locking the door, I crawled over to the two bowls left on the floor. One held water and the other boiled barley. I gulped down the water and greedily ate the gruel, licking the bowl clean.

Each day, just after sunrise, the same slave would come in with a clean pot, a bowl of barley gruel, and a bowl of water. He told me on the second day that he was forbidden to speak to me, so I never got to know him or learn anything about events in the world outside my room. Once I asked him what day it was. He told me it was three days before the calends of Junius (May 29). I had been alone in the room nearly a month. At that point, using a link from my chain, I began to scratch a mark low on the wall near the door where there was enough light to see, marking each day. Even then, in those most trying days, I had an organized and methodical mind. Every two or three days, Livianus would come in and beat me, exactly as he had the first time. I came to believe, as I was his property, he had no intention of doing any permanent damage. He spaced the abuse out allowing time for me to recover from the previous beating, and he was careful to not strike me in the face. And, while he inflicted a great deal of pain, he seldom left me bleeding. The times he did, the slave would clean the wound. I found it odd that my tormentor seemed to find real enjoyment in beating me. His visits always left him with a satisfied smile on his face. Frequently, I clearly saw an erection pushing out the front of his tunic after he beat me. Realizing how much my new master enjoyed torturing me left me despondent. I knew I would never be "sufficiently punished." I believed I was destined to spend the rest of my days in this room.

One morning, two months and three days after I had been imprisoned, Livianus entered the room, clearly upset and without his rod. 'I no longer want you,' he said. 'I've sold you to my cousin. Stand up.' I did as I was told and without warning he kicked me hard in the groin. I fell to the floor, curled up in pain. When he reached the doorway he turned and looked down at me. 'Your friend died. His wound filled with pus and he became feverish. You shouldn't have come back. It didn't do any good.' With that he pulled the door shut behind him. It would be many years before I would again lay eyes on Gnaeus Titus Livianus, and then it would be just his head I would see, jutting from the end of a pole, but that is a tale for another day.

After that, conditions improved. I was moved to a room with a small window and I was given better food. When I was strong enough, I was assigned tasks copying documents. I was grateful for something to occupy my mind, because as I grew stronger I slept less and my thoughts were more active. I spent the next few days in a kind of fog wondering why I was still at the Titus house if I had been sold. The news of Gaius' death had left me stunned, leaving me with a constant, dull ache. It was difficult for me to keep any food down, and I found myself weeping at odd times, but gradually I was better

120

able to concentrate and my handwriting, which had been shaky, improved. It occurred to me that I was being restored to my old self to make me acceptable to my new master.

A few days later, late in the afternoon, I was washed, given a haircut, and dressed. My shackles were removed just long enough for a clean tunic to be slipped over my head and then my hands were again chained. My slave collar was removed and a heavy iron collar with a chain attached was fastened around my neck in its place. The big slave led me out from the room like a dog on a leash. The atrium was strangely empty because all the slaves had been told to remain out of sight. Not even the door slave was at his post as we passed through the vestibule. As I stepped out into the street the sunlight made my eyes hurt and I felt as if I would faint. The slave roughly pulled my chain and snapped, 'Let's get moving!' Then, out of the side of his mouth he whispered, 'We can relax when we get away from the house.'

We stopped at the nymph fountain down the street. I scooped water from the fountain by the handful and splashed it on my feverish face. My guard bought two sausages from a stall under a nearby portico, and we sat on one of the stone benches across from the fountain in the shade of a small cypress tree and ate our sausages. 'I'm Gordius. We've never really properly met each other. Sorry about the chain, but if you run, Master Livianus will kill me.' Gordius had a slight Greek accent. The slave was quite affable away from the domus.

'Who have I been sold to?' I really didn't care, as I didn't care about anything at this point, but he was being kind so I thought I would keep up my end of the conversation.

Gordius laughed. 'You weren't sold. You're being used to pay off a gambling debt. Livianus bet heavily on the red team at the circus last month, and Titus didn't have the cash on hand to cover the little shit's debt, so he had to borrow the money from his patron. You, my friend are the interest on that loan.' He then looked me in the eye with a very serious expression. 'Fortuna smiled on you that day Livianus drank too much wine and bet on the wrong team. If you stayed with him, I'm certain he would have killed you.' I had a fleeting memory of the goddess as she appeared in my dream and then it was gone. An equite approached our bench, looking for a place to sit so we were obliged to move.

As we continued our walk down the street, I suddenly did care whose property I had become. The mention of Fortuna's favor had made me curious. 'You never told me the name of my new master. Where are you taking me?' I knew master Titus' patron was Marcus Porcius Cato, the famous senator, but I assumed the transaction involved me being passed along to one of Cato's other clients. I couldn't imagine he would want a sick, skinny boy with a reputation as a runaway.

'We are going to the Cato domus on the Caelian,' Gordius answered.

'I'm to be Cato's slave?' I was surprised. 'But, I'm a runaway.'

'It would be a good idea to not mention that. I'm not sure Cato was told of your taste of freedom.'

As we neared the lane leading up the slope of the Caelian Hill, I realized I might not have a chance to talk to Gordius again, and there was one more bit of information I

122

wanted. 'Do you know where my friend Gaius was buried?' It made me sad to ask, but I thought it would be nice to visit his grave if I ever got the chance. I hoped he wouldn't tell me he had been dumped in an unmarked pauper's grave outside the wall, but I knew that was most likely. If that was the case, I could at least visit the area one day.

Gordius looked puzzled. 'You mean that boy you rescued from the sewer?'

'Yes.'

'I didn't know he died. Sometimes they don't bother to tell me things though. I'd heard from the cook that Alexander planned to send him off to Neapolis (Naples) before the guy you robbed could find him and kill him. He must have died before that could happen.'

I told myself to not hope, but I latched onto the chance that my friend survived, and that sustained me, allowing me to continue living. It is strange how strongly attached I was to Gaius. In reality I had not known him very long, less than a year, but that time was a crossroads for me. Gaius had rescued me that first night and had become like a brother and best friend to me. We confided everything to each other and made plans for a future life together. Looking back, I think I was mourning the loss of my all too brief new life of freedom as much as I was mourning the loss of my friend. The possibility that he had somehow survived revived in me the conviction to one day free myself once more. Gaius had become my second family and ill fortune had snatched him from me.

Upon arriving at our destination, I was turned over to another slave at the Cato domus. Gordius and I were left silently standing in the vestibule beside Cato's door slave, while another slave retrieved a document to send back with Gordius. When this slave had returned, my chains were removed. Just before my transfer document was handed to Gordius, the slave realized the date had not been filled in. 'What day is this?' He asked no one in particular.

The door slave answered, 'Four days past the calends of Septembris (September 4).'

It wasn't until that moment I realized it was my fourteenth birthday. The slave hurried off to have the date inscribed on the document, leaving us once again standing in the vestibule in silence. When he returned, he handed the document to Gordius and that was that; I was now officially the property of Marcus Porcius Cato. Gordius and I exchanged a glance and nodded a goodbye as he left, carrying my chains. I followed the other slave, a short man with thinning gray hair into the atrium. I didn't have time to study the room, but a quick look around told me that, in spite of the sparse furnishings, my new master had more money than my former one. The frescoes on the walls were done with greater skill and had brighter, bolder colors. The mosaics on the floor contained finer detail with more complex designs around the borders. The house was kept scrupulously clean. The slave walked ahead of me, taking for granted that I would follow, leading me into a cubicle to the side of the atrium. I noticed another slave standing waiting in the corner of the room. The room was empty save for a single three-legged wooden stool in its center. Once in the room, the first slave turned to me and for the first time seemed to really look at me. He didn't seem pleased with what he saw. 'I am Miltiades. You will be working for me,' he said with a hint of regret in his voice.

124

'I thought I was Master Cato's slave,' I answered, surprised.

'I am Master Cato's personal secretary. I am told you can read and write and can properly spell in both Latin and Greek. I hope I have been informed correctly.' He looked doubtful. 'You will assist me in my duties.' With that he turned and left the room.

The other slave stepped forward. Without introducing himself, he said, 'Strip.' For an instant, I didn't comprehend what he was telling me and just stood there. 'I need to inspect you. Take off your tunic.' I did as I was told and he put his hands on my shoulders and pushed me down onto the stool. He started with the top of my head, carefully parting my hair in several places as he closely examined my scalp. 'As I suspected, lice.' He sounded disgusted. He tilted my head back and closely studied my eyes. He examined my ears and looked up my nostrils and into my mouth. He then made me stand and inspected my body from top to bottom. I began to feel slightly aroused as he inspected my genitals and this embarrassed me, but he didn't seem to notice. 'At least you don't have pubic lice,' was all he said. After he completed the examination he moved toward the door. I guessed I was to follow him, so I bent to pick up my tunic from the floor but he stopped me. 'Leave it, we are not yet finished. Wait here.' At the door he stopped and turned to me. 'The marks on your back tell me you were badly beaten by your former master. Whatever it was you did to earn such beatings, don't do it here or you will not live.' With that I was left alone in the room."

At that moment, the slave called Pollux joined us, bringing a plate of cheese. Polybius abruptly changed the subject and we discussed the weather until the man left the

125

room. After pausing long enough to be sure Pollux had left, Polybius took a sip of wine and said, "For reasons I don't fully understand, I don't like to talk about my time as a slave in front of those I now own."

Once again we were joined by a cat. This one was all black with green eyes and seemed shyer than the first one I'd met, and it didn't jump up on the couch. Polybius gestured toward it with his wine cup. "He is Hebeny. He joined our family when an Aegyptian spice dealer decided to close his shop here in Rome and return to his homeland. He didn't want the bother of bringing his cats home with him and he was going to turn them loose. I agreed to take one of them. His name means ebony, as that word found its way into Greek from the Aegyptian language." Polybius sat watching the cat for some time as it licked its fur before turning his gaze back to me. "Before I go on, I do need to make one observation. By the time I've been referring to, the practice of putting identifying collars around the necks of slaves had all but died out. After the slave revolt led by Spartacus, it was informally agreed upon that it wasn't a good idea to make slaves so easily recognizable by hanging a collar on them. The thinking was that if we knew how numerous we truly were, we'd be more likely to rise up against our masters. Of course, most slaves can tell one another on sight without any identifying marks, but our masters didn't realize this. Cato, however, in emulation of his great ancestor, continued the practice of using slave collars as another example of republican virtue. Some of his clients such as Titus followed his lead and also collared their slaves. At any rate, let me go on with my tale.

I waited for a long time when, at last, two slaves came in. One was carrying a high table. They left the room without saying a word, only to return a short time later with a basin of water, a large empty bowl, several towels, and a bottle of oil. Once again they didn't speak to me, but this time one of the slaves smiled and nodded before he left. Again, I was left waiting, standing naked in the room. I wanted to sit on the stool, but since no one had given me permission I thought it best to remain standing. Finally, another slave entered the room. He was a tall elegant looking man. Were it not for the collar around his neck, I would never have guessed him to be a slave, as this man carried himself more like a patrician. His tunic was perfectly clean, but was covered by an apron. His nails were manicured and I noticed his eyebrows had been plucked into fine thin arches, much like a rich matron's might be. In his left hand he had a pair of shears, and in the right hand he held a small wooden case. He set the shears on the table and opened the case, removing a strange looking knife with a thin curved blade. I was curious and more than a little apprehensive about the strange implement. 'Sit,' he said. 'My name is Piscius. I am the house barber and I am to shave you.' He wrinkled his nose as he said this. He started with the shears, cutting my hair as close to the scalp as possible. He then repeated the process with the sparse hair under my arms and around my genitals. I was a bit sad and disappointed to see my pubic hair float to the floor, as it had just so recently sprouted there. When he had cut as much as he could with the shears he poured oil on my head and spread it thinly around, rubbing it into the stubble left on my scalp. Using the curved blade he shaved my scalp clean. When he finished with my scalp, he moved down to my face, shaving off what little hair I had on my cheeks, chin, and upper lip. He then proceeded to shave the rest of my body. With each pass of the blade, he would rinse it in the basin of water and wipe it clean on one of the towels he kept draped over his arm.

127

Wherever there was hair, it was removed. Were it not so humiliating, the process would not have been at all unpleasant.

After my shaving, I was led, still naked, to a room behind the kitchen. This room had a stone basin built into the floor. The floor was sloped, allowing the water to flow out a small opening to the street behind the house. The room also had a well that connected to a cistern under the floor. Here I was scrubbed clean by a large, happy slave woman named Matilda. She first spread some sort of noxious smelling oil all over my body and head, explaining with a smile that it would kill the lice, 'eggs an' all if there is any left.' I was made to stand alone in the basin with this fluid congealing on my skin while a water clock marked the passing of an hour. Matilda checked in at regular intervals to monitor the progress of the clock. Finally, she used a series of different sized strigils to remove the oily substance from my head and body and then scrubbed me clean with ice-cold water. I was very embarrassed by this bath. By the time the entire process was completed the sun was setting. One of the slaves who carried the barber's supplies into the room retrieved me from the washing room and led me to a second floor cubicle. Along the way he introduced himself. 'I'm Postumus. I handle most of the deliveries, so if you ever need anything from the outside, let me know.' He tried to sound important.

'Thank you, I'm Polybius,' I answered.

The only furniture in the room I was brought to was a trunk in one corner 'Our blankets are in the trunk. Seven of us sleep here. Or I should say seven of us used to sleep here. You now make the eighth, so you need to get here early if you don't want to end up sleeping under the portico.' In a very short time, the other slaves, all male, joined us. I, being the youngest and newest member of the group, was relegated to sleeping outside the room in spite of having arrived first. As I drifted into sleep that night I had no idea I had just dipped my toe into that eternal, storm-tossed sea of Roman politics.

LIBER IX

I soon settled into a rhythm. Because of the greater
number of slaves and Cato's simpler stoic lifestyle there was
little useful work to do at the Cato domus. As a result, each of
the household slaves was set cleaning tasks each day. Often
we would be scrubbing a floor or dusting a table that had just
been cleaned a few hours before. As a result of my age and
lack of seniority, I spent a good deal of time cleaning the
latrine and the ovens. We worked from dawn to dusk, and for
at least half the day I was trained in my secretarial duties. At
that time I was being trained to take over the normal clerical
work of the Cato household. Since Master Cato had been
elected quaestor and was appointed to supervise the treasury,
Miltiades was often away from the house attending him as he
scrupulously went about his duties. I soon realized the fine
line between the public and private lives of an equite such as
Titus did not at all exist for a patrician. The leading senators of
Rome led their lives in full public view. What would be
considered privacy, if it didn't involve an illicit sexual affair,
could more properly be called conspiracy. The normal day-to-
day duties of the household secretary were, therefore, often
political. I knew the names and had collected bits of
information on most of the swimmers in the sea of politics
through my work as a copyist for Titus, but I now began to put
faces to the names I had collected in my memory.

Each morning, just after sunrise, a group of Cato's
clients would be waiting at the front of his domus for the
salutatio. I had seen Titus perform this ritual but on a much
smaller scale. Oftentimes there were three or fewer clients

waiting to speak to Titus; Cato had dozens waiting at his door. Vedius, the door slave, would open the small door to the opening in the larger door and scratch the names of those who were waiting on two wax tablets. The first tablet contained the names of the less important clients. These were the men who would be seen first. Their needs could be met with quickly. Sometimes they needed a small loan to make a rent payment or had a simple favor to ask. Sometimes they needed to bring Cato's influence to bear on one of his more important clients. That was the main reason he saw them first. Oftentimes these petitioners would be waiting in the front of the house to ask Cato to ask a favor of a man who was waiting in the same group. The second tablet was for the names of the more important clients. These were the men who had the greater political influence, and they were seen last so they could have more time. They also appreciated the opportunity to talk to each other as they waited. Not everyone was allowed in, so those who were not allowed to be seen would most often wait by the door to accompany Cato as he briskly walked, often barefoot, to the forum for the day's business.

Master Cato rose with the sun. His dressing slave, Calidius slept by his door and as the sun came in through the opening in the roof he would wake first. He would then go in and rouse Cato. Unlike Titus, Cato was quick to rise. He was up and on his feet in an instant. Cato slept naked, and, except for the coldest of days, he didn't wear a tunic under his toga, so Calidius' first task was to wrap the master in his toga praetexta, taking great care to make it seem that no care was taken at all. Most senators were scrupulous about their appearance, going to great pains to see that every fold of the toga draped just so. Cato cultivated the impression that he didn't care about his appearance. Sometimes, if his hair was not quite messy enough he would have Piscius, the barber, wet

131

it and push it around at odd angles to achieve the proper effect, and he would rarely have his face shaved before his afternoon trip to the baths.

Taking his place in the atrium, Cato would then review the wax tablets and cross out the names of those he would not be letting in. When Cato was ready, the door slave would open the door. He would point to about a dozen of the men waiting in the street and allow them into the vestibule. The ritual would then begin. Each client was greeted in the atrium by Cato himself and he would usher then him into his tablinum where, in full view of others waiting in the atrium or peering from the street through the open door, the man could have a private discussion with his patron. Eventually everyone on the list would have a private moment with Cato.

Initially, I played no part in these proceedings. I was relegated to taking dictation for the least important business transactions or the private letters of the household members. However, it was soon discovered that by employing the shorthand that the copyists had used in Titus' business, I could capture every word of a conversation no matter how rapidly the participants spoke. Because I was a slave, and a young one at that, it was assumed I wouldn't understand anything of the matters discussed. However, being an intelligent boy, I understood most of what I heard.

One of the things I learned while listening during Cato's salutatios was that Marcus Tullius Cicero was planning to run for the consulship. By his outward appearance, Cicero seemed to be no different than any of the other Roman senators hoping to one day win the top prize in Roman politics. He was just a couple of years past forty, not fat but not thin either, with thinning hair that was starting to go gray at the temples. He moved with a studied elegance that almost seemed too carefully crafted. His mind, however, was exceptional. He was a brilliant judge of character and could size up a man upon first meeting him. He was also a skilled tactician when it came to advancing his career and he was one of the most gifted orators Rome or, for that matter, the world has ever seen. Cicero knew he wouldn't, under normal circumstances, get much support from the leaders of the senate. He was a 'new man,' who had no ancestors to ever have attained the highest office and, as such, the old aristocracy didn't trust him. In those days, certain factions in the senate jealously guarded what they saw as their hereditary rights. Cicero reasoned his best chance would come in a year when the other candidates were so odious to the aristocracy that he would be the ideal compromise candidate. Cicero had spent much of his career trying to ingratiate himself with the Optimates, but he was clever enough to associate himself whenever he could with the supporters of Pompeius Magnus, the darling of the masses. He judged correctly. The support of the leading senators and their thousands of clients outweighed the wealth of Crassus, and by a narrow margin Cicero would be elected consul for the following year, but that was, at this time, still in the future.

At any rate, I seem to have strayed from my discussion of Cato. As I've already said, the summer before I came to be one of Cato's possessions, he was elected to the position of quaestor. He assumed the office three months after I entered his service. This was the first real opportunity for Cato to inflict his republican virtue on the people of Rome. Cato was appointed to oversee the state treasury and he took to this task like a rabid wolf. He sniffed out corruption wherever he could find it and then sunk his teeth into it. The first place he found it was in the senior staff of the treasury. He had the

133

public slaves in the treasury flogged, and at the same time also had his own personal slaves flogged just for good measure. That, naturally, made me hate him even more. He then dismissed most of the freedmen in senior positions and took control of the treasury himself using his own staff.

One area he paid particular attention to was the area of loans from the treasury that were made to friends of Sulla and were never paid back. He also looked closely at rewards given from the public funds to men who turned in the proscribed during Sulla's dictatorship."

At this point I had to stop him. Everyone had heard of these dark days, but this was my first opportunity to hear of that time from the mouth of someone who knew what had happened. Polybius wasn't old enough to have lived through the days of Sulla's dictatorship, but he knew many men who had. He also had access to state archives that few eyes had seen. "What really went on during that time?"

Polybius sighed. "I can only tell you what I learned second hand, as it were. This all happened over one hundred years ago. Most of what I know came from Demetrius, Caesar's nomenclator and a man who will play a lead role in this story, and from Pythogenes the physician. Demetrius was more circumspect, but also had greater personal knowledge of the events closest to Caesar, but Pythogenes was more inclined to talk, especially over dice and wine. I do not know what it was that caused the senate to appoint Marius, who was Caesar's maternal uncle, to the eastern command and deprive Sulla of his *dignitas*. I suspect it was just more of the same maneuvering for personal glory that plagued the republic until its last days. Marius was at an age when most men would have retired from public life, but at nearly seventy years of age he

134

decided he needed to fight another war to earn back his place in the hearts and minds of the people. He also wanted to ensure his land reform program would pass, and there is no one better than a conquering general to hold sway with the tribunes. Sulla felt insulted so he left Rome and joined his own army and persuaded his men that they too had been insulted by being deprived of the opportunity to win booty that the eastern war would have afforded them. It was then quite easy to convince them to follow him and march on Rome instead. This was the first time to my knowledge a Roman army had invaded the city."

I had to ask Polybius to clarify what he was saying. "Was this the war against Mithridates?"

"Yes, it was, and in a way this was when the seed was planted that resulted in you and I sitting here today. Mithridates, the upstart king of Pontus, taking advantage of the upheavals at Rome, invaded our relatively new province of Macedonia. If you will recall, I told you earlier the conflict between Rome and the home city of my mother was just a continuation of this fight. At any rate, Sulla, on his own authority, declared twelve of the opposition leaders to be outlaws, making it legal to kill them. To ensure this was done, he offered a reward for their heads. Marius fled to his still loyal clients in Africa. Amid the political turmoil, Lucius Cornelius Cinna, who was consul for that year, fell out with his colleague, Octavius, and fled to join his own army outside the city. Marius who had returned to Italia with a small makeshift army composed of brigands and freed slaves soon joined him. Together they stormed Rome. Heads were fastened to poles and set up on the Rostra. Bodies floated in the Tiber, there was blood in the streets and forum of Rome, and chaos reigned. Sulla and his family fled to Greece,

135

narrowly escaping the burning of his home. Marius and Cinna were easily elected consuls for the following year since there was no way they could *not* win, as the election was held at sword point. Marius died a few days short of a month later, leaving Cinna to await the return of Sulla.

That year was also the year young Caesar lost his father. The man died one morning while bending over to put on his shoes. Caesar was not yet sixteen years old. At any rate, as long as I've digressed again I should mention that, sometime before he died, Marius convinced his colleague Cinna to nominate Caesar to one of the most prestigious priesthoods, the office of Flamen Dialis."

"Why," I asked, "would they offer such honors to an unknown, as Caesar was at the time?"

Polybius took a pause before answering. "No one is sure, but there are several opinions. One is that Cinna wanted to use the priesthood to subvert elections and such. Another is that he simply wanted to add luster to a family that was connected by marriage to Marius. Caesar's view was very different. He told me once that he was certain Marius didn't trust him. Marius was a coarse and bitter man. He excelled as a general but had little skill in the art of politics. He wanted to be sure that after he was gone the young Julius Caesar wouldn't outshine his own son."

"How then could being elected to a priesthood prevent this?" I was a bit confused.

"Quite simply," Polybius answered, "this was not just any priesthood. This one came with several restrictions. The Flamen Dialis was not allowed to ride on horseback, nor for that matter even have physical contact with a horse. He was

136

not allowed to so much as look at an army in the field, or leave the city for even a single night, and he could not sleep outside of his own house for more than two consecutive nights. He was *not ever* allowed to view a corpse. These restrictions would effectively prohibit a man from having any sort of military or political career. The Flamen Dialis could never hold any office above praetor, and it would be difficult to gain even that without some sort of military experience. The nomination was meant to cripple Caesar as a political threat. Caesar told me he took the nomination for what it was, but had no intention of ever becoming a priest. He did, however, assume the privileges that came with the priesthood. He immediately began wearing the toga praetexta and took a seat in the senate. How ironic it is that he is now enshrined in his temple dressed as the highest priest of Rome."

"That makes it clearer," I said, "Please continue."

"In spite of his very young age, Caesar was getting a reputation as a ladies' man. It was perfectly acceptable for a young man of Caesar's station to carry on with slave girls and even plebian women, but Caesar had already developed his powerful attraction too, and charming ways with, the wives and daughters of the nobility. It was about this time that he first met and began his lifelong relationship with Servilia who was twenty-two and married. His relationship with Servilia was put on hold for a number of years though, when he fell in love with another beautiful young girl and, very much against the advice of his mother, began a passionate relationship with Cornelia, the consul's daughter. This girl was every bit as headstrong as her lover, and she went to Cinna one day to tell him she was pregnant. He was without a doubt the last to know what was going on between his daughter and the young Julius Caesar. Slaves were beaten for not having revealed it

137

and a prosecution of Caesar was organized. It was determined in advance that he was to be found guilty of conspiring with Sulla to subvert the constitution and, in spite of his young age, exiled or executed. Caesar turned his persuasiveness toward the consul. He slowly and carefully built a case explaining how the scandal would weaken the consul's position and weaken his support among the patricians just at a time when he would need to face the return of Sulla and his army. Because of Caesar's youth, Cinna came to believe he could control the young man and through him his numerous clients. Caesar also began to wear the dress and ornaments of the Flamen Dialis in an attempt to add an aura of sacrilege to any prosecution Cinna might mount. Rather than kill him, Cinna married Caesar to his daughter."

I was rather incredulous about this. It seems impossible that such a scandal could have been kept secret, and all the records indicate only one legitimate child was born to Caesar. "Why is there no record of this other child?"

"There is no record," Polybius answered, "because she never was pregnant. They were passionately in love, and when Caesar's father died he became the head of the family. From that point forward he was determined to have his way. It was all a ruse."

"And, a high stakes gamble," I added.

"A very high stakes gamble," Polybius agreed, "but this was not the last time he would gamble his life for the love of Cornelia, as darker days were yet to come."

Without warning, three slaves then entered the room, yet Polybius didn't seem the least surprised. One was carrying a tray with bowls and spoons and the other two were carrying

138

trays of food. Polybius apologized for taking the liberty of deciding what we would have for our mid-day meal without consulting me, but his menu choices were delicious. We continued our discussion while dining.

"Caesar used all his connections to keep the Pontifex Maximus at odds with Cinna. In this way he was able to stall his being formally invested as the Flamen Dialis. I was later led to believe Caesar's mother Aurelia played a significant part in this, but I could never confirm it. Rather than the month or so it would normally have taken to fill the post, the process dragged on to months and then years, eventually being forgotten all together. Cinna's goal at this time was simply to remain in power and keep the command of his army, because without that he was liable to be prosecuted for ordering the execution of Roman senators. His means to this end was simple. He used the threat of renewed force to ensure his name and that of a chosen colleague would be the only ones presented to the assembly for election to the consulship. He was able to do this for four consecutive years, but during this time Sulla had not been idle. He maintained that he was the duly appointed commander in the war against Mithridates and he prosecuted that war with vigor. Ultimately, wanting to bring the war to a close and force a confrontation with Cinna at Rome, Sulla, after having driven Mithridates out of Greece, signed a peace treaty with the king leaving him in control of Pontus and still a lingering threat to Roman interests. It took nearly a year for Sulla to settle his affairs in the east and bring his armies up to strength. During this time, Cinna decided it was better to fight Sulla on foreign soil than it was to do so in Italia, so he prepared to launch an invasion of Greece the following spring. Sulla always claimed to have Fortuna, as well as other gods, on his side and this was proven true when Cinna's long awaited invasion was launched. His soldiers were very reluctant to fight other Romans, especially in a war that promised no booty, so they were probably hoping for any sign of divine displeasure, and on the day set for the launch of the flotilla that would carry them to Greece they got it. Shortly after the start of the launch a terrible tempest arose, forcing at least one ship to be sent to the bottom of the sea and the others to be blown back to the Italian coast. Clearly the gods opposed this war. After several days of continued bad weather, while Cinna was in his tent planning strategy, his army mutinied. His own men murdered him.

This caused panic in the senate. Carbo, the other consul took shaky control of the legions, but no one trusted him to have the skill to maintain order. Carbo took as his colleague in the consulship for the following year the son of Marius, in spite of the fact that he would not be legally eligible to hold the consulship for many years. Many senators, sensing which way the wind was blowing, both literally and figuratively, fled Italia to join Sulla in Greece. Those who could not afford to make the trip would meet him when he landed in Italia. Sulla marched on Rome the following spring and after fierce fighting outside the Colline Gate, he took the city. When it became apparent he was about to lose his illegal consulship, the younger Marius chose to even the score with Scaevola, the Pontifex Maximus. Scaevola was one of the few senators who never wavered in his opposition to the illegal way Cinna and his colleagues had subverted the constitution. Marius ordered his execution I suspect as much for retribution against the man as for the gods he represented for they too had clearly let him down. Marius' mother was, you'll recall, Caesar's aunt Julia, and both she and her nephew condemned this action. The younger Marius fled to Praeneste, a small town to the east of Rome, and when he learned of Rome's surrender to Sulla, he committed suicide inside the famous

140

Temple of Fortuna in that town. It's said that when Sulla was presented with the young man's head he sadly remarked, 'He should have learned to pull an oar before he attempted to steer a ship.'

With the fall of the city, the terror began almost immediately. Sulla called a meeting of the senate beyond the sacred Pomerium in the temple of Bellona. He was required to pause several times in the course of his victory speech to regain the attention of his audience members who were distracted by the screams of captured soldiers being executed a short distance away on the Campus Martius. Soon after, Sulla's men began to execute prominent senators and equites who had opposed him or had even spoken against him in the senate. The killings were without trial and seemed entirely random. This caused many to flee Rome to their estates outside the city. In time, the nervous senate could no longer take it, and rather than demand an end to the killing, sent deputies to Sulla to ask for a list of who was to be executed so the rest could go on with their lives. Sulla complied, and the proscriptions began. Lists were posted in prominent places, first in Rome and then in other Italian cities. At first the lists merely contained the names of political enemies, mostly supporters of Marius and Cinna, but later the names of personal enemies of Sulla and his friends were added. These proscribed men had their estates confiscated and the property was often either kept by Sulla or sold at remarkably low prices to his friends and associates. Eventually, hundreds of names were added to the lists. The only "crime" of many of those named was that they were wealthy and Sulla needed the money. To legitimize his rule, Sulla put a vote before the popular assembly to grant himself the title of Dictator. Normally this office was only granted in a time of emergency, and then only for a period of six months. Sulla took the

141

unprecedented step of making his dictatorship open-ended. Of course, almost everything that happened in those few years was unprecedented. That is why I later frequently suggested to Augustus that he have the constitution of Rome set down in writing. Of course, he only partial adopted my suggestion. To have actually produced a written constitution would have either limited his authority or shown clearly that he was in fact a monarch. Everyone is happier with the fable of the Roman Republic.

Sulla was an uncompromising man and when opposed he dug his heels in and would not give way, and he was able to cow nearly the entire senate and the young nobles restricted by their youth from joining the senate. Perhaps the most notable exception was Caesar himself. As Caesar tells the tale, it was a simple disagreement between men that took some time to work out. He always made light of any past troubles, saying he trusted in Fortuna's favor and his own good sense. His mother, Aurelia, however, told me a darker version of events. She was a wise and good woman, who placed greater faith in careful planning than she did in luck. Caesar was in his eighteenth year when Sulla returned to Rome, and he had already adopted the habits required of the Flamen Dialis. Therefore, he was forced to remain in Rome during the terror. Caesar was scarcely yet involved in politics and certainly had no money so he would under normal circumstances have avoided being listed with the proscribed, but he was the younger Marius' cousin and he had married Cinna's daughter. Sulla summoned him to his house one day and ordered him to divorce Cornelia. Not knowing why the dictator had summoned her son, Aurelia went along hoping to intercede if need be, as she and Sulla had a friendship that dated back many years. They arrived at Sulla's house in the city in mid-afternoon and were kept waiting for two or three

142

hours. This was a trick often used by Sulla to unnerve people. Even then, Caesar was able to remain poised and calm. Sulla arrived home with great fanfare with lictors shouting and blowing whistles and accompanied by a large group of slaves and courtiers who attended him wherever he went. Once in the house he greeted Aurelia politely, Caesar not at all. Taking his seat on the curule chair he had set up in the atrium of his home, Sulla called Caesar before him. Aurelia says she wished at the time her son would have been humbler but, as always, Caesar met him standing tall while looking him in the eye.

'You are to divorce your wife. I'll find you another, more suitable woman,' Sulla announced.

Aurelia was relieved at this. Caesar had been looking for a way to back out of becoming the Flamen Dialis and she thought this was it. He had been married in the ancient patrician style of confarreatio, as was required for the Flamen Dialis. This marriage was difficult to dissolve in normal circumstances, but was impossible for the Flamen Dialis, but all Caesar needed to do was agree to it and he could use it as a reason he could not be the Flamen.

Caesar paused just a bit before answering, 'No.'

Aurelia was shocked and frightened. One did not say "no" to Sulla. Sulla seemed surprised and a little amused. With a small smile he asked, 'No?'

Caesar, yet again, answered, 'No.'

Aurelia started to speak, but Sulla silenced her with a gesture and said to Caesar, 'You must. I am dictator. I have imperium, and I say you will divorce.'

143

'Your imperium gives you sway over men, not over the gods, and I was married in the strictest of all possible ways. For the Flamen Dialis to divorce would be impiety. No, not just impiety, it would be worse than that, it would be sacrilege.' Caesar was firm.

Sulla was no longer smiling. 'You are not yet the Flamen Dialis, and you never will be. I am finished with this discussion. Go home, divorce Cornelia, and there will be no trouble for you.' Then, rising from his chair, he turned to Caesar's mother and said with a smile, 'It was very nice to see you again, Aurelia.' Sulla left the room and Aurelia managed to get Caesar to leave the house without another word.

Of course the reason Caesar wouldn't divorce Cornelia had nothing to do with religion. Caesar was, as I've said, one of the least pious men I've ever known. The simple fact is he was deeply in love with her. A secondary reason may already have been his growing feeling that he was in rivalry with another young man, just a few years older than himself, the twenty-four year old Gnaeus Pompeius, whom Sulla required to divorce his own very pregnant wife so he could marry the dictator's stepdaughter. Caesar was always keenly aware of others of his generation who were advancing faster than he. This Gnaeus Pompeius will figure most prominently in the later part of Caesar's story. At any rate, Caesar went home and did nothing, remaining husband to Cornelia. Of course, both his wife and his mother were spending their days living in terror, but Caesar was the head of the family and there was nothing they could do about the situation.

Strangely, Sulla never again summoned Caesar to his presence, but instead communicated with him through messengers. I overheard Pompeius at a much later date tell Caesar this was because the dictator was embarrassed by Caesar's obstinate refusal to obey him. Sulla knew if Caesar publicly refused to comply with his order again, he would have no choice but to put him to death and he was reluctant to do so for such a small crime. Instead, he first sent Caesar a message telling him his appointment to the flaminate had been cancelled and there could no longer be any religious objection to the divorce. At this, Caesar was relieved but he still did not put Cornelia aside. Instead, he began to show as much public affection toward her as good manners allowed. A few days later, the same messenger returned to tell Caesar that his marriage had been dissolved by edict of the dictator and Cornelia's dowry was to be confiscated and deposited in the state treasury. Of course, much of Cornelia's dowry was beyond reach since it consisted of land, precious metals that were stored in various places, and personal items, so this was more symbolic than anything. Still, Caesar continued to insist he was still married to Cornelia and dismissed the messenger with words to that effect. The next day a different messenger returned, this time from Pompeius, warning Caesar the next knock on the door would be men coming to arrest him if he didn't immediately and publicly send Cornelia away. An arrest order meant almost certain death.

It appeared Caesar had no choice with both his wife and mother pleading with him to comply and save his life. But, he instead gave orders to his man Demetrius to hurry on ahead and prepare supplies from his villa across the river. Taking whatever ready coins he had at the domus, he then left the house with Cornelia and took a stroll down the Argiletum to the forum, greeting friends and associates along the way. Of course, by the time he passed through the Forum Romanum and had nearly reached the Forum Boarium, word had spread that Sulla's men were looking for him. Caesar and Cornelia quickly crossed the bridge and met Demetrius and three other slaves with a horse drawn cart carrying the most basic of supplies. At this point, the sun was setting and escape would be more difficult, but so would pursuit. Caesar dismissed Demetrius, and the other slaves, not wanting to put their lives at risk, telling them to take Cornelia to the villa. Demetrius stood up to his master and insisted he stay with Caesar. Caesar could be stubborn, but he was not stupid. Realizing he might need some help in trying to hide from Sulla's men, he agreed to let Demetrius and another young slave named Norbanus flee with him.

Caesar fled with few provisions to friends in the area northeast of Rome, but agents of Sulla ranged far and wide over most of Italia. Sometime shortly after his escape, Caesar contracted a fever but still moved from place to place each night in order to escape detection and to avoid putting his friends in greater peril. Some nights the three men slept out under the stars. Eventually, a professional hunter of the proscribed, a certain centurion named Cornelius Phagites and his men caught up with Caesar. To spare his own life, Caesar had to pay the man double the price Sulla was offering for his head and gave him an astounding twelve thousand three hundred twenty five silver denarii, all the cash he, his slaves, and the owner of the house he was hiding in had on them. As men often do in times of strife, the owner of the house had buried a jar of coins in the small court yard of his home. Knowing Caesar's reputation, the man volunteered to dig up the money and pay the fee.

In the end, it was Aurelia who brought a reasonable outcome to the whole affair. She brought pressure on Sulla by organizing some of the most influential senators in the city to intercede on her son's behalf. She could be every bit as persuasive as her son and also as stubborn. What never became generally known was that she threatened a very public suicide on the Rostra in the forum, should Sulla go through with the execution of her son. Sulla gave in. This incident solidified Caesar's reputation for years to come as a man of principle and honor in the minds of many, but I truly believe his actions were taken out of an almost insane love for Cornelia."

"Aurelia sounds like a very heroic woman," I said.

"To my mind, Aurelia was not the only hero in this story."

"What other hero was there?"

"Perhaps, the greater hero was Demetrius."

"It was certainly loyal for him to remain by his master's side, but I don't see how his actions were particularly heroic," I answered honestly.

Polybius took a moment to answer me, and looked me in the eye as he did. "It would be difficult for you to understand as you value your life above all else."

"Of course, as any sane man does."

"There is one thing almost any slave will risk his life for, and that is his freedom. Demetrius knew that freedom was to be his at the death of Caesar. He knew this because he helped the young man compose his will. If Demetrius had betrayed Caesar he would have not only gained his freedom but would have also earned a substantial reward." Polybius

147

took a sip of his wine, giving me a moment to consider what he said before going on.

"At the end of the year when Sulla and Metellus Pius were consuls (80 BC), Sulla resigned the dictatorship and returned to his place as a senator. It is said he was able to walk the streets without a bodyguard, so high was the respect, or perhaps fear, others felt for him. He had returned Rome's government to where it had been a generation or more earlier. He had in effect turned back the calendar to a time when the patrician elites held much more power. In the end, when he spared Caesar, he is reputed to have said, 'They should remember, this boy they wish to save will one day bring down the party of the Optimates, which I have defended, for I have no doubt that in this young Caesar there are many Mariuses.' Perhaps to counter that, several years later Caesar is said to have remarked of Sulla, 'The man was a political illiterate when he resigned the dictatorship.'

LIBER X

"Now, it seems we have strayed far off the original path, getting lost in the weeds of ancient history," Polybius said this with a thin laugh that made him cough a little.

I had to check my notes to see where this digression had originated. "You were telling me about Cato's term as Quaestor, and how he was investigating men who had received payments from the treasury during Sulla's proscriptions."

"Thank you. You are quite right," he said, finding the thread of his thought again.

"Caesar and Pompeius were making names for themselves among the people. The faction Cato belonged to referred to this type of man as a 'Populare.' To counter that, Cato felt the need to do something to show that men of his kind, whom he referred to as the Optimates, could also take on popular causes. Of course, the horror of the proscriptions touched every level of society and was not restricted to one class or group so this was not really a "popular" cause, but Cato published a list of men who had taken the rewards for turning in the heads of men on the proscribed lists. He then began to charge these men with murder. In his zeal, Cato missed the larger point of what he was doing."

"What point was that?"

"Without intending to, Cato was questioning the legality of Sulla's dictatorship itself, and, therefore, any laws

149

or innovations he enacted. Since the dictator sanctioned the proscriptions, and the rewards were paid out of the treasury at his order, the so-called 'murders' should have been legal. Caesar, Crassus, and the other 'Populares' understood this, and backed Cato in his desire to prosecute these men. Pompeius was made very nervous about this and the rift between himself and Crassus widened."

"Why," I asked, "was Pompeius nervous? He and Caesar agreed on most political points."

"Pompeius was made nervous by the prosecutions and the Populare's support for them because his rise to fame relied on the offices and military commands granted him by Sulla with many of these honors bestowed well before he was of legal age to assume them. If the edicts of Sulla were held to be illegal, Pompeius himself was open to future prosecution. Cato's zeal in pressing for prosecutions also had an unintended result."

"What was that?"

"Well," continued Polybius, "under normal circumstances, the city praetors presided as judges during trials but from time to time, when the caseload became too great, aediles and sometimes even former aediles would act as judges. Cato's prosecutions ensured that Caesar, as the previous year's curule aedile, was called into service as a judge. This allowed me the opportunity to sit in on the trials and record the important speeches and make notes of what happened. In general trial judges then, as now, are far from impartial. It is fortunate for many of the accused that the cases are heard by juries and the judge can only exert influence over the trial."

150

"Are you going to tell me Caesar was the model of impartiality after what he had been through during Sulla's proscriptions?" I was incredulous.

"On the contrary," Polybius answered, "Caesar clearly favored the prosecution whenever he could. This was, of course, easy to do since records from the public treasury frequently provided damning evidence of the crimes committed by the men who had been rewarded for turning in a head. I was surprised by how few of the defendants tried to justify their actions based on the fact that a legally appointed dictator sanctioned them. For those who tried, this line of defense was usually ruled irrelevant and, therefore, inadmissible. Caesar seemed to relish the prosecutions of the men who profited from Sulla's dictatorship, but there was an exception. Caesar refused to sit as judge for one notable defendant. When Cornelius Phagites, the centurion who captured Caesar and released him after payment of a large bribe, was put on trial, Caesar publicly said he could not be impartial in this case because of the man's association with himself at the time of the proscriptions. This caused many raised eyebrows since Caesar showed no impartiality in any of the cases he judged. Years later, and behind closed doors, he told me he declined to judge Phagites because he would have had to rule in favor of the man; he had held up his end of the bargain and Caesar would need to honor that.

However, I was talking about my time in the Cato household, so let me continue. A frequent visitor to Cato's home was Servilia Caeponis. Cato was her half-brother and the two were very close. She would visit often, and if Cato wasn't in she would sometimes sit in the garden and read or dictate letters. When he was home they would spend time talking about family matters or discussing politics. She arrived on a spring day, several months after I had first met her, to discuss with her brother the elections for the coming year and, as was often the case, her son Junius Brutus was in tow. Cato was laying the groundwork for a possible run as a tribune of the plebs. Servilia was, for a woman, very political and held strong convictions that she wasn't afraid to express. She was pretty, or had once been. I thought she was terribly old but she was, at that time, only about forty. From my present perspective, a woman of forty seems like a young girl. Servilia had a very keen wit and was excellent at exchanging barbs when making light conversation. Brutus I found to be extremely attractive. He was in his twentieth year. The man was fairly tall with the thin muscular build of the young before fat starts to accumulate. He had regular features with a fairly prominent nose, his mother's light brown hair, and gray eyes. When he smiled he looked a bit shy. His attractiveness was diminished when he spoke, as he seemed to be working very hard to appear to be more confident than he truly was. He had his mother's wit, but was more mean spirited. His witty barbs were directed at degrading the political enemies of his uncle Cato. He spared none save Caesar and that was only when his mother was present.

On that day the three met in the tablinum for about an hour, discussing Cato's strength among the various tribes. Two or three times, Cato's voice rose in opposition to something Servilia said, but she never lost her temper. She would look at him with a smile and say, 'There is no need to shout, brother' or 'I think you're being unrealistic but I'll put my opinion in writing this afternoon and leave it for you to consider.' Sometimes Cato *was* unrealistic. He tended to overestimate the virtue of the voters and underestimate how easily a demagogue could sway the mass of men. I could hear most of the conversation because I was seated at a writing

152

table at the far end of the tablinum. Cato liked to have a slave around to find documents or make notes during important conversations so he kept me within earshot. Having the usual patrician's disdain for slaves, it never occurred to him that I might be listening to the conversation as I sat at my table transcribing speeches from shorthand. I was commonly assigned to stand in the back during important court cases or listen in near the Rostra and take verbatim accounts of what the important senators might have to say. I would then take my notes and write the speeches on scrolls that were filed in a room off the side of the tablinum. When I heard Servilia say she would be committing an opinion to writing, I assumed it would be me who would do the actual writing.

The three took their midday meal in the tablinum. Cato's kitchen slave served meals in line with his master's stoic lifestyle, meaning bland and uninspired. There was bread, hard cheese, olives, and cheap wine. As an economy measure, I was passed some of the leftovers. Brutus drank just enough wine to wash down the meal, but Cato tended to drink twice what others had. Servilia was served water in line with Cato's strict adherence to ancient republican virtue. The only time women were allowed to drink wine in Cato's house was when he hosted an important dinner party and he wished everyone's tongue to be loosened. Cato said the wine helped him relax after a hard day. It always made me smile on the inside when I heard him say that since, like most senators, his day consisted of talk, talk, and more talk. He never lifted anything heavier than a sestertius, unless it was for exercise at the baths or to raise a stick to beat a slave. It was the slaves that had the hard days. After the meal, Cato and Brutus left to spend the afternoon at the baths. Like most senators, a trip to the baths was part of the daily ritual. Many pieces of important legislation were hammered out around the pools of hot and cold waters. Very often the debates in the senate were just a formalized and organized continuation of what had been going on for days at the baths. Frequently, Cato would return from the baths well past sunset and more than a little drunk. Cato's drinking never seemed to diminish his sharp mind, but everyone was aware of it. Everyone, that is, except Cato himself. He would sometimes accuse another of being drunk when he himself was the least sober man in the room.

As I suspected, when the two had left, Servilia called me over to take dictation. She expressed her views on how three of the tribes would vote based on the results of the previous year's elections without needing to refer to notes or revise multiple drafts. Like her brother, she had a keen mind but she could better organize her thoughts before committing them to papyrus. This, fortunately, saved me several rewrites. When we had finished, I expected her to dismiss me, but instead she instructed me to get two small sheets of papyrus from my box. She then rose and paced the room reciting recipes. One was, I still remember, for a particularly spicy roasted suckling pig. The other was for a fish stew. When we had finished, she looked at my work and frowned a bit. 'Rewrite these in nicer handwriting. I want to give them as a gift.' Having seen Servilia's handwriting on several occasions, I decide, more to amuse myself than for any other purpose, to write the recipes in Servilia's hand.

Just then, the door slave walked into the room. 'Mistress Servilia, Gaius Julius Caesar is here to see you.' At the mention of Caesar, in my mind I returned to that day years before when I met him in Titus' copy shop. I noticed Caesar's name brought a smile to Servilia's face. She looked up and waved him in from where he was standing in shadow in the vestibule.

154

'Show him into the peristyle, and have Atrius bring us some wine. Not the cheap stuff though. Ask him to find something that is at least drinkable.' She said it in the most affable way.

She went out the back of the tablinum and I turned to see Caesar striding forward across the atrium. He was much the same as I remembered him, tall with a full face and dark eyes. His hair had receded a bit and he had it combed forward on his forehead, but he was otherwise unchanged. He leaned over and whispered something to the slave and they both laughed. Stepping aside at the entrance to the peristyle, the slave allowed Caesar to pass out into the colonnaded garden. I returned to my task of transcribing the recipes. I had, of course, heard the rumors of the affair between Servilia and Caesar. After having had three daughters with her second husband, Junius Silanus, Servilia was said to have rekindled an old romance with Caesar. As I said earlier, Caesar was devoted to his wife Cornelia, but, tragically, she died five years prior to this time, leaving Caesar free to resume his relationship with Servilia. Silanus, it seems, preferred younger women and was pursuing extramarital dalliances of his own, so he turned a blind eye toward his wife's activities. Caesar liked women of any and every age and didn't seem to mind that Servilia was several years older than he. Of course, even to my eye, it was obvious he was in love. It occurred to me that Servilia's insisting she put her argument with Cato in writing was just a ruse to allow her to remain in the house and meet with Caesar. After conversation and wine, the couple went into a cubicle off the garden, presumably to make love. I later learned they generally met at her husband's house, but on days when he was home they would use Cato's domus on the Caelian to meet.

155

After about an hour, they emerged with Servilia adjusting the folds of Caesar's toga. It was apparent that he had removed it. For, as you know, in order to hang properly a toga requires the assistance of a dressing slave to wrap it. Servilia may have been better at removing Caesar's toga than she was at putting it back on him. When Caesar was nearly at the vestibule, Servilia remembered the recipes. 'Gaius,' she called, 'I have those recipes Julia asked for.' This may have been another ruse to give Caesar a valid reason for visiting Servilia, or it may have been genuine. Caesar's sister was, I was to later learn, quite the epicurean. Caesar met Servilia half way, in the middle of the atrium, where he stopped to fuss with his toga. He was a fastidious dresser, and didn't like to be seen looking the least bit disheveled. He took the recipes and, kissing Servilia one last time turned to leave, but, after a few steps, Caesar stopped and turned to me.

'Can you wrap a toga, young man?' I wasn't sure he was talking to me. I was used to being addressed as 'boy,' or 'slave.'

I looked up and pointing at my own chest, asked, 'Me?' I was nearly as tongue tied as at our first meeting several years before.

'Yes, you,' Caesar laughed.

'I can try. I've seen it done, and I don't think I can make it any worse,' I said, regaining my composure.

'Excellent point. Help me out, please.'

Together with Servilia, I was able to, after only two attempts, make a very nice presentation with his toga. Fortunately, Caesar had lead weights sown into the ends of the

156

toga to help it hang better. While we wrapped him in his toga, Caesar casually read the recipes, holding them at arm's length in his right hand. When we had finished, he turned to Servilia and asked, sounding surprised, 'Did you write these yourself?'

'No, why?' she asked with a look of consternation aimed in my direction. 'I had Polybius do it. Is there something wrong?' I felt my face flush with embarrassment. I prided myself on my abilities, and I feared Caesar had found a spelling error or a problem where I had corrected Servilia's grammar at one point.

'No, on the contrary, this is quite remarkable,' he answered.

'They *are* delicious recipes, but they're not that good!'

Caesar laughed. 'Not the recipes. Here, look at this.' He said this as he handed the pages to Servilia.

She read the pages over, and suddenly they were both staring at me. I began to get very nervous. 'This is very nearly in my exact hand! How did you do this?'

'I'm sorry,' I stammered. 'I can redo it. I thought it would make it special.' I was certain I had inadvertently earned a beating.

'Redo it? No, don't you dare suggest it!' Servilia was surprised at the thought. Turning to Caesar, she said, 'Don't let Julia know I didn't write these. She'll think I went to great pains to write them myself.' I was very relieved.

157

Caesar turned to me. 'How did you learn to do this? Can you mimic anyone's writing?'

'As far as I know.' I answered with more than a little pride. 'If I had a sample in front of me, I would have done a better job.'

'You did this from memory? This is nearly perfect.' He seemed even more surprised. 'You must have excellent recall.'

'Yes, sir, I remember everything,' I replied, smiling.

'How did you learn to do this?' He was genuinely curious as he looked me in the eye, just as he did when we first met. He seemed to be studying me, trying to probe my mind. 'You are a prodigy.'

'I used to work as a copyist. Sometimes my master's clients liked to have letters written in their own writing so the recipient would believe they took extra care, just as Mistress Servilia said. I was the only copyist who could master this skill.'

'Well, I must be going,' he said to Servilia. Turning to me he said again, 'You are indeed quite the prodigy, young man.' With that, Caesar turned and walked away, but as he and Servilia reached the vestibule he turned back and called out to me. 'Polybius, was it?'

I had already entered the tablinum to gather my work to continue it in another room, so I was obliged to return to the atrium. 'Yes, Polybius is my name.'

'Do I know you?' He looked puzzled like there was a memory he was trying to chase down like a butterfly just out of reach. 'We have met before.' This time it was no longer a question.

'Yes, we met several years ago in a copy shop on the Argiletum. You were going to Hispania and needed some work done quickly. I hope you had a pleasant time during your quaestorship in the West.' I was very pleased that he almost remembered me.

'Yes, I remember. You were the remarkable boy who preferred Herodotus to his namesake. Now you seem to have become a remarkable young man.'

I was very surprised he could remember that much detail. I had, over the years, grown accustomed to having a far better memory than anyone around me. Caesar put his arm around my shoulder and steered me toward the vestibule. 'Can you remember names, faces, the backgrounds of people you encounter?' I thought the question was oddly specific.

'I can remember just about anything,' I replied.

'Thanks for your help with the toga.' And with that, he was through the vestibule and out into the street.

I returned to my work, but from time to time I would stop to think how I would like to be Caesar's slave. Then, I would need to reprimand myself and remember my goal was to be no man's slave. My goal was to either buy my freedom or to, once again, escape. Cato returned later in the day, and after reading Servilia's observations on the coming elections he was in a foul mood. He realized she was correct in her assessment, and he would need to shore up support in three crucial tribes if he was to win the tribunate. He would have to content himself with remaining merely a very influential senator for at least one more year between his quaestorship and becoming a tribune. He called me into the tablinum and dictated a letter. After reading it over, he was angry about his poor choice of words, no doubt a result of the wine he had at the baths, and cuffed my ear as if it was my fault. I hastily suggested it was just a first draft, and he could surely make it better, which we did after three more attempts. In the end, the letter was more mine than his, but Cato was at last satisfied.

By the time we finished, it was time for bed, and because I was last to arrive at our room, I was forced to take my blanket and sleep against the wall of the colonnaded portico. That night I dreamt, yet again, of Fortuna. As in all the other dreams of the goddess, I felt as if I had awakened and I could see a light through my closed eyelids, as one does when he closes his eyes and faces the sun. When I opened my eyes, I was in the forum at what appeared to be midday, but there was not a single person in sight. For reasons I don't understand, I reached up and felt for my slave collar, knowing in my heart that it wouldn't be around my neck. I didn't yet see Fortuna, but I knew she was there. 'Am I free?'

Then I heard her voice behind me. 'I am the only one who is free. All others are enslaved by me.'

'Even the gods?' I asked as I turned to face her.

'Especially the gods.' She laughed as she said this. Fortuna looked as beautiful as ever, but this time there was something even more frightening about her appearance and her laugh sounded somewhat menacing. She was sitting on a curule chair made of gold and ivory at the far end of the forum

160

where the temple of the Divine Julius stands today, about one hundred feet from where I stood. 'You so crave your freedom, Tychaeus. Look around you. Look around you and see what freedom looks like!'

I did as she said, actually making a slow turn so I could take in the empty forum in its entirety. When I turned back to face her I was startled to see her just an arm's length away from me. After a gasp, I recovered. 'This isn't how I remember freedom.'

'Are you telling me you didn't run free in this very place, after you ran away from your master?'

'It was different then. There were people. Many, many people.'

Fortuna suddenly rose from her chair, sending me stumbling back. 'Let us walk.' As she said this, she started to walk toward the center of the forum, so I followed her. 'You don't want freedom. You, like most people, believe you do, but freedom would be agony for you. You want to belong. You want a family.'

'I don't know *where* my mother is and I don't know *who* my father is. I don't have a family. I can't have a family!'

Fortuna laughed the same unpleasant laugh I heard when she was sitting in the distance. 'Then you must accept the one I give you and stop trying to run toward a fantasy. My will is impossible to oppose. Happiness comes when you accept that.'

'But I want to be free!' I would not, could not accept what she was saying.'

161

Fortuna turned toward me in anger and I felt a hot wind hit me in the face. 'Enough! You lose your freedom the instant you give your heart to someone, and you can never be happy without doing that! Perfect freedom is a torture none can endure. You gave up your freedom when you took Gaius Antistius into your heart, and you will give up your freedom many times more before I let you rest. You say your mother is gone and you have no father. I say you can find your mother and you can choose a father to give your heart to.'

'Not while I'm a slave. I don't have the freedom to do those things.' I was terrified she would become enraged, but I couldn't stop myself from answering her back.

'Dear Tychaeus, when will you hear me? No one is free.' Her anger was gone and she was smiling. 'A father can turn his family into slaves and can be the worst sort of master to them, as you have learned. A master can be a father to his slaves, as you will learn.' The light began to dim as if the sun was setting and Fortuna began to fade. Her voice sounded distant when she said, just before she vanished, 'Let the family I give you into your heart and be happy.'

With that I awoke to reality. With a start, I sat up and reached out to touch the cold wall of the portico where I had been sleeping.

LIBER XI

Two days later I became embroiled in an unusual turn of events. As was to happen frequently in the years to come, Cato and Servilia had a falling out over her relationship with Caesar. Somehow, Cato had learned that Caesar had visited her while he and Brutus were at the baths. I suppose it isn't at all surprising since Servilia and Caesar made little effort to hide their affair. If a slave didn't tell Cato, there were probably dozens of people who saw Caesar enter or leave the domus. I was working at my table in the room adjoining the tablinum when Cato angrily stomped his way into my workspace. It was amusing to see him try to stamp his feet while not wearing shoes. He grabbed the document I was working on and using the edge of my table he tore the clean bottom half off. 'I need something to write with!' he shouted looking around for pen and ink.

'Would you like me to write it for you?' I asked.

'Just give me the damn pen!' I had rarely seen him this angry. I handed him the pen, but in his anger he smeared the ink. He pushed the page toward me and threw the pen at me, splattering ink on my tunic and face. 'You write it!'

I picked up the pen and quickly reloaded it with ink. As Cato rapidly dictated, I began to write. 'My sister Servilia, you are to come immediately to my house on the Caelian. Stop whatever it is you are doing and come at once.' He snatched the page from me, but then he slid it back, adding, 'If Brutus is with you he is to come too.' With that, he took the page and signed his name. 'When the ink is dry, bring it to me!'

163

I did as I was instructed. Cato was sitting at the large table in the tablinum waiting for me. He quickly folded and sealed the parchment and handed it back. 'Have Baebius deliver this to Servilia at once.' I was glad to see he had regained his composure. I found the slave he named and told him what had happened. Leaving him with the note, I returned to my work, trying hard to draw as little attention to myself as possible, but Cato once again entered my workspace.

'When Servilia arrives I want you to remain in here and write down every word of our conversation. Keep the curtain drawn and don't let her know you are here. Tell no one about this.' With that Cato turned and left. I was both nervous and excited. I liked Servilia, mostly because I liked Caesar and she was his lover, so I didn't want to see any harm come to her. Servilia didn't come immediately. Baebius later told me he went to her house only to learn she had gone to the baths. He then went to find her there but had difficulty gaining admittance because, as a slave, he needed to be accompanied by a citizen. After going up three levels from the doorman to his supervisor's supervisor he was able to go into the baths, escorted by one of the slaves who worked there. Eventually he found Servilia receiving a massage. She read the note and handed it to a woman friend who was being massaged on the table beside her. Looking up at Baebius she said, 'Tell my brother I'll be there when I have finished my bath.'

To this, he replied, 'I'll tell him you will arrive as soon as possible.'

Servilia kept Cato waiting nearly two hours. That meant she kept me waiting as long. I wanted to go to the latrine to urinate, but I was afraid I wouldn't be at my place when she arrived and that would surely earn me a beating. I placed myself at such an angle that I could peer out at the edge of the curtain and get a good view of most of the other room. When she arrived, Servilia was immediately ushered into the tablinum. Cato ignored the niceties and started right in. 'I want to make it clear, you are to not ever bring that man into this house!'

'Which man would that be?' Servilia acted serene, but she was clearly angry.

'You know very well who I mean!' Cato, speaking between clenched teeth, didn't pretend to be anything other than furious.

'Gaius is a close friend of mine,' she replied, her tone rising just a little.

'He is no friend of mine, and he is not to be in this house!'

Servilia tried a new approach. 'Well, I don't know why. Gaius makes for wonderful company. You should invite him for dinner sometime and get to know him better. Anyway, I didn't bring him here. He came on his own.'

Cato started to pace and I was having trouble hearing him each time he turned his back to my doorway, so I leaned in closer. 'I have known Caesar most of my life, and he will never be my friend because he is no friend to Rome!'

Now it was Servilia's turn to sound angry. 'Be careful what you are suggesting, Marcus!'

Cato answered, 'It's not just me, and surely you've heard the rumors!'

'Yes,' she answered, 'and they are just rumors, nothing more than loose talk!'

'By the gods, sister, how can you be so blind? The elections last year were so corrupted the senate refused to seat the consuls! They earned convictions instead!'

'I don't see what that has to do with Gaius.' Servilia had regained her composure.

Cato stopped pacing and stood across the table from her. He too tried to sound reasonable, almost pleading with her to see his side. 'Few men in Rome have the money to finance bribes that large.'

Servilia laughed. 'Gaius has no money! Everyone knows that.'

'You're right. He spends like a fool, but Crassus has more money than Croesus, and Caesar *is* his man!'

'Caesar is his own man!' Servilia was once again close to anger.

'Watch how much he spends on the games and entertainment for the Florales and tell me he is not indebted to someone with a heavy purse.'

Servilia again changed her tone to one of calm reasonableness. She sounded almost as if she was talking to a child. 'The aedile is expected to put on a good show. Most men borrow for that purpose.' Then she added, 'It's your house, Marcus. If you don't want Gaius to visit, I suggest you tell him. But be careful whom you accuse of treason. He is quite popular among the plebs, and if you want to be elected tribune next year you just might need his help. And, you don't want Crassus or for that matter any of Caesar's other friends as an enemy. You know quite well how I feel about Gaius, but you, Marcus, are my brother and right now I am working to advance your interests and those of my husband. I'll be leaving now. I'm late for an appointment.'

Cato said nothing in reply. Before she left though, Servilia raised her voice and addressed me. 'Polybius, when you transcribe this conversation from your notes, I'd like to have a copy for my records, as well.' Then she turned and left as calmly as she entered.

Once she was gone I parted the curtain. Cato was sitting at the table, looking glum. Hesitantly, I asked, 'Master Cato, can I go pee?' He just waved me out of the room without looking up.

The morning after Servilia was summoned to Cato's house, I was set the task of composing invitations for a dinner party twenty one days hence on the nones of Maius (May 7) at the Cato domus. We had, filed away, a standard example of how the invitation should read, so it was a simple matter to compose the invitations from the list of names Cato supplied. Cato preferred dinner parties of nine, so seven people were invited to the party. To my surprise, the first names on the list were Gaius Julius Caesar and his wife Pompeia Sulla followed by Decimus Junius Silanus and his wife, Servilia Caeponis. I thought it might be dangerous to have these two couples sharing couches at dinner, but I held my tongue. I should, however, clarify this. It would only be the men sharing the couches. Cato strictly followed tradition, and since it was the custom for only men to recline at dinner parties, the women were relegated to stools. Romans have since seen the

167

foolishness of this ancient custom, and now women often join men on the couches. Marcus Tullius Cicero and his wife Terentia were also on the list. As I said earlier, at this point in his career Cicero was known to be a rising star of Roman politics and was expected to seek the consulship for the following year, as this was the first year he would be eligible, and he took pride in gaining each office he held as young as he legally could. Servilia's son, Marcus Junius Brutus was the last to be invited. Cato and his wife Atilia rounded out the nine dinner party attendees.

As I was composing the invitations, Cato confided a secret. In the room directly behind the triclinium, where formal dinners were held, there was a cabinet against the wall that was actually recessed into the wall. The division between the two rooms at the back of the cabinet was merely a wooden panel designed to resemble a fresco on the other side. I was to sit with a brass horn pressed against the wall on a specially designed bench built into this cabinet and take note of everything that was said. Cato carefully instructed me to pay particular attention any time he excused himself to leave the room for any reason. There really wouldn't be any reason for him to leave the room save a trip to the latrine, but whenever he hosted a dinner he liked to visit the kitchen and interfere with the cooks while they worked.

The day of the party, it was cloudy. On sunny days, it is possible for guests to arrive nearly at the same time, as the sundials tell them the proper time to depart. But, when the sky is overcast the time to leave home is often a judgment based on an individual's reckoning of the passage of the hours. Cato sent slaves out to retrieve the guests from their homes, and, as a result, the guest's arrivals were spaced out over nearly an hour. Brutus was the first to arrive. I surmised that this was

168

intentional on his part. He greatly admired his uncle and took every opportunity to share his company. Normally a senator would spend the hours before a party having his hair styled, his nails manicured, and the hairs plucked from his neck, but Cato, with his carefully cultivated Stoicism, eschewed any of these common luxuries so his only preparations had been his usual trip to the baths and a clean toga. As a result, the two men had time to spend together, no doubt plotting the conversation they would guide throughout dinner. Cato's wife, on the other hand, made a point of dressing in the finest clothes her husband's wealth could buy. She was even wearing a silk shawl! She had chosen a wig for the evening that was made of the black hair of an Aegyptian, cascading in curls down her back and shoulders. She also chose the most precious pieces of jewelry in her collection. Her goal was, no doubt, to test her husband's stoic forbearance. I'm certain he was seething on the inside, but he didn't rise to the bait and much to Atilia's annoyance, he said nothing.

Two by two, the other guests arrived. The women were dressed in their finest clothes and the men wore their best togas. Caesar and Cato were the only men with a purple stripe to their togas, as Caesar had been elected curule aedile and Cato was still quaestor at this time. Caesar carried the ivory rod of an aedile as if it was a plaything. At one point, he even poked Brutus in the ribs with the small gilded eagle on its end. He left his two lictors waiting on a bench in the vestibule for the evening.

That night I gathered no useful information. I, in fact, botched the task I was given. I was left in the cabinet with a stack of wax tablets, a stylus for taking notes, and a small oil lamp. I had only gotten through perhaps the first quarter hour of the party before the rising heat in the cabinet began to make me feel nauseous and light headed. However, I persevered. I was surprised by the conversation. After the initial niceties that so often start any social interaction, Brutus immediately attempted to engage Caesar in a political discussion, attempting to sound him out on the ever-lingering question of land reform.

Caesar responded politely. 'For the good of the republic, something must be done to help the plebs. So many of them have lost their farms that they're forced to beg on the streets of Rome. We need some sort of legislation that addresses the need for land reform. There's plenty of state land that can be divided among the poor.'

Caesar's wife Pompeia interjected casually, 'I always instruct my litter bearers to spit on those repulsive creatures when they approach.'

To which Caesar replied, 'Beware the day they start to spit back.' By his tone, it seemed as if an argument might erupt, but Servilia quickly changed the topic to Atilia's finery.

In an attempt to bring the discussion back to his topic, Brutus spoke up. 'There is not nearly enough land in Italia.'

Caesar answered, 'Not enough public land, but we could buy private land at fair prices and use that to help the poor.'

At that, Cicero spoke up somewhat more vehemently than the conversation seemed to warrant. 'I, for one, will never, not ever, support buying private land to give away to the poor. It is un-Roman!'

170

Brutus retreated, deftly changing the subject to that day's races at the circus, probably realizing he had waded into politics too soon, and would need to wait until more wine had been consumed. What I most remember about this conversation was how Caesar related to the women in the group. To his own wife he was short tempered but to Cicero's wife and the wife of his host he was flirtatious, saving his most risqué jokes and comments for Atilia, while to Servilia he was very proper and polite. I had expected him to be the opposite, flirtatious with his lover and proper with his host's wife.

Soon, my vision began to blur and I was having trouble forming the letters. My head felt light and I was sweating profusely. Then all went dark. The next thing I recall is waking up on the floor in front of the cabinet. Cleon stood over me, a scowl on his face, fanning me with one of my wax tablets. 'Master Cato will be furious! He did not put you in there to fall asleep!'

I started to protest that I clearly had swooned and had not fallen asleep, but Cleon would have none of it. He persisted in heaping insults on me. On his way out the door he called me stupid and lazy. A short time later two of the other slaves came in to help me to the room behind the kitchen where I was stripped and lifted into the basin. Matilda poured cold water over me in an attempt to revive me. It helped some, but not much. At her insistence, after the bath I was forced to drink some wine mixed with water and I was then taken to a small private cubicle with a high bed where I was wrapped in a woolen blanket and left for the night. This was an indication that Cleon realized I was ill, but that would not mitigate my error one bit.

Sometime later I found myself awake, and in spite of the fact that it was a warm night for Aprilis, I was shivering and needing to go to the latrine. I peered out from the doorway. At the front of the atrium the dinner guests were gathered saying their goodbyes, so I ducked back in hoping I wasn't seen. I waited, wrapped in my blanket until they left and Cato and his wife had passed my cubicle before I pushed the curtain aside again. I noticed as I left the room that the two lictors were still standing at the vestibule talking to the door slave. It occurred to me I hadn't seen Caesar with the group at the door, so I thought about going back into the room, but just for an instant. I knew I was about to have an attack of diarrhea and I did not want that to happen in the room where I would be spending the night. Running on bare feet across the atrium and to the back of the house, keeping the blanket wrapped around me, I approached the latrine. As I was rushing into the latrine, I nearly ran into Caesar as he was leaving the room. In my attempt to avoid a collision I tripped on my blanket and stumbled into the wall, dropping the blanket as I tried to keep from falling. There I stood, naked and shivering in front of Caesar. I was mortified.

Caesar didn't seem surprised. 'Don't just stand there, Polybius, take your blanket and hurry in. It seems to be an emergency.' I did as he suggested with not a moment to spare. Cato's latrine didn't have the luxury of being over a sewer. Instead, it was outfitted with four large pots, two for urine, and two for feces. I quickly took the lid off one and sat, just as the diarrhea escaped my bowels. I sat there for some time, waiting for the cramps in my belly to subside before I cleaned myself up as best I could with a wet sponge. My own stench forced me to vomit on the floor of the latrine before I left the room. On the way back to my room I noticed Caesar hadn't left. He was standing at the vestibule talking to his lictors. As I pulled

172

the curtain back to enter my room Caesar looked up and his eyes met mine. I went in and wrapping the blanket around myself, attempted to fall asleep.

A short time later I became aware that someone else was in the room. I opened my eyes to see Caesar standing over the bed. He reached out and felt my forehead. 'You are sick, Polybius.' I didn't answer. 'Did you manage to learn anything useful from the time spent in your cabinet?'

I didn't ask how he knew about the secret cabinet. 'No, I fainted too soon.'

'Too bad, I was very entertaining tonight.' Then he added something I found quite odd. 'I mean to buy you at the first opportunity.'

'Master Cato will not sell me,' I said, my voice weak and shaky. Normally I would have been intrigued by this conversation, but that night I just wanted to be left alone.

'He will. He just needs to be convinced you are no longer useful. Tonight's failure in your first clandestine assignment will go a long way toward demonstrating that you are incompetent.'

'Well, he won't sell me to you. He hates you.' I couldn't believe I was being so candid with Caesar.

'Cato hates no one. He has complete mastery over himself and, therefore, feels no violent emotions. Haven't you heard, he is a Stoic?' Caesar laughed. 'You need to appear to be afflicted in some way. You need a disorder that is both rare and frightening to your master.'

173

'I don't have an affliction,' I mumbled.

'Feign one. Did you ever see someone experience a seizure?'

I thought back and remembered standing beside Gaius Antistius in the forum watching a man lay on the pavement jolting about, his face twitching as foam frothed on his lips. 'Yes,' I told him, 'but Master Cato will beat me if I do that.'

Caesar's reply was swift. 'Cato will beat you anyway. He beats all his slaves. I, on the other hand, will not. If you're disloyal I may kill you, but I won't beat you.' He said this with a smile so I couldn't be sure if he was being honest or merely joking. 'Think about it. When you make up your mind, tell Servilia either yes, or no. You can trust her. You seem quite sick. I hope you remember this conversation in the morning.'

I mumbled, 'I remember everything,' and found myself drifting to sleep.

I did not, in fact, remember the conversation in the morning. It was not until two days later, after my fever broke, that I was to recall this strange encounter with Caesar. When I was well enough to walk, I was made to dress and was brought before Cato in the tablinum. I expected him to start with my failure to record the dinner party, but instead he began with, 'I was disgusted by the mess you made in the latrine. The pot is out behind the house. You will clean it.' I wasn't at first sure what he meant, but then I recalled my bout of diarrhea and the vomiting and the misty memory of that night started to come back. It was not until he began to berate me about the dinner party that he became physical. He started by slapping my face

174

and then he began to punch me. While I was being beaten, the memory of my conversation with Caesar came back to me. The beating continued until Servilia came into the room to find me curled up on the floor trying to shield myself from Cato's kicks.

I heard her say, 'Control yourself, Marcus, or you'll kill the boy!'

With that, Cato turned and stormed out of the room with Servilia behind him. I looked out to see him arguing with Servilia at the vestibule. In anger, he left the house. Servilia returned to the tablinum to check on me. The beating appeared much worse than it was. I had learned in the Titus house to shield my head and face, so, while my body was bruised, the only damage to my face was a small cut on the lip from the initial slap. Servilia brought me back to the room behind the kitchen and not finding a slave, she cleaned the cut herself as I sat weakly on a stool. When she was finished she led me back to my room where I lay on the bed.

'Try to sleep. I'll talk to your master,' she said, before turning to leave.

'Mistress Servilia,' I paused not sure what I was going to say. Finally, I said, 'Thank you.'

She seemed a little embarrassed by her brother's behavior. 'Just try to get a little sleep.'

In that moment, I made my decision. 'Could you do me a favor?' She turned to me and waited to hear what I had to say. After another pause, I took a deep breath and said, 'Please don't say anything to Master Cato, but when you next see Julius Caesar, can you tell him I said yes?'

She looked puzzled. 'I haven't the slightest idea what you mean, but this seems a simple request. I'll tell him Polybius says yes.' With that, I rolled the dice one more time."

Polybius looked down at the lengthening shadow cast by the table beside him and opened his eyes wider. "I'm so sorry Lucius, we are going to have to end this meeting for today. I have been invited by Rusticus to dine with him this evening and I'm afraid I'm already running late." With that he struggled to a sitting position before I could even assist him. "I'll have one of my boys see you out," he said with a gesture toward Pollux who had been sitting not far away. I helped Polybius to his feet and together with Pollux helped him shuffle over to the adjoining room. Once there, Polybius spoke again. "Pollux, my boy, please see Lucius Seneca to the door and then send Cardus up. I think I need a quick shave." We said our goodbyes and set an appointment for the following day. I had moved maybe ten feet from the door when I heard Polybius call me back. I returned and leaned into the room where he sat waiting for his barber to arrive. As soon as he saw my face poke around the corner he said, "I forgot to mention, I heard from your father that your brother Mela would very much like to join us. Do ask him if he would like to come along with you tomorrow."

I felt rather foolish that I'd forgotten to ask Polybius if Mela could come along with me, and I wondered when he had communicated with my father. My impression of Polybius was that he lived almost as a recluse, but this was, in spite of his advanced years, clearly not the case. I nodded and smiled, and said, "We'll both see you tomorrow. Thank you."

176

Later that evening, I reviewed my notes with Mela so he would be caught up with how far the tale had unfolded and wouldn't need to pester Polybius with too many questions.

LIBER XII

The following morning we arrived a bit early and sat watching Polybius finish his breakfast. Mela, as I expected, accepted Polybius' offer of food and ate a second breakfast. Once he was finished eating, we shuffled up to the couches in the room above his tablinum where a chair had been set out for Mela. Once we were settled in and the wine had been poured, Polybius shut his eyes for a long moment and then opened them and looked over at me. "I'm afraid you'll have to refresh my memory as to where we left off." I read back to him what I had last written.

He answered, "Ah yes, I didn't know what to do next." Then, with a sigh and the shake of his head he added, "So, I waited. I assumed Caesar would contact me in some way. I was certain if I gave the impression I was afflicted by some disease I'd be sold, but I knew Cato would never sell me to Caesar. The only move I made was to become less effective in my work. I began to make uncharacteristic errors or often forget to complete a task. This led to my constantly being berated by Cato and Cleon and occasionally I was beaten, but this was relatively mild compared to beatings I'd experienced in the past. I began to despair of ever hearing from Caesar when about a month later he arrived unannounced at the Cato domus. Cato was in the forum attending the courts, and it seemed odd to me that Caesar wouldn't know this, so I hoped his real purpose was to see me. I happened to be walking past the vestibule on my way to the tablinum when he was talking to the door slave. Caesar was about to leave when he turned back and asked whether he may use the latrine. Of course the slave said yes. I made a point of lingering in the atrium pretending to adjust the strap on my house sandal as Caesar passed me on his way to the back of the house. He caught my eye and removed a small scroll from the fold of his toga and to make certain I saw it waved it back and forth in front of his chest before returning it to the fold. I understood what he was telling me.

After Caesar had gone, I visited the latrine. It occurred to me that much of my communication with Caesar about this affair occurred in the latrine. I banished from my mind the brief thought of the sort of omen that presented. There were few places in the small room where the scroll could be hidden, so I quickly found it behind one of the pots. I lifted my tunic and sat on the pot while I read the scroll. The scroll contained a detailed description of an affliction called the falling sickness. Caesar displayed remarkable knowledge of this affliction and had clearly conducted research into the disease. Interestingly, he indicated that if I were asked to smell a piece of jet I was to immediately display the symptoms. He closed the note with words of encouragement and a request that I trust him to know when I was to be sold and that he would make the purchase. He included the unnecessary warning that I must commit the note to memory and burn it. I had no idea how he planned to be prepared on the day I went to the slave auction, but the tone of his message was one of confidence. At the first opportunity, I went into the kitchen and burned the scroll.

I rehearsed the falling sickness several times while cleaning the latrine that afternoon. While fulfilling that task I could be assured I would be left alone. There wasn't much room, and I had no way to observe myself, but I believed I could present a passable example of the symptoms of this

179

disease. The next morning during the salutatio I put on my first performance. I wanted the display to be as public as possible so word would get back to Caesar that I was doing my part. Standing in the tablinum taking notes, I dropped first my stylus and then my tablet. Cato looked at me with a scowl but I pretended not to notice. He grabbed me by the arm, prepared to strike me, when I began to twitch and grind my teeth. He immediately released me as if I was on fire, so I fell to the ground and flexed and loosed my muscles while twitching my hands and feet. This went on for just a short time before I simply went limp and lay as if unconscious.

'Get him out of here,' I heard Cato spit out between his teeth. Then he literally spit on the spotless floor of his tablinum. I heard several other men waiting nearby also spit. Someone, I'm not sure who since I had closed my eyes, dragged me to the sick room where I was left on the floor. A short time later I got up and attempted to leave the room. Miltiades was standing guard at the doorway and when I pulled back the curtain he started and covered his mouth and nose with his hand.

'You are to remain in this room,' he mumbled through his fingers.

I played the innocent. 'Why, what has happened?'

'Just stay in there!' was his angry reply.

An hour or so later a medicus came in to see me. He brought incense and without examining me lit it in a small brazier and recited his diagnosis to Cleon who was standing just outside the entrance to the room. 'This boy clearly has the falling sickness. Most think it is caused by a daemon entering the body, so it is important the air be purified three times a day, and no one should spend time with him since there is a serious risk of contagion. I have prepared prayers that he should recite and it would be wise to have others in the house also recite them to prevent the spread of the disease.'

'Can you cure him?' Cleon was matter of fact.

'No,' the medicus answered. 'Only the gods can cure him. 'I suggest he spend a night praying in the temple of Aesclepius, as that frequently affects a cure.'

'How will I know if he is cured?'

'One test is to hold a piece of jet up to his nose. If it causes him to fall into a fit then he is still afflicted.'

Cleon sounded incredulous. 'Does that really work?'

The medicus shrugged his shoulders. 'Sometimes it does, sometimes it doesn't. I can sell you a piece if you would like to try it.'

'No, thank you,' Cleon replied, 'I think we can find some around here.'

The incense way cloying and it burned my eyes. I sat in the corner of the room and let my mind wander. I relived the days of my summer of freedom and tried to imagine what it would be like to be Caesar's slave. After what seemed like most of the day, Baebius came in to burn more incense. He had a cloth wrapped around the lower part of his face. 'Another medical practitioner is coming in. Cleon wants to hear a second opinion.'

About an hour before sunset, Cleon held back the curtain to admit the physician. To my surprise, it was

181

Alexander! Turning to Cleon he said, 'I'd like privacy while I examine the patient.' Cleon was only too glad to let the curtain drop and back away from the doorway.

'How are you Polybius?' Alexander seemed completely nonplussed by my affliction.

'Very glad to see you. How's everyone at the Titus house?'

'All are well. Clodia and Marcus had a baby. Titus will try to make him your replacement, but I doubt the boy will have your talents.' Alexander examined me as he talked, first examining my eyes then my ears, followed by my nose and mouth. He asked me to remove my tunic and lie on the bed so he could feel my belly and press his ear to my chest. 'Have you been ill recently?'

'I had a fever last month. It lasted a few days.' I said this while sitting up.

Alexander then asked me to describe my symptoms, which I recited from memory. 'Polybius, why are you pretending to suffer from this affliction? Is this another attempt at escape?' He sounded upset with me.

'I'm not faking! This is the truth!' I wasn't sure what I did to arouse his suspicion.

'If you truly experienced the falling sickness, you would have no memory of what happened. You must have read of these symptoms and you are now acting them out.' He sounded certain of his diagnosis.

I said as I put my tunic on, 'I swear I am telling the truth.'

'No,' he calmly replied. 'You are not. You can trust me, so please tell me why.'

I knew if he told Cato the truth I would be beaten, and possibly killed, but I felt I had no choice but to trust him. 'I can't tell you why, but you have to believe it is not to escape. I want to be sold.'

'With this affliction? It is possible no one will want to buy you, and if you are sold, you will probably end up working in the mines.' Alexander was genuinely concerned.

'I've trusted you,' I said, 'now I ask you to trust me. That won't happen.' I sounded confident, but I wasn't completely sure.

Alexander sighed. 'You are still too thin. Cato should feed you more.' He paused, clearly thinking what to do next. 'I owe nothing to Cato, so I will keep your secret. I only pray to the gods you know what you're doing. I'll advise you spend a night in the temple of Aesclepius. Use the night to think about what you're doing. If you change your mind you can come back in the morning cured. Try not to contract any real sickness while you are there.'

Alexander rose to leave, but then remembered something and sat down again. Reaching into the fold of his toga he brought out the purse I had given him as payment for treating Gaius. He took my hand and pressed the purse into it. 'I can't take this,' I said. 'Master Cato doesn't allow his slaves to have money.'

'You can at least take the dice back, then,' and he poured the contents out into his own hand and picked the dice from the coins and handed them to me. I noticed two gold coins had been added to my money. 'I'll keep this for you and if you are sold to a master who lets you have money, come see me.'

I refused the dice too. 'No, Alexander, they're safer with you. If Cato finds them he'll take them from me. I know they're insignificant, but for me these dice have meaning, so please, keep them for me.'

Alexander nodded. 'Goodbye, Polybius. I hope everything works out for you.'

When he reached the door I stopped him to ask the question I had been avoiding since I first saw him. 'Alexander?' I hesitated and felt tears welling up in my eyes

'Yes, Polybius, what is it?' he asked.

'Did Gaius Antistius die?'

His look of concern changed to a broad smile. 'Why, no. His case was a complete success. After his recovery, I found him a job with a relation of mine on a farm near Neapolis (Naples).' Then, Alexander turned serious again. 'I needed to move him secretly. That man you boys robbed is a very dangerous fellow. He makes his living demanding protection money from shopkeepers in the Subura, and he insures payment by the harshest methods. He would just as soon kill you as look at you, so I would be careful when you are about in the city.'

I was overjoyed!

184

A short time after Alexander left me, I was brought in a litter to the temple of Aesclepius on the Tiber Island. This was my first ride in a litter, and it would have been quite pleasant had the curtains not been so heavy. Cleon walked beside the litter, burning incense. It quickly became very stuffy inside the curtained box, but when I tried to pull the curtain back my knuckles were rapped with a birch rod. The litter was set down in front of the temple and as I emerged Cleon took a step back from me. 'We will pick you up just after sunrise. Do not try to escape, as there are guards at both bridges. Remember to say the prayers,' he said, handing the parchment sheet containing the prayers to one of the litter bearers who then handed it to me. Cleon tossed a small purse containing four denarii at me. 'Give that to the priest at the temple steps. He will provide you with the proper sacrifice and help you with the procedure.' I turned and walked toward the temple, turning back to watch Cleon and the slaves hurry away.

The temple of Aesclepius was as imposing a temple as any in Rome. It was faced in travertine marble and the portico was supported by six ionic columns, I would suppose in honor of the Greek origin of the god. On the temple's frieze, the legend of the god's serpent arriving by ship and his slithering to the island was depicted. The tall bronze doors were open, and I could see, partially obscured by the fog of incense hanging in the cella of the temple, the enormous statue of the bearded god high atop his pedestal. There was only a single long stone bench on each side of the cella with much of the floor space left open, as the number of visitors could not otherwise be accommodated. In spite of the early hour, there were already more than two dozen sick people either in the temple proper or on the portico, when I arrived.

185

The priests at the temple were much like the first "medical expert" who visited me. Before the altar on the platform at the bottom of the steps, they heard my symptoms and prescribed prayers. Of course their prayers were said to be more effective than the ones the medicus prescribed. The prayers they offered could be had for a donation of one denarius. Much to the consternation of the priest, I opted to use the prayers I came with. In addition to the prayers, I was given the option of three different sacrifices. For three denarii I could purchase a newly born black pig. For one denarius I could buy a black dove. For two ases I would be able to provide the god with a cake made of spelt and salt. Since I wasn't really at all ill, I chose the least expensive sacrifice and insisted on being given change for my denarius. The priest warned of the dire consequences of being stingy with the god, but I stood my ground. Normally I would not have been nearly so bold, but my visit with Alexander that afternoon had caused me to recommit to saving as much money as I could, hoping to someday buy my freedom. I resolved to find a place to hide my money as soon as I was allowed to once again move about the domus. Because my donation was so small, we were done with the ritual in almost no time, and I was quickly ushered into the temple proper. Once inside, I removed the cloth belt from my tunic and folded it to make a pocket to store my money.

As my eyes adjusted to the dimly lit temple, the number of sick people filling the place struck me. The room smelled of sweat and vomit and diarrhea and incense. The incense was so heavy it formed a hazy cloud suspended in the motionless air. All around me were people with every sort of ailment. One man was missing both legs, and I wondered what he expected the god to do about that, but then I saw that the two stumps were swollen and infected. There were two women, both with watery eyes and raspy coughs, huddled together at the base of the statue. There was a healthy mother sitting along the wall with two small, nearly lifeless children and a wife with her delirious husband who would alternately moan and then shout curses at those only he could see. I could continue the list, but suffice it to say, there were many and varied ailments on display.

I went before the statue of Aesclepius and offered a prayer. I used the formula of the written prayer, but where the prescribed prayer asked for assistance in overcoming my affliction, I impiously inserted a plea for help in obtaining my freedom. At the end of the prayer I added my own apology to the god for deceiving his priests and feigning an illness. Then, I found a place in the corner of the temple and attempted to sleep. Needless to say, sleep was nearly impossible. The fits of coughing and the moaning and groaning of the sick were enough to deprive the dead of their long awaited rest. Several times during the long night, a priest stood before the statue and loudly intoned a prayer to the god. When the first rays of the sun finally filtered in through the open doors of the temple I rejoiced that I would be able to breathe the stench of the Tiber River rather than the stench of the dying within the temple walls. I got to my feet feeling considerably sicker than I had felt when I arrived at the temple. Having placed myself at the farthest corner of the temple I was one of the last to leave. I noticed, as I made my way to the door trying to avoid anyone who seemed particularly contagious, that there were three corpses we were leaving behind on the floor of the temple.

Once out on the steps, I sat and waited for Cleon and the litter bearers. I was in no hurry to find them, so I sat enjoying the sunrise and the relatively clean air of the new day. I knew when I returned I would need to bear the blame for the failure of my cure and I would, of course, be accused of being impious and risking bringing the wrath of the god on the entire household. Eventually I caught sight of Cleon and the litter as it moved to the island side of the bridge. The night in the temple coupled with my dread of what was to come later in the day had made me nauseous and I nearly vomited, but by taking deep breaths through my nose I was able to settle my stomach while walking down the steps to meet Cleon.

Cleon greeted me with, 'Are you cured?'

To which I replied, 'I think I might be. I feel very well today.' I wanted to seem as healthy as possible to avoid any recriminations sooner than was necessary. I handed the empty purse to one of the litter bearers and he in turn handed it to Cleon.

'There is no money left?' he asked suspiciously.

'I chose the best sacrifice. The priest told me it would improve my chances for a complete recovery,' I lied as I climbed into the litter and pulled the heavy curtain shut.

The ride back was much more pleasant. The streets were less crowded, so the litter seemed to glide along without the starts and stops of the previous day and the cooler morning air made the inside of the litter quite comfortable. I nearly drifted off to sleep, and, in that netherworld between sleep and wakefulness, I heard a voice I recognized as Fortuna's say to me 'Now, Tychaeus, the game begins in earnest!' The voice was as clear as if she was sitting beside me, and it caused me to jolt awake. As I collected my wits, the litter came to a stop and was lowered to the ground.

Once inside the domus I noticed the place was strangely quiet. I soon realized all the slaves were being kept away to avoid contagion. I learned through the conversation I overheard between the litter bearers that Cato had sent his family to their country villa outside the city walls to avoid me. I was immediately ushered back into the smoke filled sick room. Once again, the cloying incense was making me feel light headed and nauseous. After a short time, Cleon drew the curtain aside. Through the haze of incense I could see the first physician who had visited me was standing outside the room conversing with Cato. The man came in, and without a word spoken, produced a seal that had been cut from black stone. I guessed this to be a piece of jet that was supposed to provoke a fit if I was still afflicted. With a smile, the medicus held it up before my face. I was feeling too queasy to return his smile. He brought the black stone nearer to my nose. I had the presence of mind to wrinkle my nose and say, 'That smells funny. What is it?' the physician's smile turned into a frown.

He brought the stone so close it actually touched my nose and held it there. 'How do you feel,' he asked tentatively holding the black stone to my nose.

'I feel fine,' I answered, managing to force a smile. 'I've never felt...' With that, I made my face go blank, my eyes vacant, and, after a brief moment, my hands began to twitch as I slid to the floor where I erupted in full convulsions of my body and limbs. I managed a groan between clenched teeth. The charlatan physician scrambled to his feet and grabbed a stick of burning incense and dropped to his knees and began to wave it inches from my face. This was enough to cause my weak stomach to vomit what little it held. I then lay still as if unconscious. The physician slowly rose to his feet and announced, 'The cure has failed. The god has forsaken

189

this boy.' I heard his sandals shuffle across the floor as he left the room. Cato entered the room and through clenched teeth growled, 'Damn you to infernal Hades!' With that he kicked me in the stomach, causing me to double up in a ball, and he too left the room. Cleon let the curtain drop, and I was alone.

I remained in the room two entire days. During those two days my mind vacillated between feeling excited about what was to come and terror at the thought that I made the wrong choice. I began to doubt Caesar could come through. I knew Cato and Caesar were not on friendly terms and without a visit from Servilia I could see no way he would find out I was to be sold. My gloomy thoughts only compounded my already miserable condition, but there was no way to reveal to Cato that I had feigned the affliction without making things worse.

My food and my chamber pot were brought in by a slave who would then light incense, leaving me to eat my meager meal in a cloud of cloying smoke. To compound my misery, my meals were cut in half. The slave explained that since I wasn't working, I needed less sustenance. On the morning of the third day, a man I didn't recognize came in and informed me I would be going to the slave market. As I was put in chains I did my best to hide my panic. I had heard nothing from Caesar. I had at least expected to have Servilia visit and perhaps pass me a note, but there was not a word. I was certain Caesar had changed his mind or had forgotten about me. I believed I was abandoned.

The slave market was held each month, four days before the nones behind the Sempronian Basilica, provided there was not a festival that prohibited business. That basilica was the one that occupied the space where the Julian Basilica

190

now stands. Caesar, among the many other improvements he made to the city, replaced the older, shabbier, building with the fine structure that now occupies the space. A wooden platform was erected against the wall of the basilica and a canopy was spread over the platform. Beside the platform large posts had been planted in the ground with a heavy iron chain strung between the posts. As the slave traders brought their wares to the market, the slaves were shackled to the chain. This area was fenced in to prevent potential buyers from inspecting the slaves too closely before they were formally put up for sale. On the platform, a table was set up to handle the necessary documents for the transaction.

I was, once again, paraded through the street in chains. In front of the Cato domus a slave who had been waiting outside for the man who came to fetch me coated my foot in powdered chalk and hung a placard around my neck. I was not given a chance to read it, but I knew it would contain all the particulars about my skills as well as the fact that I was afflicted with the falling sickness. I asked the boy why he was doing these preparations here and not at the market.

'It's advertisement,' he answered, 'Maybe someone will see you in passing and come to bid on you.' I felt humiliated.

When we arrived at the market it became apparent that the man who collected me from the Cato house only worked for the slave trader who was already on the site. I was a late addition to several slaves that he had prepared to auction that day. I was unshackled just long enough for my tunic to be lifted off and my chains looped around the large chain between the posts. Since Cato didn't provide his slaves with underwear, I stood naked. Seven slaves, four women, two

191

men, and a boy of about ten years of age were already chained between the posts. As I was added to the queue I was warned that I was not to speak to the others. I prayed I would be the last to be sold since I held out hope word would somehow get to Caesar and he would arrive in time to buy me. Five more slaves were added to the group before the auctioneer announced we were about to start.

The crowd was good, as the weather was quite fair, so the bidding took some time for each slave. The child was the first to go. I was struck by the lack of emotion on his face as he was led away by his new master. Then, one by one, the six others that were in line before me went up on the platform. Each time, the auctioneer would read from a papyrus provided by the slave trader and extol the attributes of the slave. Any flaws were added almost as an afterthought. Prospective bidders were allowed to go up on the platform and inspect the slave more closely, inspecting eyes, teeth, and limbs for soundness. The women were given closer inspections than the men with one buyer even judging with his hands the weight of a slave woman's breasts. Once everyone who wanted a closer look was satisfied, the bidding began. The boy sold for nine thousand four hundred sestertii. One of the men reached nearly thirty thousand sestertii on account of his skill with arithmetic and his ability to read and write in both Latin and Greek. I hoped my talents would mitigate my flaws and allow me to be bought by a wealthier master so I could have a somewhat easier life.

It was apparent that the slaves were being sold in the order they arrived, meaning I was next to go. I prepared myself for the humiliating experience. I was feeling light headed and a little sick and I realized I had been a fool to trust Caesar. To my surprise, the slave trader skipped me and

192

unlocked the man behind me. This fellow, an ignorant brute, was sold quickly for a low price, and then once again I was skipped and the young girl behind me was brought up. She was about my age and quite pretty. She was closely inspected by several of the men from the audience. In fact, the queue to inspect her led all the way down the steps. Since she had no attributes to recommend her save her looks, bidding started extremely low. The bidding was fast and quite competitive, but eventually, she went for only about six hundred sestertii. The trader once again skipped me and went to the next in line. As he was unlocking the slave's shackles, the man who retrieved me from Cato's house ran up to him and whispered something in his ear. With that, he locked the man's chains again and turned to me. I wondered what was happening, but I was in no position to ask. I was unlocked and brought up to the platform. The pillei was put on my head. This cap indicated that the slave trader could make no guarantees of my fitness. I was being sold, 'as-is'.

Once on the platform, the auctioneer read in a loud voice, 'This boy is fourteen years and nine months of age. He was born a slave to a Greek mother who was taken captive from the city of Mytilene on the island of Lesbos. His father is unknown. In spite of his young age, he is very skilled in reading and writing in both Latin and Greek, having worked as both a secretary and a copyist. He ran away from his master once. He is of sound constitution and health with the exception of an affliction of the falling sickness, leaving him prone to fits. Experts on this affliction are divided as to whether or not it is contagious. The priests of Aesclepius say that it is caused by a daemon having entered the person and it rarely moves into another. Any interested parties may now come up to inspect the boy.' The announcement of my affliction prevented most of the men from inspecting me. One man came

193

up for a closer look but didn't dare touch me. The auctioneer then announced, 'If there are no others, we can begin the bidding.' Right then, a man pushed his way through the crowd. I recognized him from my months of freedom, as a brothel owner and this terrified me. He inspected me quite closely from my head to my feet, lingering too long for my comfort at my genitals. He even spread the cheeks of my buttocks and took a close look.

All the while he was inspecting me he carried on a low conversation with himself. 'He is quite skinny, but I suppose some will like that. He has a nice mouth. He is handsome enough.' He went on and on about my good and bad points. When he said to himself, 'He's got some scars on his back,' he raised his voice and turned me around showing my back to the crowd, no doubt to discourage other buyers. When he was satisfied he went down the steps to take a place right in front of the platform.

At that point the auctioneer announced loudly, 'The bidding will begin at five hundred sestertii!' I was shocked by the low price. My affliction and my tendency to run away must have driven down the starting bid. The fact that I looked terrified probably didn't help much either. I told myself to stand as tall as possible and look intelligent, but I stood pale and trembling with tears welling up in my eyes. Someone in the back of the crowd bid five hundred. This was followed by a pause, and I was relieved the brothel owner didn't bid. The auctioneer called out, 'Is that all? Will no one offer ten more?'

There was another pause, then from the brothel owner, 'Five hundred and five.' I waited for a counter bid and there was none. I stood in disbelief, shaking my head as tears

194

ran down my cheeks. I scanned the crowd looking for Caesar, but instead I saw Cleon near the back of the crowd.

As the auctioneer shouted, 'Sold!' I watched Cleon turn away with a satisfied smile. My humiliation was complete. The cap was pulled from my head and the placard removed from my neck as my new master counted out the sum and the documents were signed and sealed.

When the brothel owner led me down the steps, he laughed and said to no one in particular, 'He can do double duty, working as my secretary when he isn't otherwise occupied.' He didn't stop to dress me, so I would have the further humiliation of being forced to walk naked and in chains through the forum and into the Subura. It occurred to me he would probably lead me past the Titus domus. We had only gone a short distance around the side of the basilica when a well-dressed slave met us under the portico. He had a fresh, well-made tunic and new shoes for me. The brothel owner removed my shackles, saying soothingly, 'Don't be scared, everything's going to work out just fine for you.' I was not at all reassured. The slave used a cloth to wipe most of the chalk from my foot before giving me the tunic and shoes."

At this, Mela leaned forward and excitedly said, "So Caesar left you hanging in the wind? I'll bet you were angry as a harpy."

Polybius looked a little irritated, when he said, "I can tell you're one who always wants to jump ahead in a story. Please, young Mela, try not to interrupt." With that, Mela sheepishly sat back in his chair. It was quite some time before Mela would again interrupt. With a stern look at my brother, Polybius continued. "The slave then took me by the left arm

195

while the brothel owner took my right and they walked me rather quickly across the forum and along the Argiletum. As we passed the Titus domus I kept my head down and turned away, hoping I wouldn't be seen. Three blocks further on, we turned into the side street where the brothel was located. The closer we got the more I settled into a heavy despondency. Gone was the terror, as I resigned myself to a life as a prostitute for at least as long as it would take me to escape. When we arrived, I was led in through the front door. The air inside the house was cool and smelled clean. The door slave, a big burly former gladiator, let us in and bolted the door behind us. I was surprised to see there were no customers, as I could remember men waiting at the door to this place. I also didn't see any of the girls around.

This building was once a wealthy man's domus. Over the years it had first a second floor and then a third floor added. On the outside these had been converted into apartments and shops, but on the inside the cubicles around the atrium had been subdivided into still smaller rooms, each provided with a bed. Around the atrium couches and tables had been arranged for the patrons to enjoy snacks and wine while they chose their girl, and sometimes their boy. The frescoes on the walls all reflected some quasi-mythological erotic scene. I consoled myself that this was at least considered one of the high-class whorehouses. I didn't know if there was any sort of training for my new job, but I suspected I would be set to work right away. I expected to be taken somewhere to be inspected for lice and other diseases, so I wasn't surprised when I was taken into what had once been the tablinum of the house. As I was led through the atrium, I noticed the room that had been added above the tablinum was faced with an intricate latticework through which the action below could be watched without the watcher being seen. The open space at the front of the tablinum had been bricked in, but the room could be accessed through a door. I was taken through that door and immediately led up the narrow staircase to the room above. The brothel owner walked in front and the slave came up behind me; I suppose this was to prevent any escape attempt. In that moment I was feeling even lower than I had when I was led in chains back into the Titus domus.

LIBER XIII

Little did I realize, my fortunes were about to take another turn, for when the brothel owner stepped to the side at the top of the stairs, I saw Caesar sitting at the table! My intense relief must have been evident, because, setting down the scroll he was reading, Caesar said, 'Don't look so surprised, Polybius. Didn't you think I would hold up my end of the deal?'

All I could say was, 'I'm thirsty. Could I have some water?'

Caesar poured me a cup of water from the pitcher on the table.

I sat mute as the brothel owner presented Caesar with a new document transferring me to my fifth master, and my third that day. 'What did you pay for him?' Caesar asked.

'He was a bargain. Only five hundred fifty,' the brothel owner lied, giving himself an extra forty five sestertii. Caesar read the original sale document carefully and must have detected the fraud, but said nothing.

'Here is six hundred,' Caesar said, sliding a bag of coins across the table to the man. 'Feel free to count it.'

'I trust you, aedile,' the man answered while pressing his signet ring into the hot wax on the parchment.

The documents were handled quickly and efficiently and within a very short time Caesar rose to his feet saying, 'Let's go home, Polybius.'

We left through the rear door of the house. As we stepped out into the sunlight I felt reborn. I was still a slave, but I felt my future was now more certain. Other than using the back door, Caesar made no attempt to disguise that he was leaving a brothel. At the door, an older man in a tunic was waiting. This man I had seen with Caesar on the day we first met, several years prior. Caesar turned to the man and said, 'Demetrius, this is our new man, Polybius.' Then, turning toward me, 'This is my nomenclator, Demetrius. You two will be working together closely.' I would soon learn it was just a short distance to the Julian domus in the Subura on a side street just off the Argiletum.

Both Titus and Cato had insisted their slaves walk behind them in public, but Caesar didn't question that I was walking at his side. The walk down the crowded street felt easy that day despite the number of people who moved in to touch Caesar or shake his hand. Although people continually shouted greetings to Caesar and he responded to each one with a friendly smile and wave, sometimes even stopping to pat someone on the back or ruffle the hair of a matron's child, Caesar was able to carry on a conversation. Along the way, he informed me that he had grown up in the Subura. 'These streets were my playground,' he said.

This surprised me. 'I thought you came from one of the oldest patrician families in Rome?'

'You're correct, my family dates back to before the founding of the city. We lived in the Subura when the city was

199

small, in fact, before there even was a Subura. Most of the patrician families moved to the surrounding hills as the population of plebs swelled, but we stayed put.'

I had always been curious why most of the plebs live in the valleys between the hills. 'Why didn't the plebs occupy the land on the hills? The air is fresher and the views are much better.'

'Ah, that's an excellent question, but no one is quite sure of the answer, so I ask you: Why do you think the plebs stayed in the valleys?'

This led me to think. I started to say something right away, but Caesar stopped me. 'Think before you speak, Polybius.'

So I thought. I mulled it over as we walked down the crowded street. All the shops we passed provided me with an answer. 'Well, the patricians had the authority to choose the land that best suited them, but I don't think this is the only reason.'

'Go on,' Caesar encouraged me.

'In the days when Rome was small there would have been more land than the patricians and equites could occupy on the hills, so there should be some plebian families that moved to those spots. Therefore, there must have been a reason they *chose* to live in the Subura.'

'Interesting,' he said.

I was now feeling more confident. 'I think they chose to live here because the first plebeians to move to the city would have been shopkeepers and artisans, and the shops and factories were in the valley because it would be too difficult to bring the goods up the hillsides.'

'I think you may be right,' he said. 'As you undoubtedly know from your reading, Rome started as a collection of separate villages on each of the hills. When Romulus united the villages together, the space between the hills would be the logical place to conduct trade. The plebeians would have lived close to if not actually in their shops, as most of them still do.' Our conversation came to an end as we approached the Julian Domus.

From the outside, Caesar's domus was unremarkable. A wine shop on one side and a poultry shop on the other flanked the double front door to the house. Each shop had a one room apartment with a balcony above it. The wine shop was painted purple, and the poultry shop was white. As we approached, the door slave swung open both doors and stepped back against the wall of the vestibule. He must have been watching through the peephole for our arrival. Caesar entered first, followed by me, and then by Demetrius, Caesar's nomenclator. The door slave shut the doors behind us. I noticed the mosaic on the floor of the vestibule was of a fierce, snarling dog. In small black tiles the words *Cave Canum* were spelled out, warning a visitor to be wary of the family dog. Before I had time to worry about a vicious cur, a small fat dog came running up to us and immediately jumped at me, licking my hands and wagging his tail.

'Polybius, this is Antius,' Caesar said, introducing me to the door slave. 'He is as vigilant as the geese that guard the Capitoline Hill.' Then, bending down to pet the dog, he

201

said, 'This is Hercules. He is, at least nominally, my dog, but truth be told, he is much fonder of my mother.'

'Greetings young fella,' Antius said with an almost toothless smile.

Once past the vestibule and into the atrium, I had an opportunity to look around. The domus was built in the typical fashion. Before the impluvium was a small marble table. The atrium had two cubicles and an apse on each side, and each of the walls was covered with a brightly colored fresco. A balcony jutted from the second floor rooms and ran along both sides of the atrium. The floor was covered with four mosaics, one radiating from each corner, each depicting a mythological scene.

'Very good then,' Caesar said, turning to Demetrius. 'I have work to do, so see that Polybius gets situated and we'll talk more later.' With that Caesar left us and entered the tablinum with Hercules following at his heels.

Demetrius walked rapidly across the atrium. Not knowing what else to do, I followed. There was a narrow passage just past the apse on the left side of the atrium that led to a door to the outside. At the front of this passage there was an opening in the wall that contained a stairway to the second floor balcony. I followed him up the stairs and across the balcony to a room near the front. Pulling back the curtain, Demetrius stopped to let me pass in first. Once inside, he said, 'This is our room. For now, you will be spending all your time with me. You'll sleep on the floor along that wall,' he pointed at the wall that ran perpendicular to the bed. 'Please don't sleep beside my bed, as I'm inclined to get up in the night and may step on you. If you should acquire any possessions, there's a trunk under the bed where you may store them. You'll be expected to keep a clean tunic there also. We rise at first light and wake the barber so he can shave us, so don't close the curtain on the window. The master likes the slaves who accompany him to be presentable.'

Demetrius stopped talking long enough to take a breath, so I used the pause to ask the question that no one had yet bothered to answer. 'What, exactly, will I be doing for Master Caesar?'

Demetrius was about to start speaking again when he became conscious of my question, so he stopped and sighed. 'Of course, we should start there. Sometimes there is so much to do and things happen so fast I forget to attend to the preliminary details. I'm told you learn fast. I hope this is true, as there's so much you will need to remember. Please sit down.'

I looked around and saw only one stool, but I sat as I was instructed. Demetrius sat on the bed. 'I was slave to Caesar's father, and when he died I came to our current master. On the day of the funeral, my new master made a promise. He told me that when he was elected praetor he would free me. At the time I foolishly asked him why not wait until he reached the consulship, which would have prolonged my servitude a number of years, as that was the pinnacle of a man's career, but he said no. He wished to free me when I was still young enough to have some years as a free man. Caesar will be eligible for the praetorship in three years. Over time, I assumed Caesar forgot his promise, but he did not. About two months ago, he came home from a visit with Servilia and announced he had found my replacement. It will take some time to train you, but when you are ready to take over my position, I shall be given the cap of freedom.' With that Demetrius sighed and smiled.

I waited for him to continue but he just sat smiling, so I said, 'But you still haven't answered my question. What, exactly, will I be doing?'

Demetrius laughed. 'You will, of course, be replacing me as Caesar's nomenclator.'

I was shocked. For a senator or man of business, the nomenclator was one of his most important slaves. The nomenclator not only announced guests, but he was almost constantly at his master's side to remind him of the names and details of anyone they may encounter. This meant, of course, I would be required to remember the names and details of the hundreds of influential men and women of Rome."

I didn't bother to remind Polybius that I was intimately familiar with the work of my father's nomenclator.

"I began to protest to Demetrius. 'I'm only a boy and I don't know anyone of any importance and you talked about us being shaved every morning and I don't need to shave as I only have a slight moustache and a few hairs on my chin!'

Demetrius laid a hand on my shoulder to calm me. 'Polybius, when I started with Caesar's father, I too knew nothing and no one, but I learned and so shall you. Now we'll talk more as I show you around the domus.' With that Demetrius led me out of the room. While we walked along the balcony, he turned back and said, 'And, you will be shaved each morning. Caesar will not put up with even a few chin whiskers unless you are with him on a military campaign.'

204

I shook my head with wonder. An hour earlier I was certain I would be condemned to a life as a common prostitute and now there was talk of going on campaign with one of the most famous men in Rome. Fortuna certainly was as fickle as they say.

I was taken on a tour of the entire domus. I was shown each room from the humblest pantry to the master's sleeping chamber. I couldn't understand why it seemed important to Demetrius that he show me every room. He talked continually during the tour, and I did my best to listen to everything. He started at the back of the domus in the large triclinium to the rear of the peristyle. 'This is a difficult job, but not without its rewards. If you are loyal, you will be younger than I when you are granted your freedom. You will also see places and meet people few men of any station ever will. Caesar is not stingy with his slaves, so you will be properly fed and clothed.'

'Will I have underwear?' I broke in.

This caused Demetrius to smile. He had apparently heard that Cato deprived his slaves of underwear. "Yes, Polybius, you'll get fresh underwear every other day, or as it is needed. Please don't interrupt. Save your questions for later.'

He continued. 'There are times when you will need to seem invisible while in plain sight. Other times you will need to make your presence very evident, especially when you must stand up to someone who refuses to take no for an answer. It can be uncomfortable for one of our station to say no to a patrician, or even to an equite for that matter, but you'll get used to it and you may even come to enjoy it. On the street, Caesar will, as long as he holds office, have lictors to help

205

with this, but indoors you'll be the one who screens who he sees and, more importantly, who he does not see. Once you learn his ways, it will be you who makes the list, from the many waiting for the salutatio, of those who will get the opportunity to meet with Caesar. Caesar will trust your judgment as long as you don't let him down. You'll need to be at his side on the street. When someone approaches, he will probably not recognize the man so you will have to prompt him with the name and some interesting information to start the conversation. If a woman approaches him, there will probably be no need for you to remind him of her name.' Demetrius smiled and winked when he said this.

There was much more in this vein as we walked the entire house. At last we had circled around the other side and returned to the garden in the peristyle. I was led to a round, three-legged table with two chairs, where we sat. 'Now, what questions do you have?' Demetrius smiled at me.

'Could I have something to eat?' This was the first thing that came to mind. 'I haven't had breakfast yet.'

'Oh my, how rude of me.' Demetrius seemed to be genuinely embarrassed. He stopped Thestor, the garden slave, and said, 'Have Rufius bring this young man some food. And water too. There should be some chicken left over from breakfast and bread and whatever fruit there is.'

Seeing Demetrius ordering a slave to do his bidding prompted another question. 'Won't the other slaves resent me? I'm just a boy and I'll be the one at the master's side.'

I expected him to answer with some reassuring words of how we all live in harmony as a family but instead he said,

'Of course they will. Some of them may even hate you for it. You will have some slaves assigned to work for you.'

This made me very uneasy. 'How do I deal with it?'

His answer was swift. 'It is quite simple. You always remember you are following Caesar's will. If you ever come to realize you are working for your own benefit rather than your master's, take a deep breath and correct it. And, the first time you admit you are wrong and apologize to a man, you will have taken a great leap toward making a lifelong friend.'

His answer didn't satisfy me entirely, but I decided to let it sink in and I went on. 'You mentioned that Caesar will one day be consul. You sound so certain.'

This too brought a smile to Demetrius face. 'I have worked long for both this Gaius Julius Caesar and the previous one. I have met all the leading Romans of both generations, and I can tell you there is none more determined to achieve his ends than your new master.'

'What are those ends?' I asked.

'Our Caesar intends to outdo or at the very least match the deeds of all his illustrious ancestors.'

This comment brought a smile to my face. I, like everyone else in Rome, knew the history of the Julian family. 'Does he remember that the first ancestor of the Julians was the goddess Venus?'

'I'm certain he does, which should make your life very interesting. However, that should not be your concern right now. Your task for the foreseeable future is to help your master be elected praetor. That is his immediate concern so it is also your immediate concern.'

I was genuinely curious as to why. 'What makes becoming praetor so important?'

Demetrius smiled as he answered. 'Because, after his term as praetor Caesar will be posted t one of the provinces and then he can make a great deal of money and pay off his debts.' Then the food arrived and he sat quietly watching me eat.

After I ate, I was introduced to many of the slaves I hadn't yet met and then taken back to our room. Demetrius sat me on the stool again and told me to close my eyes. I did as I was instructed and he then said, 'I want you to remember our entire tour of this house. I want you to start in this very room and relive it in your mind. Remember as much detail as you can.' I could see no point to this, but since this was easier than carrying water or scrubbing a floor I did as he bid me. I was surprised at how little I remembered. There were bits that were clear as a bright day, but I was confused by the order of the rooms and I couldn't recreate in my mind most of the details. Demetrius said nothing and I was allowed quite some time to accomplish this exercise. When I was through, I admitted to him that I remembered very little.

'I'm not at all surprised,' was his reply. 'That is the way most people go through life. From this point on you must be different from the others. You must remember every detail.'

'I thought I remembered everything, but now I see I don't, and I'm not sure I can.'

208

'I know you can,' he said. You remembered the names of the people you had just met, while most forget names immediately. You remembered that Venus was the first ancestor of the Julians. You remember much more than you realize. You have the gift of remembering everything that catches your attention. You must now expand the range of what does so. The secret is to not try too hard. The secret is to pay close attention and let it happen.'

All I could say was, 'I'll do my best.'

'I'm going with Caesar to the forum for about three hours. While I am gone I want you to study every detail of this room and the next two rooms as well. I will test you on the details when I return. If anyone but the mistress of the house challenges your right to be in a room just tell him you are acting on my instructions.' With that, Demetrius got up and left me alone to study the room I was in. A placard on one wall puzzled me. It simply bore a large letter 'A.'

I found if I relaxed and didn't try to remember the details it was easier to recall them. Once again, I had no idea why he was having me spend my time on this sort of thing, but I reminded myself that it was the easiest 'work' I'd ever been assigned. I did as I was instructed and studied the rooms. I noticed the second room had a placard with a 'B' and the third a 'C.' I guessed correctly that all the rooms in the house were lettered for a reason. I thought I had done reasonably well, but I was surprised at the degree of detail Demetrius expected me to recall when he returned to question me. 'What sort of fruit is on the tree to the left of the lady in the fresco? Is the latch for the shutter on the left or the right side of the window? How many floor tiles can you see when you stand at the doorway?' I was bombarded with these questions as I ate a thoroughly satisfying meal of roasted duck and leeks, fresh from the poultry shop right outside our door.

In the afternoons, while Demetrius accompanied Caesar to the baths, I was left alone in the tablinum with a box of scrolls and a list of names. The scrolls were arranged alphabetically and contained detailed information on the prominent equites and their families. I was instructed to go down the list, look up the particular family and memorize as many details as I could about the paterfamilias of the family. The scrolls listed such things as the man's ancestors, the street he lived on, and the names of his wives, both past and present. The birthdays of the man and his family members and even the names of his pets were included. The writing was particularly small and was at times difficult to read. On their return, I was once again tested. This time I did better. I have always been naturally stronger at recalling the written word and conversations than things I have seen. I've had to train myself to remember the details of the broader events of my life.

As we were finishing up the testing, Caesar joined us in the tablinum with a plate of cheese, a pitcher of wine and three cups. 'Did your previous masters allow you wine?' he asked me.

'I was just a child when I was with Master Titus, but he did allow a taste during festivals or Saturnalia. I'm sure you know Cato deprives even his wife of wine, so he certainly doesn't allow it for his slaves.'

'You and Atilia were both spared then,' he answered. 'You couldn't pay me to drink the cheap wine he serves at home.' As he filled the cups, Caesar said, 'Just one cup for you then, Polybius, until you can tolerate more. Wine should relax one, not disorder the thinking and induce illness.' I was surprised to see my master pouring the wine for his slaves.

Turning toward Demetrius, Caesar asked, 'How did your pupil do?'

I felt my face redden. I was embarrassed by the men talking about me as if I wasn't in the room and I feared Demetrius would tell Caesar how disappointed he was.

'Remarkably well. You made a wise choice in selecting this young man.' Demetrius smiled and added, 'I believe he did far better than I did when I was first introduced to this exercise.'

Emboldened by this, I asked, 'What is the point? I understand learning the information on the families, but why memorize details of the rooms of this house.'

Demetrius smiled and tapped my forehead with his index finger. 'Just store it all away. The 'why' of it all will be revealed soon enough.'

'Is this something all nomenclators must learn?' I asked.

'Actually, very few learn this technique, but those who do become the best.' Demetrius seemed proud of himself.

I had one last question. 'Why doesn't Cato have a nomenclator? He seems to rely on his own memory and the help of his secretary.'

Caesar answered this one. 'Cato believes one should respect old-fashioned republican virtues. This in itself is not a bad thing. He *is* a virtuous man. But, these are challenging times we live in, and sometimes virtue is not enough.'

I wasn't satisfied with the answer, and I said so.

Caesar continued. 'Cato has taken the cult of republican virtue to mean that any innovation is to be avoided. Since in the time of his father's, father's, father senators didn't make use of nomenclators, he eschews the practice and relies on his own good old-fashioned republican memory that he sometimes scrambles with too much of his home-made, republican wine.'

The two men then turned to the next day's schedule. Apparently Caesar was appearing in the forum to testify for the defense in some thoroughly unimportant trial. This led to a discussion of politics. Although it was still early, the wine and the stress of the day caused my eyes to grow heavy and my head to bob. With that, Demetrius sent me off to bed. Excepting times of illness, I had not been to bed before sunset since I was a small boy.

The next day I awoke thoroughly refreshed. I had a quick breakfast of leftovers from the previous day and was allowed to sit and observe the salutatio from a discrete distance. After the salutatio, when Caesar and Demetrius left for the forum, the exercised continued just as it was the day before. In the morning I memorized rooms while in the afternoon I memorized families. This continued for twenty-three days, allowing me time to study each of the rooms three times.

It was on the morning of the morning of the fourth day that I met the dual mistresses of the house. It was time to study the second floor rooms on the other side of the atrium.

212

The women of the house had their own rooms on the second floor of the domus. In this, Caesar was as traditional as Cato. I was warned to avoid these rooms until the ladies had gone down for breakfast. When I heard them talking in the peristyle, I crossed over and began my task in the middle room, as this seemed the most interesting of the three. The two cubicles on the ends were their sleeping rooms and were nearly barren of any adornment save the frescos on the walls and an interesting mosaic on each floor. The middle room, however, was where the ladies dressed for the day. It had a table along the back wall stocked with all that is necessary in the way of combs and cosmetics and dyes and ointments. There was a cabinet that contained wigs and another, smaller one that held jewelry. Two elegant chairs were turned toward the table to catch the light from the narrow window. This room gave me a lot to study, so, as a result, it took me longer than I had expected to memorize everything in the room. When I was satisfied I had committed the room to memory, I turned to leave, almost running into Pompeia in the doorway. I jumped back to avoid the collision while stammering an apology. Pompeia had already begun to remove her stola and had slipped one side off her right shoulder baring her breast. I found myself staring, having never seen a patrician woman's breast before. It was, all in all, remarkably similar to the breast of a slave. After a moment too long, I looked up and met Pompeia's eyes. She smiled and then scanned her eyes over me, while saying, 'You must be the new slave my husband has been talking about.'

At that moment, another, older woman entered the room. 'Put your clothes back on, Pompeia,' she said sternly.

Once again I stammered an apology and asked to be excused. The older woman ignored my request. 'You are, I assume, Polybius. This is Caesar's wife, Pompeia, and I am his mother, Aurelia.' I noticed two slave women standing outside the door, trying hard to stifle their laughter.

'I am very, very sorry,' I stammered. I'm sure my face was crimson.

'Yes, you said that,' she answered. 'Are you almost finished with the room? We can come back.'

'I'm just now finished. And, I am truly sorry.' I continued to blush until Aurelia relented, smiling and stepping aside, she allowed me to escape. The younger of the two slave women gave me a wink as I scurried past. I went and hid in the tablinum until I was sure the women had left the domus.

I should comment on Caesar's relationship with his wife, Pompeia. He chose her for her family connections and her ability as a hostess. He never loved her and he only married her because he thought she would help him rise politically. Caesar rarely miscalculated, but in his choice of Pompeia, he clearly had. She was a vain, vacuous, young woman who couldn't possibly live up to the standard set by Caesar's first wife, Cornelia. Caesar had been deeply in love with Cornelia but, sadly, she died giving birth to Caesar's son, some five years previous to this time. The baby died at the same time, and this event left a scar on Caesar's heart from which he never fully recovered.

On some days, Caesar and Demetrius wouldn't return from the baths or other business until sunset or even later. On those days I would assist the secretary in clerical work. A few days after my arrival at the Julian domus, Caesar returned from the baths just before sunset and immediately changed into a fresh toga, announcing he was going out for the

214

evening. Before leaving he stopped by the tablinum where Demetrius was testing me and, leaning over my shoulder, he set a list of women's names and a small note he had written in front of me. There were about fifty names on the list. Some I recognized, but most I didn't. 'Let's make use of your secret talent,' he said. Demetrius looked puzzled, but I looked up at Caesar and smiled, knowing exactly what he would ask. 'I would like you to write a note, identical to this one, addressed to each of the women on this list in my handwriting. I picked up the note and read it. It was a simple greeting expressing hope and prosperity during the Vestalia Festival. On Caesar's copy, the place where the woman's name should go was represented by a series of 'X's'.

Demetrius looked puzzled. 'How is he supposed to accomplish this feat?'

Caesar winked at me, saying to Demetrius, 'Just watch.'

I gathered up the writing supplies and a stack of blank papyri and set to work. After studying Caesar's writing style for a short time, I began to make an almost exact duplicate of the note, substituting the first name on the list for the 'X's. As Caesar left, he said to the thoroughly astonished Demetrius, 'Leave him to his work. I want to be able to send all these notes out in the morning.' With that, I was left alone to work on my task. It was not at all uncommon for a senator to add a line or two in his own hand to a note written by a slave to a fellow senator or other prominent individual, but for a patrician such as Caesar to send notes written in his own hand to men and women of little account in the sea of Roman politics was unheard of. Many of Caesar's peers thought he was wasting his time and energy on such things, but only he

215

and I and Demetrius understood that it was my time and not his being spent, and the time was not at all wasted. While the people named on the lists had no influence in the Senate and would never rise to any prominence in the city, they had a good deal of influence on Election Day. Caesar knew that in spite of the fact that they couldn't vote it was equally important to cultivate the wives and mothers. He understood the influence a woman can have over a man. He had as examples his mistress Servilia and his mother Aurelia. When it came time to deliver the notes, Caesar made it a point to have the slave tell each recipient Master Caesar took the care to write it himself.

On the morning of the twenty-fourth day I expected to begin my study of the first room again, so I finished my breakfast quickly, but just before the salutatio began Demetrius said to me, 'Change your tunic Polybius, you will be accompanying Caesar and me today.' I guess I knew in my heart this day would come, but I envisioned it would be months, if not years in the future. I was excited but at the same time anxious. I dreaded having to try to remember the names and details of every man and woman we would encounter that day. Nevertheless, I ran off and changed into a clean tunic.

I returned to my usual place standing at a polite distance from the tablinum on the side of the atrium. Caesar then signaled to the door slave to open the door and let the clients in, but to my surprise, Demetrius stopped him. In the Titus or Cato households a slave would never have dared question the instructions of the master, but Demetrius was treated more as an associate than as the 'tool with a voice' as Cato often referred to his slaves.

'Caesar,' Demetrius interjected, 'may I have a short time with Polybius before we begin?'

'By all means,' Caesar answered.

With that, Demetrius called for me to follow him into the tablinum and sat me down. 'Pay careful attention to my instructions, as this is important.' I nodded in response.

'You are to stay by my side today. In the presence of others stand a short distance behind me and to one side, but close enough where you can observe everything. Do not speak when others are around but keep your eyes and your ears open. You may bring a wax tablet and stylus for notes, but do not write on it while we are in the company of others. People find it rude when you make notes about them in their presence.'

'I understand,' I said with a nod of my head.

Demetrius continued. 'You asked me, once or twice as I recall, why I have had you commit each of the rooms in this house to memory.' I had actually asked him at least ten times in different ways and at different times. 'Today,' he said in a satisfied tone, 'you will begin to populate the rooms in your mind. When we encounter a person of equite status, imagine him standing in the room that bears the initial of his name. Picture him reciting the important information you glean from the conversation. Try to recall anything, no matter how insignificant it may seem that will in the future allow Caesar to appear to remember him intimately. Remember to have your people stand as close to the walls of your memory house as possible as it will fill up over the years.

217

It now became clear why I was asked to recall the details of the domus. I could imagine this would be a remarkably useful tool in remembering the details.

'Do you understand, Polybius?' Demetrius asked as he stood up. I stood up with him.

'Clearly,' I answered, 'but I have one question.'

'What is it?' he asked, as he steered me with an arm around my shoulder out into the atrium.

'Where do I put the plebs and the patricians we meet?'

'Ah, an excellent question. For now, don't worry about the plebs. Later you will be spending time in another house and you'll commit that to memory as well. That house will be for the plebs. Later this summer when we go to Caesar's villa across the river you will study that as well. You will store the patricians in the villa. Caesar needs far less prompting with the patricians as they are fewer and he knows most of them quite well, but it will be important to remember the details for your own benefit when Caesar asks for your advice on matters of personal and state policy.' At that, I smiled to myself. I was certain Caesar would never be asking *me* for advice on anything.

With that, Demetrius gave a nod and Caesar signaled the door slave to let the clients in. Like Cato, Caesar saw the working class clients first, as these men had jobs to attend to. I paid careful attention to the tunic under each man's toga. No stripes meant the man was a pleb, narrow stripes meant he was an equite, and broad stripes were for the patricians and senators. It was confusing to me since some senators were

218

patricians and some were equites. This was clarified, however, as I watched Demetrius work. When we encountered a man Caesar didn't know, as the man walked across the atrium, Demetrius leaned in and quietly said his name, his social status, and some little bit of information such as, 'His daughter is getting married in eight days,' or 'His dog, Rex, died three days ago.' When it was someone Caesar knew well, he would lean over and provide me the information. With each man I reached into my memory and pictured him standing in the proper room. I then had him recite back what I thought was important.

This continued for a considerable period of time. Most business could be handled quickly. The poorest plebs came to ask for food. The formal request was part of the process. Caesar was careful to help the man preserve his dignity, so he would listen to their stories and provide a bit of encouragement before sending them off with instructions to come back in an hour and see the door slave, who would have a sack of food waiting. Others needed to borrow cash. Caesar always kept a bag of money in the fold of his toga in spite of being perpetually strapped for cash. The money he was lending to his clients he had borrowed from others. Sometimes the request was for a favor. One client would often ask Caesar to intercede with another client over some private dispute or to try to influence his ruling in a public trial he would be hearing. These men would always come with a 'gift' of money or something of artistic value. The larger the favor, the greater the value of the 'gift.' Between clients, Demetrius would make notes on his wax tablets of money lent or promises made.

The group of men kept waiting until last was composed of the young men of the senatorial class. These men were considered by most to be Populares, or populists. Cato called this group a faction and referred to his associates as the Optimates, or best men. The Populares rarely intentionally worked together on anything, but they did try to promote their own interests with the electorate by supporting laws that favored the lower classes. As a result, they often found themselves on the same side of an issue. Cato had always called what they did, 'pandering.' In spite of these distinctions, both groups frequently changed sides on issues when it would help their own advancement up the ladder to the ultimate prize, that being the office of consul. That's how it was in the last days of the republic, young Seneca. Now the factions that vie for place in politics are more often aligned with individual members of the imperial family than they are any particular cause. But, in Caesar's time the young men of the senatorial class rarely directly asked for a favor. Instead they would join Caesar as he made his way on foot to the forum for the day's business. Rather than ask, they would bring up their wishes in conversation as they walked with him.

LIBER XIV

The morning was spent on the surprise inspections of shops around the city. It was one of the duties of the aediles to inspect shops and order any corrections. Caesar paid particular attention to potential hazards, particularly fire. We walked from place to place preceded by the lictors and often accompanied part of the way by someone who was not a part of Caesar's clientela but still needed a moment of his time. When we moved through the streets of the Subura, a small crowd would often form and follow us for some distance with the two lictors keeping at bay anyone who approached too closely. Most often they could do this with a threatening glare or a not so gentle push, but once I saw an overly aggressive man shoved roughly aside. If the street was too crowded, the lictors would shout in unison, 'Make way for the Curule Aedile.' That made me feel rather important.

We had our mid-day meal at a taverna in the forum. While we ate, men, and occasionally a bold woman, would walk up and make small talk with Caesar. Because of Caesar's position, we were given the only table that had chairs around it; the rest were supplied stools or sat on benches. We sat at the back of the room facing the open front so Caesar and, more importantly, Demetrius could see people approach. Each time someone moved toward us, Demetrius would lean over and give the name and some bit of information to either Caesar or to me. At the approach of one man, he leaned toward Caesar and said, 'This is…'

At that instant I violated the rule that I remain silent among strangers and stood up, almost shouting, 'Alexander the medicus!' In unison, Caesar and Demetrius turned and looked at me. I quickly remembered my place and sat down, but I couldn't hide my smile.

Alexander walked up to our table and spoke to Caesar. 'Greetings, Aedile.'

Caesar politely answered, 'what can I do for you physician?'

Alexander then surprised all three of us by saying, 'I am actually here to see Polybius, if I may.'

'Of course.' Caesar didn't seem at all surprised by the request, but it was his way to always appear nonplussed. 'Why don't the two of you take a seat over there,' Caesar said, indicating an open table several feet away.

'Thank you Aedile,' was Alexander's response as he led me to the table.

As we sat down, I tried to contain my excitement but I'm certain it showed. My first question, before Alexander could even speak, was, 'Have you heard from Gaius? How is he doing?'

Alexander smiled and answered, 'Why thank you, I am well as is my wife.'

With that, I felt foolish and began to apologize, but the physician cut me off with a laugh. 'I have heard from Gaius. He is doing well. In fact, I have a letter from him.'

'Did he mention me in the letter?' I asked, a little too excitedly.

'You don't understand, I have a letter he wrote *to you*,' Alexander explained. 'Gaius didn't want to send it to the Titus house for fear you would never see it. I was about to write back explaining to him you had been sold to Cato when I saw you in the forum in the company of the aedile.'

'That man is Gaius Julius Caesar. I'm his slave now,' I informed him.

'I know young Caesar, I have consulted on a medical matter at the Julian house,' he replied. Then, with a wry smile he added, 'You've always been very resourceful. I don't know how you did it, but you have managed to get yourself sold to a much better master. Gaius Caesar can be trusted to treat you well.'

I have always been intrigued by gossip, so I considered asking him the details of his remark about the medical matter at the Julian house, but I knew that while most practitioners of his field enjoy spreading news of the illnesses of the great families, Alexander was discreet. So, I instead asked, 'Have you heard any news of my friend Quintus?'

'Young Quintus is well. He does most of the work tending the gardens at the Titus Villa. He asked after you the last time I visited there. He was sad to hear you had run away. I will be returning to the Villa next month. Is there anything you would like me to tell him?

'Yes, please tell him it was my intention to find him when I ran away but things didn't work out.'

223

'Things did not work out, this time,' Alexander said with a smile. 'I know you, Polybius. You will try again, but I advise against it. You are smart and capable. You also now have a master who treats his slaves well. Earn your freedom legally.'

'I'll consider your advice,' I said, 'but please give Quintus my message.'

'Of course,' he answered, 'but now you should return to your master. You have already tarried too long with me.' With that, Alexander handed me the letter, still sealed.

Standing, I inquired about the wellbeing of the other slaves of the Titus household and asked him to convey my good wishes. Then, just before I left him, I asked the one question that continued to haunt me. 'Have you heard any news of my mother?'

Shaking his head, he sighed 'After she was sold, I made inquiries, but the details of her sale were kept very quiet. All I could learn is that she was sent to a villa in Picenum. She has joined the hundreds of slaves belonging to a wealthy senator. I will continue to work to learn who bought her so you can perhaps write her a letter. Now, return to your master.'

I thanked him as I shook his hand. I was already returning to Caesar's table when I felt Alexander's touch on my shoulder. I turned to face him.

'Polybius, does your new master allow you to have money and personal things?'

'Yes, he does.'

224

With that, he pressed my coin purse into my hand, saying 'I can finally return this to you. I am not comfortable holding other people's money.' Before I left, he hugged me.

Upon returning to Caesar's table, I found a plate of food and a small cup of wine for me.

'You seem to know Alexander well.' Caesar was obviously curious about our conversation. I couldn't understand why he didn't just demand answers, but the man was polite, even to slaves.

It was because he was treating me with such respect that I chose to be honest with him. 'Alexander has an apartment attached to my first master's domus. He saved the life of someone who was a good friend to me and now he has given me a letter from that friend. You can have it, Master, before I read it. But, I would like your permission to read it when you're finished with it, as it would ease my heart to know what my friend writes. Also,' I added, 'he returned a small purse of money he had been holding for me. That too is yours if you wish.'

Caesar laughed. 'You are a perceptive young man. I was more concerned he had talked about me!'

As I thought, Caesar feared Alexander had revealed whatever the medical problem in the Julian house had been. Now I was more curious than before. 'No, Master, Alexander keeps his own counsel.' I pushed the purse and the letter across the table.

'No, Polybius,' he answered, sliding my things back, 'these are yours. Eat your food and read your letter.'

I quickly broke the seal on the letter. Gaius' poor spelling brought a smile to my face. The letter said:

To my closest friend Polybius, salutations.

I hope you are allowed to read this and I hope you aren't being treated too badly for returning to your master. I owe you a debt that I will never be able to repay and I want you to know I miss you terribly. I am doing well. I have a job on a farm south of Rome. It is my plan to join the tenth legion next year and to save my money and when I am discharged I will use it to buy you from your master and free you. We can find your mother and we can all live on a farm together like we planned. Please don't be discouraged. I believe all will work out if we have faith in the gods. I hope Fortuna smiles on you.

With great affection, your friend, Gaius Antistius.

As I read the letter, tears welled up in my eyes. Demetrius and Caesar politely pretended to not notice as they made small talk. When I finished the letter, I handed it to Caesar to read, but he declined.

Caesar glanced down at the money purse I had placed in front of my plate. 'Polybius, have you ever considered why some men allow their slaves to save money?'

I had not considered the matter before, so between bites of food I replied with what I thought was the most

226

obvious answer. 'So a slave can save enough money to buy his freedom.'

'Yes, certainly, but why would a man want his slave to be able to buy his freedom?'

'I suppose, out of kindness,' I answered. But, that immediately didn't make much sense to me. Cato didn't seem to feel any kindness toward his slaves but allowed the older slaves to save money. My own answer made me uncomfortable.

'You seem a little uneasy with what you've just said,'

'I am,' I answered. 'Cato isn't kind to his slaves, yet he lets the young men he owns have only very little money, and when they get older he allows many of them even more. He doesn't give the female slaves any money until they are past childbearing age. I was not allowed to have any.'

Caesar sat back in his chair and gestured to Demetrius, allowing him to explain. Demetrius turned to me. 'Cato gives his slaves money so they can buy their own freedom, but it is not out of kindness. You need to consider matters carefully, Polybius, as things are often not as they seem. He allows them to accumulate money very slowly. To be certain they do not amass too much, too soon, he will even charge the young men for the privilege of having sex with the female slaves.'

'Yes,' I answered, 'but eventually some of his slaves will earn enough to buy their own freedom. What motive other than kindness could he have?' I asked.

227

With that, Caesar laughed. 'Cato is following a plan laid out by his grandfather many years ago.'

Demetrius merely smiled, and continued. 'Have you noticed how long it takes Cato's slaves to accumulate enough to buy their freedom?'

'I wasn't there long, but I would assume many years,' I replied.

'Yes, many, many years. In fact, so many years, the slaves are quite old when they can afford to free themselves.'

'I would imagine,' I answered.

'Think about it,' Demetrius said, leaning back and allowing me time to consider the question.

I was tempted to speak, but I sensed this was part of my training. I was being asked, once again, to carefully consider something before I formed an opinion. I thought hard, and then the answer came to me. Smiling, I said, 'When Cato's slaves can afford their freedom, they are too old to be of much use to him. He can then use the money he allowed them to earn over the years to purchase young slaves. And, I would bet, much of the money they collected came as small payments from others and was not even his money to begin with.'

Both men smiled broadly and I knew I had the correct answer. I came to learn this would be one of many tests that would require I think deeply about matters.

Since Caesar and Demetrius had already finished their meals, I ate mine as quickly as I could. As soon as I

228

finished, Caesar announced, 'I believe it is time to inspect one of the baths. Which should we inspect today, Demetrius?'

I came to learn that this was an inside joke of theirs. Since it was the duty of the aedile to inspect the baths, Caesar could access all the amenities of the baths for free.

We left the taverna and stepped into the forum only to discover the day had become quite warm. The two men had settled on an inspection of the bath on the western slope of the Esquiline Hill. This would bring us through the Subura. As we crossed the street where the Julian Domus was, I asked Demetrius if I should find my own way home.

'No, Polybius,' he answered. 'You need to learn more so you will accompany us to the bath. Keep your mouth shut and your eyes and ears open and remember to put the people in the proper rooms in your mind.' With that, I was about to experience my first trip to a bath. I didn't question the fact that I was just a slave. I knew slaves were allowed into the baths if a citizen accompanied them. I also knew that a Curule Aedile would be allowed to bring whomever he chose into the bath. So, I prepared myself for another new experience. We arrived at the bath and were quickly ushered in. An attendant tried to separate me from Caesar and his nomenclator, indicating I wait in the outer courtyard, but Demetrius signaled to him and I was allowed to remain with them."

Turning to Mela and me, Polybius said, "You boys have grown up regularly attending the baths, but that isn't the case for most slaves. That first trip to the baths was a delight I'll not ever forget. The only time I'd ever been rubbed down with oil had been for my de-lousing when I joined the Cato household, and that was a most unpleasant experience. This,

229

however, was a wonderful sensation. The application of the oil and the removal by scraping with the strigil caused my skin to tingle. I was equally excited by the hot, warm, and cold pools of water. Since gaining my freedom, scarcely a day has passed for me that didn't involve a full bath.

This sort of thing became a daily routine for the next month. We would attend to business in the morning and attend one of the city's numerous baths in the afternoon. At first the choice of which bath to attend seemed random, but I soon realized the choice was anything but random. The selection of the bath we attended on any given day, depended on which senator Caesar wanted to 'accidentally' encounter or, equally important, whom he wished to avoid. Many of the leading men of Rome have formed regular habits, and often attend a bath close to their homes. Because Caesar was perpetually short of cash and very deeply in debt, he tried to avoid those who might pester him for repayment while at the same time making contact with other potential lenders. You may wonder why rich men would lend huge sums of money to Caesar. The answer is twofold. First, he could be very charming and persuasive when he needed to be, and second, the lenders were banking on his prospects as a politician. Every senator knew that after the consulship came a proconsular appointment to govern one of the provinces. I don't believe anyone ever returned from such an appointment without being either incredibly rich or in chains and standing trial for being too blatant about fleecing the locals.

I remember one particularly interesting meeting in Junius (June) of the same year, when Caesar's cousin, Lucius Julius Caesar, and Marcus Figulus were consuls (64 BC). The only people present in the room were Caesar, Marcus Licinius Crassus, and me. Crassus was one of the wealthiest man the

230

world has ever seen. The proverbial 'richer than Croesus' would have been literally true when applied to him. Later, Gaius Julius Caesar could have surpassed Crassus in wealth, but he was very generous with his money and gave a great deal of it away and spent at least as much enhancing not only Rome through great public works, but also other towns and cities around the empire. It was quite common, after he accumulated great wealth during his proconsulship of the two Gauls, for him to pay for the foundation of entire colonies. At the time of this meeting, however, Julius Caesar was one of Crassus' largest creditors. Crassus insisted the only people present be himself and Caesar, so Demetrius and Plautius were dismissed. I too was asked to leave, but at Caesar's suggestion I was allowed to stay.

I can still remember Caesar innocently saying, 'We both want a record of this conversation, as it involves money.'

'That would be nice,' Crassus allowed, 'but this is a very private meeting.'

'Then let just the boy stay,' Caesar countered. 'He's marvelous at taking dictation, but otherwise rather slow-witted and doesn't really understand a word of what is said. He was taught by his former master to write and spell, but is not much use for anything else.'

I recalled the conversation I had with Demetrius when I first joined Caesar's household. At that time it was made very clear to me that I was to do all I could to help Caesar advance to the praetorship so he would be in a position to pay off his considerable debts. I only worried that we wouldn't reach that goal in time to save him.

231

Crassus eyed me suspiciously, so I took the opportunity to look around distractedly with a finger in my nose. I must confess I even ate a booger to complete the illusion that I was a dullard. With that, Crassus relented and I was allowed to stay. However, while he didn't think much of the abilities of slaves, it didn't take him much longer to realize I had a significantly sharper mind than many.

Crassus began the meeting, which occurred behind the folded doors of Caesar's tablinum. Both men spoke in such low tones I needed to lean in to hear what was said. 'How much do you need this time?'

'I think fifty thousand sestertii should cover it,' Caesar answered.

'Gods!' Crassus was genuinely angry. 'What are you going to do with that much money?'

'I'm going to pay off my most pressing creditor and then run for praetor. I became indebted to half the senate in my year as aedile. I had to pay for all those spectacles.'

'You didn't need to pay for everything,' Crassus argued, lowering his voice again. 'You were not the only aedile. You should have let your colleagues carry some of the burden.'

'We both agree the people must remember that it was Caesar who paid for the most lavish spectacles.' I was impressed by the way Caesar went head to head with Crassus, arguing each point and I never grew tired of him referring to himself in the third person.

'That would be great, if it *was* you who paid for it, but it was not you. It was *me!*' Crassus' voice was surely heard outside the room, so he compensated by lowering it to a hoarse whisper when he next spoke.

'You will get your investment returned with a substantial interest, I assure you.' Caesar certainly sounded confident.

Crassus turned to me, pointing a finger. 'Be certain you write this correctly, boy. Gaius Julius Caesar agrees to pay Marcus Licinius Crassus the sum of fifty thousand sestertii one year from today. In addition, he will pay him an interest of five thousand sestertii on the loan to be spread out over the following two years.' I scribbled furiously on my wax tablet.

'Done,' was all Caesar said, not bothering to negotiate a lower sum. This surprised both Crassus and me but I continued to play the fool and didn't let the surprise show on my face. I found it difficult to comprehend the amounts of money being discussed.

With that, I was sent into the cubicle off the tablinum to transcribe my notes onto two sheets of parchment for the two men to sign and seal. I could still hear most of what was being said though, and the conversation was most enlightening.

'You put me in an awkward position, my friend,' Crassus said to Caesar.

'How so?' Caesar sounded as if he truly didn't know. 'My prospects are quite good. I'll be elected praetor in two years and then I'll be assigned a province the following year.

You'll gain back your investment with interest and, more importantly, earn my gratitude and good will.' Caesar sounded surer of his future than ever before.

'You know very well how,' Crassus was beginning once again to raise his voice. 'I am still the Censor. I'm getting pressure from your creditors to expel you from the senate before my term ends because you don't meet the financial obligations for membership. If you're not a senator, you cannot be praetor.'

'There is nothing either of us can do about that,' Caesar calmly answered.

'I *could* expel you from the senate!' Crassus' answer surprised me, but didn't seem to have any effect upon Caesar, who remained perfectly calm.

'You and I both know you won't do that. You've invested far too much in me to give up now. When I'm a success, you'll make a handsome profit, but if by some chance I fail, you'll lose everything you have invested. You and I will do great things together, that I assure you.'

'I can afford the loss,' Crassus countered.

'You can afford the loss,' Caesar calmly answered, 'but you will not take it, so let's stop all this and come up with some way to stall my other creditors.'

'You must show some political success.'

'My legislation keeps being blocked by Cato and his 'Optimate' faction,' Caesar answered.

'You must win an election.'

234

Caesar dismissed Crassus with, 'How can I do that? I'll not be eligible to run for the praetorship for nearly a year.'

'Metellus is dying.' This was enough to cause Caesar to stop talking.

Finally, after a long pause, Caesar's only response was, 'How do you know?'

'I am certain, he will be dead before the summer solstice.' Crassus didn't really answer the question.

Quintus Caecilius Metellus Pius of the great Metelli family was a former consul and for the past eighteen years Pontifex Maximus. Sensing this was of great importance, I reached for a fresh wax tablet and my stylus and began taking notes.

'It will cost even more for me to gain that office. It would be cheaper to buy an election from the people than it will be to bribe the fourteen other priests, but I suppose you can afford that as well.' Caesar was warming to the idea. 'And, it will delay the wolves scratching at my door.'

'It will be enough,' Crassus answered, 'provided, you win. You must also be elected praetor in your year.' Thus, the stage was set for Caesar to become Pontifex Maximus."

At this point, Mela hesitantly leaned forward with his hand held up before him. "Uh, excuse me."

That elicited a smile from Polybius. "You needn't fear me, Mela. If you have a question, just ask. I didn't mean to be too harsh earlier. I just ask you trust me when I tell you I will always, eventually, get to the point."

235

Mela leaned back and said, "I just need you to clarify what he meant by 'in your year.' I've heard the expression in passing, but I've never been quite sure what it meant."

"It merely refers to being elected to an office during the first year a man is legally eligible. It added to a man's *dignitas* to gain the office at as young an age as was possible. This is no longer a concern since the Emperor has bent the rules on age requirements for office for decades now." With that, Polybius took a sip of wine and was about to continue with his narrative when he stopped again and looked at Mela with a smile and a wink. "Also, young man, you need not raise your hand. I am not your grammaticus."

"I don't see how this would help," I interrupted. "I understand the significance of the post, but how could it stall Caesar's creditors? It would be scandalous to drag the Pontifex Maximus into debtor's court, but to truly come between a rich man and his money, the position would need to have serious political power."

"Ah, yes," Polybius answered. "You are only able to think of the position as the province of the emperor and more a place of ceremony than of substance. I shall explain. Originally, the priesthood selected their own head, but since before Caesar's birth, the assembly of the people had elected the office of highest priest. Of course, before this innovation could be instituted a compromise needed to be reached. The nobility argued the people couldn't speak for the gods in an election. The compromise was that only seventeen of the thirty-five tribes would vote for the Pontifex Maximus, and the college of priests would then ratify the election, giving the vote, at least in appearance, more of an advisory character. Of course, the priests who blocked the will of the people would

236

have difficulty being elected to any other post in the future. In Sulla's dictatorship this changed. Sulla attempted to bolster the power of the old nobility at every turn, so he abolished the election law and returned the selection to the college of priests. I believe Crassus originally intended to bribe at least eight of the fourteen priests who would make the choice, but Caesar's casual remark that it would be cheaper to buy an election in the assembly than to bribe the college of pontiffs hit home. Crassus, through Caesar's man, the tribune Titus Labienus, immediately had a law introduced to return the election of the Pontifex Maximus to the people. It was important this happen quickly before it became general knowledge that Metellus Pius was a dying man. Crassus' money could buy him information, but it never remained exclusively his. Soon enough, another medicus or slave would tell the world what for now only he and a few others knew. The law was introduced as part of a much broader legislation allowing all the tribes to vote for each of the priesthoods. By doing so, Caesar could promote the bill, gaining the support of the people who would vote for him, while others could whittle it down as a way of compromising with the Optimate faction to return it to the original seventeen tribes. This was of course, exactly what Crassus and Caesar wanted. If you are going to buy an election it is better to only need to buy it from half the voters."

Polybius was distracted by the appearance of a black and white cat that seemed to appear from nowhere as it jumped upon his couch. "She must be growing comfortable with you boys," he said as the cat gingerly stepped up onto his stomach and poked its face toward his. "This is Panya. In Egyptian, her name means mouse. She was called so because she was the tiniest member of the litter. You may have noticed the others around here, as I have three cats. Panya here is a direct descendant of a cat Cleopatra left behind as she fled Rome nearly sixty years ago." Polybius began to stroke the cat but he had not answered my question.

"I ask again," I interjected, "what was the political significance of the office?"

"Oh yes, I never did get to that." Polybius pushed himself back up on the cushions and continued. "The political power of the priesthoods primarily rested in their ability to obstruct politicians. A bad omen could cancel a vote or dissolve a session of the senate. The priests could also declare a day too unlucky to transact business, political or otherwise. More importantly though, the Pontifex Maximus in consultation with the College of Pontiffs controlled the calendar. You must remember the calendar in those days was not as ordered as it is today. It took the reforms instituted by Caesar during his dictatorship to bring greater sense to our numbering of days. The old calendar had only three hundred fifty five days. Since the year is ten days longer than this, over time the seasons will become out of sync with the calendar unless days are added."

At this point I felt the need to interject some bit of knowledge I assumed Polybius lacked. "There was a Greek who calculated the year at three hundred sixty five and a quarter days, but I forget his name."

"It was the great mathematician, Meton of Athens, four and one half centuries ago, but that is neither here nor there for our discussion, as the Romans at that time didn't readily accept Greek innovations," Polybius continued. "The Pontifex Maximus was assigned the task of, from time to time, inserting an extra month into the calendar to compensate for this shortcoming. The general practice was to add the month onto Februarius (February) every two years, but there was no rule binding him to this. Therefore, he could extend the year as long as he chose whenever he chose. This was quite useful in extending the year of office of his political allies or postponing the date when a law would expire. Caesar became a master of this during his climb to the top. During Caesar's time as Pontiff, we once had a year that lasted more than a month over four hundred days. This was, however, not to satisfy any political need. It was to correct the damage done in the several years when he did not extend the year, and that was due to political expediency.

At any rate, after seeing Crassus out, Caesar returned to the tablinum where I was busy transcribing my short hand notes into a readable form on a papyrus scroll. 'What do you think about this latest plan of Crassus'?'

I was surprised. This was the first time I was being solicited for political advice and this would set the pattern for the future. After an important meeting or discussion, Caesar would casually ask me for my thoughts, never publicly acknowledging he was asking for political advice from a slave. 'I think the Pontifex Maximus must be highly favored by the gods, and a large measure of success in life is a result of divine favor.' I was non-committal as I was on unsteady ground here.

'Do you think I should seek the post?' he asked more pointedly. He evidentially wanted to know what I really thought.

I decided to be honest. 'I see it as a gamble, but I believe you are favored by Fortuna.' I didn't bother to mention that the goddess had told me this herself in a dream. 'But, I see two problems.' I paused to gauge whether or not he wanted to hear more. When he remained silent, I went on. 'First, it could make you appear weak. If you fail to be elected Pontifex Maximus with the votes of only seventeen tribes, your opponents will use this against you and it will be very unlikely you will win the praetorship in your year. And, once you appear weak your creditors will pounce on you.'

'Yes,' he said, 'I had considered that.'

I went back to my writing, so Caesar asked, 'What was the second?'

'I'm sorry master?' was my response.

'You said you saw two problems. I ask you, what the second was.'

'Oh yes. I was wondering if anyone had told old Metellus Pius he needed to die this Junius.' Then, I added, 'unless, that has already been arranged.' I was afraid I had crossed a line, but at that, Caesar laughed.

'In spite of what you might suspect, Polybius, we are not murderers!' Besides, it would be most impious to hasten the demise of the Pontifex Maximus. I'll leave that to the gods.'

As it happened, Metellus Pius made what appeared to be a complete recovery, but Crassus remained convinced he was dying. In the end, Crassus was right, but it took over a year for him to die. They were, however, able to keep Caesar's creditors at bay with more extensive borrowing. Crassus realized he had already invested too much in Caesar's future

240

to back out, so he continued to finance him to pay off other debts. If anyone else had realized how deeply in debt he was, Caesar would never have survived debtor's court.

LIBER XV

The year Cicero and Antonius Hibrida were consuls (63 BC) was eventful for Caesar. In that year, it became obvious to everyone that Caesar was one of the more influential members of the Populares. He appeared in court as often as possible and chose his cases well. It was much less important that he win a case than it was to present it well and stand in favor of causes that were important to the plebs.

The events of that year were set in motion well before the end of the previous year. Crassus and Caesar had backed Lucius Sergius Catilina for consul. They felt they could influence him enough to support the legislation they wished to see enacted. As it turned out, Catilina didn't fare well on Election Day that year. I remember the walk home from the forum after the election results were read out. Catilina had lost the election and Cicero had won, upsetting the carefully crafted plans of Crassus and Caesar. Caesar was clearly displeased as were the supporters who walked with us. It was his hope that he and Crassus could exert enough control over Catilina during his year as consul to not only see the aims of the Populares enacted, but to prevent him from doing anything foolish. There were maybe thirty of forty supporters in the group, and, as we walked, the group began to split into several smaller groups. Seeing this happen, Caesar intentionally slowed his pace allowing most of his supporters to move ahead out of earshot. Left behind were Caesar, Titus Labienus, Gaius Matius, Demetrius, and me. Caesar began to formulate a new strategy. 'We can put pressure on Cicero to support the bill. He is always trying to get cozy with

Pompeius' supporters. Titus, you have connections with Pompeius, so we'll need you to use them.'

'I have connections, but I don't know how much good they will do on land reform.'

Caesar countered, 'Pompeius will need land to settle his veterans somewhere next year. Sell it to him with that.'

'I could try,' Labienus said. 'If Pompeius puts enough pressure on Cicero, he will have to support it.'

Demetrius joined in with, 'If we push the bill through right now, Cicero will have to support it. If he doesn't, the tribunes can block everything he tries to do all year.'

Matius agreed. 'There's no reason to think he won't support it. He's reached his goal. He's consul now. If we agree to help his friends next year, he'll go for it.'

I tried to follow the rule we had established of keeping my eyes and ears open and my mouth shut, but I simply couldn't. 'He won't support the bill because it's un-Roman.' Everyone stopped talking and I felt extremely foolish. 'I'm sorry, master,' I stammered.

Caesar looked puzzled and a little angry. 'Why do you think land reform is un-Roman?'

'Oh, no, no, no. That's not what I meant!' I was in a panic. 'It's not me who thinks land reform is un-Roman, no, not me.'

'Who then?' Caesar asked with a scowl. I looked to Demetrius for support, but he appeared to be as angry as our master.

243

'Don't you remember the dinner party?' I asked Caesar. By now, our little group had stopped in the street and the men were all circled around me staring like a pack of wolves.

Caesar snapped, 'What dinner party?'

'Two years ago at Cato's house. You were there.'

'I've attended many dinner parties, and those hosted by Cato are usually the least memorable.' I noticed Caesar's eyes soften when he realized I had a point. 'Refresh my memory please.'

'It was the party where I was locked in the cabinet to spy on you and the other guests. I remember Cicero telling you, "I, for one, will never, not ever, support buying private land to give away to the poor. It is un-Roman!"

'As I recall, you spent that night unconscious in your little cabinet.' Caesar was now smiling and we started to walk again.

'Well,' I said, 'Cicero's words were the last thing I remember, but I do remember them!'

Naturally, my objection was disregarded. No senator, Caesar included, put much stock in the political advice of a fifteen year old slave.

One day before the ides of Januarius (Jan. 12), the tribune Publius Servilius Rullus presented Caesar's land reform bill. At first the bill was wildly popular among most of the working urban plebs."

"Why would plebs living in the city care about agrarian reform," I asked.

Polybius took a sip of wine before he explained. "Not all the plebs cared, but the ones who owned businesses and held jobs did. Many of the plebs had been driven to the city to look for work after losing their farms. There simply were not enough jobs for them. Tens of thousands of citizens desperately needed a livelihood, and the offer of a farm on the outskirts of the city or even in a colony somewhere else in Italia was very appealing. Even the plebs who held jobs were for the bill because they thought if the number of homeless citizens were reduced, crime would also be reduced and the price for their labor would rise. Having so many unemployed workers on the streets of Rome made it easy for employers to replace workers, so employment was not always secure and wages were kept low. For these very reasons, the rich equites who employed the most workers hated the bill. The patricians hated it for those reasons too. In spite of the fact that they were officially not supposed to engage in trade, many of them did through clients from the other classes. They also detested any law that might take from them and give to those less fortunate."

"What exactly were the provisions of the bill?"

"This bill was quite complex. At this time, Caesar had not yet learned to make his legislation easy to understand. I suggested the bill be divided into three separate bills at three separate times, but was, yet again, ignored."

I was surprised Polybius said this. "Surely the senators were able to understand complex legislation."

"Most people," he answered, "are quite capable of understanding the most complex idea if they care to set their minds to it and the idea is properly explained. The problem is that most would rather not go to the trouble to understand the complex, and even those who do, don't trust it. Let me explain the bill. The first provision called for the formation of a commission of ten. Caesar and Crassus both wanted to be appointed to the commission since it would make them stand out before the masses. The commission would be empowered to buy up vast tracts of land and distribute that land among the citizens of Rome, beginning with the poorest. Some of the land was to be in the area around Rome, but since the senators held much of this land, everyone knew that wouldn't happen, so the focus was put on buying land in Italia and establishing colonies. The power held by the commissioners frightened many senators. To accomplish the task they were to serve for five years and they were to be elected by seventeen of the thirty-five tribes, chosen by lot. The commissioners were to hold the rank and the imperium of a praetor. Another clause in the law restricted eligibility to those who were present to stand for election in the city."

"Why was that important since the law affected all of Italia?"

"Quite simply, Lucius, to make Pompeius Magnus ineligible. That was another reason for presenting the bill so soon before he returned from the east. Crassus insisted on this clause. There was only enough public land to accommodate a few thousand. Other land was to be purchased for distribution."

"How could enough money be found to purchase so much land?" I asked.

246

"Ah," you see one of the problems, Polybius answered. "Money was to be raised by selling public land in the provinces, which also included lands won in the war with Mithridates in the east. Pompeius had only recently acquired some of the land that was to be sold. Another sticking point was that it was up to the ten to determine what constituted private and what was public land. So much of the public land had been worked into the private estates of the wealthy over the years that this would be only one of the problems."

"What were the other problems?" I asked. I could see many, but I wanted to hear Polybius' view as he had heard the objections first hand.

"Another problem was getting Pompeius Magnus to agree to the bill. This was accomplished by pointing out it would provide land for his veterans in Italia rather than in the provinces. He was also secretly promised that his family's estates in Picenum would not be touched. Each retired veteran becomes the general's client, and it's better to have clients close by so they can come to the city to vote. In spite of this, Pompeius' support was only tepid. You will notice the clause involving the annexation of Aegyptus was omitted. This was done because Crassus feared the command would be given to Pompeius since he was the most successful general Rome had ever known and the darling of the plebs. In fact, one of the reasons Crassus supported the bill was to have the commission of ten serve as a counterweight to the power of Pompeius."

"Why was Crassus so opposed to Pompeius?"

"Later that evening," Polybius said, "I asked Demetrius that very question and was told quite simply, he was jealous. No Roman with any political ambition can

247

tolerate seeing a rival succeed, and in the past, Pompeius had succeeded spectacularly and, at least one time, his success was at Crassus' expense. Before he was old enough to hold office, young Pompeius had, at his own expense and without any authority, raised three legions from the area of Picenum where his family had vast holdings and thousands of clients. With his legions he joined forces with Sulla. It was while working for Sulla that the dictator gave him the title Imperator and the cognomen Magnus. Caesar always thought Sulla meant calling Pompeius 'great' as a sarcastic joke, but the public and, more importantly, Pompeius took it seriously, so the name stuck. He also earned the nickname, '*carnifex adulescens,*' the young butcher. He was sent to settle things in Sicilia and Africa and was allowed a triumph before ever holding any office. After Sulla retired and even after he died, the senate continued to use Pompeius, giving him many opportunities to not only extend his patronage but also to achieve even greater military success. Naturally, this stirred deep mistrust and resentment among the other ambitious men of his generation. He defeated the legions that supported Marius against Sulla and had for years held out under their commander Sertorius in Hispania. For this he was also illegally granted another triumph. Fresh from his success in Hispania, Pompeius was sent to assist Crassus in his prosecution of the war against Spartacus and his army of slaves. Crassus had nearly completed the job when Pompeius swept in and in short order finished off the remnants of the slave army and claimed credit for winning the war. That was the beginning of the real enmity between the two men.

Two years later, and five years before he was legally eligible to hold the post and before holding any of the legally required offices that were prerequisites, Pompeius was allowed to stand for the consulship. He won, as was expected. Crassus was the other consul that year and he always resented the fact that Pompeius' popularity overshadowed his own. Two years after his first consulship, Pompeius was granted an extraordinary command. For years, pirates had been the bane of merchants and travelers all throughout the sea. At long last, the traders who were losing fortunes applied enough pressure and the senate decided to act. Pompeius was granted the command of a large force and imperium extending fifty miles inland on the coast of every Roman province. This authority set him above every general in the empire. The senate was, of course, sharply divided as Crassus wanted the command for himself, but lacking Pompeius' popularity, he was denied the post. The war against the pirates was quickly won, although this was mostly accomplished by buying them off. Officially the western part of the sea had been cleared of pirates in forty days and the eastern half in less than six months. In reality, pirates continued to plague Roman merchants until Rome gained control over all the lands touching the sea."

Polybius adjusted his position on the couch and took a sip of wine before continuing. "But, I have digressed once again. Let's get back to where we left off. What came to be known as the Rullan Agrarian Reform bill was discussed at a meeting of all the principals over what was ostensibly a dinner party. What set this party apart was that wives were conspicuously absent when the meal was finished and the wine was served. The women found their way, by a prearranged agreement, to the atrium to listen to musicians, while the men plotted. I sat in a corner taking notes. Those present were Caesar, of course, as it was in his house and the bill was his creation, Crassus, Titus Labienus, Servilius Rullus, and Gaius Matius. Demetrius, Caesar's secretary Nicandros, and I were stationed on stools in the triclinium. The invasion of Aegyptus was discussed at length with Crassus finally vetoing the idea over Caesar's objection.

'There will be no invasion of Aegyptus in this bill,' he said with finality.

Caesar countered, 'I will be elected praetor next year. After that I'll need a command. Aegyptus would be ideal.'

Crassus raised his tone, causing everyone else to fall uncomfortably silent. 'I will not take a chance on seeing that insufferably pompous ass earn another triumph!' He was of course referring to Pompeius Magnus. Since Crassus would be the one to pay the bribes needed to see the bill passed, his view won the day.

After the party, when most of the guests had left and it was just Crassus and Caesar remaining in the room, I forgot I was supposed to be an imbecile and chose to voice my opinion on the bill. This was probably because it was a rather cold day, and during the party we were all drinking wine that had been spiced and warmed. Since I was still quite unaccustomed to drinking wine, I had rather too much and it loosened my tongue. It was, of course, also before I realized how deeply opposed Crassus was to Pompeius on a personal level. In my naiveté, I said, 'With all due respect, I think you should not only include an invasion of Aegyptus in the bill, but I would specify that Pompeius Magnus should be given the command.' Caesar just raised his eyebrows in surprise, but Crassus glowered at me. I was Caesar's slave, so I didn't care so much what Crassus felt and I did want to impress Caesar, so I continued. 'It seems to me Pompeius is so popular with the plebs that as long as he's in Rome you will be eclipsed by him and be forced to live in his shadow. By including him in the bill, you will earn the support of the plebs, which I don't believe is as strong as you think it is. If you send him to Aegyptus, and he succeeds, you can take credit for the wisdom of your selection.' At that, Crassus turned to stare angrily at Caesar, as if he were the one speaking. I didn't want him to fall out with Crassus, so I caught myself and stopped talking, but it was evident I had more to say.

Caesar, with an amused smile simply said, 'Go on, Polybius.'

Perhaps it was the wine, but rather than excuse myself, I plunged forward. 'However, if Pompeius Magnus were to fail, you could lay all the blame on him and, Master Caesar, you could go to Aegyptus with three or four legions and complete the job, taking all the credit.'

With that, Crassus abruptly rose. 'It seems to me your slave is not the fool you led me to believe he was! I hope this is his own stupid thinking and he is not repeating what you have said in private.'

Caesar remained calm. 'Did I lead you to believe he was a fool? I'm so sorry about that, friend. I assure you, Crassus, while I still disagree with you on the matter, I would never want the command to go to Pompeius. I and I alone should be the man to make Aegyptus a Roman province.'

Crassus announced, 'I'll see myself out,' and turned and left the room, heading straight for the vestibule, stopping only long enough to collect his wife from where she sat talking to Aurelia, Julia, and Pompeia in the atrium. In the distance, from my vantage point in the corner of the triclinium I could look out across the atrium and see the door slave snap to attention at his approach. Caesar didn't move from his couch.

251

I was smiling at Crassus' discomfort when I noticed Caesar was not smiling. 'Polybius,' he said icily, 'you have learned much and grown a great deal in this job I've given you. Learn this. Never again make me look foolish, or we are finished.' I began to stammer an apology, but he cut me off. 'I will, for this one time, assign the blame to the wine. Go to your room and sleep. You can transcribe your notes in the morning. Get up extra early.' Once again I had crossed a line and that made me feel as if I was crossing a stream on slippery rocks. As I was leaving the room Caesar added, 'You are, however, right in your assessment.'

I felt as if I wanted to shrink to the size of a mouse and skitter out of the room. In that moment I had forgotten that my purpose was to help Caesar advance to the praetorship. Forgetting that caused me to overstep my place. I vowed to not do it again.

The next day, Caesar acted as if nothing out of the ordinary had happened.

The bill was duly presented with the support of all ten of that year's tribunes. The debate raged in the senate house and in the baths and at dinner parties throughout the cities. The deciding factor was the vehement opposition of the consul, Marcus Tullius Cicero. He was at the height of his powers as an orator and he was able to convince the senate with four important speeches to oppose the bill, and, uncharacteristically, Caesar had misjudged the enthusiasm of the plebs. Through conversations with plebs Caesar was led to believe they would support the free distribution of land, and they did so long as it was idle talk and not likely to become a reality. The poor in Rome had grown accustomed to receiving the dole of free grain and the money that was frequently

252

distributed during festivals. The *idea* of earning one's livelihood by working a small farm many miles from Rome, was far more appealing than having to actually do the back breaking labor required for one to scratch a living from the soil. Support among the plebs cooled until it was only tepid at best.

As a result, within a short time one of the tribunes broke ranks leading most of the others to withdraw their support. In the end, of the ten tribunes, only Labienus and Rullus himself supported it. The bill was allowed to die without ever coming to a vote. In spite of the great disappointment engendered by this failure, Caesar was able to console himself with the knowledge he had propelled himself into a leadership position among the Populares in the senate. Everyone except Caesar himself doubted whether that leadership role would translate into electoral success.

From late Quintilis to the end of Sextilis (late July to the end of August) we stayed at Caesar's villa on the slope of the Janiculum Hill on the farther bank of the Tiber River. During our stay there, the guests were somewhat less frequent, but I was required to memorize rooms again and start to populate my memory villa with patricians and kings and queens. The next sixteen months after our stay in the Julian Villa was one of the most taxing periods of my life. I was required to remember the names and details of hundreds of men and women from lowly (but influential) freedmen and slaves to former consuls and foreign potentates. It was during this period that I met many of the people who would shape the story of what you have referred to, young Lucius, as the downfall of the republic. During that year, I was especially gratified to be far away from the Cato household. Cato was elected tribune in spite of Caesar's efforts to prevent it. He could not prevent it primarily because Crassus didn't want to invest any money in the cause. He reasoned that Cato would, sooner or later, be elected to the office, and it was better to let it happen now and be done with it. Cato being elected tribune troubled me, but it would soon pale in contrast to the political turmoil in which I was soon to find myself embroiled.

LIBER XVI

Early that spring, Lucius Sergius Catilina scheduled a meeting with Caesar. I naively assumed it was merely a social call, as Catilina must have been feeling rather low seeing Cicero installed as Consul just a couple of months earlier. The consulship was a post Catilina much desired and very much had expected to win. I soon learned the meeting was to discuss matters of politics. Catilina was planning to, once again, run for the consulship for the following year, but he learned he was about to be brought to court for non-payment of some rather large debts.

Catilina was one of the most outspoken of the Populares, but I truly believe Cato hated him more for the way he lived his life than for his politics. A few years older than Caesar, Catilina was almost an exact contemporary of Pompeius Magnus and Cicero. As you know, Cato stressed the value of republican virtue like a devotee to one of the eastern mystery cults. Catilina was, to put it kindly, a libertine and the antithesis of Cato."

I once again felt I needed to interrupt Polybius. "From what I have read in doing my research, Catilina is described by some as a most despicable man. It is said he seduced a Vestal Virgin and had sex with his own daughter."

"Yes, and he has also been guilty of rape and murder and cannibalism if we are to believe what has been written." Polybius had an amused smile. "Think, Lucius, if the man was such a monster, how was he as successful as he was? How was he able to be so well connected with the nobility? Did he have

255

affairs with married women and men? Yes. Did he count among his circle of friends, actors and prostitutes? Yes. Did he enjoy gambling more than was seemly for a man of his rank? Yes. Was he a monster? No. Or at least no more so than several other leading senators."

"Then why were there so many horrible things written about him?"

"Because, he took the example set by Sulla and raised the stakes in the game. When the voters thwarted him in his rise to the top, he decided to usurp the government of the republic. He is so reviled, simply because *he failed*. That, and also because his charm was lost on the men of the Optimate faction."

"Tell me about him," I said. "Did you ever meet him?"

"Yes, certainly. In fact, we met several times. I first met him the year before these events transpired. I can still see him with my mind's eye, standing in his place in the 'C' room of my memory, reciting to me his name and pertinent details. The first time I met him was at the baths, but the meeting was brief and unremarkable. There may have been significant exchanges between him and Caesar at the meeting, but I was not yet sophisticated enough to detect the subtle meanings of the seemingly innocuous things said during a conversation between senators. It was mainly a good deal of joking at the expense of Catilina's companion who was a rather effeminate actor from Syria.

Lucius Sergius Catilina was a remarkable man. His family was of ancient stock, and had once held great prominence in the city but for several generations had not had

256

much success. He intended to change that. I believe he was inspired by Sulla's success. I think his original intent was to win election to the consulship and then find some means to have himself declared dictator or follow Cinna's example and serve several successive terms. He was driven by a lust for earning great distinction. In this he was very much like Caesar. He was also akin to Caesar in that he needed to win high office and the inevitable governorship of a province that followed so he could milk the province dry and pay off the mountain of debt he had accumulated in the winning of that office and all the offices that preceded it. Catilina was a large man with large appetites, and companions of low repute always surrounded him. He was always in debt, but rich men were ever willing to lend him money as he was considered a good risk. Catilina always paid off his loans on time and with interest. He did this by borrowing, embezzling, or stealing what he needed. Men of substance such as Crassus knew this but they were not concerned so long as they made a good return on their loans.

At any rate, on this occasion Catilina arrived at the Julian Domus shortly after Caesar, Demetrius, and I returned from the local bath. All morning long Caesar had been occupied, acting as judge in one of Cato's corruption trials. I had expected we would spend the afternoon at the baths where we would relax and take our meal since there was a rare evening court session scheduled for that day. Instead, we quickly bathed and hurried back home. Demetrius and I ate right away, but Caesar instructed the kitchen slave to prepare a meal for two. I was given the task of writing letters for Caesar, duplicating his own handwriting again, to his various clients and connections in the cities in the East. Caesar provided me with a list of names, each with a line or two of personal information I could use to make the letter unique to the

257

individual and a copy of a standard letter wishing good health and prosperity and all the usual blather people put in their missives. The real purpose of the letter was added almost as an afterthought at the end. Just before closing the letter, Caesar asked each recipient to fill him in on the exploits of Pompeius Magnus and the progress of the eastern war. All of Rome was speculating about what would happen when the great general returned to Rome. Posted in my usual small cubicle off the tablinum, Caesar stuck he head in the doorway just before Catilina arrived and said to me, 'Do you have wax tablets?' Seeing I did, he added, 'Be prepared to take notes when my guest arrives.'

'Should I sit closer to the door and draw the curtain?' I asked.

'If you like, but I doubt you'll have trouble hearing Sergius Catilina.' It was true that the man seemed to only be able to shout or, when he was hatching a conspiracy, whisper.

I quickly collected extra tablets because I never knew what was significant, so I frequently used shorthand to copy down almost every word. The invention of shorthand, or abbreviated writing, is now attributed to a secretary who belonged to Cicero, but this is not at all true. The man did devise a unique way to copy the great orator's words, but different forms of shorthand had been current among secretaries and book copyists for many years. Anyway, with a shout, Antius, the door slave, let Caesar know Catilina had arrived and Caesar hurried to meet him in the vestibule. At the same time, the kitchen slave hurried into the tablinum with the first course of food. As they approached, I could not hear what Caesar had said, but I heard Catilina in his booming voice say, 'The tablinum is fine. You know me, I'll eat wherever there's

258

food. We both need to get back to work today, so I can't linger over the meal anyway.' Caesar made no attempt to hide the fact that I was in the cubicle near where they sat. I hadn't closed the curtain, and both men simply ignored me. They made small talk during the first course, talking about the prospects for this year's wine vintage. As the slaves who cleared the plates and brought the second course left, Catilina abruptly changed the subject. 'You and I are not here to talk about wine.'

'No,' said Caesar, 'we are not.'

'I need your support when I canvas for the consulship.'

Caesar paused for just a bit before replying. 'What can you promise me in exchange?'

'We are on the same side on many issues,' Catilina answered.

'That's not good enough,' Caesar replied coldly. 'I need something more concrete.'

'What do you propose?'

Caesar was evidently well-prepared for this meeting. 'I'll support your bid for the consulship. Then you'll support my measures for land reform.'

'Land reform again?' Catilina failed to understand what Caesar was saying. 'You are thinking small, my friend. You will be running for praetor. Having the consul on your side can go a long way toward seeing that happens, and then in a few years you'll be standing for the consulship yourself.'

259

I looked up from my note taking to see Caesar wave his hand dismissively. 'I have already assumed you would help me with those things. I want you to also help Rullus again be elected tribune. He will propose a land reform bill that will, with our support, pass and make us both famous.'

'I'm already famous,' Catilina said with a smile.

'To be precise,' Caesar countered, 'you are infamous. But, I'm talking about lasting fame. I want people to be talking about me for generations to come, and if you help me they will also be talking about you.' That last part clearly was added as an afterthought, but Catilina didn't seem to notice.

'What sort of land reform? How far do you plan to take it this time?' he asked.

I am going to revive Gracchus' bill, but up the stakes. I will include all the land regained by Pompeius Magnus in the east.'

'He will certainly want a say in that,' Catilina countered.

'And, Aegyptus,' Caesar continued.

This last part caused Catilina to laugh. 'I think the Pharaoh may have something to say about that one. Are you still insisting his father left all of Aegyptus to the senate and people of Rome when he died?'

'It's true,' was all Caesar said.

'True or not, it would take a few legions to convince the current Pharaoh of it.'

260

'Then,' Caesar countered, 'An expedition to Aegyptus would make an excellent assignment when my year as praetor is finished.'

This caused Catilina to laugh even louder and elicited a coughing fit. When he could once again speak, he asked in his booming voice, 'And, you don't suppose Pompeius Magnus will have a few words to say about that too?'

'Leave the details to me. Just promise me you'll support my bill, and I'll see you don't face exile.' Caesar sounded very sure of himself. 'Do we have a deal, Lucius?'

'I don't know how you plan to do all you propose, but if you can see I'm not convicted and then help me gain the consulship, I'll support your land bill. I don't believe my support will make it happen, but I'll give it my best.'

'Do you give me your word?'

'Yes,' Catilina answered, sealing the deal. This was the first inkling I had of how far reaching Caesar's ambition truly was. On the slimmest of pretexts, he wanted to personally conquer Aegyptus.

I assumed the official meeting had ended. The two men had begun to engage in small talk, as men do when their business is complete and they don't yet wish to part ways. The conversation meandered toward whether or not Caesar was having an affair with Mucia, the pretty wife of Pompeius Magnus. Ever since the great general was sent east, rumors were circulating that Caesar was regularly meeting Mucia for sexual liaisons. He denied it, but Catilina knew him well, and knew he would have a hard time not having sex with the wife of one of his rivals if she made herself available."

261

"Was Caesar having sex with her? It would be dangerous to anger Pompeius Magnus, would it not?" I was very curious about matters of sex, as all young men are. Mela also became much more attentive.

"Caesar was a man with a hearty appetite for women. Each day his disliked for his shallow, stupid wife grew, and Servilia needed to manage her own household and keep her husband happy. As a result, her need for discretion kept her away from Caesar far too much for his liking. If the wife of another senator made herself available, Caesar availed himself of her."

"You're still respecting his privacy after all these years? Caesar has been dead for nearly six decades." I was a little irritated by his non-answer to my question.

Polybius smiled. "Not dead, Lucius, but rather transported to live among the gods. Forgive my old habit. I am circumspect when it comes to the personal lives of those I've loved and served, but I promised you an honest telling of my story, so yes, Mucia made herself available, and there were others as well. The other women were married to men of much less importance, so it's not necessary to record their names right now, but I can furnish you a list if you give me some time.

At any rate, I began to arrange my wax tablets so I could begin transcribing my notes when Catilina abruptly changed the subject, causing me to scramble to discreetly find a fresh tablet.

'You haven't forgotten about the other plan we discussed have you?' Catilina had lowered his voice as much

262

as possible without whispering. He had a voice that carried through a room with ease, so I could still hear him.

I looked up in time to see Caesar glance uncomfortably at me, then back at Catilina. 'Perhaps we should talk about this another time, my friend.'

Catilina didn't take the hint and went on, 'I'm going to institute a program of debt relief.'

'You mean debt cancellation, don't you?' Caesar asked, again looking nervously in my direction. But, I pretended not to notice. I could have excused myself on some pretext, but I sensed this exchange would be something worth hearing.

'Many of my loans are due for repayment on the Ides of Novembris, as I assume many of yours are. I can't repay them and neither can you. That's why I need to win the consulship and you need to become praetor,' Catilina seemed oblivious to Caesar's discomfort at discussing this with me in the cubicle just off the tablinum.

'If you keep talking about canceling all debts, you will lose. If I support your proposal, I too will lose.'

'I can win. It's not just a few dozen senators who will be relieved of the crushing burden of debt, but thousands of poor plebs. They will vote for us.' Catilina was completely taken by his idea of canceling all personal debts and having everyone start with a clean balance sheet. This would of course outrage the wealthiest men who had loaned out vast amounts of money, but he was guessing the proposal would appeal to enough of the poor plebs to carry the day.

263

Caesar was, as ever, cautious. 'You will lose the support of Pompeius and Rabirius and Crassus and everyone else you owe money to, and you need that support to get elected. As I said, if you keep talking about this, you will lose.'

The next thing Catilina said made me stop scribbling. 'If I lose the election, I'll take my place as consul by force. There are many men backing me and I want to be sure you will too. I am already raising the necessary forces.'

'This is madness,' Caesar said softly.

'Why? Cinna did it.'

'And it cost Cinna his life,'

'Sulla did it and it worked out well, as I recall.'

'Sulla's dictatorship nearly cost me *my* life,' Caesar answered.

'This time, you'll be on the winning side.' Catilina was not to be deterred.

'If you win,' Caesar responded. He then turned to me and said, 'Polybius, go get us some more wine.'

Once again, Catilina didn't understand and said, smiling at me, 'We have wine, why are you sending the boy on a needless errand?'

'This wine is too warm,' was all Caesar said, and I quickly rose and left the room.

I nearly ran to the storage room off the kitchen. The wine was kept under the floor atop the cistern beneath the house, keeping it quite cool. I took the first flagon of wine I could lay my hands on, not taking the time to find a cooler one underneath those on top and raced back, slowing to a walk as I neared the folding doors at the back of the tablinum. I stopped to catch my breath, gulping air as quietly as possible. Rather than go in, I listened at the door.

Catilina was speaking. 'You don't owe money to Rabirius, do you?'

Caesar's answer was too soft to be heard, but I knew he didn't.

'Then I want you to have one of your men bring some sort of charge against him. It'll need to be serious. This will send a signal to the other rich bastards that they can't fuck with us.'

'Why Rabirius?' This time I heard Caesar, as I had crept closer. 'He's a harmless old man.'

Catilina responded with anger, 'He's a bloodsucker! He can't be reasoned with and he will not renegotiate my loans. It's because he's an old man that he's being a prick. He's got more money than he can ever spend and he acts like he's going to live forever. He's finished in politics and he just likes to meddle for the fun of it. The old bastard's got nothing to lose, so he'll just stick the knife in my guts and twist and twist.'

'You should have thought of that before you borrowed so much from him,' Caesar answered quietly. The implication was that Caesar had thought of it and that's why he didn't borrow from Rabirius or others like him.

With that, I realized enough time had passed and I noisily opened the door and brought the wine into the room, setting it on the table. I went to take my seat in the cubicle, when Caesar dropped all pretense and said to me, 'Why don't you busy yourself someplace else, Polybius?'

I quickly left the room, leaving the door open just a crack. I walked out to the atrium, but then took my shoes off and crept back to the door behind the tablinum. I returned in time to hear the end of the conversation.

This time, it was Caesar talking. 'If I decide to join you, I'll do what I can behind the curtain.'

'That's all I ask,' Catilina said.

'If I hear my name even mentioned in any of this, I'll deny it all and it will be me twisting the knife in your guts.' Caesar's voice rose for the first time. 'Also, if I win my election, and you lose yours, all bets are off,'

'I'd do the same,' Catilina answered honestly. 'I can see myself out.'

I waited to hear Catilina's heavy steps on the marble floor of the atrium before turning to creep away. I had only taken a couple of steps when Caesar said loudly, 'Please come in here, Polybius.'

I froze. My options were limited, I could continue to creep away and deny I was listening, but then if Caesar stuck his head out and saw me I would be in for even greater

266

trouble. Perhaps he knew I was there because he was manifesting early signs of godhead, but I suspected then and I still believe he was just guessing. I was certain I was in for a beating, but I did as he said. For the first time, Caesar was truly angry with me. He started out speaking in a stern but quiet voice.

'How long have you been with me, Polybius?'

I stood before him, mute with fear. 'How long?' His voice rose some with anger.

I didn't look up. 'More than half a year, master.'

'Yes, you have been mine for nearly eight months now!' Caesar's voice and tone continued to rise. 'In that time I have placed trust in you! I have let you hear many things, private, personal things! If you wish my confidence in you to continue, you must continue to deserve my confidence! There are matters I simply will not, share with you. You are not yet the man Demetrius has become.'

'Yes, master,' I whispered, my head still bowed. In my heart I knew I needed to stay steady in my goal of seeing my master elected praetor. Once again I had faltered in staying on course.

'I trusted Demetrius with my life, because he trusted me with his!' he shouted, slamming his hand down on the table and upsetting the nearly empty wine goblets. Wine drops spattered my face and tunic, causing me to flinch. Then, in almost a whisper, Caesar said, 'You are not yet the man Demetrius is. Leave me now.'

I began to back out of the room, head still bowed when Caesar stopped me again. I looked up at him. He had regained his composure but beads of sweat dotted his forehead and upper lip. His voice was normal again. 'Polybius, do you remember the conversation we had when I first suggested you become my slave? The one where we discussed loyalty?'

I nodded but didn't speak. I recalled his words and they echoed in my head. *'If you are disloyal I may kill you...'* I stood mute with dread, until Caesar sternly said, 'I meant what I said. I feel ill, find Pythogenes and send him here immediately. Now go.' Caesar had a peculiar look to his eyes, so I hurried out to do as I was told.

LIBER XVII

In the days that followed there were several more meetings between Caesar and Catilina, but I was not privy to any of them. The day of the final meeting between them I was sent for and entered the tablinum just as Catilina was leaving. Caesar had a habit of rarely seeing his friends to the door, that honor was only reserved for those who he wished to make his friends, so Catilina left us alone and made his way across the atrium toward the vestibule. Caesar looked up from the small papyrus scroll he was reading and, satisfied with it, signed his name to it. 'Bring my seal and some twine please.'

I returned with the seal and the wax and a bit of string. He waited a moment more for the ink to dry and then sealed the scroll shut. "This will give you access to the archives in the Capitoline temple. I want you to gather everything there is to find on Gaius Rabirius. On your way, stop by Labienus' place and let him know I'd like to meet him at the baths on the Esquiline this afternoon at the eighth hour.'

I did as I was told. I was still unsure where I stood with Caesar. From the Julian Domus in the Subura, it was just a short walk to the forum. In those days, trials were held in the open spaces in the forum, and I got to hear Cicero eloquently defend a guilty man as I passed. I wanted to stop as it was always a pleasure to hear his speeches, but I didn't wish to arouse any distrust in Caesar. However, I happened to notice Labienus listening to the trial on one of the benches so I was able to avoid a trip to his house and give him Caesar's message right away. He nodded, and pressed a coin into my hand. The additional coin would be added to what I already had.

Not knowing how much information I would find, I brought two large canvas bags with me, and the requested documents filled both. The slave who managed the archives had the blank look of the functionary who whiles away the hours of his life never questioning the significance, or lack of significance of anything he is asked to do.

On my way back, I spun an unrealistic fantasy in my mind of running away and finding Gaius on the farm near Neapolis (Naples), so I made a mental note to find Neapolis on the map of Italia Caesar kept in his tablinum. Upon my return, Caesar set me the task of reading the documents in a search for any occasion where Rabirius had been accused of wrongdoing. I began studying the documents in chronological order beginning with the most recent. I reasoned if Caesar was planning to build a case against the man, more recent crimes would be easiest to prosecute. I'm a fast reader; my training as a copyist and a natural talent made reading come easily to me. Yet, in spite of combing over pages and pages of documents, I found little to report and certainly nothing offensive enough to bring to court. There was the occasional accusation of electoral bribery and some questionable loans made in exchange for favors that were beneath the dignity of a senator, but all in all, Rabirius seemed to have led a conventional life. After about three hours, Caesar leaned into my cubicle and asked, 'What have you found?'

I looked up from what I was reading. 'I'm sorry Caesar, but I've read the records going back twenty-seven years and there is nothing worthy of a prosecution.'

'Why do you assume I'm planning to prosecute old Rabirius?' Caesar asked.

I grew nervous. I had been walking on eggs since I was found to be listening in on Caesar's meeting with Catilina, and now I seemed to have stepped across another line. 'I just thought....' I began, but then I said, 'I've found four instances where he was accused of minor malfeasance. I've written a summary of each.' I held up my pages for him to see.

Caesar ignored the pages I offered and said, 'Let's go to the baths. You can finish this tonight.'

I was sent to collect Nicandros, the secretary, and Statius, Caesar's bathing slave, and rejoined Caesar and Demetrius in the Atrium.

We left for the baths on the Esquiline Hill and our meeting with Labienus. This was a smaller bath that only accommodated about one hundred people at a time, but Caesar never needed to wait to enter the baths. If it was too crowded, some of those who were lingering in the cold room after their baths were simply asked to leave. Caesar was seen as a rising star in the political world, and the owners and managers of the baths wanted to keep his good will. He was also an aedile and could simply say he was inspecting the bath, but Caesar rarely did this when he wasn't there in an official capacity. Labienus met us at the entrance to the baths and our group moved in together, leaving the lictors outside on the benches.

Once in the baths, the slaves, myself included, were required to wait in the atrium portion. The only slaves allowed in the baths proper were the bathing slaves who went in to scrape the oil from their master's bodies, unless he was carrying out an inspection. In the tepidarium, they would

271

frequently pluck unwanted hairs and trim finger and toe nails as well. Caesar was fastidious about his appearance, so Statius was kept busy at the baths. Both Nicandros and I usually brought portable desks to the baths so we could catch up on our work. Since we were not allowed into the bathing areas, I rarely saw the inside of a bath, but on occasion, when we were there very late, Caesar would let his slaves enjoy the baths themselves, if only briefly, and I relished those occasions. As I said before, I was able to enjoy the facilities during the year Caesar was an aedile, and this only made me feel the loss of the privilege even more. He preferred the bath on the Esquiline because it had two excellent tavernas with doors that communicated directly with the atrium and three conference rooms attached.

While at the bath, Caesar would spend a considerable amount of time exercising with weights. He had exercises for every part of his body. He said it was important to stay in top physical condition and thus be prepared to lead soldiers into battle. His companions at the baths usually tried to keep up with him while both exercising and conducting business discussions, but they most often failed. Labienus was one of only a few of his companions who could match with Caesar and occasionally surpass him in his exercise routine. Caesar would often take one of the heavy, iron, mock swords provided in the exercise area, and hold it at arm's length while a slave marked time by counting the drops from a water clock. He would hold it in his outstretched arm until his muscles were twitching and he was sweating profusely. On this particular day, Caesar and Labienus wagered who could hold out the longest at this particular feat. Labienus won in spite of holding the sword in his left hand. Caesar's usual routine included exercise, bathing, a small meal, and then another round of bathing. This second round was reserved for

272

socializing, but if there was important private business to discuss he would then put on his tunic and we would retire to one of the conference rooms. Today, he chose the smaller conference room, as it would just be Caesar, Labienus, Demetrius and I. There was a heavy curtain that could be pulled across the doorway, but Caesar preferred to leave it open so we could see if anyone was listening at the door.

Once in the room, Caesar turned to Labienus and said, 'This couldn't be better for us; tell Polybius what you told me.'

As we took our seats, he said, 'You didn't look back far enough into Rabirius' past.'

'I looked back nearly thirty years,' I countered.

'Not far enough into the past,' Labienus replied. 'For the past thirty years or so, Rabirius has been as pure as a vestal virgin. That is if you discount electoral bribery and heavy gambling.'

'We could go after him for the bribery,' Demetrius interjected.

Caesar winced. 'If we use that to sink his ship we will bring down a lot of others with him, myself included.'

'We could at least embarrass him with the gambling charge,' Demetrius added, not yet giving up.

'No to that as well,' said Labienus. 'Right now, he's gambling heavily on Catilina's candidacy, more than on the chariot races. We don't want anyone looking into where his money is invested right now.'

273

'What happened more than thirty years ago?' I was genuinely curious, as the man seemed to have led a most mundane life.

'Rabirius murdered my uncle,' Labienus casually remarked, as if he was talking about the weather.

Labienus, like Caesar, had a flair for the dramatic, and it became clear he wasn't going to explain until someone asked, so, after a pause, I asked. 'How exactly did he murder your uncle and get away with it all these years?' Still, he made us wait."

At that, Polybius struggled to sit up further and adjusted his cushions. I felt obliged to help him, although I felt that I was being kept waiting just as he had been those many years ago. He took another sip of wine, so I knew I was in for a rather involved explanation. I leaned forward with my stylus poised to take notes on a fresh wax tablet. "I assume you are going to fill me in," I finally said.

"Yes," he answered, "I will explain it to you as he explained it to me. It was a rather strange case even for those rather strange days when the rules that had governed the republic for centuries were no longer adequate, yet no one had come up with anything better."

Polybius took another sip of wine and used his napkin to wipe a bit or wine from his chin before he began. "Are you familiar with Gaius Marius?" Polybius asked me. "I ask you this, because that is the question that Labienus asked me."

"Only as much as we've already discussed. I know he was a great enemy of Sulla and an ally of Cinna. I also know he was consul for seven times and a remarkable man."

"That," said Polybius, "was very nearly the exact answer I gave Labienus seventy-eight years ago. Therefore, what I tell you will be much the same as what he told me. As he started his explanation, Caesar leaned over to talk to Demetrius who was familiar with the story, having lived through those times.

Labienus said to me, 'What you know of Marius is quite true. He was a most remarkable man. Marius was nearly sixty years old the year Caesar and I were born (100 BC). He was a "new man," to politics. His family was of equestrian rank, and he would be the first of the Marius family to reach the consulship, which makes his achievement of seven consulships even more impressive.'

At this point, Demetrius interrupted to ask us what we would like to eat. Both Labienus and I requested pork sausages and bread, and Demetrius left to place the order.

Labienus continued. 'You may have heard the story about the portent of Marius' success. It's said that when he was about your age, while hiking in the hills of Arpium with some companions, an eagle's nest was dislodged from the branches of a tall pine tree. Marius saw it fall and caught it in his cloak. The nest contained a remarkable seven eggs. When he brought it home to his parents, they consulted the local priests and were told it was their son's fate to be awarded the highest command seven times. I don't know whether this story is true or not, but many believe it to be so.

Marius had a distinguished military career and in the year Sulpicius Galba and Lucius Hortensius were consuls (108 BC) he ran for his first consulship and won. Marius used his authority to open military service to all Roman citizens, not just landowners. This, in effect, made the standing armies we have today possible, but it also created the problem we have today of having to find land for the soldiers after their years of service. Two years prior to his first consulship, the Cimbri arrived in southern Gaul.'

'Who are the Cimbri?' I asked.

Caesar answered this one. 'The Cimbri are a tribe of barbarians from the farthest reaches to the north. They are said to be giants, but this is clearly not true, and they were no match for the legions of Rome.'

'Quite so,' Labienus continued, 'the Cimbri were utterly defeated by forces led by Junius Silanus, but not before stirring up the Celtic tribes in our recently acquired province of Transalpine Gaul (southern France). The Optimate faction failed to do anything about the unrest in the province, so it wasn't addressed until the year of Marius' first consulship. His colleague that year was Cassius Longinus, and it was Cassius who was given the command in spite of Marius being the superior general. Cassius' legions were destroyed by the barbarians. The trouble persisted and the following year the consul Quintus Servilius Caepio marched into Gaul. He did no more than capture the city of Tolosa (Toulouse) and steal a massive treasure from their shrines. The money was never found, and legend has it that the fortune is still in the hands of the last of his descendants.'

At this, Caesar felt the need to comment. 'I can assure you this is not correct, as his last descendants are Servilia Caeponis, and her son, young Marcus Junius Brutus, and if she had that kind of money, they and not Crassus, would be financing my career.'

At that point, Demetrius returned with the slave carrying plates of food, two on each arm. He had heard what was said about Servilius, and this caused him to laugh, as he took his seat. 'If Servilia had that much money, her husband and her brother would already be consul.' We sat eating while Labienus continued his story.

The senate voted to continue Caepio's command of the army for the following year based solely on the distinctions of his family since he was clearly an inept and corrupt general. One of the consuls for the year, Mallius Maximus, was, like Marius, a new man and was, again like Marius, resented by the old established families. It was he who was chosen to lead an army into Gaul to clean up Caepio's mess, but Caepio refused to cooperate with Mallius when the Cimbri and the Teutones appeared on the Rhone River. Mallius was taken by surprise but could have been saved with reinforcements. As it turned out, Caepio refused to join forces with Mallius and over eighty thousand brave soldiers were killed at Arausio (Orange, France). This defeat left Italia and, therefore, Rome vulnerable to attack by the barbarian hordes. My father told me there was panic in the streets of Rome when people learned of the defeat.

Both convention and the constitution were ignored in the panic, and Marius was elected to the consulship for the following year. Not only was he elected while still holding command in Africa, but also the legally mandated ten years

277

between consulships was ignored. Under the threat of barbarian invasion, Marius would be elected consul five consecutive years.

The Germans proved to be as militarily inept as Caepio and failed to follow up on their advantage. They, of course, had an excuse, being nothing more than undisciplined brutes. Rather than turn on Italia and seize the greatest prize of all, Rome, the Teutoni spent the summer raiding in Gaul and the Cimbri marched into the province of Hispania. This gave Marius enough time to celebrate his African triumph and raise a new army. It would be three years before the barbarians would decide to invade Italia, and by this time Marius was well prepared. The Germans divided their forces, marching into Italia through two different passes across the Alps. Marius first defeated the Teutoni, returned to Rome to get elected consul, and then went to the rescue of his fellow consul, Latutius Catullus, and destroyed the advancing Cimbri. Catullus and Marius celebrated a joint triumph, but in the public's mind, Marius was the real hero.'

At this point, I felt I needed to ask a question, as I'm sure you do too, Lucius. I asked, rather impatiently, 'This is a fascinating history, but what does any of this have to do with Rabirius killing your uncle?'

Caesar smiled and gave Labienus a playful shove to the shoulder. 'You are being very long winded. Remember your forensics training. Stick to the point!'

Labienus pushed him back and went on. 'I'm getting there, but these things take time. Ten years later, the Italian cities allied to Rome rebelled and war broke out again.'

278

At this, I rolled my eyes, prompting Labienus to veer back on course. 'I only mention this to show that Marius was again called into service for Rome, this time fighting alongside Sulla, but he was forced to withdraw from his command due to an illness. After Italia was settled, Sulla became consul and the senate awarded him the command in the war in the east against Mithridates. That conquest was never properly settled and is finally being completed by Pompeius Magnus, nearly thirty years later. The senate, as I said, chose Sulla, but the tribal assembly chose Marius. This led to the civil war and Sulla marched an army into Rome. Marius was forced to flee to Africa where he raised an army, and while Sulla was away fighting Mithridates in Greece, he returned and seized Rome. Just a month later, Marius had a recurrence of the paralysis he suffered while fighting the Italian cities, but rather than recover, this time he died from it.'

Once again, I impolitely asked, 'What has this to do with Rabirius?'

Caesar leaned toward me and said, 'Patience, Polybius, he'll get there someday, of that I'm fairly certain.'

I leaned back in my chair, but not with any degree of patience.

Labienus continued, ignoring Caesar's jibe. 'There was a senator named Lucius Appuleius Saturninus who needed to find land for his veteran troops. In exchange for securing land in Africa for his troops, he allied himself with Marius to help him secure his third, or maybe it was his fourth consulship. That's not important. What is important is that my uncle, also named Titus Labienus, was a client and friend to

279

Saturninus. Together along with another tribune named Gaius Servilius Glaucia, Saturninus and Marius conspired to keep each other in positions that gave them imperium, and, therefore, immunity from prosecution. Marius, as it turned out, was having second thoughts about the alliance and was very seriously considering breaking it. Saturninus and Glaucia were both taking every opportunity to overshadow Marius as they both wanted to supplant him as consul and were looking toward their own political advancement, and Saturninus knew his only hope for political survival was for him to retain some office with imperium. The year before your master and I were born (101 BC) Saturninus was seeking to be elected tribune for the third time and Glaucia was seeking the consulship, a post he would not normally be legally eligible to hold for another two years, but, as I said before, these were not normal times. Running against him was the Optimate, Gaius Memmius. To ensure their electoral success, Saturninus and Glaucia hired dangerous men from the lowest classes of society to intimidate supporters of their opponents. In spite of their blatant bribery and intimidation, they still doubted their success right up to the day of the election. On the day of the election, the agents of Saturninus and Glaucia were sent out to intimidate voters. This led to fighting between supporters on both sides. Things grew more and more ugly, and Memmius made the fatal mistake of trying to personally intervene and calm the trouble. He was beaten to death by the hired intimidators while the voting was actually taking place. Of course the election was suspended and the people of Rome were outraged. Sometime during the course of the day, Glaucia got into a dispute with a fellow senator over the fact that he was not legally eligible to seek the consulship. The exchange turned violent and Glaucia killed the man before fleeing to the home of one of his supporters. Later in the

280

evening, after learning of the murder of Memmius and the rage of the senate and people, he realized all hope was lost and he killed himself.

The following day the senate met in an emergency session and formally declared Glaucia and Saturninus enemies of Rome. The senate then took the rare act of passing a law giving the consuls sweeping and undefined powers to defend Rome.'

What Labienus was referring to is the *Senatus Consultum Ultimum* or what came to be known as the "ultimate decree." The wording of the law was something to the effect of 'Let the consuls see that no harm is done to the state.' This so called "ultimate decree" was, as I said, quite rare at that time, but in later years it became much more common as the republic descended into chaos. Anyway, he continued with, 'Marius, as consul, had no choice but to arrest Saturninus and Glaucia. Glaucia was already dead, but this was not yet common knowledge, so Saturninus and his supporters, my uncle included, gathered in the forum. Marius' attempt to arrest Saturninus led to a small battle in which the poorly armed and disorganized supporters of Saturninus were scattered. A small band including Saturninus and my uncle fled up the steps to the Capitol. They were able to defend themselves, as the ways up the slopes of the hill are few and very narrow, but they were forced to surrender after the water supply was cut. Saturninus was able to negotiate a peaceful resolution, agreeing to be taken into custody and secured in the Curia Hostilia until the fates of his supporters could be decided. At the time, he was still a tribune and, therefore, his person was sacrosanct, and he could not be killed unless he was stripped of his office. Saturninus had already negotiated for his own life with exile as his punishment."

281

I had to clarify a point, so when Polybius sat up a bit to sip some wine I asked him, "What sits on that space today? Is it where the Curia Julia stands?"

"To the northwest of the present curia between it and the Basilica Porcia," he answered while noticing Mela struggling to stifle a yawn. "Don't worry," he added with a smile, "we're almost there."

I was grateful, but said nothing as I set down my wine cup and took up my tablet and stylus.

Polybius continued. "Labienus also assured me the end of his tale was near. 'Saturninus and his band of followers were all arrested and taken to the curia, but it didn't take long for word to spread of the deal Saturninus had secured to spare his life, enraging members of the Optimate faction in the senate. Memmius was a tribune and his death not only offended the senate and people of Rome, but also the gods. The senators attempted to force their way into the curia with the intention of dragging Saturninus out into the forum for some informal justice, but they were driven back by the guards posted at the door. Some of the younger and more physically able members of the band climbed onto the roof of the curia in an attempt to get in. Rabirius was among this group. After removing a few tiles, they realized it was a foolish plan since they had no ropes with which to lower themselves, and even if they had brought ropes they would have been easily captured and probably killed by the group in the curia. Someone got the idea to use the roof tiles as weapons with which to pelt the helpless group of men being held in the curia. Several of the men were killed before they could find refuge beneath the benches that had been stacked along the walls to make room for the prisoners. Some of the survivors later testified that it was Rabirius who threw the tile that killed my uncle. He also tried to take credit for killing Saturninus, but the witnesses confirmed that that dubious honor belonged to the slave of one of the other senators. And that, young Polybius, is how Rabirius murdered my uncle.'

Demetrius gave his opinion first. 'I don't see how you can make this work for you, Caesar. Without a conviction you will be seen as nothing more than a petty nuisance and since it is all so long ago it will be nearly impossible to win a conviction. I'm sure most of the witnesses are either dead or far from Rome and to the members of the jury this will all be so much ancient history. If you drag doddering old men into court to testify to these events they will be easily discredited and you will be made to look like a fool.'

Caesar frowned, but said nothing. He sat back in his chair and took a few moments to consider the matter. 'You're probably right, Demetrius. I guess I hadn't really thought enough about it.' Then, turning to me, he said, 'Find out anything you can about the case anyway, Polybius, and keep digging into Rabirius' past. There must be something we can use.'

I nodded, but then a thought occurred to me so I asked the question, 'What if there was no jury? What if he was simply tried by a judge?'

Caesar smiled and shook his head. 'There isn't a law that allows a senator to be tried without a jury.'

Now it was my turn to smile. 'Respectfully, master, I believe you are wrong.'

'Really?' he asked.

283

I brought up a story from my past. 'A few years ago, when I was still working as a copyist for Titus, there was a senator named Horatius who fancied himself a legal expert and was looking to expand his law library. Every month or so, he would bring in scrolls he had borrowed to be copied for his own collection. He took a liking to me and would sometimes try to engage me in conversation. The man was an insufferable bore and all the older copyists managed to avoid him. Since his only two passions in life were Roman law and Greek law, his idea of idle conversation was to expound on the most obscure laws he could think of. As a result, I learned of several long forgotten laws.' I paused for effect, but this only frustrated my audience.

Finally, from Labienus, 'And?'

'Well,' I continued, 'I learned of an obscure law called *lex perduellio*.'

Demetrius nodded, and said, 'I've heard of this law.'

I didn't' want to be upstaged by Demetrius, so I quickly added, 'The wording of this law was something like, "The Law of the Twelve Tables compels that a man who has incited an enemy or who has handed over a citizen to the enemy is to be punished with death," if my memory is correct.'

'And your memory is always correct,' Caesar said with a smile.

I ignored the compliment and continued. 'The punishment was to be either thrown from the Tarpeian Rock or hanged to death.'

284

'That seems rather harsh in this case,' Caesar said.

Labienus ignored him and focused instead on the law. 'Does Rabirius' crime correspond to the law?'

I tried to look as wise as possible. 'Horatius told me the law was used in ancient times by King Tullus to convict a man of murder. It has also been expanded to include usurping the functions of elected officials and violating the rights of a tribune. Those two points clearly apply in this case. And, even better for you, the case is not tried by a jury, but rather by two judges called duumvirs and it can be brought to court by a tribune such as yourself, Titus Labienus.' I leaned back with a satisfied smile.

The meeting ended with Caesar agreeing to have me do the research needed to see how Labienus could introduce the case. We finished our meals and left the baths as a group and as was usual a small but growing crowd followed us through the street. At the bottom of the hill, Labienus and his followers parted ways with us, he heading toward the Caelian Hill and our group going along the Sacra Via and onto the Argiletum into the Subura. I knew I had a long evening of research ahead of me, but I enjoyed that sort of work and looked forward to solving difficult problems. Although I was looking forward to the work itself, I was troubled by the whole business in which I had played such a large part.

We walked most of the way home without my adding a word to the conversation, being occupied with my own thoughts. Caesar noticed my withdrawn silence and asked me about it. 'What's bothering you, Polybius?'

Since it had been a successful day for me I thought I might have redeemed myself, by some small measure, in

Caesar's eyes, so I felt free to tell him the truth. 'I feel as if I may have condemned a man to death today. Do we have to kill him?'

Caesar didn't answer at once. In fact, we were at the door of the house before he said, 'Come see me as soon as you've had your bath and we will talk about this. Demetrius you come too.'

Demetrius and I bathed in special water filled basins in a room behind the kitchen reserved for the slaves. Unlike most masters, Caesar allowed his slaves to bath almost every day. He was meticulous about his own appearance and he considered us to be an extension of himself. After we bathed, we got dressed and went to join Caesar in the tablinum. As we crossed the darkening peristyle, I looked over at Demetrius. We hadn't discussed the case at all since arriving home and I wondered how he felt about the matter, but he moved with his eyes cast down at his house slippers and seemed lost in his own thoughts, so I let him be. The tablinum was glowing with oil lamps. When we were not sleeping we always had lamps burning. The Subura fills the valley between the Viminal and Esquiline Hills. With tall buildings on either side of the domus and the hills with their own structures beyond that, it was only at mid-day that a significant amount of light made its way into the peristyle or through the roof opening in the atrium. Any time spent in the house was spent in either darkness or a kind of artificial twilight. The folding doors on the front of the tablinum were open and Caesar occupied his usual spot at the table, facing the atrium. Demetrius and I took the two other chairs at the sides of the table.

After I had already taken my seat, Caesar, always cautious about eavesdropping, pointed to his wife berating a

286

slave in the atrium and said to me, 'We don't need anyone listening in. Polybius, please shut the doors.' I wasn't sure if he didn't trust the slave or his wife, but I suspect he was cautious about both. After drawing the doors shut, I reached into my cubicle off the tablinum and grabbed a fresh wax tablet from the stack I kept on the small table, when Caesar stopped me. 'There won't be any record this time.'

Caesar turned to me and looked directly into my eyes. 'You did well today, Polybius. You used that elephantine memory of yours to solve a serious difficulty I was having.'

I couldn't help myself and I did what no slave should ever do; I interrupted my master. 'But do we have to kill him?'

Caesar sighed. 'If Rabirius is found guilty it will have been I who will have killed him. Caesar and Labienus will have blood on their hands, not you. Today you acted in your capacity as a talking tool.' The phrase he used was one I had never heard him say about a slave before. In Latin, it is *instrumenti genus vocale*.

'Why,' I asked, 'does he need to die at all?'

'He did kill a man. There is no time limit on justice.'

For the first time, Demetrius weighed in on the subject, and I was surprised to see he took my side. 'Justice requires a fair trial. The man can hardly get a fair trial after all these years.'

'Are you saying the Duumvirs cannot be fair?'

'Perhaps perduellio has faded from use because the entire process is inherently unfair and, as our system of justice advanced, the Roman people came to understand that.'

'He is clearly guilty of the crime. The public record attests to that.'

'If he is clearly guilty today,' Demetrius countered, 'his guilt would have been even more evident immediately following the crime. Why was he not convicted then?'

I began to get the sense that this was something that occurred frequently between Demetrius and Caesar. This give and take seemed to be one of the ways Caesar thought through difficult questions. I had seldom seen it because it only occurred behind closed doors. Caesar thought for a moment and then answered him. 'Tempers ran too high then. Saturninus was guilty of killing a tribune.'

'Saturninus did not kill the tribune. It was his hired agents.'

'In law, it is the same thing.'

'Perhaps he was never tried, indeed none of the senators on the roof of the curia that day stood trial, because the consuls didn't call for it.

'Anyone can initiate a prosecution.'

'The senate had issued the 'ultimate decree' empowering the consuls to restore order by whatever means necessary. On that day, the consul had the authority to do whatever he chose to do.'

288

Both men stopped talking and paused to think. Caesar broke the silence. 'It seems we can serve two ends with this trial. I need to give a serious fright to Catilina's creditors. His political survival is at stake. But, young Polybius here, by remembering an obscure law, opened another door to us.'

This time it was Demetrius who interrupted. 'Your political survival is also at stake. Both you and Catilina went to sea in the same leaky boat.'

Caesar dismissed this with a wave of his hand and went on. 'The other opportunity before us is a chance to bring into question the extent of authority the 'ultimate decree' gives the consuls. Rabirius killed the man after order had been restored. The Optimates in the senate are too eager to issue a decree that should be reserved for true threats to the people of Rome as a means to stop those of us who support the rights of the plebs with our programs. We also need to question whether or not once the senate declares a man to be an enemy of the republic he loses all legal standing or does his outlaw status last only so long as he continues to be a threat. Those men had surrendered and should, to my mind, have regained the protection of the laws.'

After a moment of silence, I asked, 'Caesar, how can you be certain the judges will find Rabirius guilty? If they find him innocent, all this will be for nothing.'

'That's a good point, but in all honesty, I'm really starting to lose hope for Catilina. It might be time to cut the cords that bind us together, or to use Demetrius' metaphor, to push him from the leaky boat we share. If I'm tied too closely to him and he fails, I might sink with him. Prosecuting Rabirius will at least serve our second aim. Let's do our best

289

to keep Catilina's hands off this one. The man's too desperate and he will probably do something stupid and make a mess of it.'

I still wasn't fully satisfied. I had played an important part in setting a man up to face a capital charge. I had to remind myself that this was another small step toward helping my master be elected praetor. Still though, it didn't feel at all right. Caesar ended the meeting with, 'It's getting late. I need to go read up on whatever tomorrow's damned senate debate is about. Polybius, go back a few more years in the official records. Find out what Rabirius did or didn't do on that day. Let's build a case.'

I was feeling rather gloomy as I dragged myself to my feet. I recall thinking I wouldn't ever have to do this sort of thing when I gained my freedom, Then, Caesar threw me a rope of sorts by saying, 'See if you can't find some way the judges can find him guilty but we can still get him off the hook. We need to scare him, but we really don't need to throw the old man from a cliff.'

We had very little time to prepare the case. Caesar wanted it brought right away so it wouldn't be too close to the elections scheduled for Quintilis (July), I worked closely with Labienus' secretary, Pelonus. He resented working with one so young, but he was most loyal to his master and never seemed to express an original idea of his own. He was competent and acquiesced when Labienus told him I would take the lead in forming the case. I had determined to find some loopholes large enough through which a good advocate for the defense could squeeze the fat old man and win an acquittal, and as it turned out I didn't need to try very hard. As I suspected, we could only find four witnesses from those days. There were actually several men still alive and active in Rome who were reputed to have been on the roof of the curia with Rabirius that day, but each denied it and refused to testify for fear that they too could be put on trial. For each potential witness an informal meeting was scheduled. Labienus, as the tribune bringing the case to court, would meet with the man and question him as to what he could recall. Pelonus took notes at these meetings and I sat in the corner of the room listening closely to what they each had to say. I believe my presence in the meetings was to ensure everyone was aware it was Caesar behind the prosecution. Of the four witnesses who were willing to place Rabirius on the roof that day, one's eyes had become so clouded with age he wouldn't have been able to point him out at the trial, another was known to spend most days quite drunk, and a third was of such low moral character that he would be easily discredited. There was only one man whose testimony might hold up in court. He was a client of Labienus' and had been hiding under a bench in the curia that day, so his motives for testifying were sure to be suspect. The entire case needed to rest on the official archives, so I was confident there was a good chance Rabirius would escape punishment.

I still needed to accompany Caesar when he made his rounds of the forum, but I had time to work on building the case on the days when he acted as a judge or as an advocate in a trial. That spring, there were many days he was called on to sit through more than one trial a day. At this time in the last days of the republic, Rome had become a very litigious place. There were more trials than the sitting magistrates could handle, and former praetors or aediles were frequently brought in to serve as judges. Caesar was more than willing to do this service, as it kept his name on the minds of the voters. When he was sitting in judgment or arguing a case, he had no need

291

for a nomenclator, so I was free to work with Labienus, interviewing witnesses. Half an hour before the expected end of the last trial I would go to the forum and take a position off to one side and wait for the proceedings to end. One day, I arrived just as the great orator Hortensius was about to begin a speech for the defense. Since the man never made a quick speech in his life, I knew I was probably more than an hour early. With extra time to fill, I decided to indulge a whim and visit the scene of the crime, as it were, and poke my head into the curia. I had only been in the curia a few times and that was just to rush in and hand Caesar a note, so I never had an opportunity to really examine the place. I knew the curia I would be studying was not the place where the murders had occurred, but rather was the new, larger building constructed by Sulla. But I was still curious about the layout of the structure and I had heard it said Sulla constructed his curia as a larger version of the Curia Hostilia. I walked up the steps, looking around to see if anyone would challenge me. At the top of the steps I grabbed the large metal ring projecting from the heavy bronze door and was able to pull it open a bit. I peered in not knowing what to expect. I was fairly certain there would be at least one slave inside to challenge me, but there wasn't anyone at all and this emboldened me further. I knew I wasn't allowed unescorted into the curia, so it was a bit of a thrill to even take a single step into the place. I slid sideways through the small opening I had made and pulled the door shut behind me. The room was long, maybe more than one hundred feet and about half as wide. Sulla had ordered it made nearly twice as large as the old building, so it could fit most of the six hundred Roman senators. To the left along one of the long walls were three rows of low wide marble steps with inlaid wooden benches on them. To the right was a marble altar and to either side of the altar was a statue.

292

Tradition dictates the senate can only meet in a sacred space so, even today, every senate house is also a consecrated temple. At the back between two sets of smaller doors was a platform with the consuls' chairs set in the center and a longer bench behind them. High up on each of the long walls were three large windows covered with an ornate latticework. The space was cool and dark after the bright sun of the forum.

I moved to the center of the chamber and looked all around taking it in. I moved among the rows of benches where the great debates of the senate took place. I imagined the space filled with senators, sometimes sitting at rapt attention while one of their own makes an eloquent, impassioned speech or at other times bickering and shouting at each other. I looked up to the rafters supporting the roof and I could see the bottoms of the red clay tiles and imagined them being torn loose and thrown down on me. Lost in my reverie, I didn't hear the door open behind me, but I became aware of a brightening of the room as it did, and I did hear it quietly shut. It was one of the smaller doors at the back. I was paralyzed with terror.

LIBER XVIII

In that instant, my heart and my mind both raced. The only excuse that occurred to me was to say I was looking for my master and Caesar had told me to meet him there. I hoped Caesar would back my story when I was returned to him after what I was certain would be a flogging. I turned to see who had entered the room, but all I could see was three men in togas standing in the shadowy corner of the room. The togas dashed any hope of it being a sympathetic slave who had discovered me, so in a panic I slowly backed toward the front door with the intention of turning and making a run as soon as I thought I was near enough to open the heavy door and escape.

As I turned, one of the three spoke in a loud, clear voice. 'Don't run. Six of my lictors are guarding the front door and you will not get past them.' I knew the voice but couldn't place it.

I stopped where I stood and slowly turned around. I was having difficulty finding my voice and I gave up any attempt when the three men stepped forward into the light. On each side was a tall, well-built lictor with the official bundle of rods over his shoulder and in the middle stood Consul Marcus Tullius Cicero. At this time of his life, Cicero was forty four years old and at the height of his powers, and by that I mean much more than politically. He was a brilliant writer, speaker, and thinker. I'm certain that generations from now people will still feel great respect and admiration for his speeches and his prose. When looking at him, however, one was not very impressed. Cicero had a rather large head with thinning and receding brown hair, flecked with gray at the temples. He was somewhat thick around the middle but was otherwise well-proportioned. When Cicero moved and gestured it was with an easy elegance. Up until this meeting, I always took pleasure in hearing and seeing him speak.

'You are, unless I am mistaken, Caesar's new Demetrius. Polybius, I believe?'

I still couldn't speak, so I simply nodded.

'I watched from the portico of the basilica across the forum as you snuck in here. I'm not one to let an opportunity pass.'

I could feel sweat dripping down my sides and I felt nauseous. 'I'm so very sorry Consul. I'm looking for my master. He told me....'

'Don't bother,' Cicero cut me off. 'We both know Caesar is sitting on the judges' platform hearing a case just across the forum. I myself snuck into the old curia when I was about thirteen years old. Of course I am a citizen and you are a slave.' Cicero looked around the chamber as he was comparing it in his mind to the room he visited as a boy. 'That room was much smaller, but the senate was smaller in those days as well. We also have the opportunity, that our fathers lacked, to stare into the stony faces of Lucius Cornelia Sulla on one side and his protégé, Gnaeus Pompeius Magnus on the other,' he added, gesturing toward the statues along the wall. He began to walk toward the benches, but not knowing what was expected of me, I simply stood rooted to my spot on the marble floor. When he reached the benches he turned and sat and only then noticed I hadn't followed. 'Come, sit.'

I walked over but didn't sit. 'I think Consul, it would be more appropriate if I were to stand.'

'Suit yourself,' he sighed. 'Tell me, what's all this business with old Rabirius?'

This was unexpected. 'I am helping my master's client, Titus Labienus, prepare a case against the man who murdered his uncle.' I was able to find my voice because Demetrius had coached me on what to say when someone inevitably asked. 'He waited until now to bring the case because now he is a tribune.'

'I have made inquiries about you, Polybius, and I know you are not stupid. Please don't treat me as if I am.' Cicero sounded cross, but kept his composure. I knew he wasn't stupid. In fact, I believed then and I still believe he was one of the most intelligent men to ever reach the consulship. He rose to the top in that dangerous world without any family connections; his political career was a result of his own intelligence and hard work.

I couldn't tell him the entire truth since it would have been foolish on my part to be disloyal to Caesar, so I told him a half-truth. 'I don't know why they decided to prosecute him, but I have been directed to build a case against the man. I know Catilina is somehow involved. I am just doing as I was instructed, Consul.'

'I knew there was more to it than a thirty-seven year old murder. How is that drunken viper Catilina involved?'

'I don't know. I know he talked about this with my master, but I have no idea what it's all about. That is all I know, Consul. I swear to the gods.'

296

'If that is truly all you know it is because it is all you choose to know.' I could tell by the change in the tone of his voice Cicero was getting down to the real purpose of his joining me in the curia. Caesar seems to give you a good deal of latitude in your travels. I have heard you are often sent out alone on business.'

I nodded, wondering where he was going with this.

'You could find yourself in no small amount of trouble for this little adventure, sneaking in here like this. It would be easy to believe you intended to steal something or perhaps lay in wait and do harm to a senator or maybe even one of the consuls.' With this, he looked me hard in the eyes. In spite of my efforts to remain composed, I'm certain he could see I was terrified.

With that, he got up and began to pace back and forth, as if about to launch one of his famous orations. 'Perhaps, we could help each other. I will forget I ever found you here, and in return, you will agree to help me. *Quid pro quo*. I'm sure you can recognize my man Tiro. Each morning your master is in court, I want you to meet him in the taverna near the west end of the Basilica Aemilia. Don't make him wait; be there first thing before any other business. I want to know what your master is up to. I want to know what Catilina and any other friends he might be talking to are up to. It is your duty to report to me anything your master or any of his associates might be doing to subvert the constitution, but I never expect a slave to do anything from a sense of duty, so I will make sure you are rewarded.' At this point, he somehow made a purse appear from the folds in his toga. He emptied it into his hand and leaning forward pressed some coins into my hands, holding them tightly and looking into my eyes. 'If Tiro brings me any useful information, the next time he meets you he will have more money for you. Add this to what you are saving and it won't be long before you can buy your freedom. Do we have an agreement?'

I was in no position to say no, so I simply nodded my head and said, 'Yes, Consul, we have an agreement.'

Cicero gestured to the two lictors and they joined him as he moved toward the front door of the curia. He turned to me at the door and said, 'Leave by the back door.' With that one of the lictors pushed open the heavy bronze door and they were gone. I knew the consul had twelve lictors, and since he left with two and had six waiting on the steps, I reasoned there would be four guarding the back doors to the curia, but they were no longer there when I left. I tucked the money into my belt and didn't dare count it until I was safely at home. It was three full denarii and I was that much closer to freedom.

I was in a quandary. That evening, just at sunset, I requested leave to retire early, telling Caesar I had a headache, which was true. I lay in bed staring up at the shadows cast by the oil lamps flickering down in the atrium, as their distant light played on the ceiling. I had no idea what I should do about Cicero, but I knew I needed to figure it out very quickly. I wanted the money Cicero was offering, but I had no doubt that if Caesar were to find out I was spying on him, he could quite possibly kill me. At last, I made up my mind. I decided it was more important to remain loyal to Caesar. I threw off my blanket and found my house slippers. When I reached the tablinum I was disappointed to see Demetrius was still with Caesar, joking and sharing a flagon of wine; I had hoped to speak with him alone. I thought about asking Demetrius to leave, but that would have been an insult and I was fairly certain Caesar would share what I had to say with him anyway. Neither of them noticed me in the shadows until I spoke.

'Master, I have something I need to tell you.' Both men looked surprised. I rarely referred to Caesar as 'Master,' and never in private.

'Have a seat, Polybius,' Caesar said this while sliding his chair back to reach an empty cup on the shelf behind him. It was Caesar's rule that this shelf was always stocked with empty cups in the event an unexpected guest wants to share his wine. Tonight I was that unexpected guest. Pouring my wine he said, 'What's on your mind?'

'A strange thing happened today. I should have told you right away, but I did something wrong and I didn't want you to be angry with me. However, it is important you know about it.' I planned to use my sneaking into the curia as a cover for why I didn't tell him immediately, as that would have been the loyal thing to do. 'Today, while you were delayed in court, I snuck into the curia. Over the past month I had been reading and talking about the building so much I just wanted to see what it looked like. I know only certain slaves are allowed in the building but I let my curiosity get the best of me.'

'Why are you telling me this? You could have said nothing and I'd never have known.' Caesar swirled the wine in his cup. 'There's more to this story, isn't there?'

'Yes, master, I was found out by someone.' I expected him to be angry, but he wasn't.

299

'Who caught you? If it was one of the guards, I'd expect you to be nursing some bruises right now?'

'It was the consul.'

Both Caesar's and Demetrius' eyebrows went up. 'Really?' Caesar asked, 'which one?'

I was about to answer when he stopped me. 'No, wait. Let me guess. If it were Hibrida, you would have been flogged and returned to me in irons. I would have paid a fine for it too. That man's a fool. So, it was Cicero!'

'Yes, master. He wants me to spy on you.'

'How much is he paying you?' Caesar seemed genuinely amused by the situation.

'He didn't say, but he did say I could make some money. Today he gave me a full denarius,' I lied. I thought about offering to give the money to Caesar but decided not to.

'He won't pay that much in the future. That was just to buy your cooperation. He will probably offer a sestertius. Insist on two.'

'I don't plan to sell him any information! I'm loyal to you.' I was surprised at Caesar's attitude.

'On the contrary, make as much off him as you can. I only insist we decide together what you tell him.' Both Caesar and Demetrius were smiling.

'When are you meeting him again?' Demetrius asked, joining the conversation for the first time.

'He wants me to meet his man, Tiro, each morning Caesar is in court.'

'That's no good,' Demetrius replied, 'It doesn't give us time to prepare what to say, and there could be several days between court appearances. When you meet Tiro, insist on a regular time and place.' Then, turning to Caesar he asked him, 'Why don't we have them meet at one of the baths every fourth day. While you're bathing, I'll make myself scarce and leave Polybius alone.'

'That's perfect,' said Caesar. 'I'm in court tomorrow. When you meet Tiro tell him you have no news to report, but use the opportunity to negotiate the time and place. And also, don't forget to discuss your price.'

'Push for more money,' added Demetrius. 'It will make it appear you are being truly disloyal. In the morning, I'll instruct you as to what to say.'

I felt as if a great weight had been lifted and my headache was now gone. I stayed up listening to Caesar describe the pros and cons of various military strategies he had been studying in his spare time until the oil lamps began to flicker and the flames began, one by one, to sputter and die and it was time for us all to go to bed.

I awoke early in spite of having gotten little sleep the night before. I had the same feeling of excitement and fear I remembered from my escape from the Titus household. It was at once thrilling and uncomfortable. Demetrius went over what I should say to Tiro four or five times requiring, each time, I repeat it back to him. I knew I could remember what to say, but I was afraid it would sound too practiced. After the salutatio, Caesar immediately went out to the street to talk

301

with the people who had gathered to accompany him to the forum that morning. This was his way of keeping contact with those who didn't rate an actual face-to-face meeting in his tablinum but still had a vote in the comitia. This was very inconvenient for me, but, naturally, Caesar didn't care as the voters were more important to him than my convenience. I was forced to gather my tablets and stylus and rush to put my street shoes on. As I was sitting in the vestibule hurrying to pull on my shoes, I asked Demetrius, 'What happens if I'm found out?'

He could see my distress, and it caused him to smile. 'Tiro will be angry, and Cicero will be furious, but nothing will happen to you. Cicero will try to find some way to punish Caesar politically, but what can he really do. He is already opposed to most of the programs Caesar supports. Remember, he is the one who is trying to have a man's slave spy on his master. If word of this becomes public, he will lose the trust of every man of influence, so stop worrying. This game is being played between Cicero and Caesar, and you are just a pebble on the board.'

'Why will Tiro be angry? He's just the messenger.' I was starting to relax.

'Demetrius smiled again. 'I'll leave that one to you to figure out.'

My meeting went surprisingly well and it didn't take me long to figure out what Tiro's stake was in the game we were all part of. The taverna we met in was at the corner of the basilica and had two entrances. The main entrance was the wide opening in the front, but there was also a side door. I arrived as scheduled and looked around for Tiro, but he was

302

not yet there and the place was filling up with customers. I took a seat near the back at the edge of a bench and placed my tablets and my canvas bag on the space next to me, trying to save a seat. I began to worry when almost every seat was occupied, as I knew it wouldn't be long before someone insisted I move my things.

I was scanning the throng of people moving past under the portico in front of the taverna, looking at each face trying to spot Tiro's, when I heard a man lean in next to me and say, 'Can you move your things, I need to sit?'

I did as I was asked without looking up. I was resigned to the idea that something had gone wrong and began to peel the boiled egg I had purchased. Just then the man leaned over and said, 'You are Polybius, correct?'

'Yes,' I said without taking my eyes from the egg, 'and you are Tiro?' For the first time I glanced over at him to be sure I was talking to the right man. Satisfied, I went back to methodically picking the remaining bits of shell from my egg."

At this point, Polybius attempted to take a drink of wine, but it dribbled down his chin. Realizing he had slid down too far on the cushions, he said with a raspy chuckle, "Please help me become vertical enough to drink my wine." After helping prop him up, I wiped his chin with the napkin from the table. He seemed genuinely surprised by this gesture and said, "Thank you, Lucius,that was certainly kind of you." I must confess I too was surprised I did it.

He then continued. "You must understand how I had conceived of Tiro in my mind. He was somewhat of a legend for his loyalty to his master. I imagined him to be much older than myself, but the reality was that when seen up close, I realized he was not yet thirty. I imagined him to be upright and proper, but he was quick with a joke and always had a sharp verbal barb to sling at someone. I assumed he would be quick and efficient and all business, but he was frequently willing to take an opportunity to linger over wine. All of the finer qualities I thought he possessed were a result of gossip overheard. As I'm sure you are aware, masters frequently complain in private of the sloth and inefficiency of their own slaves while comparing them to the model slaves of others, while publicly they boast of their own as paragons of hard work and good behavior. I came to realize that what I had believed true of Tiro was a result of what I had gleaned from overheard conversations in the Cato and Caesar households. Cicero frequently extolled the virtues of the man and it came to be widely believed. In a way, Cicero was right. When he needed to be, Tiro was all the things Cicero expected him to be. The reality was that he was accomplished at seeming one thing to his master and yet at the same time he would serve himself as much as possible. I learned much from this man over the years.

I was about to launch my prepared speech I had been practicing in my mind since I had sat down, when Tiro spoke. 'I'm supposed to offer you a sestertius for each bit of useful information you have, but I'm authorized to go as high as four. If you insist on four I'll look bad and Cicero might think I tipped you as to how high he would go. I propose I tell him you insisted on three, but we have to split that last one with two and a half for you and half for me. Occasionally, if you have something good, we'll say you asked for four and you'll get the full three.'

This surprised me. Later I realized if he told me he was authorized to go as high as four he could probably pay five, but at the time I had planned to ask for only two, so I was satisfied. 'Sounds good to me,' I replied. 'I don't have anything for you today, but I'd like to set up a regular meeting since I probably won't have much you can use every time Caesar has to attend court. What if we meet at one of the baths? Caesar likes to rotate through four different baths so he can make contact with more people.'

'Good idea, this place is too crowded. Someone's bound to overhear us talking,' he answered. 'Cicero does the same with three baths, but I can talk him into changing his schedule to put us both in the same place on the same day. The man has achieved the consulship but he still feels insecure enough about his position to crave information the way a drunkard craves wine. He has been building a network of spies that rivals the court of the Parthian king. Can you make it the bath on the Quirinal Hill?'

We worked out our schedules and settled everything rather quickly. Since Cicero had expected us to take quite some time, we made small talk and began to get to know each other a bit. I found that to my surprise I liked the man. We never quite came to completely trust one another but we did understand one another. I would feed Tiro the half-truths Caesar, Demetrius, and I agreed on to keep Cicero off balance and Tiro would repay me with money and the half-truths about Cicero that Caesar requested. I think we both knew the other was lying but as long as I was getting my money and Tiro was getting information to bring home we were both happy. I would write out what I had to tell Tiro to save time so we could enjoy a couple of hours of freedom. Our transaction would never take more than a quarter of an hour, and often much less time, and then we would either retire to the taverna beside the bath or to one just down the street. The one down the street from the bath was more fun. The men there spent their time playing at dice, and the drinking was more enthusiastic. Tiro enjoyed gambling with other patrons, but I scrupulously avoided it. After a couple of experiences losing money I opted to simply watch others lose their money. I was saving my earnings to buy my freedom. The owner of the taverna didn't allow slaves in his establishment, but since it was generally accepted policy to avoid having one's slave wear any badge identifying his status, he couldn't do anything to bar us. This was common practice, especially since the Spartacus rebellion. Slave owners feared that if we recognized each other on the streets of Rome we would come to appreciate our true strength and rise up against our masters. The irony is that even without any identifying marks or badges slaves always recognized one another. We could tell by the way our eyes met in recognition or the way we carried ourselves around each other. We were far more aware of our numbers than our masters. To this day I can tell a man or woman is a slave even if he or she is dressed like a wealthy pleb or his wife. We were not allowed to wear togas, but that did nothing to distinguish us from the vast majority of the city's plebs.

As winter turned to spring, Caesar began to provide more accurate information to Cicero, because Catilina's position continued to weaken and Caesar felt his association with the man was becoming a greater liability. By allowing Cicero to know what was really going on, we felt it would make it easier on him when Caesar decided to push Catilina out of the leaky boat.

Two days before the nones of Martius (March 5), Labienus brought charges against Rabirius. It was our expectation that less than enthusiastic judges would be selected as the duumvirs hearing the case, but Catilina had other plans. Using borrowed money he bribed the praetor in charge of supervising the lottery that selected the judges to choose Caesar as one of the trial judges. This infuriated Caesar. In a rare display of anger, Caesar with me in tow marched to Catilina's town house and raged at him, calling him stupid and dangerous and, the worse epithet of all, a political illiterate. Of course he contained himself until he was safely past Catilina's vestibule and had regained complete control before we set foot out the door, but I was frightened by the display. Catilina's zeal to secure a sympathetic judge in the case had a result that further infuriated Caesar, but amused everyone observant enough to figure out what was going on behind the scenes. Catilina paid the praetor a generous sum to see that Julius Caesar was a judge assigned to the case, but he didn't specify which Julius Caesar he meant. Afraid of losing his commission, the praetor played it safe and arranged for the names Gaius Julius Caesar, and Lucius Julius Caesar to both be drawn in the lottery. That's how both Caesar and his cousin were chosen as judges.

At this point, Caesar's main goal in having Labienus bring Rabirius to trial was to call into question the extent of the consul's authority when the senate issues the ultimate decree. He had by now all but decided to abandon Catilina in this election year. Caesar was always living in the present day, but looking ahead toward the future. He knew that the electoral process was becoming less stable over time and he saw opportunities there. I believe he was looking toward a time after his forty-first year."

307

Polybius paused, so I asked, "What was so special about that year?"

"Think, Lucius," was his reply, so I thought. I must admit the first thing I thought was that if I was Polybius' age I wouldn't be so patient. With time so short I would do things as fast as I could, but when it became apparent he wasn't going to answer me until I gave him my thoughts, I thought some more.

"His forty-first year would have been the year he completed his first consulship."

"Exactly!" Polybius smiled showing his old yellow teeth. "Caesar knew he would have achieved the ultimate prize as early as he legally could. He wanted or I should say needed to know he could still hold positions with imperium. He needed to know that he too could have several consulships as Marius had. Caesar saw the unstable politics of his day as an opportunity for any clever, resourceful man to gain and keep power for as long as he chose, but he knew the senate would try to block that. Each senator was and to a lesser extent still is in competition with every other senator as they climb the political ladder. One important tool for such purpose was the ultimate decree. He also knew Pompeius would have the same idea, and that rival had a head start in the game. As it turned out, Caesar was a man who was far more clever and resourceful than even he understood. In the end, however, he wasn't clever or resourceful enough to save his own life.

Caesar's cousin Lucius was a man with the character of soft clay. He was pliable enough that the trial was run as if there was only one judge. The structure of the perduellio law was such that the defense was almost irrelevant. The trial

308

judges started from the point of assuming the accused was guilty and the defense consisted of providing an excuse for the actions of the accused. It was a very quick trial. Charges were presented, supported by the official documents retrieved from the vaults in the Tabularium, witnesses were called to confirm Rabirius was present that day, and speeches were made for and against condemning him to a grisly death. Most of the senators failed to appreciate the significance of what was happening, but Cicero was, of course, the exception. As a result, he spoke for the defense during the trial, and also at every other opportunity.

Caesar didn't mind condemning the man to death, and I had even warmed to the idea because we were confident we had provided a means for Rabirius to be spared. The charge of perduellio provided for the convicted man to appeal to the comitia. His conviction could be overturned by a vote of seventeen of the thirty-five tribes, selected by lot. Caesar had also bribed the praetor to choose the tribes in which he had the least support and to select tribes that were most likely to favor Rabirius. Unfortunately, as was so often true in the confusing alliances formed by patrons and clients and marriages and divorces and shifting political support, many of those same tribes also supported Catilina. To eliminate this threat, Caesar made it very clear to Catilina that if he meddled in the process in any way, the two were finished as allies. He had also made it clear that Catilina was to see to it his supporters stayed home on the day of the vote. As trial judges, it was up to the two Caesars to set the date for the comitia vote, once the lottery for the tribes was held. Caesar delayed the vote as long as he could, giving Cicero a chance to make four more persuasive speeches as he argued before the people, laying out the reasons Rabirius should be spared. I recorded these speeches and I can still recall some lines from one I found

309

particularly interesting, as it made clear that Cicero understood that while Catilina's motive may have been to alleviate some of his debt, Caesar was using it to question the authority of the senate to pass the ultimate decree. In the first speech, Cicero said:

'The true plan of this prosecution is to banish from the republic the ability, passed down to us from our ancestors, which the majesty of the state and our dominion enjoys. What are on trial here are the authority of the senate and the imperium of the consul and the unanimity of the all good men to be used against any mischief or ruin designed to undermine the state. Therefore, as a handle for the destruction of these great obstacles to these designs, the infirmity, the old age, and the solitary condition of this one man is attacked.'

In the end, we were convinced even the gods were on our side. The weather turned very hot that spring, and as each day grew hotter, Caesar decided it was time to call the vote. It is difficult enough to get men to stand half the day in a queue waiting their turn to vote on a cool day; on a sweltering day voter turnout is always lower.

The day of the vote came and we rose early and confident. Caesar was in high spirits as we made our way to the Campus Martius for the vote. He loved any opportunity to appear before the people in any official capacity. The sky was dark and heavy that morning and it appeared the gods had decided to help us even more. We were forced to take shelter under the portico of the Basilica Aemilia when the skies opened and rain began to pour down. I beamed at Caesar. 'Nobody will come out to vote on a day like this!'

310

A slave was sent back for cloaks and when the rain lessened we continued on our way.

As it turned out, both the gods and Catilina had conspired against us. The storm passed quickly, and in its wake a gentle cool breeze followed. Shortly after we arrived at the corrals that had been set up for the voting, the tribal assembly began to arrive. Early on, it became clear Catilina had not lived up to his end of the agreement. The earliest to arrive were Catilina's men and they were shouting slogans and moving through the crowd making arguments in favor of condemning Rabirius. Caesar dispatched me and several other slaves to gather information about what was going on in the corrals and none of it was good. Catilina's men were being very persuasive. One of their strongest arguments was that seeing an old man thrown from the side of the Capitoline Hill would be a great show. Many of the rabble-rousers had also been provided full coin purses to persuade those who were the most influential in their tribes or those harder to convince.

I began to grow very concerned. You see, Lucius, the only reason I was willing to see Rabirius condemned was because I was certain the voters would acquit him; I knew he was innocent. During my interviews I had spoken to several slaves who were present at the curia that day and they each independently told me Rabirius did not and, in fact, could not climb up to the roof that day. I was most convinced by the testimony of an old slave who had served as Rabirius' nomenclator. He informed me that two days prior to the events, Rabirius had slipped climbing the steps of the Temple of Concordia, breaking his right wrist. His wrist was tightly bound and immobile, and, in any event, it was too painful for the man to pick up a stylus on that day, much less use his arms to scale the side of a building. It became apparent to me that

311

the guilty party was his cousin, a man also named Gaius Rabirius and long since dead."

"Why didn't you provide that evidence to Cicero so he could introduce it in court?" I immediately knew the answer as soon as the question left my lips.

"Because, Lucius," Polybius answered, "slave evidence can only be admitted at a trial when it is obtained under torture. I was not about to give Cicero the information that would compel him to have even a single one of those old men and women tortured."

"I ran back to Caesar who was by this time pacing back and forth on the temporary wooden tribunal erected for this occasion. My arrival interrupted his pacing. 'Caesar,' I panted, trying to catch my breath, 'He will be convicted! The vote is going very badly for him.'

Without a word, Caesar began to pace again with the fingers of his right hand pressed to his forehead, as if this extra pressure would force an idea to come to him. After a moment or two, his pacing slowed but didn't stop. I grew very concerned that I had helped condemn an innocent man to death, when Caesar spun around and grabbed me by the shoulders. 'The flag!' he said excitedly, staring into my eyes and giving me a shake. I had no idea what he was talking about until he pointed to the Janiculum Hill across the river. He grabbed a sheet of papyrus from one of his clerks who was about to add it to a growing stack on the nearby table, and without stopping to see what was on the sheet began to scribble a note on the back of it. While he was melting the wax to seal it before the ink was even dry, he said to me over

312

his shoulder, 'I hope you've found your breath; you're going to have to outrun death!'

LIBER XIX

Run I did, and I arrived just in time to save Gaius Rabirius' life."

At that point, Castor came into the room carrying a bowl of nuts of a type I had not seen before nor since. They were small with a hard pale shell that was split on one end. Polybius explained to me he imported them from Syria on the advice of a Greek physician. 'It is said they will help prevent the sudden death that occurs so often to the elderly.' As the nut matures the shell splits open making it easier to eat the meat of the nut.

Once Castor left the room, Polybius seemed distracted by the shelling of a difficult nut, and he sat quietly looking down at his fingers as they worked to separate the halves of the shell. Finally he put it back in the bowl and took another. "Perhaps you'll get that one and younger, stronger fingers can remove its shell."

My curiosity overcame my manners, and I asked, rather more impatiently than I intended, "What was in the note Caesar wrote?"

This brought Polybius out of his reverie and, tossing a shell on the floor, he continued his story. "The solution Caesar hit upon was elegantly simple. Whenever a vote is being taken on the Campus Martius, sentries, under the supervision of a praetor, are placed on the Janiculum Hill. This is an ancient practice that has served no practical purpose for hundreds of years but is still adhered to even today. In the

314

old days when Rome was surrounded by enemies and the army was drawn from the same men who would be voting in the Comitia Centuriata, it was thought prudent to keep watch for any surprise attack when so many men would be outside the city walls and unarmed. A bright red flag is flown on a tall pole that can be seen across the entire city, even from certain vantage points in the Subura. If the sentries ever detect danger, the praetor orders the flag lowered and the voting is immediately stopped so the men can hurry back into the city and defend it from the threat. Caesar's note instructed the praetor, Quintus Caecilius Metellus Celer, to lower the flag.

When I arrived, soaked in sweat and coughing and wheezing, I found Celer and some of his men playing at dice. One of his lictors moved to stop me as I ran toward the praetor, but I brushed past him. I was finally blocked by another, but at this point I was close enough to be recognized, and Celer said, 'Let him by, he's Caesar's.'

I fell to my knees in exhaustion before Celer and handed him the note. Gasping for breath, I coughed the words, 'Caesar…read…now.'

Celer took the note, and, after eyeing me suspiciously, he examined the note, trying to decipher the writing on the outside. 'Please sir,' I panted, a bit more in control of my words, 'it's what's inside.'

Celer cracked the wax and began to read the smeared writing. He abruptly stood up from his seat, and while still reading, pointed toward the flag with his left hand, shouting, 'Pull down the flag! Pull down the flag now!' The flag was lowered, and I was given water and sent on my way back across the river. I knew it had worked, because as I made my

315

way back toward the Campus Martius I encountered a stream of men moving in the opposite direction back into the city. Later that day, when I was walking home with Caesar, I asked him what the note said. All he would tell me was, 'I let Celer know it would be in his best interest to lower that damned flag at once.'

That day marked the final break in the personal relationship Caesar had with Catilina, but Caesar still needed to support Catilina politically if there was any chance of the land reform bill becoming law. I expected Caesar to again return to Catilina's home in a rage, but he simply ignored the man. Sometime later, when I asked him about it, he simply said to me, 'If you play with a snake, you shouldn't be surprised when it bites you. I had hoped he wouldn't betray my trust, but the man was desperate. He did what he felt he needed to do.' The Rabirius case was quietly allowed to fade away. A new vote was never called and it would be a long time before any renewed charges would be brought against the man, but after that day, Caesar let it be known it was always his intention to see the old man acquitted and it was Catilina who nearly had him convicted and killed. This event began the rapid erosion of the little support Catilina had left in the senate, although Caesar and Crassus continued to support Catilina in the build up to his trial, as they needed him to be eligible to run for the consulship as long as there was a tiny sliver of hope he might win.

Cato used his influence in the senate to twice delay Catilina's trial. At first Catilina, Caesar, and Crassus welcomed the delay, as it afforded a greater opportunity to persuade potential witnesses for the prosecution to develop lapses of memory. After the second delay, Cato's real aim became clear. As long as he was facing trial, Catilina was not

316

eligible to stand for the consulship and Cato intended to see that the trial date would ensure he couldn't be elected that year. The delay actually helped Catilina's case, for although Cato's reputation for integrity steadily grew, his actual influence with the senate declined as was inevitable when the end of his term of office drew near. In addition to this, many senators had begun to lose interest in the cases and Catilina was able to use his remaining connections, Caesar's influence, and Crassus' money to make more than one witness change his mind. An old freedman who had been a treasury slave at the time of the proscriptions conveniently died thirteen days before the start of the trial. It was rumored that Catilina had a hand in the man's demise, but, as the freedman was quite old, nothing ever came of it. As it was, Catilina was found to be not guilty of the charge with just enough time to announce his candidacy for the consulship.

Catilina's trial had served to remind everyone of the man's reputation for debauchery and questionable dealings as propraetor during his stint in Africa. The latest trial also reminded the public that he was found not guilty of extortion in that case two years previously. Demetrius counseled Caesar to publicly state he had abandoned Catilina's cause, but since it was common knowledge he had given the man his word, this wasn't an option. Caesar did not want to gain a reputation as someone who fails to honor his commitments. At the time I thought Caesar was being rather foolish since everyone who mattered could tell by Caesar's silence about Catilina's candidacy that he had withdrawn his support.

While all this was happening, Crassus and Caesar continued to plot Caesar's election to the office of Pontifex Maximus in spite of Metellus Pius' stubborn refusal to die. Each time they met, Crassus would assure Caesar that

Metellus' death was eminent. As it was, Metellus Pius did not die as scheduled. He managed to cling to life throughout the spring and into the summer. Crassus changed his mind in Junius of that year and counseled Caesar to skip the election for the post since Caesar had already begun canvassing for the praetorship. The vote for the consulship had been, since the time of Sulla, scheduled for the nones of Quintilis (July 7), meaning the vote for the praetors would be held two days later. Caesar was noncommittal on the question of whether or not he would seek to become Pontifex Maximus."

"Why," I asked, "did Sulla move the vote to Quintilis (July). I noticed in doing my research, elections for consuls and praetors had always been, prior to his dictatorship, held in Novembris."

Polybius took another sip of wine, as he tended to do when he was about to explain something in detail. "In the earliest days of the republic there were only the two consuls. This was adequate when Roman territory was limited and wars were being conducted with our close neighbors. In those days one consul would be able to lead the army into battle against an enemy while the other governed the city. As Roman imperium expanded throughout Italia, we were more and more frequently fighting wars on two fronts, calling both consuls away from the city. As a result, the praetorship was instituted, because it was deemed necessary to have an official with imperium who could lead our forces. Over time the number of praetors increased as the population of Roman citizens increased. One became two and two became six. This put great pressure on our election process. The law and our ancient cutoms required elections be completed in one day and the vote for six praetors had stretched that to the extreme. If an election couldn't be completed in one day the entire vote

318

would need to be rescheduled. Sulla increased the number of praetors to eight, making it impossible to complete the vote in Novembris because the amount of daylight was too short, so the election was moved to Quintilis (July)."

"Why not hold the election on two separate days?" I asked.

"The official reason is that the gods ordain certain days as good for elections."

"And the real reason?" I asked.

"The real reason is that an election over two days would mean the ballot boxes would need to be protected and secured by the very people with the greatest interest in the outcome of the vote. No man running for the praetorship wants his political enemies taking the ballot box home over night. An election that was costly enough to secure could fade away in the darkness of night. At any rate, the elections were delayed that year as a result of the charges of corruption that were leveled against the men running for the consulship. The bribery was so flagrant and so great as to make it impossible to ignore, and Cato vowed to prosecute whoever won the consulship. However, I was at this time not focused on that. My goal was to help Caesar be elected praetor. The vote was rescheduled for the nones of Sextilis (August) that year, meaning the election for praetors would not be held until two days after that. Crassus and Caesar were forced to be more circumspect in their bribery to avoid the charges spreading like a contagion from the men running for the consulship to those seeking to become praetor. This, of course gave us more time to shore up support before the official canvassing began and more time to spread out our bribery, but it also gave the same opportunity to Caesar's opponents. The election was again delayed as the debate raged on in the senate as to how to deal with the corruption until it couldn't be delayed any longer. The date was set for the nones of Novembris (November 5) as in the old days. Voting for the praetorship was then set to start at the first sign of the sun on the horizon two days later and would be hurried along at the pace of a chariot race.

At this time another meeting occurred between Catilina and Caesar. This was the third that I was aware of, but there may have been many others. When Caesar would attend private dinner parties I was rarely required to go along, and he frequently came home with bits of information that would come up in strategy meetings in the following days, leading me to believe Catalina attended some of those same dinner parties. This particular meeting happened at the baths on the Esquiline Hill. I was sitting on a bench having a clandestine meeting of my own with Tiro when Caesar and Catilina came strolling into the exercise yard with Catilina guiding my master along by the elbow and leaning in close to talk directly into his ear. He led him across the yard to the small conference room where a tall man who was, for once, unknown to me joined the two naked men. I recall he had golden hair and eyes the color of the sky. I was to later learn he was a barbarian from the north. After they entered the small room, Tiro abruptly cut me off in the middle of a lie about Caesar's finances. 'What's your man meeting with Sergius Catilina about?'

I looked directly into Tiro's eyes and was able to speak to him with complete honesty for a change. 'I don't have the slightest idea. Catilina and Caesar are old friends. For all I know they could be discussing the games for the Roman

Festival.' This conversation took place during the annual sixteen-day festival honoring the people of Rome.

Tiro looked down and tried twice to stomp on a spider with his bare foot as it scurried across the paving stone before him. The spider managed to put enough distance between itself and Tiro to live another day. 'There is an election very soon and they are both standing for office. We both know they are talking electoral politics.'

'What my master discusses with Sergius Catilina he doesn't share with me.' I was again uncharacteristically honest with Tiro. It gave me a strange feeling to be able to tell the truth.

Tiro was still looking down at the paving stone when he said to me, 'There is talk Catilina means to become consul by whatever means he can.... constitutional or not.'

'I haven't heard anything about his plans,' I answered. I could have speculated based on small bits of conversations I had overheard and cryptic lines in letters Caesar had dictated to me, but I sensed I was, once more, stepping onto those slippery rocks and said no more.

'If you do hear anything of Catilina's plans you will tell me, won't you?' I could tell by his tone that this information would be valuable to Tiro because it was important to Cicero.

'Of course. That is as long as your master is willing to pay the right price.'

My talk of money seemed to convince Tiro of my sincerity, but in my heart I wasn't sure what I would do. In those early days, I believed there was a price for which I would betray Caesar, but I wasn't at all certain how high that price was.

Tiro put his hand on my shoulder and squeezed. 'Let's put our shoes on and run down the street to roll some dice. Your man and mine have a meeting with each other this afternoon, so we have at least two hours before they notice us missing. I'll buy you a flagon of the good stuff.'

Tiro probably thought wine would loosen my tongue, but even then I knew that while I sometimes said more than I should while drinking, I was always on guard about what was truly important. I enjoyed his wine enough for Caesar to notice as we walked home in the deepening twilight. All he said about the matter was, 'Exercise caution when you let Tiro buy you wine. I need you to be thinking clearly when you meet with him.'

Metellus Pius finally died four days before the calends of Octobris (September 26) of the year Cicero and Antonius Hibrida were consuls (63 BC). More frequently, Caesar was setting other tasks for Demetrius and relying solely on me to act as his nomenclator, so I was with him when he learned of Metellus Pius' death. One of Crassus' slaves met us with a note from his master, as the trial Caesar was judging was adjourned at mid-day. On the way home, Caesar turned to me and asked, 'Do you realize what day it is?'

'Yes, Caesar I do,' I answered, smiling at him. 'It's the day we honor Venus Genetrix with a festival.'

'Do you suppose she's trying to send me a message?'

Venus was widely believed to be the ancestor of the Julii and was revered by the clan, but Caesar never seemed to take omens seriously unless they could be used to his advantage. 'You will be better equipped to answer that yourself, once you become Pontifex Maximus,' I was in high spirits. Caesar's confidence was infectious, but when I thought about things more deeply, my mood soured. I believed the goddess might be sending me a message as well, binding me closer to his service. I frequently needed to remind myself that in spite of the fact that Caesar was the best master I had yet known, I was still a slave and I had resolved to gain my freedom.

Caesar noticed my mood shift. 'What's the matter, Polybius? Don't tell me you've sided with Crassus on this one? Are you afraid I'll lose?'

Rather than tell him the truth and admit my real fear was that he would win, entwining our destinies more tightly together, I forced a smile and said with all honesty, 'I guess I'm just a little nervous about the future.' At this time I was at two minds. I was working every day to achieve the goal Demetrius laid out for me when I first joined the Caesar household; we needed to see Caesar elected praetor. At the same time, I strongly desired freedom.

Upon arriving at Caesar's domus, we were met by one of Crassus' slaves. He too had heard the news and wanted to learn Caesar's intent. 'Tell your master I intend to seek the post.'

'In that case,' the slave answered, 'I'm to ask you to meet with Master Crassus in two hours to discuss the matter.'

Caesar replied, 'I'll see him at his house at that time.'

The slave replied, 'Master wishes you to meet him at the temple of Venus on the Esquiline Hill.'

'Very good then,' was all Caesar said, pressing a coin into the man's hand and sending him on his way.

'The temple will be packed with people,' I said. 'Why does he want to meet there?' I was confused.

'He's arranging for us to run into each other by accident,' Caesar said. 'Now, let's find Demetrius and get to the bath quickly so we can attend to our religious duties this afternoon.'

On the way to the meeting with Crassus I asked Caesar the question that I had been asking myself for some time. 'Why do you want to be Pontifex Maximus?' Caesar had never appeared pious.

'It will make it easier for me to be elected praetor and that moves me one step closer to governing a province,' was his simple answer.

When they met, Crassus again tried to dissuade Caesar from running for Pontifex Maximus, but once it was clear Caesar wouldn't change his mind, Crassus intended to see him elected. The election for Pontifex Maximus was scheduled for twenty days past the funeral of Metellus Pius, making it only thirteen days before the election for praetor. Since the two elections were to be so close together, it was decided that he would combine his canvassing for both Pontifex Maximus and praetor. A loss in the run for the Pontifex post would doom any chance of being elected praetor, but Caesar insisted he was going through with it.

What seemed a thoroughly unremarkable meeting happened the following day. Or, I should say, at the time it scarcely seemed worth remembering. I only recall it because of an unusual occurrence of three days prior, that many doubt happened, but which I can safely vouch for. On the morning seven days before the calends of Octobris (September 24), I was sitting on the steps of the curia where I was frequently stationed during senate debates. Several senators liked to have their slaves wait out on the steps of the senate house should they need to send a message to someone during the session. Cato thought this practice lowered the dignity of that august chamber, but Caesar and other like-minded senators didn't care. In his constant need to plot his next political move, Caesar needed me to be able to run the latest news from the senate out to one or more of his supporters. At this time I was frequently running to find Labienus or one of the other tribunes, should Caesar feel the potential need to have some piece of legislation vetoed. On the particular morning in question, about an hour after the session of the senate had convened, a senator came rushing up the steps of the curia looking as disheveled as a drunken soldier on leave. I immediately recognized the man as Gaius Octavius, husband to Caesar's niece. I had always liked the man, because he, like Caesar, treated his own slaves and those of his acquaintance more as a father would rather than as an owner. I rose to my feet as I saw him huffing his way up the steps and saluted him warmly. He only stopped for a moment to say hello. 'I've no time to talk my boy, as I'm already quite late for the debate.'

'Is everything alright?'

A great smile broke across his face as he said, 'Everything is splendid! My wife just gave birth to a son this

325

very morning. That's why I'm late!' With that, he pushed his way through the small crowd on the steps and into the curia.

It has since been said that the senate was debating the fate of Catilina on that morning, but that would not occur for almost two months. They were, however, debating how to deal with the corrupt ways leading members of the senate were attempting to buy votes for the upcoming elections, and Catilina was a prominent member of that group, as was my own master. I followed Octavius up the steps and pushed my way right up to the open doorway to watch the reaction of the other senators to his news. The members of the senatorial class tended to become quite ebullient when one of their own produced a son. I couldn't hear what was said but a group of senators came down from the benches and crowded around Octavius, clapping him on the back and shaking his hands.

Now, at that time there was one member of the senate who was a frequent embarrassment to the house. Publius Nigidius Figulus fancied himself to be an accomplished astrologer. He was often going around warning people of portending trouble or cryptically suggesting a change in their fortunes. Of course, he was often right, as trouble sooner or later visits every man and there is not a day that goes by that one's fortunes are not liable to change. Most people, myself included, simply thought he was a madman. On hearing the news, Nigidius stood up, throwing his hands into the air and letting his toga nearly slip off, shouting, 'The ruler of the world has been born this day!'

I remembered this because two days later, rather than return home after our midday meal in the forum, Caesar led the way up the slope of the Palatine Hill. I recall looking wistfully back from the steps near the top at the place where

326

Gaius and I spent many nights during that summer of freedom just three years prior. On the way up the steps I asked Caesar, for the third time, where it was we were going. The previous times another had interrupted him before he could answer, but this time he turned to me with a smile and a wink and said, 'We are going to meet the ruler of the world.'

Knowing he was referring to Figulus' proclamation in the senate house, I smiled back, saying 'I am deeply honored.'

Standing at the southwest corner of the Palatine Hill, the Octavian Villa was small, but it was situated in what was then and still is the most fashionable neighborhood in Rome. When one stood on the steps in the front of the villa there was a fine view of the forum to the right, and if one were to walk to the corner of the house there was a magnificent view of the Circus Maximus and the homes and temples on the Aventine Hill just beyond that. If one had a sharp eye, it was possible to watch the races in the circus from that vantage without actually attending. The villa was very near the reputed house of Romulus, *alleged* to date back to the founding of the city."

I smiled at Polybius' skepticism about anything old in the city. He saw me smile. "You think the house truly does date back some seven centuries or more?" Now he too was smiling.

"That is what I've been told," I answered politely. I looked to Mela for help, but he was playing with one of the cats.

Polybius laughed and shook his head. "It scarcely looks the same today as it did when I was your age. It is constantly being repaired and rebuilt, so it is no more what it

327

is purported to be than the Regia, which has also been repaired so many times that nothing of the original structure remains. Now let me go on with my story. The Octavian villa was small, as I said, but nicely built to neatly fit into that little corner of the hill. The door slave announced Caesar's arrival and ushered him through to the atrium. I held back, waiting in the vestibule. When Caesar was nearly at the atrium, he realized I wasn't at his side and he stopped and turned. 'Don't you want to meet your sovereign lord, Polybius?'

'That would be you, Master Caesar,' I playfully answered. 'Besides, I think it might be improper. This is a family event.'

'Nonsense! Come along and meet my great nephew.'

We stepped into the atrium together to see Caesar's daughter, Julia, who had arrived at the villa about an hour earlier with her grandmother and with the new baby in her arms. The baby's mother, Atia, was just behind, hovering at Julia's elbow as a nervous new mother does when she reluctantly gives up her baby into the arms of another. Behind her was Caesar's sister, Julia, and Octavius, beaming proudly.

Caesar stroked his daughter's cheek with his left hand while simultaneously kissing Atia on her cheek. He then turned and gazed at the baby for a long moment before looking up over Atia's shoulder and saying, 'You have a fine looking son, Octavius, my friend.'

Atia eagerly took the baby from Julia's arms as everyone gathered around cooing and tickling his chin. I moved back, and watched the tableau of the family inviting a new arrival. That was my first look at the future Augustus Caesar. At the time, of course, we called him baby Gaius."

Sensing a pause in Polybius' story, I broke in with a question. "Do you really think Nigidius was able to foretell the future?"

"Lucius, I have seen many strange and wondrous things over the long span of my life, so I have come to accept that it is possible for a god to speak to us through the mouth of a feeble old half-mad senator. Of course, my belief would be stronger if I hadn't later found out he had made that same prediction on hearing of the birth of a baby boy every few months for two or three years. We are all capable of foretelling the future. It requires divine inspiration, however, to do so accurately. Now, I seem to have once again strayed from my primary account.

What struck me as more remarkable at the time was a speech I happened to hear on the day baby Gaius was born. It was by chance that I was near enough to the door of the curia to listen in as the senators spoke. Had I not followed Octavius up the steps, I would have been blocked by the crowd gathered under the portico. As it was, it was too packed with young men standing near the doorway for me to easily force my way back down to my place on the steps, so as long as no one objected, I simple stood pat and listened to the proceedings in the curia.

Once the excitement of the birth of Octavius' son had died down and the consul Cicero was able to restore order to the house, Catilina, looking peeved at the interruption, resumed his speech. 'As I was saying...' Hating to be upstaged, Catilina stared daggers at Octavius while he spoke. 'Rome is not the single great republic my esteemed colleague, Tullius Cicero professes to lead. No, my friends, there are two republics, each like a hideous monster in its makeup. The teeming masses of Roman citizens are like a giant creature, stumbling around without a head, while my opponents, dare I say my enemies, in this house form a separate republic. This second monster is like a massive ravenous head without a body since it is made up of men driven by a lust for personal wealth and for personal glory and there is no real substance to the support of these arrogant leeches. I cannot help the bodiless head. I cannot help the men among us who purport to lead in the name of the senate and people of Rome but only work to bring those of us with a long and illustrious family history of service to Rome down to their level.' At this, Catilina was staring and gesturing toward Cicero. 'I can, however, be the head for the great and powerful mass of true citizens of Rome, giving the leadership these good and humble citizens have longed for, for so many years.'

There was much more in this vein. I think I still have the complete text somewhere in my collection of documents. I'll find it and have one of my boys make a copy. This speech brought the house to its feet with most of the members denouncing Catilina as a slanderer. But, while several men seated near him moved away to the far ends of the benches, a surprisingly large number of supporters stayed near him, and a few more even joined the group, filling in the seats left empty by the others.

I soon put concerns about Catilina's intentions out of my mind, as I was kept very busy for the next two months. Politics in Rome have always been part theater, as my master was soon to teach me, and each man was expected to play his part. Through Crassus and his money, two days after the death of Metellus during the Equirria festival, a delegation of five of the other Pontiffs publicly asked Caesar to run for the office. The large crowd of citizens from the Subura gave Caesar an opportunity to feign surprise, and then in a loud voice he shouted out to the crowd, 'Let's see what the people who will be making the choice think! What should I do, citizens of Rome?' this particular festival always led to raucous behavior and feelings had been running high all day so, quite naturally, there were cheers and impromptu speeches imploring him to seek the post. It was all great fun and in the end Caesar humbly accepted the endorsement of the people and decided to run for an office he had been plotting to win for over a year. As you are no doubt aware, the Equirria festival is one of our most ancient festivals in celebration of the might of Roman arms. This festival honors the Roman cavalry in particular but as the festivals date back to the time of Romulus, there are always chariot races in addition to the races between men on horseback. With racing comes gambling and the high spirits generated by competition and wine. The good feelings enjoyed by the people can work to the advantage of an energetic and persuasive politician, but they can also make a crowd difficult to control. That day, Caesar managed his mob of supporters masterfully.

LIBER XX

Following by two days the announcement he would seek the Pontifice, Caesar publicly announced from the Rostra what everyone had known for some time; he was running for praetor. During those two days, I was engaged in writing letters, in Caesar's hand and that of other, both to and from the propraetors and proconsuls serving in the distant provinces formally requesting an endorsement. At least half of those men had already sent letters endorsing Caesar's candidacy, but they were being held from public view until Caesar was officially a candidate. I was charged with copying out the letters so that duplicates, in what appeared to be the original author's hand, could be posted in several prominent spots throughout the city and be delivered to surrounding towns to be nailed to their senate house doors. That Caesar would seek the praetorship had been a foregone conclusion, but now the two elections were linked in people's minds and he had doubled his number of opponents. With the second announcement came the formal start of canvassing. Each morning we would make our way to the forum with a large group in tow. Caesar wore the traditional toga candida, bleached with sulphur and powdered chalk to a white so bright that on a sunny day it hurt my eyes to look at him up close. During the first few days of Octobris, we made a tour of the neighboring towns around Rome. This was my first visit outside the walls of Rome any farther than the Janiculum Hill. During these visits Caesar was feted by friends at public banquets held in the local forum or on the steps of a temple. This was also the first time, while studying the map of Italia we now carried with us, that I got a sense of the size of Italia.

This in turn induced me to further study the map of the world kept by Caesar in his tablinum. I was stunned by how vast our world is, and by how much of it is controlled by Rome.

It was illegal for a candidate to give gifts or provide banquets for voters, but it was perfectly acceptable for his friends to do so. Of course, Caesar, using money borrowed from Crassus, was paying for the banquets. In each city the banquets fed nearly one thousand people. I found the amount of money spent to be staggering. With each banquet there was a series of speeches made first by local friends of Caesar and then by the candidate himself. Each day was a repeat of my earlier education as nomenclator. Demetrius would fill me in with the names and particulars of the men I had not yet met and I would store these with the appropriate image in my memory houses. In the towns closer to Rome I already knew many of the locals from their frequent visits to the city, but, as we moved further out to the more remote communities, there were many more men and sometimes even women to commit to memory. In the evenings I was kept busy collecting and copying out letters of endorsement from dignitaries of the Italian towns. The number of friends Caesar had from all levels of society and all walks of life was astonishing.

It was during this tour of the towns surrounding Rome that I got a glimpse into Caesar's political philosophy. I was working on some letters while Caesar and Demetrius discussed the next day's agenda. As Demetrius turned over the functions of the nomenclator to me, he began to focus on managing Caesar's personal household and the staff of slaves that did so much of the legwork for the campaign. The topic somehow turned to the possibility that Caesar might not win the upcoming election.

333

Demetrius said, in a matter-of-fact way, 'You can run again next year, and with a year to work on it, you will surely win.'

'I intend to win this election and the election for consul in my year, just as I have done my entire career.' Caesar was emphatic.

Demetrius countered with, 'I'm sure if you make a good showing, Crassus will finance you for another year.' He had misread the intent behind Caesar's words. I could sense it, so I looked up from my work to watch the exchange.

'I come from a very ancient and illustrious family, so it would insult *my* dignitas to not earn the distinctions that come with the people choosing a man to hold office. It would insult *my* dignitas.' By the way he emphasized the word "my," I assumed the reference to his family was simply a matter of good form, but once again, Demetrius didn't pick up on what was meant.

Mysteriously, Caesar seemed to be growing angry at this. Fearing he might embarrass himself, I tried to rescue Demetrius by joining the conversation and turning it in a lighter direction. 'Master Caesar, I've no doubt you'll win every office the first time you are eligible to run, but how will you do it?'

Demetrius looked over at me, but spoke to Caesar. 'Your father was a most dignified man, as was his father before him, and neither of them won office in their year. Neither of them even gained the consulship.'

Caesar pretended to ignore what Demetrius had just said and spoke to me instead. 'Polybius, more than any man of my generation, *and perhaps a generation or more before me*, I understand how to win office, and I'll use what I know to gain and keep imperium for the rest of my life.'

Demetrius looked incredulous at what Caesar had just said.

'What do you know that your opponents don't?' I asked. Talking about his plans seemed to lift Caesar's mood a bit.

'The people cannot possible know us, and I'm up against men who are paying just as much for votes as I am, so money can only keep us even. The secret is that people will vote for a man they *like*.'

'How can even a tiny fraction of the voters ever get to know you enough to like you?'

'They can't,' he answered bluntly, 'and if they could, there's a good chance they would dislike me.'

'That seems a paradox.' I was genuinely interested now.

'Not at all. The secret is, when you are with a man or a man's wife,' at that he smiled, 'you must for that moment treat that person as if he or she is the most important person in the world. Have you noticed, no matter how much the business of my life distracts me, I never let the person I'm talking to see distraction.'

I had noticed that, and I said so, but then I added, 'Of all the voters, few get to actually speak with you face to face.'

'All the better,' he answered. 'As I said before, many of them might not like me. The secret is to always keep in mind a man's public life is like the theater. People will like a man who *appears* likeable. I always laugh a little louder and smile a little wider when there is an audience. And, as much as possible, I let the crowds only see me with the people who do like me.'

Later that night, I considered the matter. I had noticed, especially since the campaign began in earnest, there seemed to be two Caesars, the man I knew as my master and the one who was ready to clap a common pleb on the back or kiss a matron's baby on the head. I realized, whenever we stepped out of the house, a show, of sorts, began. And, while canvassing for office, the show seemed to never end.

Along each road we traveled, we posted signs announcing Caesar's candidacy for the praetorship. It was considered unseemly to use signs of this nature to gain votes for a religious office, but the signs were frequently decorated with drawings of the symbols of office of the Pontifex Maximus.

What Caesar needed most in this election was an endorsement from Pompeius Magnus. As each day passed without a letter of endorsement, Caesar grew a bit more nervous. He never showed anything but total confidence when he was in view of even a single voter, but in private discussions his concern was evident. He was not simply worried that Pompeius would fail to endorse him, as that would be bad enough, but his greater concern was that he would endorse one of his rivals, and that would be disastrous. In typical fashion, Caesar decided to take a calculated risk. I was provided a sample of Pompeius' handwriting and my

336

master dictated his own endorsement from the great general. The hope was that the election would be over by the time Pompeius heard of the forged endorsement and could respond to it, but this was a long shot. Even in those days there was an excellent road system with posts at regular intervals all the way to the east, and Pompeius would probably receive the news in just a few days. If he was angry enough, he could have a response read out in Rome five or six days after that.

After the endorsement was posted and read out in not only the surrounding communities but also in Rome itself, Caesar called a meeting to plan how we would deal with the inevitable wrath of Pompeius Magnus. Crassus, as was his way, suggested Caesar bribe the general. Matius suggested Caesar offer to support a run by Pompeius for the consulship the following year. Demetrius even suggested Caesar offer Pompeius marriage to his daughter Julia. Caesar dismissed that idea at once. Labienus and Vatinius both argued for a massive bribe and the offer of support in any future election in which Pompeius should choose to participate. This was nearly our settled course, when I had an idea. 'Master,' I said as unassumingly as I could, 'I know I'm supposed to listen and not talk during these meetings, but if I may suggest an idea...' Crassus broke in and tried to stop me from finishing, but Caesar cut him off with a wave of his hand

'What's your idea, Polybius?'

'It seems to me that Pompeius has nearly as much money as Crassus.' In truth, he probably had more, but I wasn't going to say that in front of the proud man. 'I don't think a bribe will impress him much. From what I've heard, he's also very confident and his accomplishments support his confidence, so, while I'm sure he would welcome your

337

support, I doubt he feels he *needs* it to be elected to any office in the republic.'

Crassus was irritated by talk of Pompeius' wealth and accomplishments so he broke in. 'You said you had an idea, boy. You are simply telling us why you think the ideas of older, experienced men of substance won't work. Remember, you are a slave and we are the men who run an empire.'

I almost stopped talking, but my anger rose and I could tell by the look on Caesar's face that he wanted me to finish, so I ignored Crassus and, as calmly as possible, went on. 'What Pompeius never tires of is public honors. You can save a great deal of money if you simply arrange for the senate to vote him some extraordinary honors.'

The group fell silent, waiting for either Caesar or Crassus to speak. They both spoke at once.

'It will never work!' Crassus said, glaring at me.

At the same instant from Caesar came, 'You make some very good points.' And then while looking at me he spoke to Crassus. 'You're just saying that, Marcus, because you can't stand the thought of Pompeius being honored again. We need to talk about this.'

In the end, Crassus reluctantly agreed to the proposal, mainly because of the size of the bribe that would be required to buy the famous conqueror's support. He would be the one who would have to come up with the cash, increasing Caesar's debt to him substantially. A short time later, Labienus proposed that extraordinary triumphal honors be granted to Pompeius in recognition of his conquests in the east. None of

338

the senators, nor any of the other tribunes, dared oppose the measure.

As luck would have it, two tribes Caesar had great influence with were chosen by lot to be among the seventeen tribes that would vote for Pontifex Maximus. These were the Fabia, Caesar's own tribe, and the Suburana, the tribe that represented many of the citizens living in the part of the city near the Julian domus, and we knew we would carry them both quite easily. How much strength he had among the voters of the other tribes remained in doubt. I was both excited and nervous when the day set for the election of Pontifex Maximus arrived.

The evening before, surrounded by oil lamps, we made final preparations. The meeting was attended by perhaps thirty of Caesar's closest associates. At the start of the meeting Pompeia was present, but, as was usual when politics were discussed, she feigned a headache and left. The doors to the tablinum were fully opened since there were too many people to fit in the room in spite of its large size. Strangely, Caesar was perhaps the least active of the principals in attendance. Matius led the meeting with significant input from Aurelia. The campaigning was done for this election and the focus of the meeting was getting influential members of each tribe to the voting area of the Campus Martius as early as possible. Aurelia showed a remarkable command of tribal politics and frequently was allowed to overrule Matius' choice of who was to put pressure on an important member of a tribe. I was used to provide written instructions to each member of the group after final strategy had been decided on. It was well past dark when the meeting ended, but Crassus had provided a sizeable personal guard for the gathering, so the men left in two groups protected by his well-armed men. The guards escorted the first group who lived to the north and west home and then returned for the group living to the south and east.

Demetrius asked Caesar's permission to retire to bed, pointing out that the next day would be hectic, and Aurelia kissed her son on the forehead and made her way up to her cubicle, leaving me alone with Caesar.

'You know,' he said to me, 'perhaps I should have taken the money Catullus offered and dropped out of the contest. I could have then concentrated on becoming praetor.'

Catullus was one of the other two candidates for the office. Nearly a month prior, when Catullus sensed Caesar was gaining ground, he offered him a substantial amount of money to withdraw his name from consideration. Instead, Caesar spent even more money he didn't have and redoubled his efforts.

'That would have been an affront to your dignitas and would haunt you for years,' I said.

Caesar sighed and shook his head. 'Yes, Polybius, you are right about that, but if I don't win tomorrow, I'll have risked everything and lost. The case against me is ready to be brought to trial. Everything I own, and that includes you, will belong to someone else, and I'll be forced out of Rome.'

I hadn't considered that I would need to change masters. I was now as concerned as Caesar. 'Surely,' I said, 'Crassus will be able to stall the others for a month or more. Once you win the praetorship you will have imperium and they won't be able to bring you to court for a year.'

340

'If I lose tomorrow, I won't stand a chance at the praetorship.'

'It will take some time for your creditors to prepare a case, probably a month or two. That will give you time to come up with something.' I tried to sound upbeat.

'Crassus has already been preparing the case for some time now.' He said this with a sigh. 'I'll be brought to trial before the nones of Januarius (January 4).'

I was shocked, and said so.

'You have misread the relationship Crassus and I have. He's a businessman, and I'm an investment. Sooner or later I need to start paying off or he will cut his losses and get what little he can. You and I have given him plenty of evidence against me.' He sounded resigned to the possibility he might lose.

'When did I give him evidence?' I was hurt and surprised.

'You were the instrument I used to give him the evidence then. You were my talking tool. Don't you remember the promissory notes you wrote for me to sign?'

'Yes,'

'Did you ever hear a word about me making good on any of them? Did you ever write a second note clearing the debt?'

I was quiet. It is true that after that first loan of fifty thousand sestertii that I had witnessed, I prepared documents for at least three others, although Crassus didn't let me listen

341

in on the negotiations. I knew then my position with Caesar was even more precarious than it had been with Titus and Cato. That night I counted my money before going to sleep. Sadly, it was not nearly enough to buy my freedom. I looked at the frescoed walls of the cubicle I shared with Demetrius, and in the dim flickering light from my small lamp the images seemed to dance. It appeared Demetrius was sleeping in a garden on a hill overlooking the sea. Two lovely young girls picked flowers near his feet. I thought I would miss this place, but then reminded myself of the promise I made to the gods and to myself to live life in freedom. Once again, I resolved to plot my escape. As I lay down to sleep, I wondered if Fortuna would visit me in a dream, but I slept fitfully through the night without a single dream and woke with the sun. I was still on edge.

The morning was unusually cold, but the day was clear and sunny. Demetrius shook me awake early and we both dressed quickly in fresh tunics. There was a thin sheet of ice covering the water in the bowl on the table. Since I had so rarely seen ice, and never before in Novembris, I was reluctant to break it, but, after a nudge from Demetrius, break it I did. I splashed some water on my face to chase the sleep away and wrapped myself in a cloak. I could see my breath like fog in the crisp air, but there was no time to light a brazier, as there was much work to be done. Our task that morning was to hand out small, red, earthenware bowls filled with hot wheat porridge in front of Caesar's house and remind voters he was standing for the praetorship. Each bowl was inscribed on the inside with Caesar's name and the office he was seeking. The hope was that the recipient would keep the bowl and use it each day between now and the election. And, it was hoped that after every use he would think of Caesar. Hundreds of them had been made and distributed already, and there was an order

342

with the local potter, awaiting the result of today's election. Before letting a prospective voter go, we would remind him that Caesar needed his help that day in the election for Pontifex Maximus.

I was about to go back inside to request another batch of porridge from the cook, when the door swung open and Caesar and Aurelia stepped onto the low porch. Julia stood in the shadows in the vestibule, but Pompeia was nowhere to be seen, and I assumed she was still sleeping. She never rose until at least an hour past sunrise and some days it was even later than that. Aurelia stopped Caesar as he was about to join the waiting crowd in the street.

'I pray the gods, *and the voters*, favor you today.' I could tell she too was nervous about the election, but she smiled bravely, realizing the people in the street would be taking cues from both her and Caesar. At that moment I couldn't tell who the better politician was. Aurelia had certainly learned a lot helping first her husband and then her son navigate the city's political storm-tossed sea.

Caesar turned to her and kissed her goodbye. He lowered his voice so only Aurelia and I could hear him and said, 'I feel like a gambler about to throw the dice. Once I let them go, it's up to Fortuna to decide the outcome. I don't want to let them go so soon.'

Aurelia kissed him again and said, 'The time has come. Recall the proverb, *the voice of the people is the voice of god.*'

Remembering his part in the show, Caesar turned so the waiting crowd could see his face and said loudly enough for many in the gathered crowd to hear, 'I'll either return

343

home today as Pontifex Maximus, or not at all.' With that, we were off to Mars Field and the future.

Two stories are told of that pivotal election. The first is that Caesar won by an avalanche of votes. To hear this version, one would think that every member of every tribe came from the far reaches of Italia to vote for him. That this story is still to be seen in the works of reputable writers is a tribute to Gaius Matius and his pliable relationship with the truth. He worked very hard to give everyone the impression that Caesar was loved by all of Rome so that the voters in the upcoming election for the praetorship would want to back a certified winner. The truth is the voting was very close and if there had been only two men in the running, Catullus would have won. As it was, Lutatius Catullus and Servilius Isauricus split enough of the votes to give Caesar the slimmest of margins. It was late in the day by the time all the votes were tallied, but we walked home under a darkening purple sky with the sun setting at our backs, confident in our victory.

The following morning I was trusted to visit each of the fourteen Pontiffs and invite them to a meeting in the Regia. The Regia, as you are well aware is one of the oldest buildings in the city. Its antiquity is unquestioned, and is also patently false."

I once again felt compelled to interrupt Polybius and question what he had just said was unquestioned. "Everyone knows the Regia dates back to the time of the kings and probably to the founding of the city!"

"Yes, most certainly, there was a building on that site that served the same function, but, if you examine it closely, you will see there have been so many repairs that virtually

344

nothing of the original structure save the foundation stones remains. But, that is neither here nor there and I mention it only in passing. The meeting I was helping arrange was to plan Caesar's investiture as Pontifex Maximus and, more importantly, to turn over the keys to the Regia and the Domus Publica. Caesar wanted to move closer to the forum as soon as possible and with as much fanfare as we could arrange.

This mission to visit the fourteen Pontiffs took me much of the morning as they lived in three different areas of the city, and I was made to wait in the queue for the salutatio for two of the Pontiffs just to deliver my message. It took so long to see the first eleven pontiffs that the last three had already left to conduct the day's business in the forum, and I needed to locate them there. All in all, it was a very pleasant way to spend the morning. It was another unseasonably cold and sunny day, but the sun on my face and my wool cloak kept me warm. I must confess, I took some extra time after the last message was delivered and visited some of the places where I'd spent so many days during the months I was free. Sitting on the slope of the Palatine Hill where I'd spent nights sleeping with Gaius' arm over me made me sad, so I decided to return home before the melancholy mood took hold and made me miserable for the entire day. Twice that morning I gave serious consideration to never returning, but I had made no preparations and my money was stored in the strongbox in Caesar's house, so I realized that to run away was, for now at least, only a dream. I was on my way home when I encountered Caesar on the Argiletum almost at the forum. He had Demetrius by his side and an even larger crowd of supporters than on any other day.

He greeted me with a huge smile, throwing an arm around my shoulder. 'All finished with your mission?' he asked. 'I've already received replies from half the Pontiffs, so the meeting is on for tomorrow.'

'Yes, Caesar, I had to track some of them down in the forum, but I managed to put your summons in the hands of each of the Pontiffs.' My melancholy mood had evaporated and I was feeling good again.

Caesar said to me, as we walked rapidly into the forum, 'There's something I need you to do for me.'

'I am yours,' I replied with the formal answer of a slave to a master.

'I have had some boxes of documents and scrolls brought over from the Regia. When we get home from the bath today I want you to start figuring out what I'm supposed to do in this job. I'll need to learn the rituals. I've seen most of it, but to be perfectly honest I often didn't pay close attention. It'll be up to you to keep track of what I need to do each day. I'll want a report at least twelve days in advance, and I'll need to know the religious significance of every one of our damned festivals and such. You'll have to teach me, but just what I need to know to make a good show of this.'

'Me?' I asked rather stupidly.

Caesar ignored my consternation. 'You're far more pious than me. I've noticed you mumbling a prayer each time we pass a shrine on the street. You'll be great at this!'

And with that, the Pontifex Maximus of Rome put a fifteen-year-old slave boy in charge of the state religion.

We spent the rest of that day as we spent every other day for the past month, canvassing for the praetorship in the forum in the morning and then canvassing for the praetorship at the baths in the afternoon. The evenings were spent with Demetrius, planning the next day's meetings and such. Most often Caesar wasn't involved in this planning since he needed to attend a different dinner party almost every night. When all this was done, late into the night, wrapped in a cloak with a smoky brazier by my feet and two oil lamps on the table in my cubicle off the tablinum, I studied the rituals of Roman religion and the duties of the Pontifex Maximus. I was getting little sleep during this period of time. Caesar was dividing his time between the Domus Publica and his home in the Subura, and this was most inconvenient for me. Caesar liked to be briefed on his religious duties in the morning before the salutatio. This meant that I was constantly shuffling boxes of scrolls between the two homes. It also made planning his schedule more difficult since with Pompeia permanently installed in the Domus Publica, my master had greater opportunities for trysts with Servilia at his house in the Subura and time needed to be allotted in the middle of the days when she was available. Since Servilia's husband was canvassing for the consulship, he was seldom home and she could meet Caesar quite often. It seemed impossible to me that Pompeia could remain unaware of Servilia's frequent visits to the Julian Domus, or that both Servilia and Pompeia knew nothing of the less frequent but still regular visits by Mucia, but nothing was ever said. As it would later turn out, Pompeia really didn't care.

As I've said before, Caesar was quite particular about his appearance, and, as you might imagine, the artificially whitened toga candida shows dirt far more readily than the regular toga a man wears. This led to frequent toga changes,

347

and on one occasion, Caesar's toga was splattered with animal manure thrown up by the wheels of a fast moving cart. As we were near enough to the domus, I was sent home to fetch another whitened toga. This was the occasion of my first meeting with Cornelia, the laundry girl for the Domus Publica. I remember feeling flustered as I spoke to her, as I had so little experience with girls my own age and I found her vivacious personality and natural beauty tug at the strings of my heart. But, I had much work to do so I put her out of my mind.

LIBER XXI

Three days prior to the consular election, I learned of Catilina's plans. As you well know, every election is solemnized with sacrifices and other religious observances. In fact, an election cannot take place until an auger and a haruspex are consulted. I'm not too sure what would happen if they said an election could not occur, but I believe, after a great deal of fuss, the vote would be rescheduled. As a result, Caesar was kept busy not only with his own campaign but also with religious ceremonies all through the days leading up to the election. This meant I too was kept very busy. Caesar was often forced to meet with the college of pontiffs or the Virgo Vestalis Maxima long after the sun had set. On this particular night, Caesar had called the pontiffs to meet at the Regia, right across the way from the Domus Publica where he was now staying almost full time. As usual, I was awake and working in my small cubicle just behind the tablinum. I preferred my work room at Caesar's house in the Subura better, as it was smaller and easier to keep warm; in this workspace, I often found it necessary to drape a cloak over my shoulders as I worked. I was writing notes thanking prominent men for their support when I heard a sound in the tablinum. I knew Pompeia and Caesar were both out for the evening, and both Julia and Aurelia were asleep, so I got up to investigate. As I stepped in through the open back of the room, I could see a figure silhouetted against the dim moonlight coming in through the open roof of the atrium. The figure stood motionless.

'Who is it,' I asked with more than a touch of fear in my voice. Since my brief escape to freedom, I've always been unnerved by strangers approaching in the night.

'It's Marcia.' Her soft, quiet voice almost sang the name.

I sighed in relief and irritation. "My master is out. He is expected to be quite late, so you can either leave a message with me or return at sunrise.' I turned to go back to my work.

'I didn't come here to see the pontifex. I came to see you, Polybius.'

I was once again nervous, and I swallowed hard and turned to face the silhouette. Marcia was now much closer, she was, in fact, close enough to reach out and run a long, slender finger across my chest, which is exactly what she did."

At this point, Mela interrupted to ask Polybius, "Who was Marcia?"

"You do have a way of interrupting the dramatic flow of my story," he answered, sounding a bit peeved. Mela turned red and looked at his folded hands.

"I'm afraid I lost the thread of your story," I said, coming to my brother's rescue.

"I'm getting there, but if you boys insist on knowing, I'll tell you straight out. Marcia was one of the vestal virgins. She had told me when we first met, just after Caesar and his family moved into the Domus Publica, that she had been a vestal for eight years, which would mark her as eighteen years of age. It was her special task to carry the most important

350

messages between the Virgo Vestalis Maxima and the Pontifex Maximus. The Virgo Vestalis Maxima was a very pious woman, and observed all the traditions including the tradition of appointing one of the younger vestals to act as the go between with the chief pontiff. She wanted the world to know there was no impropriety in her relations with him. On the very day we met, Marcia seemed to me to be very forward for a vestal. She looked me up and down the way a matron appraises a duck hanging in a poulter's shop. Marcia had long, blond hair braided down her back and large gray eyes. Her waist was small, but her bosom was full for a girl her age, and she had a way of parting her lips that seemed to invite a kiss. This unnerved and frightened me."

"As I was saying," Polybius said, pausing to take a sip of wine, "Marcia ran her finger across my chest. I jumped like a willow switch had flicked me. I swallowed hard enough to make a gulping sound, and stammered, 'W-why do up w-want to se-se-see me?' I knew quite well why she wanted to see me.

'I find you very much to my liking.' She actually licked her full lips as she said this.

'I have work to do' I tried to sound in control, but I could feel sweat trickle down my sides.

'I won't keep you too long.' She had leaned in close enough so I could feel the heat of her breath on my cheek.

'But you're a vestal virgin.' I thought this might save me.

'You are a slave, silly, so it doesn't count.' She laughed as she said this.

351

'I believe it does.' I not only believed it, I knew it. Regardless of the standing of the man, a vestal virgin had sex on pain of death, for both herself and the man.

Marcia leaned in even closer and kissed me deeply on the mouth. I must confess I felt an excitement I had not before felt and I began to kiss her back. She took my left hand in hers and guided it to her right breast. Her nipple was hard as a stone. With her other hand, she took my right hand and brought it up between her legs. It was then I realized she had pulled her tunic up in the front and tucked it into her belt. I felt my hand buried in her pubic hair and pressed tightly against her vulva. I was at once thrilled and terrified. She let my hand go and grabbed my stiff penis, stroking it through my tunic.

I thought I would ejaculate just then, when a voice took away the thrilling spell of sexual arousal and replaced it with thrill of pure terror. The doorman was talking with someone in the vestibule. To be caught, projecting an erection while in a darkened room with a vestal virgin with her vagina exposed, would mean certain and horrible death for a slave. Marcia let out a small groan of disappointment, but seemed otherwise nonplussed. Taking my hand, she led me toward the back entrance to the tablinum. Just as we were about to step out the back more voices rang out from the direction in which we were moving. I never learned who it was, but I suspected it was some of the other household slaves. The public slaves attached to the Domus Publica were so numerous it took me almost a month to meet them all.

At this point, fear caused me to take control. I pulled Marcia back in the other direction, intending to slip out into the shadows in the front of the room, but it was too late. The door slave, oil lamp in hand, was already leading two men across the atrium. Now, Marcia did lose her composure.

'What should we do?!' I had to clamp a hand over her mouth as I dragged her, one hand on her waist, to the side of the room. Hidden in the wall, was a small narrow space. The hinges were so cleverly concealed and the door matched the rest of the wall so perfectly, it was undetectable with even the closest scrutiny. I myself would never have found it if there was not a reference to a 'secret listening-room' in one of the former Pontifex Maximus' private records. Old Metellus Pius had installed the room to have a slave listen in on private conversations he wanted a record of. There was only room for one in the small space, but I managed to force my way in behind Marcia. In hindsight, I realize I should have pushed her in alone and made up a story as to why I was fumbling around in the dark tablinum. I may have sounded suspicious, but not criminal. As it was, I was pressed in against her, and there was barely enough space to force our way in far enough to shut the narrow door. I was certain the three men in the tablinum would hear the sound of my beating heart.

'Master Caesar will be with you very soon,' I heard the door slave say, 'I will have wine sent in for you while you wait.'

With that, the man left the two visitors alone. I recognized Catilina's voice at once.

'Are things ready up north, Gaius?' I cursed the fact so many men were named Gaius.

'Lucius, you have asked me the same question seven or eight days in succession. If you win tomorrow, it won't matter, but, yes, we have three good legions,' the stranger

353

replied, 'and if you can get Caesar to make a speech or two in the next couple of days, you might just pull off a win.'

'You and I both know I don't have a fucking chance.' Catilina was in a sour mood.

'I'd put it at even odds,' the mysterious Gaius answered. 'Just get Caesar to support you. If he does, Crassus will come along.'

'If he doesn't, Caesar can die alongside Crassus!' Catilina was speaking with his characteristically indiscrete volume'

'Quiet, Lucius! Do you want the entire city to hear? It's said the walls themselves have ears in this house. Is it still on for four days before the calends?'

This time, Catilina lowered his voice to nearly a whisper, but thanks to the closeness of our hiding space, I had my ear pressed to the inside of the wall. The man named Gaius didn't realize how accurate he was about the walls of the Domus Publica. 'You'll get your order when the time is right, but here's where things stand now: Just after sunset, Sextius will have his men put the Subura to the torch in three or four different places. There's a torchlight ceremony that night tied in with the festival and all the important senators and the magistrates are involved. I'll have agents ready to attack Cicero and Hibrida and their followers as they leave their houses for the forum. Any who survive will have to deal with our forces as we march on the city. One way or another, I'll be master of Rome at the start of the year. Either I win the election and become consul on the first day of Januarius, or I lose the election and become dictator on the calends of

Novembris (November 1). If I get Caesar's support tonight, we can take his name off the list.'

Gaius sensibly answered, 'Many of those men will have lictors with them.'

'My men will have gladiators,' Catilina countered.

The torchlight ceremony was part of the fourteen-day festival of the plebes, and as Pontifex Maximus, Caesar's presence was required.

At this point, Marcia pulled up my tunic and began to fondle my penis. My body refused to listen to my mind and I became aroused again. Marcia was giggling at my discomfort as I tried to push her hand away in the hot, cramped space. I managed to push my lips right up against her ear and whisper, 'You will get us both killed, *vestal virgin.*'

I believe it was the reminder of her status as a vestal that caused her to release my penis. I'm certain it was not out of any sense of religious duty, but rather the knowledge that the punishment for any vestal who breaks her vow of chastity is to be entombed alive.

The two men moved the conversation to more conventional politics with talk of canvassing and offering late bribes, when I heard Caesar enter the room.

'Gaius Manlius!' Caesar was being his friendly public self, and I now knew who the mysterious Gaius was. Gaius Manlius was of the branch of the Manlii who were outside the senatorial class. He had made a fortune serving under Sulla in the civil war but managed to lose it through bad investments and gambling and expensive women. The

355

gambling and expensive women were probably the reasons he became an associate and supporter of Catilina. You know the old saying about "birds of a feather."

Apparently, Caesar acknowledged Catilina with a nod or gesture, as I didn't hear him speak his name. I missed much of this new conversation because Marcia shifted position, forcing me back, and I now found my ear pressed against her breast. I was afraid to reposition myself, as I wasn't sure whether or not Caesar knew of the secret space where we had hidden ourselves, but I knew he would not be content to assume mice in the walls produced any sounds we made.

The meeting was brief and soon I could hear the men saying their goodbyes. I decided to take a chance and gamble that Caesar would, since Manlius was not among his intimate friends, walk the two men to the vestibule. My plan was simple but risky. I would open the door of our cramped space enough to be sure they had left the room and then we would slip out through the back of the room and into the peristyle. Once I got Marcia out of the tablinum she would be on her own. I knew if one of the virgins was missing for too long there would be a search and sooner or later the Virgo Vestalis Maxima would realize the only unguarded door out of the villa of the vestals leads directly into the Domus Publica. This door was fitted with a very clever lock that could be unlocked from either side. There was supposed to be only two keys to this lock. One key was in the possession of the Virgo Vestalis Maxima and the other key under the control of the Pontifex Maximus. Either the door had been left unlocked, or there was at least one extra key. If we made a sound, Caesar might turn around to look. There was also the chance one of the household slaves would still be up and about. The plan was dangerous, but it was the only option.

We managed to slip out without being seen by the three men as they walked along the portico of the atrium toward the vestibule in the front. The peristyle was dark with the moon being the only source of light. Once out of the secret space in the wall, I pushed Marcia toward the back and I turned toward the latrine, planning to use that as my cover should anyone see me. Marcia grabbed my wrist and pulled me toward her and tried to kiss me, but I turned my head down and away and her lips landed on the top of my head. I wrenched my arm free and turned quickly and walked away, hoping she wasn't foolish enough to follow. While passing from the doorway to the latrine, I heard the small sound of metal on metal from the lock on the back door. I sighed with relief and slid down on the floor next to the door, pressing my sweat-soaked back against the cool wall.

Because my duties as nomenclator forced me to work odd hours, I was given a small cubicle all to myself. In reality it was little more than a closet, but it was a treat to not share a cubicle with four or five other slaves. After a quick stop in the latrine, I went straight to my cubicle where I could figure out what to do. I knew if I warned Caesar of Catilina's plans he would be furious I had spied, but if I didn't warn him it would mean civil war for Rome, and more importantly, death for Caesar. He was the best master I could hope for, and while I was still determined to find freedom, I knew I was better off with him for the time being than I would be with almost any other master.

LIBER XXII

I peeled off my tunic that was wet with sweat, and bent over to find a fresh one in my trunk. Just as I was slipping it over my head, I heard a female voice say, 'Polybius?' My heart skipped a beat as I imagined Marcia had returned. I quickly fumbled to lower my tunic before turning to face her. Rather than seeing Marcia, It was Cornelia who stood in my doorway smiling. 'I didn't mean to startle you,' she said apologetically. I was both relieved and frightened. My fear turned to near panic when she said, 'I saw you with the vestal.'

'It wasn't what it looked like,' I quickly said.

'Don't worry, I won't tell. I just wish you were with me.'

'Really, it was not what you think. She forced herself on me, and then we had to quickly find a place to hide.'

'You shouldn't be fucking vestals. It's just stupid to put yourself in a position that will get you killed.'

It suddenly became very important to me that she believe me, so I laid out as much of the story as I could. I told her about the way Marcia had tried to seduce me and about the secret listening space and about our narrow escape.

'Spying on Master Caesar may get you whipped, but you did nothing more seriously wrong.' She was looking into my eyes and she sounded concerned. After a pause she added,

358

'Why are you still so nervous? What are you not telling me? You can trust me Polybius.'

I realized she was holding my hand, and for reasons I still don't understand, in that moment, I did trust her, but I didn't tell her about the Catilina conspiracy, as it came to be known. I didn't yet trust her that far.

I slept little that night, but shortly before sunrise to the sound of the first chirping of the birds I drifted into a fitful sleep. In times when I have grave concerns on my mind I seem to have no trouble falling asleep, but I often do not stay asleep. I wake several times and find myself turning my troubles over in my mind, and on this night my mind was deeply troubled. I had the problem of how to warn Caesar of Catilina's conspiracy and the danger he faced. I also had the problem of dealing with Marcia. Caesar was Pontifex Maximus for life, and Marcia would be a vestal virgin for at least another twelve years before she was released from her vow. When in Rome, it would be impossible for me to avoid her forever. When sleep did come, Fortuna, once again, visited me. She came to me in my dream as she had in the past. I noticed the light through my closed eyelids and thought I was awake and it was the light of dawn streaming through the small window of my cubicle, so I sat up rubbing my hands over my face. Instead of sunlight, the light streamed from the goddess sitting at the foot of my bed. I could actually feel the warm glow of her light as if I was sitting before a small fire. She was smiling and I smiled back, genuinely happy to see her, after so long an absence.

Her voice was still like music. 'You thought I had forgotten you, Tychaeus.'

I could only nod my head.

'The gods have memories that span centuries, and some of us forget nothing. I remember all that has happened and all that is yet to happen.'

'I don't know what you want from me.' I found my voice.

'I want you to trust in your abilities. You have been given certain talents so you can use them to help pilot Rome's ship on the course I have charted. I've put many hands on the rudder but the vessel will not go in the right direction without yours.'

'Tell me what to do,' I pleaded.

Fortuna only smiled. 'You will discover what you must do. You were right to trust Cornelia. Continue to trust her.' She got up and briefly stood looking at me before moving toward the door. I remember thinking it odd that a goddess would need to use a door. As she turned to leave, she said, 'And, quit worrying about that other silly girl.' With that she was gone and I awoke, sitting up in bed, staring into the dark. I should tell you how Fortuna appeared when she visited me. She was incredibly beautiful with full lips and dark curly hair. Her dress was a shimmering gold cloth, and she was wrapped in a pure white mantle. On her head she wore a golden crown. On this night she held a cornucopia brimming with natural bounty in her left hand and in her right she held the sort of oar used to steer a ship, but her oar was attached to the globe of the world. Behind her and moving with her was a golden wheel with the shape of a human skull on its hub.

I lay down and was able to fall asleep easily and when I finally did awaken, the sun was already higher than usual. I had to hurry, so I splashed water on my face and used the chamber pot rather than run down to the latrine. I felt bad that another slave would need to empty and clean my pot, but I had no choice. I ran down to the tablinum expecting to find Caesar there, but instead I found an elderly slave named Phoebe polishing the furniture. I never came to like her because she was always in a sour mood. Her teeth hurt constantly and she never smiled. She turned to me with a scowl and said, 'If you're looking for the master, he's in with the barber.'

I ran to the room where the barber worked and slowed to a walk as I approached the doorway. Caesar was looking at his reflection in a mirror the barber was holding in front of him. His eyes shifted from his own reflection to mine. 'Did you oversleep, Polybius?'

'Yes master, I'm sorry.' I tried to sound my usual self in spite of my lingering anxiety from the night before.

Caesar pulled off the cloth the barber had wrapped around him to catch the hair clippings and handed it to the man as he rose to his feet. 'Walk with me,' he said, so I followed as he walked to the dressing room. 'I know what you did last night.'

I felt a wave of nausea and broke into a sweat. 'I'm sorry master. I'm so sorry. How did you find out? Let me explain!' I was in a panic and I felt light in the head as one does when he is about to faint.

'No reason to explain,' he said. 'I saw the laundry slave leave your cubicle. A young man needs female

361

companionship. In fact, an old man needs a woman too.' Caesar clapped me on the back as he said, 'If you want to have sex with her you may. Just don't get too attached. If all goes according to my plan, in just over another year we'll be leaving for a province.' With that we were at the dressing room and Faustus was waiting to wrap Caesar in the toga candida. 'Just don't let your fun with the girl make you late for work again.'

I was intensely relieved. 'Don't worry. It won't happen again.'

It was another long day, dealing first with the ever-growing salutatio, followed by an appearance in court, and campaigning in the forum. It took twice as long to get to the baths since Caesar now had to stop at every corner as we made our way through the Subura and make a short speech, oftentimes standing on a bench or the low wall of a fountain. At each stop, I would need to point out and provide names for all the influential people he needed to pretend to know and then I would listen to the speech yet again. After I had heard it two or three times, I began to truly appreciate what a naturally gifted orator Caesar was. While men like Cicero mastered the art of public speaking through endless practice, Caesar was the master of improvisation. He could recite the same speech five times in the span of an hour or two and make it sound fresh each time by changing his tone or inflection to suit the mood and character of each new crowd that gathered. Once again it was past dark when we made it back to the domus at the edge of the forum. Normally I would be afraid to walk the streets so late at night, but since Caesar began campaigning, there was always a crowd of men to accompany him. I had assumed this would cease after he won the praetorship, but, in reality, the crowd that joined him continued to grow for the rest of his life.

More in answer to what Fortuna told me than out of any real belief she could help me with my problem, I sought out Cornelia when I finally finished my work for the night. I knew she usually stayed up later than most of the others in the house. After everyone else had gone to bed, she would go around gathering up the dirty laundry we would each leave by our door or in a designated spot near the laundry room. She said laundry was much easier to do if the clothing was allowed to soak overnight. She also needed to prepare the more delicate or more heavily soiled garments so they could be taken to the professional cleaners in a shop about a half-mile down the Sacra Via.

I found her leaning over a tub in the laundry room. 'Hello Cornelia.'

She jumped up turning quickly. 'Polybius! You startled me.' Then with a smile she said, 'I suppose it's only fair, after I snuck up on you last night.' She shook the water from her hands and carefully pulled a lock of long black hair from her face, tucking it behind her left ear.

'I didn't mean to sneak up on you.' I was embarrassed.

'Last night, it *was* my intent to sneak up on you,' she answered. 'I'd hoped to see you with your tunic off. I was just an instant too late, but I liked what I did see.' She laughed teasingly. I liked her laugh. It wasn't the silly laugh of a girl, but it wasn't the loud crude laugh of a rustic slave woman. She laughed like she could actually be descended from the aristocratic family that matched her name.

363

What she said made me blush. I didn't understand at the time why I was suddenly attractive to these pretty young women. Looking back with hindsight, I now understand that much of my attractiveness was derived from my close association with Caesar. The more famous and important he became the more important and appealing I became. I was also uneasy about the fact that I didn't really know if I found these girls attractive."

Mela interrupted, as was his way. "If you didn't find them attractive, why was your prick stiff?" I was both embarrassed by my younger brother and glad he asked the question, as it had also been on my mind.

Polybius surprised me and embarrassed Mela with his candid answer. "As you no doubt know, young Mela, at your age a stiff wind can lead to a stiff prick. I'm sure you've had to hide more than one erection, perhaps after looking at a statue of Venus or maybe even a plate of vegetables. While most of my teen-aged masturbatory fantasies involved the men and boys I knew, I often thought about girls and women as well. I once or twice and only very briefly, imagined how Servilia would appear naked, but since she was Caesar's mistress and old enough to be my grandmother, I quickly decided she was far from my liking. I was, in those years, a very sexual creature and my tastes had not yet narrowed.

But, you have once again caused me to stray from my story. Let's return to that laundry room of so long ago. 'I need your advice,' I said to Cornelia. She smiled and stepped closer, drying her hands on a towel. As she got closer I began to feel nervous. 'It's about what we talked of last night.' She dropped the towel and put her hands on the back of my head, lacing her fingers together. I didn't know what to do, so I did

364

nothing, while she leaned in and kissed me, she parted my lips with her tongue and I responded with both my mouth and my penis." With that comment, Polybius looked at Mela.

"Cornelia broke the kiss off and leaned back far enough to focus on my face. 'I've been told Master Caesar has given you permission to be with me.' Nothing remains a secret among household slaves. With that she took my hand and led the way back to my cubicle, where I made love for the first time. I was a little clumsy but I said a small prayer of thanks to Venus when I was able to bring Cornelia pleasure before I reached my own climax. I quite expected it to be over for me when it had only just started for her.

After making love, we lay together on my pallet with her back pressing against my chest, her soft round buttocks pressed against my loins, and my arms wrapped around her. It was warm under the wool blanket and I felt very comfortable and very much a man. '*Now* can we talk about my dilemma?' I laughed, but I was concerned. I didn't tell her about my encounters with Fortuna until years later, but I took divine advice seriously and I wanted to trust Cornelia, so I went ahead and told her everything. I told her about the conversation I'd overheard and about how I alone knew what the magistrates and the leading men of Rome were completely ignorant of; the Roman republic was in the gravest of danger.

After I'd told her everything, Cornelia shrugged and said, 'You may be concerned about nothing.' Cornelia was matter-of-fact. 'Catilina could win the consulship and then you have nothing to worry about.'

'That would take a miracle,' I answered.

'Then pray to the gods, that's what they're for.'

365

I had learned enough about Roman politics to know Catilina didn't stand a chance, but I took her advice and prayed frequently to every god I thought might be interested in the outcome of the election.

The day finally came for the election of consuls. As was usual, we began the morning with the salutatio. What was most unusual, though, was the size of the crowd waiting to see Caesar. Many of my master's clients looked to him for advice as to how to vote in that day's elections, but by this point Caesar had practiced his stock answers and managed to say a lot while saying very little. He feared backing the wrong charioteer, as the saying goes, and if his man lost it would hurt his own chances in the election for praetor two days later. Caesar did relish the opportunity to greet more voters, shake more hands, kiss more babies, and charm, and charm, and charm the people. With the men of influence, of course, Caesar put as much space between himself and the doomed candidacy of Catilina as he could. Everyone who understood Roman politics knew Catilina didn't stand a chance; everyone, that is, except Catilina himself.

He seemed to have convinced himself he could win, but he hadn't entirely deluded himself. He knew that if he failed to win the consulship his career was finished. The consulship would give him imperium and the immunity from prosecution that came with it. After the consulship he would be guaranteed the governorship of a province and proconsular imperium would delay prosecution even longer, and, more importantly, it would give him the opportunity to steal enough money to not only pay back his massive debts, but to make him a very wealthy man. Failure would mean he would quickly find himself in debtor's court where he would lose everything. Assorted crimes would also be dredged up from

366

his murky past, and Catilina would most likely find himself exiled to some lonely desolate province. To make matters worse, he made it clear that he believed a loss would insult the dignitas of not only himself, but of his ancient patrician family. Exile to a villa on the sunny shores of Cisalpine Gaul would be bearable, but the injury to his dignitas would not.

We spent the day talking to the voters as they queued up to cast their votes for consul. By mid-morning I realized all my prayers served no good purpose. All the snippets of conversation I was able to overhear told me Catilina would lose. The results as they were read out later in the day confirmed what I already knew. Junius Silanus, Servilia's husband, and Licinius Murena had won the election. Catilina had lost. I realized I should already have had a plan to deal with this situation, but I couldn't go back and change things, so I tried to formulate a plan that day. There were too many distractions for me to think clearly, and as the day wore on I grew more distressed. I just wanted the problem taken care of, so I resolved in my own mind to tell Caesar the truth and face my punishment. I was going to tell him as soon as we reached home. I was sad for Demetrius, because I knew that once Caesar realized I couldn't be trusted, Demetrius would have his old job back and, for a time at least, be denied his freedom.

We walked back into the city following the Flamian Way along with crowds of voters returning to their homes after the election. It was unusual, but Caesar decided to skip a trip to the baths since it was late in the day and he had a dinner party to attend at Silanus' villa just outside the city. He was clearly looking forward to seeing Servilia even if it was at a party to celebrate the electoral victory of her husband. I was grateful for the din coming from the hundreds of voices surrounding us. The noise crowded my thoughts and chased the worry from my mind for the moment. Of course, my concerns resurfaced, and just as I began to feel nauseous in anticipation of what was to come, I thought I heard a woman's voice behind me say, 'Continue to trust her.' Those were the very words Fortuna had said as she left me. I was glad to have an excuse to change my mind and not tell Caesar about what I had overheard. I decided to consult Cornelia before I did anything else.

I busied myself in my cubicle until Silanus' slave came calling to escort Caesar to the party. Silanus was a thoughtful host and dispatched slaves at the appropriate time to escort his dinner guests back to his house. This practice ensured everyone would arrive at his home at about the same time and they could all enjoy the evening together. As was typical at this time, Caesar's wife Pompeia didn't join him at the party. Instead, his mother and his daughter accompanied him. Shortly after Caesar left for the party, there was a banging on the door and the door slave let in three or four people Pompeia had invited to one of her symposia. I'm afraid, at these gatherings the emphasis was placed less on high minded discourse, and far more on the consumption of wine. I always tried to remain in the far end of the house when Pompeia entertained. I much preferred she spend her time at the townhouse in the Subura, but Pompeia was growing to like the notoriety living in the Domus Publica afforded her. I made my way toward the laundry room to find Cornelia, trusting that Pompeia and her friends would never venture anywhere near a place where labor occurred.

I expected to find Cornelia bent over a washtub, but she wasn't there. I turned to leave the empty room when Cornelia nearly walked right into me. 'Oh!' she said. At the time I believed she was genuinely surprised, but I now realize

368

she may have arranged to bump into me as an excuse to kiss me, which is what she did. She tried to get me to respond to her passion by becoming even more passionate, but I was clearly distracted, so she took a step back. 'What's wrong?' Cornelia pouted.

'Catilina lost,' I answered sullenly.

'Oh, I see,' was all she said.

I sat on the edge of one of the tubs, elbows on my knees and my head in my hands. Cornelia sat beside me and put her arm through mine. We sat like that for a long time before I rubbed my face and turned to her. 'I must tell Caesar the truth.'

'You will almost certainly be beaten,' she said. Then after a long pause, 'And, then you'll be sold. I'll never see you again.'

'If I don't warn him, Caesar will die.'

'Perhaps you will be freed in his will.'

'I doubt that,' I answered sullenly. 'I've only been Caesar's man for two years.'

'But you might!' Cornelia tried to sound hopeful.

I had thought about the possibility of gaining my freedom, but in the end, I couldn't bear to let Caesar die for it. He tried to make the lives of his slaves as bearable as possible and we had grown closer with the passing of time. I felt he'd become more than just a master to me. Caesar was a man of his times and could do no more for me than he did, but I knew from experience, he certainly could have done less for me.

369

'I must tell him,' I finally said, getting up to leave. I'll tell him as soon as he returns.'

Cornelia grabbed my hand as I turned to leave. She was crying.

'I'll be okay.' I tried to sound optimistic. I felt sorry that I had involved her at all. I also regretted having had sex with her, for now she was growing attached to me and my problems. I left the laundry room resolving to sit up all night, if need be, waiting for Caesar's return. I went to my work cubicle to plan how I was going to tell my master that I had betrayed him.

It wasn't long before I saw the dim glow of an oil lamp with its wick trimmed low, making its way toward the open door of the cubicle where I was sitting in the dark. Cornelia appeared in the doorway behind the glow of the lamp. 'There you are,' she said. 'I've been looking all over for you.'

'I've been here.'

'I see,' she said, leaning on the table beside where I was sitting, my chin resting on my arms. 'I've had an idea.'

I looked at her for a long moment and when she didn't speak I snapped, 'Well, what is it.' She was obviously pleased with herself and wanted me to ask rather than volunteer what she had to say. I found myself irritated, yet, at the same time, looking for an answer.

'You can write him a note. And don't get pissy, Polybius. I'm just trying to help.'

370

This was precisely my idea, but it didn't solve the problem. I had planned to write it all out and leave it for Caesar to find. I would then sit in my cubicle and wait for my inevitable punishment. 'That will only delay the pain.' My mood was getting bleaker by the moment.

'No. He doesn't need to know it comes from you. Do you have any money?"

'Some,' I said.

'It'll take a copper coin. I don't know which one, but I can tell you if I see it.' Cornelia apparently had formed a plan.

'I think you mean an as,' I said. I was intrigued.

'You write a note, and I can bring it with me when I go to drop off the woolens at the launderer. The boy there will do anything for a copper coin. I can have him slip the note in with the return laundry that he delivers the day after tomorrow to the house here. Caesar will never know it came from you.' Cornelia was pleased with herself, and I started to see a glimmer of hope. The plan had merit, but, in my own usual, methodical way, I began to look for the flaws.

In the style I had seen Caesar debate ideas with Demetrius I began to question Cornelia. 'What if the boy talks?'

'He won't. His master would punish him.'

'What if Caesar pays him to talk? Maybe he pays him a lot more than we did.'

371

'That won't matter to him. He's saving up to buy himself and his sister. If he sells out for a higher price, nobody will ever trust him in the future. He's not stupid. I've talked to him many times. He has his eyes on the future.'

Cornelia had her plan well thought out and I was impressed by her sharp intelligence. I had begun to warm to the idea, but then I saw another flaw in the scheme. 'Caesar isn't stupid either. He may not know it came from me, but he will suspect. Catilina has a long list of the most prominent men in the city he plans to kill. If Caesar is the only one who gets a warning, he'll know it came from someone close to him, and how many of those close to him can't warn him to his face?'

This appeared to be a problem for Cornelia, so she sat staring at the lamp for a long time, watching the wick sputter and die. I too stared at it. Finally in the dark, lit from behind by the moonlight coming through the open roof of the atrium, she said, 'Many of the prominent men in the city use the same fuller for their woolen togas. They have them sent to Caeso, he's the best. So, we will warn them all.'

'In Catilina's own hand,' I said, improving the plan.

'How will you get Catilina to write a warning to the men he's planning to kill?' Now she was finding an objection and I was defending the plan.

'Don't worry about that.' I said. She couldn't see my smile, but I'm certain she heard it.

'It will cost more,' Cornelia said.

'How much more?'

'I don't know. Maybe one of the silver ones?'

'I'll send you with one of those, and the big bronze one. Try to get him to do it for the bronze coin. If you need to give him the silver one *and* the bronze one *and* the copper one, do it. Five or six notes should hide my involvement.'

'Can you have them ready by tomorrow morning?'

'I wasn't planning to sleep tonight anyway,' I answered. 'Let me find a light.' With that, I went out to the atrium to find a lamp that was still lit. I found one hanging on the stand near the vestibule. The door slave was fast asleep and never saw me take it. There were four on the stand, so the one wouldn't be missed. When I returned to my cubicle, Cornelia was curled up asleep in the corner, wrapped in the cloak I kept hanging from the hook for cold winter nights. I thought about waking her, but it felt good just knowing she was there, so I let her sleep. I spent the next two or three hours copying Catilina's handwriting onto seven identical notes, warning the most prominent Roman citizens to leave the city on the impending day of the start of civil war. I worked fast to ensure I would finish before Caesar returned, but I took extra time and care with the note addressed to Caesar. This one had to be an exact example of Catilina's writing. Caesar had seen enough of my work to detect a fraud, were I not entirely accurate. Sometime just after the middle of the night I had each note sealed with wax and twine and stuffed into a canvas bag.

I woke Cornelia and led her sleepily back to my cubicle, just as Caesar and his family returned. He was laughing at something his mother said as the family made their way into the domus. Caesar sounded a little drunk, but I knew

373

he wasn't. He often pretended to be drunk so others would let their guards down. Caesar drank little and even when he did, he almost always retained control. I suspected he was just continuing the show he had started at Silanus' house. Cornelia and I made our way back to my sleeping cubicle without being heard. I stuffed the bag containing the notes under the clean tunics Cornelia had lain on top of my trunk, and after guiding Cornelia onto my mattress I slid under the blanket beside her and wrapped my arm around her. I slept soundly for the first night in many.

The next morning I was awake with the first light, so I gently shook Cornelia awake. I discovered she was not as cheerful in the morning as she was later in the day. After more than a little encouragement, I managed to rouse her enough to explain the plan. I made her repeat it back to me three times to be sure she understood. Most of my money was kept in Caesar's strong box, but I always kept a little hidden in my mattress, so I pressed what I had into Cornelia's hand and sent her on her way with the tunic I had slept wrapped around the bag of notes. Since Caesar had given us permission to have sex, there was really no reason to hide that she had spent the night with me, but both Cornelia and I whispered our goodbyes. I sent her off with a quick kiss on the lips and a silent prayer to Fortuna that she not make any mistakes in carrying out her end of the plan.

The day was spent campaigning in the forum, but all I could think of was how things worked out between Cornelia and the slave at the laundry. I trusted her to perform her part well, but the delivery boy was an unknown element. I worried he would be careless with the bag of notes or he would mention it to someone.

The day seemed to last a month, but when it was nearly dusk we returned from the baths. Cornelia was waiting for me in my work cubicle. I only had a very short time before I needed to join Caesar and his most loyal supporters for a meeting in the tablinum. He was going over final strategy for Election Day, and I needed to take notes and supply the details and names of the important people among the tribes. 'Well?' I sounded more irritable than I intended when I approached Cornelia.

'Don't worry, everything was fine.' She smiled and kissed me, a quick peck on the lips. 'I had to pay him the silver one, but I kept the other two coins. I put them back in your mattress.'

I was actually relieved. If the delivery boy had agreed to do the job for a lesser amount, I reasoned, he would have been more inclined to tell someone about it. I joined the meeting feeling good about our plan.

We were up much of the night planning strategy while Aurelia and Julia were hosting the wives of several prominent men in the garden of the house, surrounded by smoldering braziers to keep the autumn chill at bay. As usual, Pompeia had one of her headaches and retired to her cubicle where two slaves played soft music for her. It has always struck me as quite strange how men, and women for that matter, engaged in planning political or military strategy seem to have the ability to thrive with very little sleep. Caesar was exceptional in this way. He seemed more full of life after a long, successful strategy session than he did after a night of sound sleep. When I finally packed away my notes and writing tools and made my way to my cubicle, Cornelia was already laying on my mattress. I was forced to nudge her aside to slide

375

in. I remember being irritated by this. I felt as if my life had changed too fast. I certainly didn't want to deal with two masters, but now was not the time to put up a fight, so I pretended to fall asleep quickly so Cornelia wouldn't begin to pester me for sex.

It seemed as if I had just shut my eyes when the morning light roused me from sleep. The window of my cubicle was too high up to let the light strike me in the face and wake me right at dawn, so I adopted a strategy used by Demetrius. I took a polished brass mirror and suspended it from the wall opposite the window at just the right angle so the first light of dawn would shine directly on my face. On those rare days when I was allowed to sleep later, I simply draped a cloth over the mirror and was able to enjoy an extra hour of slumber. Of course, this didn't work on cloudy days, and those are the days I often found myself scrambling to be ready for the salutatio. The day of the election was bright, but quite cool. I knew there was much to do and it would be best to rise quickly, but I took some time to lie looking at Cornelia as she slept. At that moment, I realized I was in love with her. Some people seem to need months or years to fall in love, but I loved Cornelia so soon after meeting her because I had opened my heart to her and she responded. Sounds from the other room reminded me of my duties and I scrambled quickly out of bed and woke Cornelia.

'The boy will be delivering the clothes to everyone today? You're certain, right?' I dispensed with the cheerful morning greetings.

'And a good morning to you too, Polybius,' Cornelia answered as she rubbed her eyes.

'I need to go, and I must be sure what to expect tonight.'

'Don't worry. If the clean laundry isn't delivered today it will be sent over by tomorrow at the latest. The boy is reliable.' Cornelia was becoming cross, so, as she sat up, she said, 'Go now before I get angry with you.'

I felt bad, so I leaned in and kissed her on her forehead and said, 'I'm sorry. I'm feeling quite anxious about this whole thing and I just want it to be over. This could mean war for the city. People could die.'

'People will die,' she said softly. 'They always do. Our master and the men like him are like little boys playing king of the hill. They take turns fighting their way to the top and what does it get them? Some grandson or great grandson gets to boast of their illustrious achievements, but they still end up dead just like us. They are men, after all, not gods.'

With that, I smiled at Cornelia and left the room to join Caesar and Demetrius in the tablinum. That conversation came back to me on the day the senate voted to declare Gaius Julius Caesar a god of the Roman pantheon, and I have never forgotten it since.

The salutatio was brief that day, as everyone wanted to proceed to Campus Martius and begin the election. I arranged for Caesar to be escorted by six of the lictors allocated to the Pontiffs rather than the usual one he allowed himself. I reasoned it would look good to have Caesar appear as if he was already a praetor so the voters would have that image in mind when they cast their ballot. I made the decision without consulting him and I was gratified to learn Caesar found it to be an excellent idea.

377

LIBER XXIII

The voting went rather quickly, and at least three hours before sundown we knew Caesar had been elected. It is traditional for a newly elected official to host a dinner party for his closest supporters, so we hurried home as soon as the results were read and posted. I would have liked to visit the baths, as I wanted to learn from Tiro if Cicero had any inkling of the Catilina threat, but Caesar had other plans. I didn't write a note warning Cicero, because he was one of Catilina's bitterest enemies. I wanted my warning to seem as if it was from Catilina himself to friends he wished to spare, so I was careful to send the warning to Caesar's opponents as well so there would be no suspicion the warning came from Caesar's household. Caesar's plan for the rest of the afternoon was to use the small private bath in the Domus Publica to get cleaned up for the dinner party and then spend an hour or so with Servilia at her house before her husband returned home.

When we entered the vestibule, I knew at once the warning note had been delivered. I could see Faustus, the dressing slave, waiting in the atrium with the sealed letter in his hand. I had wanted to stop by the kitchen for a snack, but I thought it might be more important to stay close and see how things developed, so I went straight to my work cubicle. Caesar spent a short time in the tablinum before shouting for me. Quickly sliding from my tall stool, I made my way to the tablinum, trying to seem casual. I could see the note opened and face down on the table and I expected Caesar to show it to me, so I was prepared to appear surprised. Instead, Caesar ran his hand over his unshaven cheek and said, 'Write a note to

Servilia telling her I won't be visiting her this afternoon. Include my sincerest regrets and let her know I will make it up to her. Tell her how sorry I am. Then, write another to Crassus and tell him I need him to come here immediately. Write it is extremely urgent, and send them with two of the fastest boys we have. Pick slaves who know their way around the city and won't get lost.'

I stood waiting for further instructions, but Caesar looked at me crossly and said, 'Now!' making a shooing motion with his hand. I quickly did as I was instructed.

The note summoning Crassus was not necessary. It turned out the boy I sent running to his house with the note nearly ran into him at the front door of the Domus Publica. Not knowing what was in the sealed document and not wanting to risk disappointing Caesar, the young man dutifully handed it to Crassus on the front steps of the domus. Crassus was reading Caesar's message as the door slave ushered him into the atrium. Antius was about to announce him when Crassus cut him off, pushing past and moving straight for the tablinum where he could see Caesar reading for at least the fourth time the warning that was sent to him. Caesar saw Crassus approaching and waved him forward.

'I see you've received one too,' Crassus growled, slapping his warning message alongside the note Caesar had again set down on the table. 'I came as soon as I read it. You're praetor elect, and one way or another you'll have a hand in dealing with this.'

Caesar picked up the note Crassus threw down and compared them side-by-side. 'The text is identical.' I had expected to be asked to leave the room, but the two men ignored me. Normally, Caesar would not be so careless as to allow a slave to be privy to such information, but it had been a long day, and he was quite distracted by the development that met him on his arrival home. Caesar began to pace as he read the note aloud. *'You have in the past been my friend and for that I repay you with a warning. Five days before the calends of Novembris the corrupt body of men who claim to rule the state in the name of the senate and people of Rome will be brought to justice. I warn you because we will need able men to manage the affairs of Rome when the traitors have met their just ends. On that day, death and destruction will be brought to the city and if you wish to spare your life and those of your family leave Rome.'*

'Do you recognize the hand that wrote this?' Crassus asked taking up the copy Caesar had laid on the table.

It was at that moment Caesar seemed to realize I was in the room. He looked at me hard, a crease forming between his eyes. 'Come here, Polybius. You've read letters from every leading man in Rome, and many from beyond. Do you recognize this writing?'

I pretended to study the note carefully. I then asked Crassus if I could see his note and compared them side-by-side. 'I can't be certain,' I said at last, 'but it appears to be the work of Sergius Catilina.'

'I thought as much!' from Caesar.

'That bastard son of a wolf bitch!' Crassus added.

Caesar read the warning yet again, carefully examining the writing and then he looked at me, narrowing his eyes. I was afraid he suspected my involvement, but, if so, he

381

never mentioned his suspicion. I suppose he reasoned there would be no way possible for me to come by such information if it was indeed true that I was the author, and there would be no reason for me to fabricate such an elaborate hoax, were the information not true.

The two men agreed to do nothing with the warnings until they could determine whether or not the coming civil war was a genuine threat. Later that night, after the wives left the dinner party to have a dessert of dried apricots steeped in honey while playing some word game beside the pool in the garden, Calpurnius revealed that he too had received the warning. This prompted Septimus to admit that his dressing slave had found one wrapped in his best toga. It began to be apparent that only men of patrician families had been sent the warning, as Labienus and Spurius had not received one. This had been intentional on my part. I knew the pride Catilina took in his standing as a patrician, and how he resented Cicero as a 'new man,' so I thought this would dispel any doubt as to the author of the documents.

I learned all this from one of the slaves serving dinner when Caesar sent him to fetch me. I stood in the doorway of the triclinium, looking as humble as possible with my hands folded in front of me, as Caesar proceeded to instruct me. 'Polybius, take two or three of the big men who handle the deliveries as guards and visit as many of the pontiffs as you can find at home. Without revealing too much, ask them if they have received any unusual correspondence of late. Any of the fourteen that say they have, ask to join me at tomorrow's salutatio. Have your escorts bring clubs and lamps.'

I succeeded, I believe, in hiding my disappointment at the assignment. I was extremely tired and didn't want to spend the night running around the city, visiting senators. I took it as part of the role Fortuna had given me in whatever her plan might be, and did as I was asked. That was the only time I regretted writing the warnings.

Within three days, nine warning notes had been revealed to Caesar as having been delivered to prominent Romans."

At this point, Polybius struggled to adjust his position on the couch so he could better sip his wine. I scanned my notes, not sure whether I detected an inconsistency in the account, when Mela, less conscious of courtesy, blurted out, "You said there were only seven warnings! I heard you."

I looked crossly at my brother and felt a bit embarrassed for his ill manners in spite of having just found in my notes that he was correct.

Polybius only smiled and pointed a bony, crooked finger at Mela. "Ah. What I said, young friend, is that I wrote seven warnings. Two more than the seven I wrote turned up. The two were quite different from mine, merely saying get out of the city five days before the calends of Novembris or be embroiled in civil war. They were both written in a different hand than Catilina's or my close facsimile of his work. After careful analysis of the warnings the two extras were determined to be in Manlius' hand and it was later discovered that both men owed him a considerable sum of money and he wished them to survive so the money would not end up in Catilina's purse. This was a lucky break for me, because it provided independent corroboration of my forgeries. A gathering of all the interested parties to debate what to do with the information followed the discovery of the notes. Some were of a mind to leave the city, while others thought it prudent to send word to Pompeius in the east and have him begin a march on Italia. This was deemed too risky because before word could return to Rome confirming that Pompeius received the summons it would be too late to prevent catastrophe. Crassus was, for personal reasons, dead set against Pompeius', involvement in rescuing the city, and his influence tipped the balance away from the idea. In the end it was decided to follow Caesar's suggestion and turn the warnings over to Cicero as the senior consul. Caesar adroitly pointed out the longer the group delayed revealing what they knew, the more it would seem they were involved in the conspiracy. As Caesar was already suspected of having secret dealings with Catilina, he didn't want his name tainted any more than it was already. His reasoning was sound. Although Cicero was no soldier, he would be able to stall an attack on the city until the consuls elected for the following year could assume office and take the field against the rebels. Crassus and the two pontiffs, Domitius and Vibes, were chosen to present all nine of the warnings to Cicero.

Amid all this political turmoil, Cato with his usual poor timing and lack of foresight decided to stir more mud into the already murky waters. As soon as the court clerks arrived at their offices he filed the necessary document to initiate a prosecution against Murena, the consul elect for the following year on a charge of electoral bribery. This seemed to take everyone by surprise; everyone that is but me. The evening of the election I reminded Caesar of Cato's promise to prosecute whoever won the election, because there was such blatant bribery by all the candidates.

384

To my polite reminder, Caesar merely scoffed. 'Even Cato wouldn't be stupid enough to do that with so much uncertainty. He'll wait and see which direction the wind blows.'

I smiled to myself. During my brief time as his slave, I came to know Cato far better than his fellow senators did. I was certain he would live up to his promise. In spite of the perilous situation he would create were he successful in removing one of the two most senior magistrates during a constitutional crisis. I understood that Cato would stand on principle to enhance his reputation for righteousness.

Cicero took some time from his duties as consul to head the defense of Murena. His co-counsels for the defense were Hortensius and Crassus. Hortensius was acknowledged to be second only to Cicero himself as an orator, and Crassus was in the best position to buy an acquittal should that be necessary. Crassus' money wasn't needed though. The jury understood that in spite of Murena's obvious guilt, it would be a mistake to start the new year with the removal of one of the consuls. Cicero barely presented any defense, preferring instead to ridicule Cato as an idealist who barely had a grasp of political reality, ready to threaten running the ship of state onto the jagged rocks to be true to his principles."

Polybius must have seen me wrinkle my nose at his expression, because he quickly added, "The phrase was Cicero's, not mine. He was clearly not at his best, no doubt due to fatigue."

I nodded and Polybius continued. "That though, was merely a distraction. The most important events were happening just out of sight of most citizens.

On the day after the Armilustrium, the annual purification of Roman arms in honor of Mars, the warnings were brought to Cicero. This day was chosen because there would be a large gathering of the legions just outside the city walls and swords, spears, shields, and armor would be plentiful within the walls should Catilina's forces attempt to move on the city when the conspirators learned the plot had been revealed. It was also an opportune time to approach the consul, as little official state business was carried out on that day.

If Catilina heard what was happening, he did nothing. Cicero took the following day to verify reports of the conspiracy through his own network of spies. I had a meeting with Tiro the day after the warning letters were delivered to Cicero, which was far from our usual convivial meetings over wine and dice. This meeting was a brief and somewhat threatening interrogation. I, of course, pretended to know nothing.

Caesar arrived at the senate meeting early on the second day after Cicero was made aware of the threat. As a result, I was seated right outside the door to listen and record as much of the proceedings as I could overhear. I sat in my usual spot to the left of the door while, after an initial nod of greeting, pretending to not notice Tiro sitting to the right of the door eyeing me suspiciously. Once the chamber was full and the portico was filled with the sons and the slaves of the senators inside the curia, Cicero launched into a carefully constructed speech. Unlike most of his speeches, this one was short on personal attacks on Catilina's character and was instead meant to concisely lay out the legal case against Catilina and his unnamed coconspirators. Cicero called the recipients of the warning letters to stand at his side before

386

presenting them to the senate. He then argued that the plan was for Manlius to initiate the rebellion four days before the calends of Novembris (October 27). He further asserted that Catilina would lead his men in massacring the patricians and leaders of the senate and put Rome to the torch on the following day. Several witnesses were brought forward to provide circumstantial evidence, but perhaps the most damning evidence came from Quintus Arrius who testified he had witnessed Manlius mustering troops in and around Etruria. After all the evidence was presented, the motion was made to pass the *Senatus Consultum Ultimum*. The ultimate decree was that far-reaching law that was used in the most extreme times of threat or calamity, authorizing the senior consul to protect the city by whatever means he thought necessary. Cicero accepted the decree and then, wisely realizing his military experience was not up to the task, gave Metellus the commission to gather and command the troops in the area of Rome to protect the city from the threat of attack. It is fortunate that two generals were preparing to celebrate triumphs early the following year. They hadn't yet disbanded their troops but instead had billeted their legions on the outskirts of the city so they could participate in the triumphal celebrations.

Catilina attended the senate as usual, but rather than being surrounded by friends, he was left to himself on the benches with each member of the senate having avoided sitting within five paces of him. This made for an especially tight situation for the rest of the senators, especially since that august body had been called to meet in the temple of Jupiter Stator, as the temple occupied a more defensible position. In his speech indicting Catilina, Cicero made much of how his spies provided him with excellent intelligence and reported on Catilina's every move. This was just so much theater, but since Catilina would be the only one who could verify the truth of what Cicero had said, but was in no position to do so, the claims made quite an impression on the senate and later, via rumor, on the people of Rome.

The ultimate decree caused a sensation in the city. In the past the decree had only been used when the threat to the city was so dire that immediate action was needed. The decree was first used to avoid appointing a dictator after Sulla made that office odious in the eyes or, perhaps more appropriately, the nostrils of many. In essence, the ultimate decree gave the senior consul the authority of a dictator without the title. Word of the coming disaster spread quickly and for several days people made preparations for an attack on the city. There was little anyone could do, but men sharpened kitchen utensils to use as weapons and stones were brought up to the top floors of the insulae to be used as missiles against an invading force. The coopers in town were kept busy making barrels to store water and pails to deliver it to fight the coming burning of the Subura promised by the warning letters. Crassus, always the practical business man, set the leaders of his fire brigade of slaves to recruit extra men and further train and condition the existing members. He also began to negotiate the purchase of properties in advance, should the Subura be put to the torch. Women baked extra bread, men filled barrels, and the children helped in any way they could."

The mention of the slave fire brigade intrigued Mela, and without waiting for Polybius to pause in his story, my brother interrupted him. "I don't understand. Why did Crassus have a brigade of slaves just to fight fires?"

Rather than finding the interruption a nuisance, Polybius welcomed it. Instead of looking at Mela, he looked at

388

me and said, "Mark in your notes where I left off. I must get up, as nature compels me." Then, turning to Mela, "I'll answer your question when I return. For now, please go and find one of my boys and ask him to bring us some cheese and fruit." Mela did as he was asked, and I was surprised he didn't complain. I took the opportunity to fill in my notes so I could more easily turn them into a coherent narrative when I returned home.

When Polybius had again settled in, he proceeded to answer Mela's question about the fire brigade. I already knew the story, so I took the time to finish polishing my notes.

"A large part of Crassus' fortune was a result of the careful buying and selling of real estate and many of the properties he traded were in the Subura. As I'm sure you are well aware, the poor construction of the insulae in that part of the city makes the dangers of collapse and fire very real. As evidence, one need only look to the new forum constructed by Augustus. Great care was taken to build a tall, marble-faced, stone wall along the entire side abutting the Subura to act as a firebreak. Crassus, as a young man, saw the potential fortune to be made from the frequent fires, so he trained a group of slaves to fight fires. Shop owners in the subura were paid a fee upon reporting a fire with the money going to the first one who alerted Crassus or his man when fire broke out. Upon hearing of a fire, Crassus would interrupt whatever he was doing and run with his brigade of burly slaves to the spot with a handful of already prepared transaction documents. He would then, if it appeared his crew could save the structure, negotiate the purchase of the building with the owner. The longer the owner haggled, the less valuable his property became and the price fell accordingly. If it appeared the structure couldn't be saved Crassus would then turn his attention to the neighbors downwind of the flames and negotiate the purchase of their building before they too disappeared in flames and smoke. Once a deal had been struck, his slaves would rush in and either put out the fire or tear down the neighboring building so the flames couldn't spread any further. During hot and dry weather Crassus was able to buy up entire blocks at discount prices and then either sell them at a huge profit in the future or manage the properties and collect the rents. As he grew older, more influential, and wealthier, he rarely visited a fire himself, instead sending a trusted freedman to handle the negotiations."

Polybius paused to eat a date and a small wedge of cheese from the plate Castor had set on the table between us and said to Mela, "I hope that satisfies your curiosity. I will now continue. Lucius, remind me where I left off please"

I was prepared, and read back from my notes where he had stopped his narrative.

Polybius continued. "The city was as tense as a drawn bow for those few days, and on the day when the attack was set to occur no business was transacted save the purchase of barrels and pails and of animals to be used as sacrifice. Throughout those days, the temples and street side shrines were in constant use with people from all walks of life and from every part of the city beseeching the gods to spare Rome. The Temple of Concordia was especially popular, as people prayed to the goddess to maintain peace and amity. The patricians and wealthy equites had fortified their homes and set guards at the doors. In a show of support for the consuls, almost no senators fled the city outright, but more than a few found some pressing business in one of the neighboring towns or down in the port city of Ostia that required their personal

390

attention. The shops were all closed and men spent their time gathered in the streets, speculating amongst themselves as to what might happen, all the while keeping kitchen knives and farm tools at the ready. Women and children continued to run to the fountains bringing water to fill the barrels that lined many of the narrow streets.

When the day came and then faded into night without incident, people seemed to be both relieved and disappointed. Caesar, taking a leadership role as praetor-elect chose to spend those few days at his home in the Subura. He sent Aurelia, Julia, Pompeia, and several other relations, including Atia and baby Gaius, to his villa across the river with transports and supplies at the ready to send them out to another villa at a safer distance should the need arise. We spent those days on the streets sharing the concerns of the plebs in the neighborhood so, when nothing happened, I was able to witness their concern turn to suspicion of Cicero's motives and anger at being duped. The prevailing view was that Cicero had manufactured the entire affair in an attempt to hold imperium past his term of office. It was even suggested he planned to make himself dictator.

The following morning the mood of the people changed as word spread quickly through the streets that Manlius and his troops were on the move in the countryside to the north of the city and picking up recruits along the way, so Caesar made speeches that day in support of Cicero. The first was an impromptu speech in front of his house just after the morning salutatio. The second speech was made from the Rostra in the forum, and the third was made in the Temple of Jupiter Stator during the meeting of the senate. Caesar was being very careful, after spending months being noncommittal

391

in his support of Catilina, to make it clear to everyone that he didn't support the aims of the conspirators.

Everyone was shocked to see Catilina himself making his way through the forum toward the temple. He moved with studied poise, acting as if nothing out of the ordinary was happening. He stopped to chat with anyone who would be engaged in conversation, and because of his notoriety, there were several people who wanted to be seen with him. As we watched from our vantage point on the steps of the temple as Catilina made a slow progress along the Sacra Via, I asked Caesar why anyone would risk being in his company. He didn't even stop to consider the question before answering, 'So many crave fame so much that, strangely enough, they will accept infamy as a reasonable substitute.' With that he turned and entered the temple. I forced my way right next to the open door so I could listen in on the proceedings.

Catilina joined the meeting in the middle of a speech by Valerius. At first the senator didn't notice, but when he did he stopped speaking and a murmur rose from the assembled men. Catilina took a seat as if nothing had happened, but those near the place he had chosen moved to the other side of the chamber. Since the cella of the temple was full, they were forced to stand. After a series of speeches denouncing the activity of Manlius outside the city and accusing Catilina of conspiring to bring down the constitution of Rome, Cicero rose to make a speech formally requesting an indictment of Catilina. After the speech Catilina rose to answer the charges. Since there was not yet any direct evidence tying him to the conspiracy, he merely denied all the charges and offered to, as a sign of good faith, place himself under arrest in the home of either Metellus or Cicero. As there had not yet been any

392

rebellion, there were no real grounds for arresting Catilina, so both consuls declined the offer. It was shrewd of him to offer himself for arrest. Since neither Metellus nor Cicero wanted him in their homes, it would be impossible to ask anyone else to take him, and it was unprecedented to place a patrician with such an illustrious heritage in the Carcer prison on hearsay evidence with only unsigned letters as "proof." As a result, the meeting came to a thoroughly unsatisfying conclusion and Catilina was able to repeat his slow progress in the opposite direction.

Caesar arranged for regular reports to be sent to him from clients in the cities around Rome. I was charged with summarizing the reports and presenting them to Caesar and his supporters each evening. As a result, I knew in detail what was happening in the area around Rome. The day after the senate meeting Cicero sent one of the quaestors, Publius Sestius, with a few hundred men to secure Capua, a town not far from the bay of Neapolis (Naples). This town was considered particularly vulnerable because it was legendary for its wealth and was also lightly fortified. It was also true that both Marcus Cicero and his brother Quintus owned villas in the area. He also sent troops to fortify Praenesta to the south east of Rome, and this proved to be a very prudent move, because forces under one of Manlius' lieutenants tried to seize the city on the calends of Novembris (November 1). The reports all indicated they were easily repulsed. On the same day, reports were presented to a meeting of the senate that the city of Faesuae, north of Rome, had risen up in support of the conspirators. Cicero dispatched two of the quaestors with sufficient troops to put the city in line.

Each day, more witnesses were brought forward to testify to Catilina's involvement as the leader of the

393

conspiracy. I was saddened to hear the testimony of slaves read out to the senate, because I knew the men had been unnecessarily tortured before providing the evidence.

Three days prior to the ides of Novembris, (November 7), Lucius Aemilius Paulus formally indicted Catilina. This followed an attempt to assassinate Cicero. Two equites who were in league with Catilina were turned away at the door to Cicero's house during the morning salutatio. They were found to be armed with daggers and wearing breastplates under their togas, as was the consul they meant to kill. It later came to light that a patrician lady named Fulvia, who was engaged in an affair with one of Catilina's supporters, had warned Cicero of his impending murder. As she came to realize it was becoming less and less likely that Catilina would succeed, Fulvia informed Cicero of the plot and threw her fate into the hands of the consul. A day later, (November 8), Cicero called a meeting of the senate to be held, once again, in the Temple of Jupiter Stator. I must add, this temple was chosen not only because it was easy to guard, being set on a hill and with high walls on its three sides and only a narrow staircase leading up to the Rostra in front, but also because it both represented Jupiter in his role as the steadfast protector of the Roman people, and to honor Cicero's co-consul since the Metelli family had built the temple. Catilina was expected to flee the city, but instead he arrived at the emergency meeting of the senate to hear his indictment read out. Cicero gave much the same speech he had given a few days prior, but this time it was more formally structured and more polished. It was also nearly twice as long as his earlier effort. Catilina again denied that any conspiracy existed and spoke at length recalling the illustrious achievements of his ancestors and contrasting the nobility of his own ancient family with the humble background of Cicero. His fellow senators attempted to shout down this speech, but he wasn't deterred. Concluding he had done nothing wrong, Catilina insisted he would go into voluntary exile in Cisalpine Gaul to spare the city any more trouble and to save his family name from dishonor. Later in the day, he left the city on horseback with a small group of supporters. He got as far as Etruria where he joined Manlius and his troops. It was reported that along the way Catilina had adopted the regalia of a consul and was being accompanied by twenty-four men bearing the fasces of lictors.

Four days before the ides of Novembris (November 9) when the fourteen-day festival honoring the plebs of Rome was at its height, Cicero mounted the Rostra and delivered a speech summing up the actions he had taken to save the city. Cicero spoke of the great victory it was to have Catilina no longer in their midst. The speech was designed to persuade the plebs that the consul had the situation under control and that he, not Catilina, had their best interests at heart. Cicero pointed out that he had sacrificed his popularity among the nobles to protect the plebs of Rome from the Catilina conspiracy, saying: *'At length, my fellow Romans, we have dismissed from the city, driven out, and pursued when he was leaving of his own accord, Lucius Catilina, a man mad with audacity, breathing wickedness, impiously planning to bring the worst sort of dangers to his city, threatening fire and sword to you and to Rome. He is gone! He has departed! He has disappeared! I say he has disappeared! He has left the city! No injury can now be perpetrated against the city walls, nor within our walls by that monster and prodigy of vile wickedness!'* there was much more in this vein, and the speech was quite well-received. And, for those who could not be nearby in the forum, the speech was copied out and read throughout the city.

The senate had been waiting to test the mood of the people before taking any further action, but after the effect of Cicero's speech swayed the public to trust the consuls and senate to protect the city, the senate felt free to declare by vote Manlius and Catilina to be public enemies. Amnesty was declared for those who deserted Catilina's cause, and dates were set where any deserters who remained with the conspirators would also be declared public enemies. Official letters to the senates of the cities of Italia were drawn up explaining the amnesty, but since there was still a good deal of trade and movement throughout the areas around Rome, Caesar thought it prudent to personally advise his most influential clients of what was happening at Rome. I was charged with writing the letters in Caesar's hand to the thirteen most important men, but I was allowed to recruit literate slaves from Caesar's household and from the slaves attached to the Pontifex to accomplish the task for the great number of less important clients. Out of this event I was able to keep one young man named Agamedes as my own personal assistant. It felt odd to have a fellow slave working for me. What was equally strange was that he was five years my senior.

LIBER XXIV

Two days after the ides of Novembris (November 15), word reached the city that Catilina and his army had arrived at the outskirts of Faesulae. It is said by some that it was there they discovered they had become, by senatorial decree, public enemies, but I doubt this to be true. There was enough traffic between the city and all parts of Italia that they had probably received word of this the day after the senate took its vote, if not even the very same evening. Since it was to be expected, I'm sure the conspirators didn't really care what the senate called them.

Around the same time, small disturbances broke out among the tribes in Gaul and the cities of northern Italia, but these proved to be of little consequence. Lieutenants of Catilina instigated some of these local uprisings. This I knew to be true because of the regular dispatches Caesar was receiving from clients throughout Italia. One evening toward the end of Novembris Caesar was discussing the situation with Matius, Labienus, and Demetrius. Normally, I excused myself from those meetings and went to my work cubicle to finish up the day's business and plan for any religious matters scheduled for the following days, but on this night I was feeling excited by recent events and since no one raised an objection, I stayed behind and listened as Demetrius read out the reports on Catilina's activities and the activities of his subordinates.

When Demetrius finished reading, there was a pause lasting some time, as everyone digested the information.

Caesar spoke first. 'It's probably good that Catilina didn't become consul. He has no skill at organizing troops.'

'It's not all his fault,' Labienus countered. 'The best he could put together was a pretty raggedy lot of men.'

'Even so, he should have kept them together. His cause was finished as soon as he began to split them off. With his full contingent of forces he may have had a chance. I would have marched up and down the Adriatic coast picking off cities and building my army. I would have avoided a pitched battle with any real legions until I was stronger. Now he's finished.'

Caesar almost seemed sad, and this prompted me to ask, 'Are you worried you won't find anyone to support the land reform bill now?'

For the first time since the meeting began, Caesar seemed aware I was in the room. 'I gave that up a long time ago.' He said this while leaning back in his chair to bring an extra cup from the sideboard behind him. 'Pour yourself some wine, Polybius.'

Emboldened by being invited to join the group I asked, 'What of your lasting fame?'

Caesar thought a moment and then his face lit up as he remembered the conversation he had with Catilina months earlier. With a big smile, he said to me, 'You really do remember everything. I'll find some other path to lasting fame. I'll make certain your grandchildren know my name.'

This was then followed by a conversation critiquing each of Catilina's military decisions. I have many times in my life seen a group of men find fault with one general or another while they pick apart his decisions like a flock of carrion birds picking at the flesh of a dead soldier. The only difference is the men do all their picking one hundred or more miles from any battlefield. I have only met three men in my life that I would trust to do this with any credibility, though."

I had to ask who they were, but I surmised he would name both Caesar and Augustus. "Which generals would you name to that list?"

"Of course, the first on the list was Gaius Julius Caesar."

I nodded.

"The second was Pompeius Magnus. The third was Marcus Agrippa."

My surprise showed on my face, prompting Polybius to ask, "You don't approve of my choices? I'm sure there are others that could be added to the list, but I'm only referring to generals I've personally met."

"Doesn't the god Augustus qualify?"

Polybius snorted a small laugh. "Study your history carefully. Augustus was superb at the politics of managing an empire, but it was Agrippa who won his battles for him. Now, let me return to where I left off before I forget anything."

I found it difficult to accept that even at his advanced age Polybius would forget something, but I leaned back signaling him to go on with his tale.

As the days went on, Catilina's lieutenants were, one by one, being captured and tried and imprisoned. Caesar was right, of course, about Catilina having made a grave error when he split his army. The army he had would have been sufficient to make a stand against the legions and perhaps even to have prevailed were they adequately armed and trained. Unfortunately, he lost some of his best-trained men and their armor and weapons when the cohorts he split from his main army fled or were captured or killed. He needed to wait until he could gather the extra supplies but he was running short of time so he tried a very different tactic.

When he saw that his forces would be overwhelmed if he acted too soon, Catilina realized he needed to provide a distraction to draw away the legions gathering against him. There was a tribe called the Allobroges from the southern part of Gaul who were, after nearly a century of contact with Rome and living under Roman rule, now as civilized as much as any of the people living in the allied cities of Italia. This tribe had been heavily taxed by Rome and for many years had no problem financing this tax. In fact, they knew the benefits of Roman rule far outweighed the burden of the tax demanded by the senate. Unfortunately for them, the previous two summers had been particularly dry resulting in very poor harvests. This calamity was followed by a long winter, which was colder than usual. As a result, the tribe was unable to pay the money owed Rome. In an effort to ease the debt or arrange a way to make payments over time, the tribe sent an embassy of leading men to petition the senate. The ambassadors were staying in the city when the conspiracy led to rebellion. Hoping to persuade the group to side with Catilina and his party, Catilina's man in the city approached the Allobroges with an offer of amnesty from their debt and five years free of taxation if they would agree to support the conspirators and create a diversion in Gaul. The idea was that the tribe would rise in rebellion against Rome drawing the forces under Metellus away from Italia. Once Metellus was engaged with the Gauls, Catilina could strike against the city and gain possession of Rome, barring the gates behind him.

None of the leaders of the senate seemed to have the slightest idea one of their number was involved in the conspiracy and was acting as Catilina's agent within Rome. It turned out Publius Cornelius Lentulus Sura had been persuaded to join with Catilina for personal reasons. Lentulus and Catilina had been associated with each other throughout the years, mainly thorough their mutual friends. Both men led lives others considered to be debauched. Cato frequently railed against Lentulus for his love of gambling, excessive drinking, and the seduction of the wives, daughters, and sometimes even the sons of other men. Lentulus once tried to seduce me. He made eye contact with me as I sat on the back bench during a trial Caesar was judging, and he then signaled from the side for me to join him. Thinking it may be important news for my master, I left my place and went to him. Suffice it to say what he proposed was direct and to the point and involved us going to the area behind the temple of Castor and Pollux where Gaius and I had spent so much time during my period of freedom. For some reason, those of us who are physically attracted to members of our own sex seem to recognize one another with just a look. It is the same with slaves, as we are able to identify other slaves on sight. Needless to say, I didn't take him up on his offer, not that I wouldn't have were Lentulus younger and more attractive and were it possible to disappear from my place on the bench without later having to explain my absence to Caesar. At any rate, personal friendship with Catilina drew him into discussions of revolution, but Lentulus seems to have joined mostly because of an old

401

prophecy he put great stock in. The Sibylline Oracle once declared three Cornelii would come to rule Rome. Lentulus assumed Lucius Cornelius Cinna was the first, and Lucius Cornelius Sulla was the second. In his mind, Publius Cornelius Lentulus was destined to be the third. He was convinced of this soon after Sulla became dictator and his conviction led him to behave in rash and unpredictable ways. Because he so firmly believed it was his destiny to rise to the top, he felt he had license to flaunt social conventions and even defy authority. When he was quaestor under Sulla, the dictator accused him of squandering state funds on personal luxuries. Rather than fear for his life, Lentulus arrogantly refused to provide any account of how he spent funds allocated to his discretion and instead presented the calf of his leg to Sulla to be struck with a stick, as young boys do when they are chastised for making a mistake while playing a game or when they interrupt a schoolmaster's lesson. For this action he was given the nickname Sura, meaning the calf of one's leg, and he used that name proudly throughout his life. For a time, I understand, this endeared the man to Caesar, for he too had defied Sulla's orders. But, since Caesar had no Sibylline prophecy he could rely on, Lentulus' behavior exceeded even what Caesar could tolerate. Lentulus had been expelled from the senate several years earlier on account of his immorality but, trusting in the prophecy, he failed to change his ways. Later, the senate reinstated his position, but since his support was so weak it seemed very unlikely he would rise beyond the position of praetor, which he had won for that year by the slimmest of margins. Since he was blocked from rising to the top through election, he was quite willing to join in a revolution and agreed to assist Catilina. How he planned to supplant Catilina as ruler of Rome, I have no idea; perhaps he trusted in the ancient Sibyl to take care of that, as well.

Lentulus presented Catilina's proposal to two of the ambassadors and added an additional five years of tax amnesty when *he* became master of Rome. The ambassadors without giving any real commitment led Lentulus to believe they were open to the idea but needed to discuss it with the rest of their group. After considering the idea and judging what they had to gain against what they could lose, the members of the embassy decided it would be better to spy for Rome than risk everything in a venture rife with peril. They returned the next day to Lentulus asking for a written confirmation of the agreement signed by the leaders of the conspiracy. It took several days to obtain all the required signatures, but even before the ambassadors had the document in hand, they went in a body to the Allobroges' patron in the city, Quintus Fabius Sanga. Sanga went to Cicero with the information that very day, sealing the fate of the conspirators who had remained in the city. Cicero instructed the Gauls to play along with Lentulus so they could secure written information about the plot. The day after the calends of Decembris (December 2), an envoy of Gauls was assembled to carry two letters from Lentulus to Catilina. Cicero had two praetors and a handful of picked men stage, as a ruse, a fake ambush on the Allobroges as they crossed the Mulvian Bridge just after nightfall. The Gauls played their parts well and pretended to reluctantly turn the letters over to their attackers, supplying Cicero with the evidence he needed while disguising the role the Allobroges played in the ruse.

One by one, Cicero invited each of the conspirators to attend a private meeting at his home. Once each "guest" arrived, Cicero's lictors arrested the man and bound his wrists and stuffed a cloth in his mouth so he couldn't alert the next man already on his way to the domus. In all, five men were arrested that same morning. The conspirators were then, each

403

in turn, forced to admit their guilt. The men were locked in the Carcer while Cicero considered what to do with them. By this time it was already Decembris and Cicero's tenure as consul was growing short. He realized he needed to act swiftly and decisively to ensure his legacy.

Calling together the prefects, quaestors and, somewhat reluctantly, Caesar in his capacity of Pontifex Maximus, Cicero secretly held a meeting in the Temple of Concordia. Of course, a meeting at the northwest end of the forum at mid-morning didn't remain secret for very long, as the parade of elected officials and their lictors and their followers making their way across the open space between the Sempronian and the Aemilian Basilicas drew a great deal of attention. The reason for the meeting was to gather men to guard the formal meeting of the senate and make certain the prisoners remained in custody. I was called to the temple along with other slaves and freedmen and left waiting under the portico, shivering in a cold Decembris wind. After a short time I was instructed to run ahead and gather the lictors of the pontiffs to the forum near the Rostra. Other slaves gathered remaining lictors that had not accompanied the men to the forum. Since elected officials moved with fewer lictors while within the walls of the city there were always some in waiting. This was all accomplished very quickly and the lictors were posted around the temple to guard the prisoners and protect the proceedings. Young, strong equites were chosen by Cicero from his own clientela to augment the guard of lictors.

Those arrested were Lentulus, Cetheges, Statilius, Gabinius, and Caeparius. They were all brought, hands bound behind their backs, to the Temple of Concordia where they were placed under guard. I was then dispatched to call the remaining pontiffs to the temple while other slaves were sent

404

to gather the most distinguished members of the senate. An inquisition was conducted and all five conspirators were found guilty. Later Caesar, as well as others, would argue that the decrees that issued from this meeting had no legal standing as there was not a quorum of members and, therefore, it was not truly a meeting of the Roman Senate. That same day upon searching Cetheges' home, a cache of arms was discovered. The weapons were declared to be arms for the rebel army, but plainly this wasn't the case. The number of weapons was too few to have made any significant difference in the fighting ability of Catilina's so called legion. Cetheges' explanation that they were part of a private collection also didn't ring true as there was nothing at all special about the armor and weapons. In all likelihood, the cache was meant to arm those who would be sent to assassinate Cicero and the other leading senators and set fire to the Subura. The prisoners were given over to leading members of the Senate, and both Crassus and Caesar were charged with the duty of keeping one of the captives. At the time, Cicero said it was a gesture of trust in the men, but Caesar suspected this was an attempt to draw them out as partisans of the plot and Caesar was certain his homes were being watched by Cicero's agents. On the grounds that it would be sacrilege to keep a prisoner in the Domus Publica, Caesar had his prisoner, Cetheges, sent to his town house in the Subura. He called on a number of his own clients to furnish a guard both in and around his house. Demetrius was put in charge of providing accommodations for the prisoner, whom Caesar chose to treat more like a guest than an enemy of the state.

Later that day, Cicero, surrounded by his lictors, mounted the Rostra and delivered a speech informing the citizens of the great danger from which he had rescued them. Like all his speeches, it was elegantly composed. I can still

405

recall his opening lines: *'This day you see, Oh men of Rome, the republic, and all your lives, your goods, your fortunes, your wives and children, this home of our most illustrious empire, this most fortunate and beautiful city, by the great love the immortal gods have for you, by my labors and wisdom and by the dangers I have faced, snatched from fire and sword, and almost from the very jaws of fate, and preserved and restored to you.'* This caused widespread celebration in the city that went on until well past nightfall. The days of tension had been broken and the people acted as if there was no longer any danger whatsoever in spite of the fact that Catilina was at the head of a sizeable army and quite near the city. Out of relief that the internal threat to the city was eliminated, Cicero was hailed as a hero.

The following day was the day when the festival of Bona Dea was celebrated, and this delayed the meeting of the senate until the afternoon. The senate once again met in the Temple of Concordia where the five prisoners were forced to stand, gagged and in chains, listening to the debate. This time, nearly every senator in the city attended and there was scarcely any room for the senators to move. During this meeting, rewards were voted to informers and the senate voted an amnesty for any of the conspirators or their followers who turned themselves in on or before the ides of Decembris (December 13). This prompted Lucius Tarquinus to attempt to implicate Crassus in the plot. Tarquinus' so called evidence turned out to be nothing more than innuendo and rumor, but many in the senate were inclined to believe him until Crassus rose to defend himself. He pointed out to his colleagues that the chief appeal of the plot was that Catilina promised a cancellation of all debts and that many of the conspirators including Catilina owed him substantial sums of money. From my vantage at the open doorway I noticed Caesar's head snap

406

up from the document he was reading so he could glare at Crassus. Since Caesar also owed a fortune to Crassus and several other wealthy senators, I'm certain he didn't appreciate Crassus pointing out how the plot would appeal to men such as himself. Should he himself have been named, Caesar would have had a much more difficult time defending himself. Cicero then moved to adjourn the meeting and called for another meeting of the senate in the same place the following day. The agenda for that meeting was to debate a fitting punishment for the five captives. He seemed to take their guilt as self-evident, and never once mentioned a proper trial. As a matter of form, Cicero asked Caesar, in his capacity as Pontifex Maximus, whether the day would be an auspicious one since it fell on a religious festival. Caesar looked toward the door of the temple and, spotting me, raised his eyebrows. I slowly nodded my head as casually as I could, hoping none of the senators, or anyone else for that matter, would notice that a fifteen year old slave boy was making pronouncements of the highest importance on matters of state religion.

As soon as we were safely in the vestibule of the Domus Publica, and the door was barred behind us, Caesar said over his shoulder as he hurried toward the tablinum, 'What damnedable festival is it tomorrow?'

'The Faunalia. It's not much to worry about. It's an agriculture festival so you don't need to do much. After a quick sacrifice at the shrine dedicated to Faunus, the rest is handled outside the city walls. It's not even on the official calendar. I've made a list of your duties, and put it in the box on the table. Most of it can be passed off to one of the other pontiffs, so there shouldn't be any problem making it to the meeting.' I said the words so casually that I surprised myself with my impiety. I silently said a prayer to the god asking his

407

forgiveness and promised myself I wouldn't let Caesar's impiety corrupt *my* relationship with the gods.

From the tablinum, Caesar shouted to me, 'Gather your scrolls and brief me on this afternoon's ceremony while I have a shave.' I was already prepared, having memorized his list of duties the night before. I took the scrolls out of the rack in the room off the tablinum, but I was confident I wouldn't need them. That evening was the feast of the Good Goddess and, as I'm sure you boys are aware, the main ceremony was barred to all men. For that reason, Caesar's duties were few. Late in the afternoon, after assisting the Virgo Vestalis Maxima in performing a sacrifice at the goddess' temple near the Circus Maximus on the lower slope of the Aventine, Caesar needed only escort the vestal virgins to Cicero's house, where his wife and daughter were hosting the main ceremony.

I was always surprised at how Caesar could never seem to remember what festival was celebrated on which day, but once I reviewed his duties with him he was able to recall them and perform them flawlessly even hours after I had briefed him. As I stood off to the side in the deepening shadow of the Aventine Hill watching Caesar assist the Virgo Vestalis Maxima perform a sacrifice to the good goddess while shivering in the cold Decembris wind, I said a private prayer to the goddess, once again apologizing for my master's lack of reverence. The sacrifice took place on the altar in front of the temple, and Caesar, being a man, was not allowed to cross the threshold and enter the temple. So, for a time he had to stand facing the open door of the temple watching the Virgo Vestalis Maxima and the rest of the vestals perform the most important rites inside the temple. To all who saw the ceremony, Caesar fit the role of Pontifex Maximus perfectly, but I knew in his heart he lacked reverence for the gods.

408

That night, in spite of the events of the day, Caesar hosted a dinner party for the husbands and sons of the most prominent women attending the Bona Dea ceremony at Cicero's house. I rather enjoyed those rare occasions when Caesar hosted a party for only men. His manners were less refined and he was to my eye even more charming. I suppose this is because masculine charm is more to my taste. The next day's debate was certainly on everyone's mind that evening, but, by unspoken agreement, each of the men avoided bringing the topic up. There was an exaggerated air of good humor at the party in spite of the fact that the next day they would help decide whether five prominent Roman citizens would live or die. The few opportunities I had to glance in on the party, Caesar seemed lost in thought. I'm sure his guests noticed this and because the host was not being his usual charming self, made excuses to leave early. Usually Caesar's dinner parties lasted well into the night, but this particular party was over just two or three hours past sunset. This turned out to be a boon for the household slaves as much food was left over and we were allowed to divide it amongst ourselves. That evening Cornelia and I sat in my work cubicle and shared some sort of small duck seasoned and roasted to perfection.

Cornelia had wanted to make love that night, but Caesar required my assistance as he reviewed our laws and religious traditions as it pertained to the punishment of Roman citizens. This kept us up until nearly daybreak. He was determined to argue against the execution of the five prisoners. I pointed out this would make it seem he sympathized with the conspiracy and draw suspicion to himself.

To that, Caesar answered, 'One day it could be me in that position. The men who voted for the "ultimate decree"

409

scarcely realize how dangerous it is to give that much power to a single man. I think it may take a dictator to cure the sickness that our republic suffers from, but Cicero is not that man, and now is not the time. The guilt of these men should be determined in a legal trial, and the punishment should be meted out as it always has been. We do not execute Roman citizens until juries find them to be guilty.' With that I left the subject alone and spent the night helping Caesar compose the speech he would give in the senate.

The following morning I once again briefed Caesar on the duties he needed to carry out for the Faunalia festival. We managed to pare them down to what was absolutely required of the Pontifex Maximus and then assigned the rest of the lesser duties to two of the other pontiffs. Once again I found myself tired and shivering in a cold wind as a sacrifice was made followed by a quick trip back to the Domus Publica for a change of Caesar's toga and then off to the other end of the forum and the meeting of the senate in the Temple of Concordia. This time the five conspirators were not present at the meeting but were instead held in the Tulianum awaiting the outcome of the debate. Cicero, in a well-crafted oration, quickly proposed the conspirators in custody be put to death without delay and those still at large as soon as they are apprehended. He then called on the consul elect, Junius Silanus to speak. It was common in any debate held close to the end of the year to hear the opinion of the men who would be piloting the ship of state for the following year. Silanus provided a graphic description of the death and destruction that would follow should the conspirators not face the 'ultimate penalty.' He was an excellent politician and left himself enough room to slip free of his own words by not mentioning the word execution. The elected officials all in turn rose to speak in agreement with him. Then the former

410

consuls were chosen to speak. The debate moved on to the rest of those who were set to assume office for the following year and it was soon Caesar's turn to speak. Caesar rose and spoke against killing the men. He cited long tradition and laws that made it illegal to execute citizens without benefit of trial and the right of an appeal to the people. To blunt the impression that he felt sympathy for the conspirators, Caesar refused to make his argument about the five prisoners, but instead warned against the implications of a Roman oligarchy taking such drastic measures against the people. Rather than kill the men, Caesar proposed they be banished and held each in separate towns in Italia. Being stripped of their property and any right to seek office and not allowed to communicate with one another, the men, Caesar argued, would no longer be able to threaten the republic.

I have a copy of Caesar's speech to the senate somewhere on that table over there." With that, Polybius pushed himself into a sitting position with the intent, I suppose, of shuffling over to find the document.

I stopped him with a touch on his arm. "We can find it later, and I can add it to my notes."

Polybius eased back down on the couch and closed his eyes to better look back in time nearly eight decades. "I can probably recall the speech, as I studied it carefully in the days before Caesar delivered it. I disagreed with him on this matter and it was my intent to compose a rebuttal to his position. The events of the day, however, prevented me from ever doing so. Let me see if I can recall the closing argument."

With that, Polybius paused and then began to speak:

411

"However, when our republic grew in power and our citizens, due to their vast number, split into factions, men began to condemn the innocent as well as the guilty. This led to other abuses of power and it was then that the Porcian and other laws were devised to allow condemned citizens to go into exile rather than face execution, the one punishment that cannot be amended. The leniency of our ancestors, Conscript Fathers, I present as a very strong reason why we should not adopt new measures of greater severity. There was surely greater wisdom and merit in those men who raised so mighty an empire from such humble beginnings than there is in us who can scarcely preserve what they so honorable gained. You might ask, is it my opinion that these conspirators should be set free allowing the army of Sergius Catilina to be increased? Far from it. I recommend that their property be confiscated and that they themselves be kept perpetually in custody in those municipalities of Italia that are best able to bear the expense of their confinement. I further propose that no one hereafter bring the case of these men before the senate of Rome or speak of it to the people of Rome and that the senate, here and now make it law that any man who acts contrary to this will be regarded as acting against the general safety of the republic and the senate and people of Rome."

Polybius took a sip of wine while he considered his words and then with a satisfied grin said, "That's close enough. I'll have one of my boys find the transcript before our next meeting. The mention of the Porcian laws was, I must admit, a nice touch. Caesar was forcing Cato to argue against a law established by his most famous and illustrious ancestor.

At any rate, I was once again forced to pretend to not notice the accusing stare of Tiro, as my master spoke against his master's proposal. I wanted to tell him I agreed with

412

Cicero, but I remained loyal to Caesar. This was the beginning of Caesar's lifelong policy of clemency toward enemies of Rome and even toward his personal enemies, and many times in the future I would secretly disagree with his forgiving attitude. I suppose one could say I was right, for in the end it was some of his personal enemies whom Caesar had forgiven, who took his life.

When Cato rose to speak, a shiver ran along my spine. Each time I heard him speak with passion or in anger, his raspy voice rising as he went on, I was reminded of the cruel treatment he heaped on me when I belonged to him. I couldn't see him from my vantage point, but I could imagine his pinched expression, the scowl, the narrowing of his eyes the reddening of his face, the spittle spraying from his mouth. I could well imagine the wild gesturing with his hands as he made each point. I muttered a silent prayer thanking the gods for delivering me from him. Cato, that strict defender of republican virtue, actually argued against the Lex Porcia. This law, enacted by a relation of his more than a century before, allowed for any citizen to appeal a sentence of death. Cato argued the men were so dangerous to the republic they must be immediately put to death to serve as a warning to those contemplating following Catilina in a march on the city. The evidence all pointed toward the legions assembled by Manlius and led by Catilina marching on Rome four days after the ides of Decembris (December 17). I hoped this wouldn't happen as that day was the start of the Saturnalia festival and I certainly didn't want anything to dampen that annual small taste of freedom granted to slaves. Cato was unyielding in his insistence that the men must die.

Caesar rose in answer to Cato's speech and in his usual calm and reasonable way presented a strong rebuttal.

413

Sensing he was losing ground, Cato made his argument more personal, suggesting that Caesar was sympathetic to the conspiracy and may even be a co-conspirator himself. I had a chance to witness this part of the exchange up close for just a few moments before a slave I recognized as belonging to Servilia forced his way to the top of the temple steps. The man struggled to catch his breath as he looked around in distress. The sun was low in the sky by this time, and it was difficult for him to see clearly in the shadows. Finally, he spotted me and pushed his way forward. Had he been a shorter man he may have missed me, as there were several others standing between us.

'Bring this note to your master. It's most urgent. Don't tell Silanus who delivered it.' With that he slipped back out through the crowd but then turned and, in a loud whisper, added, 'or Cato!' Then, he was gone.

I was curious why he warned me to not tell Silanus or Cato where the note came from, but then it struck me that it was from Servilia, Silanus' wife and Cato's sister. I was amused by her boldness, and relished the idea of presenting the note to Caesar as he debated with his lover's self-righteous brother. I quickly explained to the man at the door that I had an urgent message for my master and I was allowed in. I walked rapidly to Caesar with my head down and my shoulders hunched, presenting myself to the senate as a humble slave. Interrupting Cato in mid-sentence, I handed Caesar the note, which he quickly read and tucked into a fold in his toga. I waited for instructions, but Caesar simply waved me out. I paused for a moment watching Cato's face twitch as he eyed both my master and me with suspicion.

414

As I turned to leave I heard Cato's shrill, angry voice shout, 'Ah ha. This is probably a message from one of the conspirators, perhaps even that viper Catilina himself! I *demand* Gaius Caesar read this message to the entire senate. If he is innocent he will not hesitate!'

The room fell silent, all eyes fixed on Caesar. 'I would rather not read the note, as it refers to a personal matter and is not at all about state business.'

Even I had to admit Caesar appeared uncomfortable at the thought of reading the note to the senate. Cato interpreted his manner as reflecting guilt. I stopped near the door and turned to witness the exchange.

'I *demand*,' Cato shouted, most dramatically with his left hand on his breast and his right hand flailing above his head, 'This traitor read the message. If he is guilty let this entire august body know of his guilt, and if he is innocent let the note exonerate him!'

This was met with encouraging shouts from all around. I suspect the senators were by this point filled with curiosity about the message that was urgent enough to interrupt such an important meeting. Caesar's reddening face seemed to demonstrate his guilt, and he knew he would have to prove he was not a traitor.

'It is just a romantic note from a lady.' Caesar said it so quietly most of the house couldn't hear him.

'A love note?! Is that what they call correspondence between traitors, now?' Cato shouted so all could hear.

With that, Caesar simply nodded and handed the message to Cato. As Cato read the page filled with passion and graphic detail, his lips characteristically moving as he silently shaped each word, his face was first drained of color and then, when he reached his sister's signature at the bottom of the page, it began to flush red.

At this point Cato was no longer acting and had clearly lost control of his emotions. He stamped his feet and crumpling the papyrus, threw it at Caesar, shouting, 'Have it back! Have it back you filthy drunkard!' Caesar calmly picked the letter up from where it fell at his feet and flattened and folded it as best he could, tucking it into his toga amid the laughter and cheers from the hundreds of men surrounding him. Years later, when recalling this incident, it occurred to me that this had been a pretense devised by Caesar and Servilia to embarrass Cato. The timing and the audacity of the note could have served no other purpose.

When the house finally returned to order, Cato, having regained his composure, called for a vote on the matter of the five prisoners without further delay. Silanus and Cato had both put forth proposals to execute the men, and by rights Silanus' proposal should have been the one to be voted on, but it was agreed by the senior members of the senate that Cato's proposal was more accurately worded and that was the one chosen to formally present to the full house. The senate voted to support immediate execution of the men, and the elected officials as well as the most prominent members of the senate all moved the short distance to the Tulianum.

News of the debate carried out to the portico of the temple and then down to the crowd gathered in the forum. When it was learned that Caesar had argued for leniency for the conspirators in custody, the crowd grew angry with him. While the plebs had little sympathy for the Optimate faction of the senate, they had spent more than a month fearing a conspiracy that had as one of its goals the torching of the Subura. Cicero and his lictors ensured Caesar's protection from the angry mob as the senators left the temple. The men crowded into the small upper chamber of the prison and packed themselves together in the open space in front of the place. Then, each of the five conspirators was brought up from the lower room one at a time to be strangled by one of Cicero's former slaves who had been freed the day before so he could act as executioner. Caesar told me later that Lentulus was the last to be brought up from the pit. He said he didn't react at all to the sight of the corpses of his associates, each propped into a sitting position side by side against the wall. There was a delay in his execution when Caesar quietly asked Cicero, 'You will then kill a praetor of Rome? He has not formally given up the office.'

After a brief discussion, it was agreed that Lentulus needed to affix his name and seal to a document attesting to the fact that he resigned his office. Without the document, it would require a vote of the full senate to remove him. This led to Tiro coming out of the prison to look for writing implements. I had my case with me so I was able to lend him a sheet of parchment and a pen and ink. Once back inside the prison, Cicero dictated the necessary document testifying to Lentulus' resignation from the post of praetor and the man willingly signed the sheet. Years later I had a chance to see the page and was surprised Lentulus' signature appeared to have been written by a steady hand, while Cicero's shaky signature as witness attested to his nervous state. Lentulus was then strangled in his turn. Tiro never did return my pen and ink.

417

Cicero, followed by the others, then went out into the forum. Seeing the large crowd that had gathered, he mounted the Rostra and made a brief speech to the people. He opened with, 'They have lived.' The speech that followed was short and to the point. I'm quite certain he would have liked to speak at greater length, but the sun had set and the evening was quite cold, so he allowed himself to be escorted home in an impromptu torchlight parade that he would latter refer to as 'triumphal.' Caesar crossed the forum directly behind the consul to the Domus Publica surrounded by his own lictors and a guard of equites for protection. I was grateful to cross the threshold into the house that night, as random cries from the darkness threatened Caesar as we made our way home. Caesar thought it wise to give the people a chance to see the reasons he took the side he did and sent Vatinius and Labienus out the next day to spark public discussions of how his position was really in support of the people against the tyrannical rule of the Optimates.

LIBER XXV

It was the established practice then, as I assume it still is today, to have a female slave wait, just after sunset, at the door between the Domus Publica and the connecting passage to the atrium of the home of the vestal virgins. At that time, the appointed slave was a very old, wizened, white haired woman named Primilla who spent her days weaving the cloths used to clean up the blood and gore from the sacrificial animals. She took this as a sacred duty and was quite serious about it. Each evening as the sun went down, she would shuffle over to my cubicle and check the special box where communications between Caesar and the Virgo Vestalis Maxima would be waiting for her. She would then take the small sealed scroll and sit on a stool beside the door waiting for the knock from the other side. When the knock came she would open a very small door within the door, large enough to pass a message through but too small for the smallest of bodies, and pass the message along. Most days, there was nothing to communicate, but Primilla would wait to pass that information along.

On the night after the senate meeting where the fate of the five conspirators was decided, I was busy in my work cubicle. We had spent the day secluded at home, remaining out of sight of the still angry plebs. Caesar had been exhausted and demoralized by the long debate and didn't wish to see anyone but Servilia in the afternoon. The salutatio had been limited to just a few of his most important clients; the rest of the morning he had spent reading military history, while the afternoon was spent relaxing, and at least twice Caesar retired

419

to his sleeping chamber with Servilia. As a result of Caesar's desire to stay home, I was able to spend the day catching up on his important correspondence. This would mean a chance to get to bed early and perhaps make love to Cornelia. About this time, I'd taken up with a young slave from the secretarial staff, named Philon. We enjoyed each other's company, but more importantly, he enjoyed engaging in sex play with me. I convinced myself I was remaining faithful to Cornelia as long as Philon and I only masturbated together. On that night, I made it a point to avoid him so as to not allow myself to be tempted into finding release with him, because I wanted to be eager for Cornelia's attentions. I heard Primilla as her house slippers shuffled across the marble tile, the sound growing louder as she came toward my cubicle. She leaned on the doorjamb as she poked her head into the small room.

'It is so cold in here, you should light the brazier.'

'I'm okay,' I answered her with a smile. 'I'll put my cloak on. The lamp is enough to keep my hands warm.'

Primilla shrugged, leaning into the room and setting the lamp she was carrying down on my table to pull her pila more tightly around her. 'Does Master Caesar have any messages tonight?'

'Not tonight,' I said, my eyes focused once again on the page before me. I didn't look up as Primilla shuffled away.

A short time later, I heard the shuffling sound again growing louder. I assumed Primilla was coming back to see if I'd put my cloak on, so I jumped off my stool and, taking the cloak from the peg, quickly threw it over my shoulders as I sat down. I appreciated the concern of the other slaves, but found

420

it irritating that most of the older women of the household felt it their duty to be a substitute mother to me.

When Primilla returned, she didn't seem to even notice I'd put my cloak on. 'The vestal would like to speak to you,' she said, a surprised look on her wrinkled old face.

'Me?' I said stupidly. 'Not Caesar? Me?"

'Yes, she was clear.'

My heart sank. I was afraid it would be Marcia and I was in no mood to fight her sexual attentions. As I made my way to the back of the house, I resolved to tell her as firmly as possible she was to no longer bother me. I grew even more nervous when I came close enough to see the door to the passageway had been opened slightly. Lamps had been lit on the other side of the doorway, but the door wasn't opened enough to allow me to see who was behind it. I wrapped my cloak tightly around my shoulders more for protection from Marcia than from the cold.

I stopped at the door. 'Hello?'

'Please come in.' I didn't recognize the voice from the other side, but it clearly wasn't Marcia.

'I'm not allowed.' I tried to not sound nervous.

'Don't worry. The door on the other side is locked, and I'll allow it,' she said.

I stepped forward and opened the door to see who was on the other side. Her face was in shadow, but I recognized the dress of Rutalia, the Virgo Vestalis Maxima. She was sitting on an ornate ivory chair that had been set with its back against the other door leading into the home of the vestals. A stool had been set in front of her and slightly to the left. I was actually sorry it wasn't Marcia.

'Please, come in.' Her voice was reassuring, but I wasn't at all reassured. 'Sit.' Rutalia gestured toward the stool. I had no choice, so I did as I was instructed.

I looked at the floor until she said with a laugh, 'It's okay Polybius, you can look at me.' When I looked up I was surprised. She was the same woman I had seen several times at religious observances, but on those occasions she always appeared so stern. This night, her wrinkled face had one of the kindest smiles I'd ever seen. She seemed so relaxed and at ease in spite of her sitting arrow-straight posture in the chair with both feet on the floor and her hands folded in her lap.

I had no idea why she had called me there, but I expected a most important message, so I was surprised by what she said next. 'You know, two of the virgins find you very attractive. You are right to be frightened when you're called anywhere near our house.' She must have seen the panic on my face, because she laughed and leaned forward to put a hand on my shoulder. 'Don't worry; you're not here about that. I don't mean to hurt your feelings, but I don't at all understand what they see in you. When I was young, I was excited by gladiators. At any rate, I had a talk with the girls and they will not bother you again.'

That made me wonder how many of the Vestal Virgins had taken an interest in me, but I had no time to worry about that.

I gathered the courage to speak. 'Why *am* I here, Virgo Vestalis Maxima?'

422

'I don't know,' she answered. 'I was hoping you could tell me. I had a dream last night. Do the gods ever come to you in your dreams? They sometimes visit me.'

'Only one,' I answered, revealing my secret for the first time.

'Which one?' She seemed genuinely curious and took me seriously.

'Fortuna has visited me.' I began to relax somewhat. It was a relief to be able to tell someone who wouldn't doubt me.

'Fortuna? She is a great power. You are lucky to have her on your side. Bona Dea came to me last night. The Good Goddess said you are worried about something and I should speak to you and set your mind at ease.'

'Did the Good Goddess tell you what it was?' I knew immediately this was Bona Dea's response to my prayer before her temple and was afraid of the consequences of discussing Caesar's lack of piety.

'No, she said I must hear it from you, and I *never* argue with a goddess.'

I took a deep breath. 'I prayed to the goddess because I'm worried the Pontifex Maximus is not pious enough.' I said the words rapidly, while I still had the courage to betray Caesar to the Virgo Vestalis Maxima.

I was shocked when she laughed at my response. I thought she didn't believe me and I would be punished for falsely accusing Caesar of impiety. 'I have known Gaius

Caesar since he was a boy. He was impious as a child and I don't expect he has come to take the gods any more seriously as a man. Did you know his mother and I are cousins?' I was about to answer when she asked, 'Do you assist him in understanding what he must do?'

Once again, her question frightened me. I was often terrified someone would find out I was guiding the Pontifex Maximus as he acted as the bridge between the people and the gods, and now the Virgo Vestalis Maxima was asking the question outright. 'Yes,' I answered quietly.

Rather than show any surprise or anger, Rutalia seemed to move the conversation down a different path. 'I believe the gods sometimes do speak to us through the voice of a single man or woman, but, more often than not, they also speak through the collective voice of the Roman people.'

We had been speaking Greek, so, recalling the words of Caesar's mother on the day of his election as Pontiff, I softly said, '*vox populii, vox dei deorum.*' and translating to Greek repeated, 'The voice of the people is the voice of the gods.'

'I have come to believe that.' Rutalia sounded quite sure of herself. 'Did Caesar get elected to the post of Pontifex Maximus?'

'Yes,' I answered.

'Then the people, *and* the gods, have made their choice. It is the duty of the Pontiffs to unite the voices of all the people of Rome and speak with their collective voice to the gods. It matters very little, if at all, how pious the pontiff is. What is important is the faith and reverence of the people

424

who chose him, the people he represents when he stands before the altar.'

'Not all elections are honestly won.' I came dangerously close to saying Caesar had bought the election.

This didn't seem to bother the Virgo Vestalis Maxima in the slightest way. 'Do you think the gods don't know how we handle elections in this city? Perhaps a little bribery is their chosen method of seeing the right man elected. I remember once, when I was a first made a vestal, a man announced his intention to run for Pontifex Maximus. The day after he made his announcement his house was struck by lightning and in the ensuing fire he was burned alive. The gods know how to fix an election and prevent the wrong candidate from winning the post.'

Without moving her eyes from mine, Rutalia raised her voice and said, 'Don't worry, Gaius. Polybius is not telling any of your secrets.'

I quickly turned my head to see Caesar standing in the shadows just outside the door. Before I could stammer an apology or an explanation, Caesar answered her. 'I keep no secrets from you for him to tell, Rutalia. I just hope you're not freeing my favorite slave behind my back.' By the tone of their voices as they spoke to one another, it was clear they had a long and loving history."

I must have looked puzzled, causing Polybius to pause in his story and explain. "I assumed you knew. One of the powers granted a vestal virgin, in addition to being able to sit in the front row of seats at gladiator matches and in the circus, is the power to free a condemned criminal or a slave with a touch and an invocation to the gods. You must believe

425

that thought raced through my mind when the Virgo Vestalis Maxima first laid her hand on my shoulder."

"I hadn't known," I answered. "The vestals are certainly interesting women."

"Yes, they are. Allow me to continue," Polybius said, after taking a sip of wine. "I wasn't surprised when Caesar referred to me as his favorite slave. I had heard him refer to Demetrius and at least two other slaves the same way. It was a sort of joke we all participated in. I was, however, surprised by what Rutalia said next.

'You chose well when you picked this young man to guide you in your duties. You almost never make a mistake.'

She was teasing him, but Caesar answered her seriously. 'When I do err, the mistake is mine, not his. It's because I sometimes choose to not listen to what Polybius tells me.'

The Virgo Vestalis Maxima rose to her feet, and I quickly stood up as well, not wanting to remain seated while she stood. Being shorter than me, she needed to look up into my eyes as she laid a hand on my arm. Once again I had the fleeting hope she would free me with her touch. 'I hope this little conversation has put your mind at ease.'

'It has helped. Thank you,' I answered.

'Now, help me pull this door open when I get it unlocked.' As she said this she made a key appear from somewhere in her sleeve. 'The door is quite heavy.'

Walking back to the tablinum at Caesar's side I expected him to have much to say about what he overheard, but all he said was, 'Fortuna visits you in your sleep?'

I nodded.

'That is quite interesting,' he said as he scratched his head with a single finger so as not to disturb his hair. 'I have a meeting tonight with young Marcus Antonius, so you needn't wait up. He's quite upset about his stepfather.' With that, Caesar gave me a squeeze on my shoulder before walking away." Polybius leaned over to take a piece of dried fruit from the plate on the table between our couches when he saw my puzzled look. "I'm sorry. I forget that not everyone is as well-versed on the family connections of the cast of characters in the great drama that was the fall of the Roman republic. Antonius' stepfather was Lentulus Sura, Catilina's man in Rome. It was Lentulus who tried to get the Allobroges to join sides with the conspirators. I kept my opinion to myself, but I believed it was dangerous for Caesar to continue to associate with a man so close to the conspiracy.

LIBER XXVI

These tumultuous few days were followed by several days where almost no news came from outside the city. In the absence of real news there were rumors, but for the most part the city returned to normal. Cicero continued to arrange to have Tiro and I meet, hoping to gather even more information. Caesar agreed to continue the arrangement to confirm his innocence. This caused me to reflect on the guilt of the five conspirators. I wondered how much of what Cicero learned of their movements came from meetings like the ones I had with Tiro. It occurred to me Tiro may have been meeting with the slaves of many influential men. Should I have wished to implicate Caesar, I could easily have made up 'evidence' that could lead to his arrest. Perhaps the men were not as guilty as they seemed. I wondered if, perhaps, there may have been other slaves who could mimic a man's handwriting and fabricate letters like the ones used to establish their guilt. Perhaps this was the reason Caesar insisted they should be given a proper trial.

It was during one such meeting with Tiro, two days after the executions, that I actually might have helped bring the crisis to a swift conclusion. After the usual exchange of money and lies, Trio and I relaxed in the back of our regular taverna. The place was crowded since the wind continued to blow cold and men wanted to spend more time indoors. Over a cup of wine I casually mentioned something that may have influenced Cicero to act.

'Tiro, I think you've read me wrong.'

428

'How's that?' he asked.

'I agree with your master. I hate to admit it, but I guess that means I agree with Cato too. Those men should certainly have been killed.'

Tiro nodded but didn't say anything, so I went on.

'I just don't understand why Cicero isn't shouting it to the world.'

Tiro snorted. 'Haven't you been listening? He stood on the Rostra and made speeches. I thought you were there.'

'Don't get sarcastic,' I countered. 'Cicero made the argument that the executions would convince others to abandon Catilina's cause. Of course what is said from the Rostra can eventually be heard all across this wide world, but that does takes time. Why doesn't your master dispatch riders with copies of the news to post on temple doors in the forums of every town in Italia?'

Tiro was quiet for a moment and then without looking at me he nodded. 'Perhaps he will.' At sunrise the next morning, riders left the city gates bringing the news to every city within a two days ride of Rome. Cicero announced this in a speech to the senate as just one more way he was insuring the safety of our republic.

Two days after the ides of Decembris (December 15), news began to flood into Rome of a large number of desertions from Catilina's army prompted, it was said, by the executions of the five conspirators. Even Caesar had to admit this was one positive outcome of what he had taken to calling the 'murder of Roman citizens.'

While the city remained on watch and troops were posted outside the walls, the good news allowed for a very happy Saturnalia festival. I'm not sure how strictly your family observes the festival, as I've heard that the rituals are not as carefully observed as in the old days. This may, however, simply be the musings of some of my old friends, who seem to believe life was always better a generation or two earlier. For this Saturnalia my master was the Pontifex Maximus, so we needed to be much more involved in the public celebrations. Our day began early with the unbinding of the statue of Saturn in the god's temple in the forum. In this part of the ceremony the statue, which normally has its feet bound in wool, was symbolically set free by having the wool wrappings removed from his feet and lower legs. This was then followed by a sacrifice in front of the temple. The main sacrifice, carried out by Caesar, involved slitting the throats of three suckling pigs. This was followed by each of the other pontiffs doing the same. The actual ritual itself doesn't require a sacrifice of this size, but since the meat was roasted and presented to the people in a public banquet, the extra meat made the festival that much more enjoyable. This was one of the few times the forum was filled with color, because it was a day of great license from what was considered proper decorum, and most of the people dressed in the Greek style with colorful clothing.

After the public banquet was finished, we all retired to our homes for the private celebration where the slaves were served by the masters at a banquet of our own. On that day we were allowed to act and dress as we pleased and to treat our masters as if they were the slaves, all within reason of course. After our banquet, everyone in the household, both slave and free, mingled freely and drank and gambled and played a variety of games. Caesar always brought in professional

430

illusionists, musicians, and comics to entertain us. On the day of gift giving, which falls eight days before the calends of Januarius (December 23), Caesar gave me a new, fine woolen tunic and a magnificent writing set with a matching set of a bone stylus and pen, each inlaid with gold. This festival was celebrated with extra gusto because of the many days of heightened fear and tension in the city.

The day after the end of Saturnalia (December 25), word reached the city that Catilina had attempted to move his legions through a pass in the Apennines but was blocked by Metellus Celer and his forces. At the same time, Antonius and his forces were approaching Catilina's army from the rear. The forces of Catilina were hemmed in for ten days. Five days past the calends of Januarius (January 6) Catilina moved his army of about three thousand men south, choosing to take his chances against Antonius' army while it was still gathering. Antonius and two cohorts of foot soldiers had not yet joined up with the main army, but near the town of Pistoia the legate Petrius gave Catilina a chance to surrender. Being a proud man in a desperate situation and probably realizing he would be strangled in the Tulianum like his friends, Catilina chose to fight. That day, almost to a man, his soldiers fought to the death and Catilina fell with them in battle.

Around this time, Quintus Caecilius Metellus Nepos returned from the east. He was one of the tribunes for the year but had been absent from Rome for most of his term of office. Nepos was brother in law to Pompeius Magnus, and along with his brother Metellus Celer, was one of the great general's most trusted lieutenants. Nepos' return was widely seen as the first step in Pompeius' return to an active role in Roman politics. Caesar was very keen to bolster his own reputation by being viewed as an associate of Pompeius, so the day after

Nepos returned to Rome, he was invited to meet with Caesar at the Domus Publica. I wasn't present during the meeting that lasted through the midday meal and nearly to sundown, but when Nepos left the two men were on very good terms.

The result of the meeting was almost immediately obvious. On the last day of Decembris (December 29), the tribunes Bestia and Metellus Nepos vetoed Cicero's attempt to address the people from the Rostra during the traditional ceremony where he lays down the regalia of the office of consul to be taken up by the next consul. They said they took this action because Cicero had executed Roman citizens without the benefit of a trial. This insult didn't prevent the Senate from honoring Cicero with the title "Father of the Country" for having saved the republic with his swift action. Nepos then went a step further and along with Caesar proposed a law recalling Pompeius from the east to put down the Catilina rebellion and to restore order to the city. This further confirmed he was working as an agent of the great general and went a long way toward repairing Caesar's tarnished reputation with the plebs. To the common citizen, Pompeius was held in the highest regard.

On the same day he took office, (January 1), Caesar launched a surprise attack on Quintus Lutatius Catullus. This man had been Crassus' colleague in the censorship and made a career of opposing anyone who had been a partisan of Marius in the years before Sulla's dictatorship. Of course, this included Caesar. Throughout the time leading up to the death of Catilina, Catullus consistently attempted to implicate Caesar in the plot. As his first official act on assuming the praetorship, Caesar mounted the Rostra and accused Catullus of corruption in his handling of the restoration of the temple of Capitoline Jupiter. Several years previous, the temple had

432

been severely damaged by fire. Catullus had been allocated funds and charged by the senate with the supervision of its restoration. Since the temple was still operational, though not yet as grand as it had once been, Catullus was quite slow in completing the project. Caesar accused him of spending the money allocated by the senate on personal luxuries. When Catullus began to mount the Rostra to defend himself, Caesar added to the insult by ordering him to speak from ground level. Caesar then proposed a bill transferring the task to someone more competent. The man he favored for the job was Pompeius Magnus. At this point in his career Caesar most strongly wanted to be associated with the famous general to enhance his own reputation and to gain Pompeius' support three years hence when he would be running for the consulship.

There were two bills to be voted on, this one and the one recalling Pompeius from the east to finish off the Catilina rebellion. On the day of the vote, Nepos called, as was usual, a meeting of the Roman people in the forum. Rather than address the plebs from the Rostra, the scene of Cicero's recent speeches, Nepos chose to address the crowd from the platform that jutted out from the portico of the temple of Castor and Pollux. It was common for tribunes to address the people from a temple at this end of the forum to demonstrate by physical separation their political separation from the senate. On this day, Caesar had his official chair of office placed beside Nepos' chair on the platform to lend his support for the bill. Cato, who claimed to have decided to run for the tribunate so he could stand in opposition to Nepos, arrived at the meeting with his fellow tribune, Minucius Thermus and a large group of supporters, intending to veto the bill as soon as it was presented. Cato, not content to stand by at the base of the platform, marched up the temple steps and took a seat between

433

Nepos and Caesar. Half the crowd seemed to be shouting in support of Cato while the other half supported Nepos. Nepos gave the bill to one of his clerks to loudly read to the gathered crowd, but Cato used his veto to prevent the man from presenting the bill. Nepos then rose and, after calmly adjusting his toga, began to read the document his clerk had returned to him. Cato, knowing he would be unable to stop a fellow Tribune from presenting the bill, stood and slapped the document from Nepos' hand and stamped his foot down on the crumpled papyrus scroll. Nepos calmly began reciting the bill from memory without missing a word. With that, Cato roughly grabbed Nepos by the shoulder with one hand and clamped his other hand over his mouth. Physically assaulting a tribune was a capital crime even for a fellow tribune, and Cato had either lost his temper or was taking a huge gamble in making this move. From my vantage point behind the men near the temple portico I could see first Caesar and then Nepos give a prearranged hand signal to supporters in the crowd. A riot then ensued. At first men used fists and sticks but soon some in the mob produced daggers and from where I stood I could even see a sword or two. Cato and Thermus were both roughed up in the fight, but ultimately Nepos and his supporters were forced to withdraw. Caesar and I, with our own smaller group, retreated into the temple and waited until both sides had dispersed. I was utterly unnerved, but Caesar calmly made small talk with his men while we waited. Later that day the senate met and once again enacted the "ultimate decree" giving the consuls authority to restore order. A proposal was put before the senate to strip Nepos of his tribunate but it was later dropped because Cato himself opposed it. Cato clearly understood he needed an opponent if he wished to stake out a position among his fellow Optimates. Nepos called another meeting in the forum to formally accuse

Cato and his followers of plotting against Pompeius. Although it was a violation of his office for a tribune to leave the city for more than three days during his one year term, Metellus Nepos soon fled Rome and returned to the island of Rhodes to once again join Pompeius at his winter headquarters.

Aside from these incidents, the close of the year of the consulship of Cicero and Antonius Hibrida was a welcome event for most citizens, but the senate was still in turmoil. The year had been one of uncertainty for the city, and the people as well as the senate all looked forward to a better year, but it would still be some days before the situation would return to normal. It would have been better for Cicero had the rebellion been crushed before he laid down his office, but since it ended just a few days after his term expired, the next consul was not able to steal his credit, so, in the end, Cicero's term as consul ended well. Unfortunately for Caesar, his year as praetor began quite poorly. In fact, he was nearly deprived of his praetorship largely due to his own actions.

I rather enjoyed the feeling of self-importance that my close association with Caesar engendered, as it allowed me to forget, from time to time, that I was a slave. Since I was working on serious matters of state and not fetching water or scrubbing floors or cleaning a latrine I felt superior to many free men. In spite of this, the feeling of uncertainty was beginning to wear on me. I was only able to ignore my slave status for brief intervals, and when I did remember I became keenly aware that since I had been elevated somewhat above many of the other slaves I had further to fall should something happen to Caesar. In his craving to rise to the top and achieve the highest imperium, my master frequently took risks. He trusted in Fortuna perhaps more than I did. Most often his ventures paid off, but sometimes, though rarely, Caesar

435

miscalculated. Choosing to associate himself so closely with Nepos was clearly one of those times. Caesar assumed Nepos would win the day since his closeness to Pompeius would grant him immediate popularity with the plebs. What he failed to take into account was that the influence of Pompeius had been diluted by time and distance and the Optimates held an advantage by being in the city.

On the day Nepos set sail there was a meeting of the senate. Caesar didn't seem to feel anything was amiss and this day started as any other. At the vestibule of the Domus Publica we were joined by Caesar's three lictors and made our way out to the Sacra Via."

I found I was confused and told Polybius so. "Caesar was a praetor at this point in his career, right?"

"That is correct."

"Praetors have six lictors."

"Ah," he answered, "outside the Pomerium, the sacred and ancient city boundary, the praetor has six, but within the city limits he has only two. I'm very familiar with this, because I often had to arrange for the other four to meet us at a particular gate whenever Caesar needed to leave the city. If he changed his mind about his route or destination I was in charge of sending slaves on ahead to alert the lictors to change their meeting place. The four outside the Pomerium also had the special fasces with axes bound to them."

"I see," I answered, "but you said there were three lictors with you. Why three?"

"The third lictor was a lictor curiatus. There were thirty of these and they were at the command of the Pontifex Maximus. It was at his discretion how they were distributed. In theory, all thirty could attend the Pontifex Maximus himself, but tradition dictated they would be distributed among the other priests. Since it was the duty of these lictors to assist at religious ceremonies and sacrifices, it also became my duty to dole out these lictors among the priests based on the religious calendar. A lictor curiatus also accompanied any vestal virgin when she appeared in public. Caesar was usually accompanied by only one lictor curiatus as he went about his ordinary business. In public, I would walk on Caesar's left side, the lictor curiatus would walk behind Caesar and a little to his right, and the two other lictors would walk in front. The principal lictor who gave the orders to the others was always on the right and the closest lictor to Caesar. Clients, petitioners, and the usual crowd that joined us when we went out, filled in behind or lingered at the sides of our group. I found it quite thrilling to walk the streets with Caesar. I felt very important when I accompanied him in public. Of course this minor pageantry would pale in later years when he became dictator and we were surrounded by seventy-two lictors with four lictor curiatus' behind, all keeping a crowd, often numbering in the hundreds, at bay.

Once again though, I have left my original story behind. So allow me to continue before I lose the trail of my thoughts. Without Nepos for a target, Cato and his allies turned on Caesar. A proposal was made by one of Cato's men that Caesar should be expelled from the praetorship. Cato didn't make the proposal himself because he wasn't certain it would carry. He need not have worried though for, although it was close, the senate voted to deprive Caesar of his office. I was stunned as I watched the proceedings from the doorway. I must have appeared the fool as I stood, mouth open, under the portico of the Curia. On hearing the consul say, 'The measure has passed,' I dropped my wax tablets and stylus. I was looking around for my stylus that had rolled off somewhere, having just retrieved my tablets from the marble slabs of the portico floor when Caesar stormed out of the meeting and without looking back, said, 'Let's go Polybius.' I left my stylus, grateful it wasn't my good, ivory one and quickly followed him. The group of men who had followed Caesar through the forum on his way to the meeting was much smaller on the return trip to the Domus Publica. There was some confusion for the two lictors as they had also heard the senate deprive Caesar of his office, but they chose to err on the side of caution and quickly caught up and accompanied us home. Along the way, Caesar made it very clear he didn't accept the judgment of the senate and let the two men know they should inform the other four lictors that they still worked for him. Being equestrians and all handpicked from his clientela, his lictors were glad to go along with Caesar's view of things.

The lictors blocked everyone from following us as we crossed the threshold and entered the Domus Publica. Once inside though, Caesar called the door slave, Antius, to him and sent him back out for Labienus, Vatinius, and young Marcus Antonius. I was surprised Antonius was invited back, thinking Caesar was still misreading the situation. By associating with Antonius, the bitter stepson of the executed Lentulus, I feared Caesar was simply providing stones for the slings of the Optimates in the senate. I thought it would be best he avoid any reminder of the role he played in arguing for leniency for the conspirators. I realized, however, that it was neither the appropriate time nor was it the proper place to voice my concerns. My overriding worry now was that Caesar

438

would be exiled and once more my life would be turned end over end.

As was often the case, Aurelia seemed to know something was very wrong. She came from the back of the house to greet her son. I suspected she had spies of her own throughout the city. The proceedings of the senate were almost always carried out with the doors open. As a result, there was a constant flow of information that ran from mouth to ear like a waterfall down the steps of the curia and out into the crowd in the forum. Aurelia always seemed to have a trusted slave or freedwoman running an errand near the curia on days when important matters were being discussed.

'The vote went against you?' she asked this as she hugged Caesar to her breast. For just an instant, my master looked like a weak, defeated, boy and then he broke the embrace as his genius rallied his inner strength.

'We must plan what to do next,' he said to Aurelia. 'Where's my wife?'

Aurelia understood immediately. 'She said she'd be at the house in the Subura. I'll send someone to keep eyes on her.'

Caesar was all action then. Another surprise in a day filled with surprises came when he said to his mother, 'When you've that taken care of that, join us in the tablinum.' Then, turning to me, 'Find Demetrius and bring him to the meeting.' With that he signaled to the group of men waiting in the atrium and they all entered the tablinum and shut the folding doors behind them.

Demetrius had been freed on the calends of Januarius (January 1) but had not yet left the house. In fact, he would never actually leave Caesar's service until the ides of Martius (March 15), some eighteen years later. Demetrius was put in charge of Caesar's financial and business affairs. A freedman had the ability to go places and attend to matters a slave never could, so as Caesar's agent he could buy and sell property and negotiate loans. For now he was working out of the cubicle next to my small workspace. I found him there poring over a scroll of Caesar's accounts. When he saw me, he jumped up from his high stool and adjusted his toga. Apparently, Aurelia had warned him what to expect, so without a word, he moved past me and I followed him into the tablinum, stopping by my workspace to pick up a stylus and three fresh tablets. When we joined the men, the meeting was already underway, and without interrupting what he was saying, Caesar signaled for me to get wine for Demetrius and myself.

'I want every one of you sending out inquiries to all your clients,' Caesar was saying. 'Find out who is really behind this. Cato isn't smart enough to have hatched this plan.'

Aurelia answered him. 'Maybe it's not a plan. Maybe he's just taking advantage of the situation.

'Fine. If that's the case I want to be sure.'

The meeting went on in this vein for some time with the discussion of the motives and personalities behind the attempt to strip Caesar of his office until Demetrius, always the practical one, changed the subject. 'We can debate this well into the night, but right now we should figure out how to proceed. What are your options, Caesar?'

440

It was Labienus who answered. 'You will have to resign. You can't oppose the entire senate.'

Caesar looked at him crossly and replied, 'First of all, it's *not* the entire senate I would be opposing. A little more than half sided with the proposal.' He paused to take a sip of wine and collect his thoughts, so I did the same.

'And your second point?' This was from Vatinius.

'When I was studying oratory in Rhodes I learned one very valuable lesson. When backed into a corner while arguing a case, reject your adversary's premise.' Most of the group seemed puzzled. Only Demetrius, Aurelia, and I knew where this was going. I could now see how useful it was to spend so many long hours with Caesar. He continued, 'I will simply state that it is plainly obvious the senate hasn't the authority to remove a duly elected praetor, and ignore their *suggestion* that I step down.'

For the first time, Marcus Antonius spoke. 'That, as recent events clearly demonstrate, is plainly not the case. They can remove a praetor with lethal results.' This surprised me as it sounded like a reasonable statement and I hadn't expected that from Antonius.

Everyone sat back to absorb this statement. It had been just over a month prior that Lentulus was forced to resign his praetorship just before being strangled to death.

The silence began to grow awkward, so I spoke. 'If you do take that position, you will be accusing Cicero as well as most of the senate of committing an illegal act.'

441

Caesar smiled for the first time that afternoon. 'Yes, so we had better rouse our supporters.'

Then, however, Antonius added, while punching his right fist into his left hand, 'We should kick some asses and knock some heads. I could easily get a couple of dozen men willing to help me do it.' This once again lowered my opinion of the brash young man.

With that, Aurelia, arguably the best political manager in the group, began to issue orders. She set every man present a task. She made certain any client or client of a client to anyone in the room would be contacted and instructed, persuaded, cajoled, and, if necessary, bullied and threatened to whip up support for Caesar's position. She then added with a cold stare at Antonius, 'We will, however, not be kicking any asses or knocking any heads.' At this point in the meeting, Antius rapped gently on the door and announced Crassus' arrival. Demetrius went out to inform him of what had happened up to that point and Crassus joined the strategy session. Crassus was plainly furious, but was doing his best to keep his temper under control. He saw Caesar as an investment and he didn't want his time and especially his money to go to waste.

After just briefly listening to what was being said, Crassus voiced an opinion. 'This is all good to a point, but we need to put more pressure on the bastards in the senate if we're going to pull this thing out of the fire.'

Aurelia challenged him, most impressively. 'We will be putting pressure on the senators who matter. They all want to be elected to the next office on the ladder. Every man dreams of one day being consul. They'll listen when the voters start screaming loudly enough!'

'That'll be too little and it will come too late!'

'What do you suggest, Crassus?' With this, Caesar reentered the discussion.

What he said next seemed to cause him actual pain, as he detested dealing with other men's slaves and Demetrius had been, until just a few days before, among that group. 'Demetrius and I will get together and make a list of every man who has dirt under his nails. We'll find out who has spent the family's fortune at the circus. We'll find out who drinks away his evenings with cutthroats and pimps in the lowest tavernas of the Subura. We'll find out who is whoring around with what girl or *boy*.' At that, he paused and stared straight at Antonius, causing the younger man's face to redden, but he didn't look away. He met Crassus' stare with a cold stare of his own, telling me his face reddened with anger, not shame. 'And, then,' Crassus continued, 'we will threaten to visit fathers and brothers and wives and lovers and tip up the rocks to expose where that dirt all came from.'

It was then Demetrius spoke. 'We'll need Polybius.'

My head snapped up to see Crassus on the verge of choking. He began to shake his head no and started to spit out a reply when Demetrius cut him off. 'I've been out of it almost a year. We'll need Polybius for the latest scandals, and you'll want fresh dirt.'

Crassus stared at me, thinking it over. So, before he could say anything I spoke up. 'Cicero has the best network of spies in the city, and his man Tiro knows everything his

443

master knows, or nearly so. I've been dealing with him for months, so with a purse full of your coins, I could buy a lot of information.'

Crassus' eyes narrowed as he made up his mind. Turning to Caesar he said, 'With your permission, I'd like to meet with these two tomorrow morning.'

Caesar answered, 'You can have Demetrius all day, but I need Polybius in the morning. I have court in the forum and I'm not even sure of the names of those involved in the trial.'

Everyone in the room looked at him in surprise. Labienus was the first to speak. 'You can't be serious about going out tomorrow. You have been stripped of your office. You can't sit in judgement at any trials!'

Caesar was calm but definitive in his reply. 'I was elected praetor by the people of Rome. The senate does not have the authority to change that, so I will discharge my duties. It would be an insult to my dignitas and the dignitas of my ancestors to do otherwise.

With that, Crassus rose with a sigh. He knew Caesar well enough to know that once he made up his mind on a matter of personal honor, the discussion was over. Turning to Demetrius he said, 'We can meet after the trial. Bring the boy.' He didn't look at me as he turned to leave. Uncharacteristically, Caesar walked Crassus out of the room with me following at a discreet distance. The older man put his hand on Caesar's back and leaned forward as they stepped a few feet from the group and into the atrium. Caesar leaned toward him to hear what Crassus had to say. Crassus lowered his voice and said, just loud enough for me to hear, 'At the least don't be seen with Marcus Antonius.'

Caesar stopped and looked at Crassus with the utmost innocence. 'Why not?' He made no attempt to lower his own voice.

'You know perfectly well why not!' Crassus hissed the words.

'No, I don't. Tell me.'

'He is a degenerate young man. He drinks too much, he gambles too much, and he whores around too much. He's not yet twenty-five and he's already run through his family's fortune. He's even said to be having an affair with that other young man he's seen with all the time. What's his name?'

Caesar smiled. 'Except for the drinking and the affair with the young man, you could be talking about me at his age.' Then he smoothed the hair down on the right side of his head where it had a tendency to curl up. 'In fact, people said I was involved in a relationship with a man when I was a few years younger than Antonius is now.'

I was, to say the least, shocked by what I heard. This was the first hint I'd heard of Caesar's rumored affair with the king of Bythinia, said to have occurred over fifteen years earlier. I was also intrigued by the possibility that Antonius shared my attraction for the male sex. I glanced over at him, and noticed him in a new light. Briefly, I thought he was more attractive than I'd previously noticed. I continued to busy myself scratching meaningless marks in the wax, hoping the two men wouldn't realize I was listening.

445

Crassus was clearly frustrated and wanted to raise his voice, but Marcus Antonius was just a few feet farther away from them than I was. I wondered whether he too was listening. 'I would also advise you to stay away from your younger self. In fact, I'd suggest you stay away from your present self if that was somehow possible.' Crassus tried to sound as if he was making a joke but his tone said otherwise.

Caesar answered him evenly but firmly. 'When I was a boy my father tried to tell me to stay away from some other boys I'd befriended. I didn't follow his advice. If as a child I wouldn't let my own father choose my friends, whatever makes you believe I'll grant you that privilege? Now go home and get some sleep. You are, I believe, appearing as an advocate at the trial I'm presiding over tomorrow, and I want you at your best.'

Crassus and Caesar began to walk toward the vestibule. I was watching their backs and didn't hear Antonius walk up beside me, so it gave me a start when he said clearly and loudly, 'Crassus!'

When Crassus and Caesar turned, Antonius said for all to hear, 'Natalis.' Crassus looked puzzled, so he added, 'The man's name. His name is Marcus Natalis.' Antonius didn't wait for a reply, turning back to join the others in the tablinum. An awkward silence filled both the atrium and the tablinum, only to be replaced by a higher level of animated talk that made the men sound like actors on a stage. I found Antonius' response to Crassus' gossip to be quite refreshing. I appreciated the fact that he stood up to the fabulously wealthy and arrogantly famous Marcus Licinius Crassus. I used my wax tablet to make a note to myself to find out all I could about this man, Natalis.

446

The following morning, Caesar spent more time than usual with his prayers and the offering to the household gods. I stood in the distance, but close enough to hear him say the start of a prayer to Fortuna before his words trailed off and his prayer became a silent one, said with his heart rather than his lips. A short time later he held his salutatio as usual and then with his three lictors and just a slightly smaller group of followers, we proceeded to the forum. Along the way I made note of all the men who avoided Caesar. He wasn't a vindictive man and Caesar never seemed to carry a grudge, but I thought the information might come in useful at a later time. Caesar, of course, needed to know the names and pertinent details of the men who approached him. On the other side of my tablet, I noted those men's names. Caesar made a point of stopping to talk to Antonius and even made a show of throwing his arm over the young man's shoulder. I'm certain this was a message to Crassus who was watching, with a scowl on his face, from a short distance away. When Caesar mounted the platform and took his seat, there was a murmur through the crowd. I watched nervously for a club or dagger to appear, but everyone calmed down and the trial proceeded as it normally would.

Just before the trial ended, Demetrius joined me on the back bench and waited for Caesar to adjourn the proceedings. We met briefly with both Caesar and Crassus and we then parted ways with Caesar, following Crassus back to his house. Rather than try to hide the fact that he was meeting with both Caesar's former and current nomenclator, Crassus guided us on a winding tour of the forum to ensure we were seen by as many men as possible. We spent that afternoon compiling the list, and it was extensive. I surprised myself with the sheer volume of scandalous knowledge I had picked up on the private lives of the leading senators. My method was

447

the same as always. I would shut my eyes and make my way to the appropriate room in my 'memory house, and then imagine myself standing in front of the man in question as he responded to my inquiries.

We were allowed two meal breaks while we worked, and during these breaks we were forced to eat the regular fare Crassus afforded his slaves, which was every bit as good as the food Caesar served to his dinner guests. I could then see there are real advantages to belonging to a rich master.

It was close to sunset when Demetrius and I left Crassus' house. On the way home I had my first opportunity to talk to Demetrius since he had been granted his freedom.

'May I ask you a question?' I said.

Demetrius was in a playful mood; adversity seemed to bring that out of him. 'You just did. Would you like to ask another?'

I smiled and answered, 'Yes, and probably a few more after that one.' He nodded. 'I'm curious. You had years to save money. Why didn't you save enough money to buy your freedom? Why did you wait until Caesar freed you? Surely he would have let you buy yourself.'

'We stand in a unique position, Polybius. Caesar is one of the best masters a slave can have.'

'He is a good master. Crassus, however, has better food.'

Demetrius laughed. 'I made a promise to serve Caesar's father, and when he died I made the same promise to serve your master.'

'What about yourself? Isn't it important to do what's best for yourself first?' I had made myself a promise to gain my freedom, and I could never understand why Demetrius didn't feel the same.

'Not always, I remained a slave for love.'

I didn't understand, and I told him so. 'For love? What do you mean?'

Polybius, I told you everything there is to know about a thousand Roman citizens, but I've never told you that which is most important about me. When I was just a few years older than you, I fell in love. I was mad with love for Aurelia's flower arranger, a girl named Phyllis, and in time she came to love me too. We have a daughter together. We named her Pandora. She's a beautiful girl already nearly ten years older than you. When our daughter was three years old, Caesar's father needed money quickly. I won't go into details, but I will tell you he was selling assets. Phyllis and I had each been saving money. We agreed that whichever of us had saved enough money to buy the other and our daughter first, would do so. I had greater opportunity to accumulate money, so I had nearly enough to buy both of them, but she had saved much less. Our master started selling the slaves he had no real use for. Of course, a three-year-old girl contributed nothing to the house, but our master, the elder Caesar was, like his son, a kind man, and he made it clear he wouldn't sell my daughter. But, I saw this as an opportunity. I knew that together we didn't have enough to buy both Phyllis and our daughter and

449

we couldn't bear to separate them by freeing just one. I also knew it would be a mistake to take advantage of the elder Caesar's financial straits by offering a price that was too low for both, as I certainly didn't want to engender any ill feelings between us. It was Phyllis who came up with a creative solution. I was able to negotiate a quite reasonable price for Phyllis and bought her freedom. She then borrowed money from your master, the younger Caesar, to raise enough to buy our Pandora. Caesar didn't have the money himself, as he was not yet considered a man. At first he said no, but when he saw how desperate we were, he arranged a loan from Marcus Licinius Crassus, who had just recently come of age. That was the first money Caesar ever borrowed from him.'

'I never knew that.' I didn't know what else to say as I tried to imagine Demetrius as a young man in love.

He continued. 'Phyllis works as a florist now. She used to have a shop in the stall now occupied by the poultry shop attached to Caesar's domus in the Subura, but her business grew and she now rents a place in the Basilica Aemilia. Pandora and Phyllis live in the loft above the business. We see each other ten or twelve times a month for an hour or two and sometimes I'm able to spend the night with them. Next month my family will be moving with me to Caesar's domus in the Subura. When they do, you will meet them. At any rate, we could have bought my freedom some years ago, but then there would have been no money for difficult times, and since Caesar promised my freedom when he gained the praetorship, we chose to wait. With the way things have been, we thought it prudent to save for difficult times. Besides, I wouldn't have wanted to leave Caesar's service until he had found an adequate replacement. Then, he

450

found you. You're not yet my equal, but I've no doubt, one day you will best me at what we do.'

That last part made me feel proud. We walked the rest of the way without speaking. I said a prayer to the goddesses Juno and Fecunditas to not let Cornelia get pregnant until I was free. I would have said a prayer to Venus to not let me fall in love, but it was too late for that, as I was already in love with Cornelia. At that time, I was convinced no one had ever been more deeply in love, but I would one day learn that a much deeper and more powerful love was in store for me. Not entirely trusting the goddesses, I made a promise to myself to keep track of Cornelia's monthly cycle as added insurance. In that I felt confident; the spare hours I spent in the company of Alexander and Lydia served me well throughout my life. They were two of the very few adults who are willing to treat children as if they are adults merely lacking in understanding. They were able to explain things to me in a way I could understand. As a result of their tutelage, I probably knew more of the workings of the human body than many of the most learned men in Rome. I now endeavor to do the same." With that, Polybius looked long at Mela who blushed and turned away.

"Speaking of human bodies," Polybius said, "mine is beginning to feel stiff. I propose we take a walk." With that, Polybius pushed himself up to a sitting position. I was surprised to see Mela spring up to assist him and was embarrassed that I hadn't thought to do the same. Quickly we were both helping Polybius to his feet. From the shadows in the corner of the far end of the room, I saw Castor rise from his seat and approach us. I hadn't noticed him there and this surprised me. I briefly thought about how much I take our own family slaves for granted.

451

"I won't be requiring your assistance, Castor," Polybius waved him off. "These two young men and my staff will be enough for now." As we shuffled along on our slow journey out to the garden, Mela on one side and I on the other, Polybius remained silent, concentrating his effort on walking, but once we found ourselves seated in chairs around a table, he became more animated. With a wave of his hand he caught the attention of one of the slaves working nearby and had the boy run inside for a pitcher of water and three cups. Polybius had me check my notes to remind him where he'd left off, and we went on.

LIBER XXVII

"At any rate," Polybius continued, "our efforts to construct a list of scandalous charges to hurl at the leading men of the senate ultimately came to no good end. Crassus was very careful to not directly engage the enemy. Instead, he enlisted clients of Caesar's supporters to, whenever Caesar's name was mentioned at dinner parties and business meetings, bring up various details of the private lives of leading senators. After several days of this, it became apparent that the strategy was having an effect. Certain men stopped attending the meetings of the senate and others avoided associating with those who had been accused. However, it turned out both Caesar and Crassus had misjudged the mettle of their opponents in the senate while all the while thinking they were scoring hits against the opposition. Both were quite pleased when a written request for a face to face meeting was delivered to Caesar by two freedmen, one from each of the two consuls. Caesar sent back a reply that he would be happy to meet with the consuls to settle any differences between them and himself. He then invited them to meet him the following midday in the gardens of the Domus Publica.

Caesar planned the meeting carefully. He was dressed in the toga praetexta of a Roman magistrate and his three lictors were stationed discreetly, but obviously, several feet behind him. I and the three secretaries, Agamedes, Nicandros, and Plautius were stationed at the sides to take notes of what was said. A cold meal of fruit, various cheeses, and dried meats was laid out with plenty of the best wine at the ready. At the meeting were Crassus; the tribune, Rufinus, to act as an unspoken threat to veto any legislation that might be proposed against Caesar; the Chief Vestal; the eldest of the pontiffs; Labienus; and Marcus Antonius. Caesar invited Cicero to add political muscle to his side, but the former consul claimed to not be feeling well and declined.

I asked Demetrius why Antonius was there. I believed then and I still believe his continued presence only served to diminish Caesar in the eyes of the senate. At first his reply was in line with what Caesar said to him; 'Your master likes him and thinks he has potential.'

I looked at Demetrius with a smirk, prompting him to add, 'He also has a reputation as a volatile and potentially violent young man with little to lose. He's a bow that has been drawn too tightly and might free its missile with the slightest jolt. Perhaps Caesar thinks this may prompt the consuls to think twice before doing anything rash.'

The group had been left sitting and impatiently making small talk for what I guessed to be about an hour past the appointed time for the meeting when the door slave came in and announced the two freedmen who had delivered the original invitation to meet.

Caesar was clearly irritated when the men approached. 'Have the consuls been detained?'

One of the two men stepped forward. 'The consuls will not be coming. We are instructed to tell you that the senate will be asked to vote to authorize the consuls to exercise all necessary means to compel the former praetor Gaius Julius Caesar to give up any pretense of office, by force if necessary. That is all.'

Caesar, and indeed the entire group, was speechless. It was not until the two men turned to leave that Crassus spoke. 'Please tell your masters that this course of action is unwise. Both men stopped and turned back. Crassus, carefully considering his words, continued, 'There has been much loose talk. Talk can turn into legal action.'

The one freedman who spoke for both drew a small scroll from his toga. 'As you can see from the way I'm dressed, I'm a Roman citizen and, therefore, I am my own master, but if you are referring to the consuls, they are not worried.' Turning from Crassus to Caesar, he said, 'Have your slaves stop writing.'

Caesar signaled to me and the two others to stop taking notes and nodded at the man. Without checking to see if we had set down our styli, the freedman calmly unrolled the small scroll in his hand and said, 'There is abundant and irrefutable evidence that the formal praetor Gaius Julius Caesar is currently, or has in the recent past, engaged in carnal relations with Servilia, wife of the consul Junius Silanus and sister to Marcus Cato as well as Flavia, wife of Hosidius; Vibia, wife of Saturninus; and at least four other wives or daughters of men of senatorial or equestrian rank. Legal action is being contemplated and the information has been passed along to the censors.' There was no law against sex with a married woman, but Caesar could be expelled from the senate on moral grounds.

The men turned to leave, but the second man, the one who had not yet spoken, turned back. He stopped and looked first at Caesar, then at Crassus and then back again at Caesar. 'My colleague failed to mention there is also strong evidence that Gaius Julius Caesar has been engaging in a sexual relationship with Mucia, wife of the proconsul Gnaeus Pompeius Magnus.' With that, both men left the suddenly quiet room.

After a long, uncomfortable silence, Caesar turned to me and said, 'Polybius, make sure the three accounts of this meeting agree and then set the exact text to papyrus and leave it for me in the strong box. Be sure it is securely locked.' I did as he ordered. Then, after another moment, he said, 'Make certain all those wax tablets are scraped clean when you finish.'

The meeting in the garden went on for another hour or so, but I wasn't sent for. At last, Caesar leaned into my cubicle and said, 'There's food left over. Fix yourself a plate and bring one to Cornelia.' I nodded, not knowing what to say. 'At least for now,' he continued, 'I'm dismissing my praetorian lictors. I need time to think.' With that, he entered the tablinum with Crassus and Labienus. The men didn't emerge until well past sunset, but I noticed Antonius left at the end of the formal meeting along with the others.

The following days, Caesar carried on life as a private citizen. He didn't attend court or for that matter any other official business. He didn't put on the toga praetexta, and since the month of Januarius had few religious days, he only put on the robe of the Pontifex Maximus once. He spent much of his time in systematic thought. He let it be known through his clients that he intended to retire from public life. He even told the household staff this was his intention, but I certainly didn't believe it. I knew he was planning something. The day after he announced his retirement, a large group of plebs began to gather on the Sacra Via just after sunrise. By noon there was a group of several hundred men and women

456

singing songs and chanting Caesar's name. I was sent up on the roof to look over the crowd over and estimate its size. The mass of people spilled over into the forum and word of the demonstration spread quickly. Labienus and Antonius stopped by the house to tell Caesar there was talk among some senators of restoring him to his position. With that, Caesar went out onto the street, and made a short, eloquent speech thanking the people for their support, but urging them to return to their homes and businesses. Those members of the senate who still longed for the distinction of office were naturally intimidated by large demonstrations staged by voters. I've no doubt Caesar, through his clientela, had orchestrated the start of the gathering, but even he seemed surprised by how large the crowd had grown by midday.

On the fifth day after the meeting in the garden of the Domus Publica and one day after the demonstration on the Sacra Via, Caesar asked me to bring a papyrus scroll and pen and ink into the tablinum. He then dictated a list of the names of seventeen women. I took down the names without question, but I was certain what they all had in common. After the ink dried, he took the scroll and bid me to join him. I said nothing as we walked across the forum, but as we approached the curia he said without looking at me, 'Do you trust Fortuna has a plan for me?'

I thought I should pretend to not understand the question, but I knew that would make me appear weak in his eyes, so I answered him honestly. 'I am certain she has a plan for *us.*'

Caesar looked at me and smiled. 'I'm rolling the dice, Polybius. As you've no doubt guessed, the list you made contains the names of married women I've had relations with all of them within the last two years. Either the senate will forget all this nonsense or I'm throwing myself on the sword politically, and I'll bring scandal to many of the most prominent families in Rome.' I then noticed Caesar was, quite literally, rolling two or three dice around in his right hand.

'You are bold,' I said, but when I thought about it, I hadn't lied. I was certain Fortuna favored us and I knew things would turn out, one way or another, according to her design, but I was worried about the outcome. I was grateful though that Demetrius had the foresight to purchase a villa for Caesar just outside Massilia in southern Gaul, in the event the goddess' plans were not as straightforward as I would have liked.

I was a little disappointed Caesar could arrange a meeting between himself and both consuls without my knowledge, but I admitted to myself that it was vanity that led me to believe I was at the center of his world. The meeting took place in one of the antechambers of the Curia Hostilia. By the number of lictors waiting outside I knew both consuls were present. After just a short time, Caesar emerged from the curia, smiling. I quickly got to my feet and followed him as he made his way down the steps.

'Fortuna still favors me, Polybius,' he said, clapping me on the back. 'We won't be moving to Gaul.' Sometimes he seemed to be able to hear my thoughts. 'Send for my lictors.'

Caesar took a chance and faced down the consuls. Silanus, it was said, loved his wife in spite of her infidelity with Caesar and didn't want to be forced into having to divorce her. Caesar's many affairs were common knowledge, but once they were officially recognized, husbands and fathers would be forced to act. No one wanted a scandal of such magnitude to be brought to light. There was also the possibility that many of the leading men would find their own indiscretions made public. My master had been able to secure his position, but I wondered at what cost, having made enemies of some of the most powerful senators.

The restoration of Caesar's office didn't sit well with all the senators. Cato was particularly upset, but he was smart enough to know it was not the time to stir up more trouble. He was keenly aware his sister was having an affair with Caesar and he didn't want to call Caesar's bluff and have him announce it to the world. Others, though, thought they were clever enough to outflank him. I never learned who was behind the move, but Quintus Curius was somehow persuaded to level a charge of treason against Caesar. The Catilina conspiracy had just recently been put down and suspicions ran high. Curius was originally a member of the conspiracy but was persuaded by his mistress to betray the whole affair to Cicero. He was rewarded with restoration to the senate but he agreed to not seek office for at least ten years. This, in effect, ended his political career so he had little to lose. A few days after Caesar was restored to the praetorship, Curius presented to a meeting of the senate a list that he claimed contained the names of surviving members of Catilina's plot. Caesar's name was third from the top and was the most distinguished and prominent name on the list. Curius was able to produce a witness to corroborate his accusation. An obscure equite named Lucius Vettius came forward to announce he had a letter written by Caesar to Catilina. Vettius said he would produce the letter only after Caesar was arrested. In his defense, Caesar called on Cicero to make an account of his actions during the crisis and Cicero steadfastly maintained Caesar had been not only loyal to Rome but most useful in rooting out the would-be rebels. As a result, Curius was deprived of the reward he expected. Caesar then, in his capacity as praetor, commanded Vettius to appear before the Rostra. Upon mounting the platform, Caesar recounted all the blemishes against Vettius' reputation going back many years. He was able to do this at short notice because Vettius was one of the names that came up when Demetrius and I met with Crassus to dig into the private dirt of Caesar's enemies. While Vettius was never important enough to be a target for Crassus, his name continued to surface when we investigated the questionable dealings of Caesar's real enemies. This had the added benefit of embarrassing men Vettius was involved with, though Caesar was discreet enough to not actually name them. When he was done haranguing him from the Rostra, Caesar ordered his lictors to give the man a good beating and had him hauled off to the Carcer. A few hours later, Caesar ordered the man's release with a warning to cause no more trouble.

Caesar had started his year as praetor with an ambitious political agenda in mind. He had been formulating plans to align himself with Pompeius Magnus when the conquerer returned from the east, but first he was going to push a series of Populare causes that would gain him even greater favor among the plebs. In meeting after meeting during the early part of the year everyone close to Caesar gave him the same advice: Don't stir the pot until at least summer. Finally, it was Aurelia who persuaded her son to accept that his position was too precarious for bold action and Caesar was convinced to spend the next few months walking down the center of the road. He was more than competent at the job, since it mainly consisted of acting as a judge in civil cases. The ease with which he handled the duties of the praetorship left Caesar time to cement alliances with the associates and clients of Pompeius Magnus. He felt he could trade his support for Pompeius' ambitious legislation for settling things in the eastern provinces for the general's support for his own social agenda in Rome. During these months Caesar was frequently bored with his duties, often telling me how he craved greater imperium and the right to lead armies against Rome's enemies. Where Caesar's high level of confidences sprang from, I have no idea, but he was always certain he would be greater than even Pompeius Magnus once he was given legions of his own to command.

For a time, our lives seemed settled, however, in Aprilis of that year, my personal affairs took a turn.

LIBER XXVIII

Near the end of that month, Cornelia announced to me, in spite of my careful calculations and close scrutiny of the calendar, that she was pregnant. We visited Lydia and had the matter confirmed. After that visit I was able to sneak her into the Titus Domus and introduce her to my former slave family. We were there for quite some time before one of Porcia's slaves forced us to leave. With the impending birth of my first child my hopes for freedom were complicated. My relationship with Cornelia was also strained, as she had, at least for the first few months, a difficult pregnancy and this severely limited our intimacy. About this time I again took up with the young slave named Philon to relieve my sexual tension. I, once again, convinced myself I was still being faithful to Cornelia, because for the sake of our impending child I wanted to build a solid family. So, Philon and I only masturbated together when the urge arose.

At any rate, as winter turned to spring and then to summer, Caesar settled into a mostly unspoken agreement with the powerful Optimates in the senate. He would not take any extreme positions and they would grant him a lucrative province to govern for the following year. It looked as though the year was going to finish uneventfully when scandal broke yet again. Remarkably, while Caesar was at the center of the scandal, it wasn't of his making. This time it was Caesar's wife who brought shame to her husband and indeed the whole of Rome. I'm quite certain you've heard of the famous Bona Dea scandal, so I won't bore you with the details."

462

With that last comment, Mela looked crestfallen. Both my brother and I had heard of the Bona Dea scandal, but, as it took place nearly eighty years previous, we actually knew very few of the details. I didn't want to seem eager to hear of scandal, so I said with a smile, "I know it's about sex, so you'd better fill us in with the details or Mela will be very upset."

"It was a tedious affair and it's been written about so many times, I'd rather not bore you."

I wasn't quite sure, but I suspected Polybius was having fun at our expense, so I made the case for him telling the story. "There's no reason to cover eighty year old salacious gossip that can be easily researched in a library, but in the interest of historical study, I'd like to hear the account from someone who witnessed it firsthand."

With that, both Mela and Polybius smiled. "I am quite certain there is not any witness to the events still among the living." Polybius took three or four sips of wine, indicating he was going to tell the story. "I'm afraid I can only tell you what was pieced together through conversations since no man is allowed to be present during the rites, and it was then that the scandal took place. My Cornelia witnessed some of the events, but she was sworn to secrecy and took her oath seriously. I probably could have pressured her to reveal the secrets, but I would never risk the wrath of the goddess by doing so. As you know, the festival of Bona Dea is mainly an affair for Roman women. The public rites are held during the day and a priest, most commonly the Pontifex Maximus is present at that time, but the most sacred ceremonies take place at night behind closed doors and those rites are only ever attended by women. The wife of one of the senior magistrates always hosts the rites, so for that evening all the men of the household including the male slaves retire to some other place. Since Caesar was both praetor and Pontifex Maximus, it was deemed appropriate that his wife conduct the ceremonies at the Domus Publica. It was also most convenient that Caesar had another home nearby in the Subura where all the males could while away the hours. Generally, one of the other senior magistrates hosts a dinner party for the man whose wife is hosting the sacred rites, and all the men of the household are invited. Since Caesar was either at odds with or deeply in debt to many of the other senators, he chose instead to have an informal party for his closest friends and his male household slaves. He called the evening a "Saturnalia preview," and a great deal of latitude was extended to the slaves, putting us on an almost even footing with Caesar's freedmen.

It is important at this point you understand the relationship Caesar had with his wife. His marriage to Pompeia was one of convenience. She was young and pretty and a gracious hostess. She was also vain and vacuous with almost no interest in the arts or literature or politics. In my estimation, she was one of the stupidest women I'd ever met who was able to pass for normal. In short, Caesar and Pompeia had nothing in common save the fact that they were married. Caesar was kept very busy maintaining sexual relationships with never fewer than two, and often three or four women at the same time. He didn't believe it would be appropriate for Pompeia to have the same freedom he gave himself, but he didn't keep her on a very short leash, and throughout their marriage she was rumored to have had two or three affairs.

At that time, she was hopelessly infatuated with a brash young man named Publius Clodius Pulcher. Clodius was a brilliant politician, but was also somewhat of a rogue. In many ways he resembled Caesar. Both were charismatic, good looking patricians, meticulous about their appearance and ambitious enough to abandon the Optimates and make names for themselves by supporting the popular causes. Clodius was born a Claudius during the consulship of Flaccus and Herennius (93 BC). He adopted the plebeian spelling and pronunciation of the family name after he had himself grafted onto the plebeian branch of the Claudians through a purchased adoption. Unlike Caesar, Clodius was far more sexually adventurous than either convention or the law allowed. He was at various times accused of having incestuous relations with his two full sisters. Clodius also liked to have sex in public places or sneak into the home of a lover while her husband was home. He was able to stay out of serious trouble by spending several years away from Rome, attaching himself to the staffs of several prominent proconsuls. Cicero tried to link Clodius to the Catilina conspiracy, but this went nowhere, as there was absolutely no evidence to support the charge. Even Cicero soon realized there was no reason to suspect Clodius of plotting against the state and he let him join the band of young equites who acted as his bodyguard during the crisis. In spite of being married to a respectable matron of the Fulvia family, Clodius sought to sleep with the wives of as many senators as he could. He pursued Pompeia, I believe, simply because she was married to a praetor who was also the Pontifex Maximus.

Aurelia spent many days preparing for the Bona Dea rites. By tradition the wife of the magistrate plans the evening, but since Pompeia had little interest in religion and virtually no organizational ability, she was only nominally involved in the planning. My Cornelia had been relieved of any strenuous duties around the domus, as she was just days from giving birth, but there was a significant role for her in the Bona Dea

465

ritual. Pregnant women, even slaves, have a special role in the rites, but, as a man, any knowledge of what role she played was denied me. What the actual rites entailed I have no idea since she and all the other women present swore the most dreadful oaths to ensure secrecy. The rites themselves were followed by music, dance, and feasting.

I'm not certain whether the idea for an assignation on this most sacred occasion stemmed from the abysmally empty mind of Pompeia or the perverted thoughts of Clodius, but between the two of them they hatched a ludicrous plot whereby Clodius would sneak into the Domus Publica dressed as a woman and the two would profane the rites and put all of Rome in peril by engaging in intercourse while the other women continued the festivities. Clodius was able to pass as a woman because he was sufficiently plump to bind his chest with a silk sash forcing his pectoral muscles to form cleavage. He was then able to pad the lower part giving the appearance of full breasts. He also had the habit of having his barber pluck the whiskers from his face rather than shave it, so his cheeks were smoother than those of many of the matrons in attendance at the rites. Clodius took the disguise of one of the slaves brought in to perform music for the women. He was let in a side entrance by one of Pompeia's personal slaves who was in on the plan. This slave then went off to find Pompeia, leaving Clodius waiting, with flowers in one hand and a flute in the other. He was already a little drunk and he grew restless. Some say he was looking for someplace to piss, but I suspect he was just bored with waiting and curious about the house, never having been invited into the Domus Publica. At any rate, he wandered off and was found, apparently lost, by one of Aurelia's slaves. She persistently attempted to coax the not too pretty musician to join the group in the other room. Finally he had to tell her he couldn't follow her because "she" was

466

waiting for "her" friend. This gave him away, as he was either too foolish or too drunk to disguise his voice by attempting a falsetto. Aurelia's slave ran off screaming about the male intruder. Since the lictors that attended the vestal virgins had been placed around the house to act as guards, he couldn't escape, so Clodius hid in the room of Habra, the slave girl who let him into the house. Aurelia had the house searched from top to bottom by groups of women carrying torches and kitchen knives. When he was found, she pulled off his wig and examined him closely. Once she was certain of his true identity, the women drove him from the house. I later heard from one of the lictors that he had heard the ruckus from inside the house but thought it was part of the ritual. When a crowd of angry women chased a man in a peplos dress from the house he had no idea what to do, so he just remained at his post and watched him disappear into the darkness.

Pompeia tried to pretend she was as horrified by the sacrilege as everyone else, but Aurelia saw through her. She kept giggling and snickering at the outrage of the other women. Aurelia was certain of Clodius' identity because he was a close friend of Pompeia's brother and had visited the house in the Subura with him on several occasions. Apparently he had taken to visiting Pompeia without her brother as well.

Aurelia, accompanied by the Virgo Vestalis Maxima and her lictors, went straight to Caesar's house in the Subura. Soon there would be a wild ruckus in the street, but for now we had no idea anything was amiss, so it was a complete surprise when Antius crossed the atrium on his way to the triclinium. Philon and I had just come from my sleeping cubicle, having taken advantage of the absence of the women for a quick sexual encounter, when we saw from the balcony

467

overlooking the atrium the two women overtake Antius on their march toward the back of the house. I had never seen more determined looks than they had on their faces. I noticed the two lictors they left standing near the vestibule seemed puzzled. I could hear Aurelia's raised voice coming from the back of the house but I couldn't make out what was being said. Philon and I looked at each other. He seemed amused, but I was horrified. I knew that for the women engaged in the sacred rites to leave the house, something must have gone horribly wrong. I feared the goddess' wrath for both Rome and the Julian house.

Soon, Aurelia's voice faded into a murmur that issued from the triclinium and a moment after that, there was silence. Caesar came out to the atrium, looking around. He spotted me on the balcony and shouted up, 'Polybius, take a few of the boys and round up the pontiffs. Bring torches and clubs; I want everyone to get back safely.'

"Yes master.' I now guessed something unprecedented had happened. 'Should I bring them here?'

'No,' he answered, 'to the Regia.'

It took a couple of hours to make the rounds of all fourteen houses. The pontiffs each made their own way to the Regia, bringing their own slaves and lictors, so when my small group arrived with the last of the pontiffs there was already a considerable crowd gathered on the Sacra Via. The gathering crowd of slaves and lictors around the portico of the Regia attracted an even larger group of people from the surrounding homes and tavernas. Patricians mingled with equites and plebs as word of the events of the evening spread. As the lone lictor of the pontiff I was accompanying attempted to force a path

468

through the mob, the people suddenly parted being pushed aside by the twelve lictors clearing a path for the senior consul who was departing the Regia. The second consul and his lictors followed them. Once again, the crowd filled in and we had to fight our way through to the courtyard. Once in the courtyard there was more freedom of movement. I was surprised not one of the women was there. I later learned from Cornelia that the women were each being questioned, one by one, by Aurelia and the Chief Vestal in the small room between the Domus Publica and the atrium of the vestals. This was the very room where I had had my unusual interview with the Virgo Vestalis Maxima.

Caesar was meeting with the pontiffs in the center room of the Regia. The room to the west was dedicated to Mars, and the one to the east was the Ops Consiva. These two rooms were deemed sacred and no one but priests and the chief vestal were allowed to enter them. The east room was, as a matter of fact, so sacred that only the Pontifex Maximus and the Virgo Vestalis Maxima were allowed there. These rules were, however, regularly violated, as such august persons were not about to sweep or scrub floors and walls, so one of the vestals was given special permission to, with the Virgo Vestalis Maxima in attendance, enter the sacred spaces and do the monthly cleaning. The central room was used as an office and meeting place of the Pontifex Maximus. Caesar didn't like the place, so most of his work was conducted in the Domus Publica, but on special occasions this room was used. The space was trapezoid shaped to correspond to the triangular shape of the building, and it had a high ceiling supported by columns of travertine marble. The wall near the entrance and the two side walls were decorated with frescoes depicting mythological scenes. There were four windows, two on the front wall above the door and two high on the back wall. The

469

center of the room was dominated by a heavy polished wooden table. Along the back wall, which was of plaster stained the color of blood, stood statues of gods and goddesses. When Caesar took possession of the Regia, he had a nearly life sized statue of Fortuna added to the collection.

One of the other priests took the last arriving pontiff aside and filled him in on what had happened. I saw no reason to stay in the room, so I bowed my way out and waited beneath the portico. As I backed out of the room, I noticed someone had left a pair of dice on the table. There was little else that could be done that night, so Caesar's lictors dispersed the crowd and he sent the pontiffs home, agreeing to meet again after the emergency meeting of the senate, which had been hastily called by the consuls for the following morning.

I followed Caesar and Demetrius back to the Domus Publica. Throughout the night Caesar maintained his composure, but once in the house he demonstrated how furious he was. He stormed into Pompeia's room and slammed the door. Through the heavy door we could hear him yelling, but we heard not a sound from his wife. When, a short time later, the door swung open, she was sitting on the floor sobbing. As Caesar walked past Demetrius and me he said, 'Be ready to leave early tomorrow. I'm going to bed.'

The following morning the senate voted to form a commission to investigate the whole affair and decide how to handle the unprecedented events. Never before in the history of Rome had the Bona Dea rites been polluted in this way, and the people were frightened and outraged. Caesar wanted as little to with the commission as possible, but as Pontifex Maximus he was chosen as one of the principle players. It was decided that afternoon at the first meeting of the commission

470

that the entire festival would be restaged on the ides of Decembris (December 13). After meeting with the college of pontiffs and the Virgo Vestalis Maxima, the commission ordered the formation of a special tribunal to try Clodius for his crimes. Caesar was deeply embarrassed and wanted there to be as little fuss as possible, but this wasn't to be the case. He was sent a summons to testify before a meeting of the tribunal in the Temple of Concordia five days before the ides of Decembris (December 8). The meeting was being held indoors to better protect Clodius from the angry mob that would inevitable form and demand blood.

Caesar called a meeting of his closest friends and associates for the evening of two days before he was to testify. Attending the meeting were Crassus, Labienus, Antonius, Cornelius Balbus, who recently arrived in Rome from Hispania, and a few others. Aurelia, of course, was also there. What was said at this meeting, I was never told. However, after the meeting he called me into the tablinum. 'I fear for my political future. What we do now will determine what province I'm to get. I thought Illyricum was a sure thing, but now it's all thrown up in the air.'

Caesar poured himself a cup of water from the pitcher on the table. During a crisis he rarely drank wine because he wanted to keep his thinking clear. 'Bring pen and ink, and two parchments, not papyri.

I did as he asked and quickly returned to him. 'Will you be using it, or do you want me to write?'

He reached for the sheets of parchments and then pushed them back across the table to me. 'I'll tell you what to write, but do it in my hand and write it in Latin, not Greek.' I

471

was by now practiced enough in my master's handwriting to not need a sample from which to copy. So, I smoothed the tip of my reed pen and dipped it into my inkpot as Caesar began to dictate. 'To Pompeia, sister of Quintus Pompeius Rufus. Take your things for yourself.'

I looked up at Caesar. He had spoken the ritual phrase that ends a marriage. 'Are you sure, Caesar?' I asked.

He nodded and continued dictating. 'As of now we are no longer husband and wife. I wish you the blessings of the gods and a long and happy life.' Caesar stood and looked over my shoulder approving the document and then said, 'Make a second copy to post in the forum. Leave them for me to sign and seal.'

With that, Caesar was divorced. The ritual requires the husband actually speak those words directly to his wife, and this I'm certain Caesar did so, but as this was a very private moment, I wasn't witness to it. He may have even spoken the words the night of the scandal when he was alone with his wife in her room. Demetrius made the arrangements for Pompeia to return to her brother's home. She left before we returned from the forum that day and her things were all moved within three days. Servilia spent nearly every afternoon with Caesar. What she told her husband she was doing, I have no idea, but I suppose the lovers were making an attempt to spend as much time together in the last days before Caesar was posted to his province. Caesar had been granted the post as propraetor of Hispania Ulterior.

At the same time, I began to formulate a plan of my own.

472

LIBER XXIX

I was charged with gathering information on the province. This gave me access to maps and naval charts detailing the whole of Europe. I used the opportunity to study the most probable route and I formed a plan whereby I would escape from slavery while travelling to the province. My plan was simple. Once the strongbox was loaded onto the ship at Ostia, I knew it wouldn't be again opened until it was secure in Hispania. My money was in a separate bag tagged with my name, so the night before our departure I planned to substitute my coins with metal slugs and flat stones to approximate the weight and bulk of the bag. I doubted anyone would ever open the bag and check as Demetrius, Caesar, and Aurelia were the only other people with a key to the box. I knew our ship would dock for a day or two at Massilia in Cisalpine Gaul as Caesar longed to see his new villa there. Once in Gaul, it would be a simple matter to go out for a walk around the town and never come back. As Caesar needed to move on to his province, his party couldn't spend more than a few days looking for me, and I was certain I could hide long enough to elude detection or even disappear into the countryside to the north. I even convinced myself that what I was doing was in the best interest of Cornelia and my soon to be born son or daughter. I had already composed the note of apology, explaining my actions to Cornelia, which I would leave behind for her to find. I had also convinced myself that our love was strong enough to endure a long separation while I worked out a plan to win the freedom of Cornelia and our child. In retrospect, I was a bit of a fool, but what eighteen year old man is not." With that, Polybius looked at me with an arched eyebrow.

"On the day of the meeting of the tribunal, Caesar's testimony was surprisingly brief. He refused to implicate Clodius, saying he knew nothing of the events as he was at his home in the Subura. When asked why he then chose to divorce Pompeia, Caesar now famously answered, 'Caesar's wife must be above all suspicion.'

Some found it odd for him to speak in the third person, while others simply found it amusing. Cato was heard to say it indicated Caesar's arrogance. I, and perhaps just a few others, knew that when Caesar spoke referring to himself by name he wished the quote to be recorded and repeated. He spoke in the third person so there would be no confusion when others repeated it. Caesar made no public comment on why he chose to not testify against his wife's lover, but on the way home from the forum that day he did joke with me about it, referring to his inaction as a courtesy, 'From one philanderer to another.' I forced a smile at this remark, but I didn't appreciate that my master could so easily joke about so sacred a matter."

Polybius went quiet for some time, causing my brother to grow impatient. Finally, Mela asked, "Did you run away?"

"You, young Mela, always want me to get ahead of my story. A narrative is like a journey one takes. Each sentence is a step along the path, and if one looks too far ahead, important places along the way can go unnoticed. At first Caesar had wanted to go to his province by water, sending his entourage along the overland route some twenty

474

days prior to his departure. This plan was changed, he said, by the weather. In actuality, a man named Pontius altered it. This senator had almost no political influence, but he was quite certainly acting for men who did. On the same day as the Bona Dea scandal became public he sent Caesar a demand for repayment of a loan. The loan demand stated it was now six months past due and must be either paid or answered for in court on the nones of Januarius (January 5). The demand was presented directly to Caesar, so I had no opportunity to see it, but I did see the color drain from his face as he read it. We were crossing the forum when, from the crowd before us, a man shouted Caesar's name. As was my habit I immediately looked to see where the shout originated since I would in all likelihood need to name the person. Caesar spotted the man, waving his arm above his head some twenty paces ahead of us.

As I suspected, Caesar leaned toward me and said, 'Who, in Jupiter's name, is this now?'

I remembered his name but very little else about him. 'It's Lucius Pontianus, freedman of Gaius Pontius.' This brought a scowl to Caesar's face.

The man boldly sidestepped Caesar's lictors and thrust a folded sheaf toward him. Caesar tried not to accept it but the man pressed it into the fold of his toga. This rough handling caused the lictors to grab Pontianus, one on each side, and pull him back. It was about to become violent when Caesar waved the lictors back. Without reading the document, he said to the man, 'Tell Pontius I'll meet him tomorrow at the bath on the Esquiline.' The freedman smirked as he turned and disappeared into the crowd. As soon as we left the forum and were on the Sacra Via, Caesar broke the seal and read the

475

document. This is when his face lost all color and he stopped in the street in front of the Domus Publica. 'They are like Parthians, taking one last shot at me.'

At the time, I had no idea what he meant, but later that day, Demetrius filled me in. Caesar had borrowed quite heavily from several senators. It was easy to avoid being brought into court over the failure to repay a small loan, so Caesar only borrowed large sums from men who were rich enough to never need the money. He reasoned such men would be less likely to demand repayment before he could secure his own fortune. Normally, this would be true, but Pontius was motivated by his associates among the Optimates. He had been persuaded to purchase the debt Caesar owed to some of his other creditors, bringing the total debt owed Pontius up to the staggering sum of eight hundred thirty talents. The whole affair was a ploy by Caesar's enemies to deny him his province, and end his political future, as he was clearly incapable of repaying such a large amount."

Mela had been playing with one of the cats, bobbing a ball of twine tied to a string in front of its paws. There were cat toys such as this in nearly every room of the villa. He stopped and asked, "What did Caesar mean when he said they were like Parthians?"

Polybius looked at him for a moment as if he was trying to comprehend the question, and then he remembered what he had said just before. "He was referring to the Parthian mounted archers. A very effective strategy of the Parthians is to mount archers on horses. These archers are so well-trained they can shoot both while riding toward an enemy, and again while riding away from him. They manage to guide their horses using just their legs and verbal commands so they can

476

fire multiple arrows in a single charge. They will first charge an enemy line while shooting, and then wheel around and release another volley, looking back over their shoulders as they wheel away from the enemy."

Polybius adjusted his position before continuing, "In the end, Crassus once again saved things. He assumed Caesar's debt and was able to pay a third and negotiate a three-year extension for the balance, but before anything else could go wrong, Caesar changed his travel plans. A meeting was called to discuss the changes, and I, as usual, was sitting in the corner of the room.

Caesar got right down to business. 'We'll be leaving on the ides with the rest of the household (December 13).' I was disappointed; I had been looking forward to Saturnalia.

Demetrius interrupted. 'Should I try to get the deposit back on the merchant ship?' Demetrius had, some days previous, secured passage for Caesar and his party aboard a merchant ship traveling to Gades (Cadiz).

Crassus answered for Caesar. 'Absolutely not! That money's gone. We want them to think Gaius will be remaining in the city until after the start of the new year. Let them think they have time, should there be any other traps they wish to lay.'

With that, the matter was settled. The rest of the meeting involved planning the logistics of sneaking out of Rome in just six days. Now that I think about it, this may be why Caesar declined to testify against Clodius. He would have been compelled to stay in the city until the trial ended if he was listed as a witness and his testimony was extended. As it was, we left Rome long before Clodius' acquittal.

477

As we left the meeting, Demetrius clapped me on the back. 'Don't look so glum. There will be other Saturnalia festivals, but you're starting on a new adventure. You should be grateful you're not sailing to Gades. Even if the pilot hugs the coast, sailing in Januarius is rough business.'

'It's not just the festival,' I answered.

'Cornelia.' He laid a hand on my shoulder. 'And, the baby. I warned you your feelings would change.'

Mela interrupted. "Were you feeling down because your plan to escape was ruined?"

Polybius paused and collected his thoughts. "No, Mela, I still could have run away had I wanted to. Even travelling overland, we would have stopped in Massilia. I was sad because the night before I had gained something very precious, and now I was being asked to leave it behind. You see, Mela, the previous night, my son had been born. At that moment, I realized Demetrius was right. Until my son was born, I had every intention of escaping when we stopped in Massilia. I knew we would spend at least one night at Caesar's villa near the city and saw that as my opportunity. Were I to disappear into the countryside of Gaul, there would be no time to search for me before the party needed to move on. Of course, I knew almost nothing of Gaul or how I would live once I was free, but I had been successful in my first escape and I told myself I could live by my wits. Once I held little Tychaeus in my arms though, I wasn't at all sure. I had no idea how Caesar would react to my running away, other than that he had promised to kill me if I were to ever betray him. But, I knew it wouldn't be good for my new family. I was also deterred by something else. Right after our baby was born,

Lydia came out of the room and beckoned to me. She was grinning broadly and said in a whisper as I approached, 'You have a son, Polybius.' I was about to slide past her into the room, but she took me first by my shoulders and hugged me to her breast. I was eager to see the baby, so I broke free rather quickly, and went into the cubicle. Cornelia's hair was wet with sweat and she looked exhausted, but she too was smiling broadly as she looked down at our son. She was on the bed wrapped in blankets, so I slid onto the bed beside her and looked closely at the baby. Without warning, Cornelia passed my son to me. Instinctively, I took him and pressed him to my chest. I remember my heart was racing. This was a feeling I'd never before experienced. We just sat close like that for a long time. Cornelia and I didn't speak.

Finally, Lydia came into the cubicle with Caesar. She stepped aside and Caesar approached the bed and studied the baby for a moment. Turning to Lydia, he said, 'Is the child healthy?'

'As far as I can tell,' she answered.

'Is he whole?'

'Ten fingers, ten toes. Strong limbs and a sound cry, as you no doubt heard.' She was aglow with the successful birth.

Caesar turned to me. 'Polybius, I need to speak to you in private.'

I was nervous when I stepped into the hall, expecting to follow Caesar away from the room, but he stopped just a few feet from the doorway and he too took me by the shoulders with both his hands. 'Do you want to keep the child?'

Until I had held the boy I would probably have answered differently, but with tears in my eyes and a smile on my face I nodded to him. 'Yes.' I said this almost as a whisper. I was then truly surprised when Caesar wrapped his arms around me and pulled me close to his chest. Briefly, I thought, this must be what it's like to have a father, but then I dismissed the thought, remembering both my son and myself were his property.

I returned to Cornelia and my baby boy and Caesar followed. As you are no doubt aware, there is a ritual with the birth of any baby. When the child is freeborn, the father enters the birth room and the midwife or another woman attending the birth lays the baby on a blanket at the man's feet. If he turns and walks away, the newborn is taken outside the walls of the city and left to the elements and the will of the gods. If, however, he picks the child up, the baby is acknowledged as his son or daughter. The same is done for slaves born into a household, only it is the master of the house who makes the choice, and not the baby's father. Before Caesar entered the room, Lydia had already set the blanket on the floor. As he entered, she took my son and laid him on the blanket, expecting Caesar to step forward. When he hesitated, my heart skipped a beat and I felt as if I would faint, but then he said, 'This is for you to do, Polybius. He is your son.' I immediately stepped forward and scooped the baby up into my arms, holding him tightly against my chest. I was crying as I beamed at Caesar. He too needed to wipe a tear from his cheek.

It was arranged that Cornelia and I would spend the night together in that cubicle. Throughout the night, we seldom spoke, but when we did it was to express our dreams for our child's future. At one point I looked Cornelia in the eyes, trying to comprehend what her expression was saying, guided only by a single beam of moonlight coming in through an open space between the shutter and the wall. 'I'll talk to Caesar and see if I can stay here with you and the baby. Just for a while. He can do without me until spring.'

Cornelia put her finger to my lips. 'Don't talk like that!' She was trying to whisper, but failed. 'You are his nomenclator. And, you are finally free of Demetrius. This is your chance to make some real money. You can provide direct access to the Propraetor of Hispania Ulterior. People will pay good money for access to the governor and you can use that money to buy our son's freedom.'

At once I knew she was right. 'Maybe I can make enough money to buy all three of us.' I allowed myself to dream of a different sort of freedom. So, to answer your original question Mela, no, I did not run away. My new focus was on money, as much money as I could get my hands on. Unfortunately, Hispania Ulterior wasn't the richest province in the empire. I didn't sleep much that night, but at one point when I closed my eyes and entered that place between sleeping and wakefulness, I heard Fortuna's voice echo in the distance. 'Let the family I give you into your heart and be happy.'

I was happy.

I spent three days as a new father before we set out. Although there was nothing illegal about setting out for the new province before the term as propraetor actually began, the move was unprecedented and was meant to catch everyone by surprise. Caesar let it be known that he was sending almost all his baggage ahead with the group traveling overland. There was nothing unusual about this as it is foolish to risk sending precious cargo on a ship in the winter. Properly speaking, Januarius in that year occurred in early spring because the calendar had been allowed to drift out of synchronization with the seasons, but it was, nonetheless, Januarius."

Since both my brother and I appeared confused, Polybius explained. "In those days, before Caesar revised it, the calendar only accounted for three hundred fifty five days. The additional days were made up for by inserting an additional month every five years. The Pontifex Maximus was in charge of this, and due to his prolonged illness, Metellus had failed to do so. When Caesar took the position, he chose not to extend the year, as he was hoping a change of magistrates would result in a better outcome for him personally. Therefore, the date had been allowed to drift nearly two months from what the sun the moon and the stars, not to mention the weather, said it should be.

LIBER XXX

The excuse Caesar invented for leaving the city was elegantly simple. Lollius, Pompeius Magnus' legate had come to Rome to pave the way for the general's imminent return. Since the great conqueror had been awarded a triumph, he would need to forgo crossing the sacred boundary of the city before celebrating his triumph. As a result, Pompeius planned to stay at his villa in the Alban Hills. It was only natural Caesar would want to curry favor with Pompeius, so he scheduled a day trip to the Alban hills some ten miles or so southwest of the city to meet with Lollius. We headed out through the Sanitarian Gate on the way south from the city. After walking about three miles out from the city, we stopped at an inn where Caesar procured horses for his traveling party. Since I had never in my life so much as sat on a horse, I was assigned a mule to ride. We made better time after that, but more importantly, we were spared the seven-mile walk. We did actually spend the night at the villa and Caesar had a private conversation with Lollius that lasted well past dark. In the morning, he sacrificed at a small shrine in the neighborhood, and the local haruspex conveniently declared it more auspicious for Caesar to go directly to his province.

After a quick breakfast, the entire party was summoned to meet in the spacious courtyard of the villa to finalize our plans. The slaves were the only ones surprised by the announcement of our sudden departure from Italia. It seems Caesar had already discussed his plans with the rest of the group. When I realized this had all been plotted well in advance I was quite angry with Caesar. Since I was often treated as though I was a free man, I had grown accustomed to Caesar's trust. I wasn't sure whether I was angrier about his lack of faith in me or about not being allowed time to say a proper goodbye to Cornelia and our son. Fresh horses were added to the ones we already had so we could make better time. The plan was to circle around the city by some of the minor roads and link up to the Via Cassia several miles north of the city. In this way, it was hoped word would not reach the senate that Caesar had departed until it was too late to summon him back to Rome to explain his actions. Caesar had achieved his goal of gaining a province meaning I had attained my goal of helping him get there. I now had a new aim, and that was freedom for my family."

With that, Polybius yawned and stretched his arms. "This seems a good place to end my narrative for today. Shall we make arrangements to meet again tomorrow?"

Mela and I quickly agreed and rose to help Polybius to his feet. After helping Polybius return to his tablinum, we saw ourselves out, both looking forward to the continuation of his most interesting story.

POSTSCRIPT

As it would turn out, it would be more than a month before we would return to Polybius' narrative. The following morning, just as we were preparing to set out, one of his slaves arrived at our front gate bearing a message. Polybius had taken ill in the middle of the night and was at that very moment in the throes of a fever and was no longer conscious. For several days it was presumed he would die, as he suffered from several bouts of both chills and fevers. On the sixth day Mela and I were allowed to visit him, but, in his weakened state, he was barely able to speak. We surprised ourselves by how emotional both my brother and I became upon seeing Polybius stretched out on his bed. In observing how heartbroken his slaves were, particularly Castor and Pollux, I knew Polybius had been wrong in assuming they would welcome his death.

We returned home believing the next correspondence we would receive would be the notification of Polybius' funeral, so we were delighted when, some ten days later, a letter, in which he actually apologized for his illness, was sent by Polybius himself. Of course, he had dictated the letter to one of his slaves, but the tone and style of the message indicated he had regained the use of his mind and faculties. It was, however, to be some time before Polybius was strong enough to continue with his tale.

I am currently working with Calistus at compiling the next set of codices, and I will send them along to you as soon as they are bound.

Affectionately, your friend Lucius Seneca.

For a richer reading experience, and to see updates about the sequel to Initium, visit nomenclatorbooks.com to learn more about the world and times of *Nomenclator: Initium*.

I hope you enjoyed *Nomenclator: Initium*. If you did, please write a review at https://www.goodreads.com/

Made in the USA
San Bernardino, CA
01 July 2018